SHADOW
OF
LIGHT

SHADOW
OF
LIGHT

MOLLY E. LEE

Entangled Publishing, LLC
10940 S Parker Road
Suite 327
Parker, CO 80134
rights@entangledpublishing.com

Entangled Teen is an imprint of Entangled Publishing, LLC.
Visit our website at www.entangledpublishing.com.

Edited by Liz Pelletier and Heather Howland
Cover design and illustrations by
Elizabeth Turner Stokes
Interior design by Toni Kerr

ISBN 978-1-64937-099-0
Ebook ISBN 978-1-64937-111-9

Manufactured in the United States of America
First Edition November 2021

10 9 8 7 6 5 4 3 2 1

an imprint of Entangled Publishing LLC

ALSO BY MOLLY E. LEE

For Stoney. Thanks for braving a haunted hotel with me. Only you could get me to laugh that hard in the face of terror. As far as Scooby Gangs go, I think we've nailed it.

Author's Note: This book depicts issues of emotional and physical abuse, violence and gore, kidnapping, animal abuse, and sexual content. I have taken every effort to ensure these issues are handled sensitively, but if these elements could be considered triggering to you, please take note.

If you are suffering from abuse, please know that you have done nothing to cause this, and there are places ready and willing to offer help and guidance.

For ChildHelp National Child Abuse Hotline, call 1-800-422-4453 or visit childhelp.org.

For the Domestic Violence and Intimate Partner Violence Hotline, call 1-800-799-7233 or visit ncadv.org/get-help.

If you or someone you know is contemplating suicide, please know you are not alone. Visit bethe1to.com and help save a life.

PROLOGUE

DRAVEN

Sulfur and tar singe my nose as something hot presses against my back.

Somewhere, Harley screams. The sound is muffled and too far away, urging me to pry open my eyes.

Shadows skitter along my skin, a smooth, cool caress as they combat the heat slipping through the cracked, black stone I lay against.

My bones feel brittle, but I manage to stand. My shadows gather around me, a shield of darkness among the red light that flickers in and out of the room.

Footsteps echo, and I whirl around.

A man saunters toward me. He looks human enough in a suit of black, his hair dark as midnight. But his *eyes*…they're orbs of molten red.

My shadows recoil—no, they *tremble* as he approaches. Power ripples from him with each step he takes, but I hold my ground.

Fighting is pointless—I gave Harley everything she needed to shut the gate, and I can feel the drained remnant of my power trying like hell to restore itself. I don't regret it, not for a second. Marid and his brethren couldn't be set free. They would've destroyed everything in their path.

Dying felt like an easy choice when Harley's life had been at stake.

I just hope she finds happiness, in the end.

"You are not the girl," the man says, his voice seeming to come from everywhere at once. It's a deep rumbling tone that shakes the walls of slick black stone. He closes his eyes, inhaling through his nose. "But her scent *drenches* your skin."

The girl? There is only one girl's scent that would be on me, and that's Harley.

Something yanks at my soul, that chain of connection burning bright between Harley and me even now, even *here*. The pain radiating through it is an agony jerking at me from the other end.

"Who are you?" I sound like I've been screaming for days. Maybe I have. Maybe time doesn't work the same in death.

The man slides his hands into his pockets, a vicious grin forming at the corners of his mouth. "I've been given many names." He tilts his head. "Many by humans with little understanding of who I truly am. Some by your kind and the bastards you answer to." The red of his eyes darkens, their centers swirling with a glittering black.

I swallow back the urge to puke.

"Morningstar," he coos. "Dark Lord. Osiris. *Devil*." He rolls those red eyes at the last one, and my blood turns to ice. He shrugs, such a casual, *human* gesture. "My true name, the one those like you never bother to know, is Rainier."

Whenever I thought of dying, I thought of many things. Light. Peace. Torture. Revenge from the ones I'd been forced to send to this place. I expected a hundred different scenarios.

Not this.

Not *his* realm.

A sharp tug from that chain inside me has me stumbling to the left. What is happening with our connection? Is it dying because *I've* died? Can Harley feel it, too?

Rainier's eyes narrow as he studies me.

I draw on what little power I have, curling shadows around me in an attempt to hide that connection. To hide the truth. To keep her safe.

His eyes widen, and he roars a dark laugh. "You would!" he shouts to the sky. "You would make one of your soldiers her soul mate."

The word blows through me.

Soul mate.

A rarity among Judges. Sacred.

Harley…I suspected what she was the moment I touched her and didn't drain her of power and life.

I can't believe it's true.

She's my soul mate.

Another title forced on her…

No. I can't allow that. And she cannot choose me.

She can't be chained to me, not when I almost destroyed her… and still may if the Seven find out and Order me to kill her. If they do that, I wouldn't even know it was her. I'd be nothing but the assassin they've always used me for. Or, best-case scenario, they put me in the Divine Sleep and she's mated to a ghost.

Fuck, she deserves better than anything I could ever offer. And I'll make damn sure she gets it. All I have to do is ensure she doesn't choose me back.

The Seven—especially Aphian—always said I was evil because of my siphon powers. He made a point to remind me any chance he got. But somehow, a kernel of hope had kept me from truly believing I'd be drawn elsewhere in death, instead of—

Another hard pull on that chain inside me, and my vision flashes from pure darkness to Rainier before me.

A throne of black rock and velvet cushions appears behind him, and he sinks into it with a fluid grace. He props his chin on a fist. "It's abhorrent how much they don't tell you, Judge," he says, shaking his head. "How little you truly know about the real world."

Among the sulfur and smoke, the smell of fire and lilies teases me—Harley's scent. But *how*? How can I smell her—

"Well, go on," Rainier says, motioning his free hand toward me. "Tell me about the girl," he says impatiently. "The Key."

My stomach bottoms out, and I flinch at another yank inside me, this one stronger than the last. "I don't know anything."

"Oh, come now. It's not the time to be humble, *Draven*. You're quite the naughty little Judge, aren't you?" He inhales deeply, his eyes drifting shut. "You're a siphon, and your best friend in the world is an angel of death. Not common, among the divine," he murmurs, then his eyes open, pinning me in place. "Your brother—he's in the Ather."

Nausea washes over me. Is this what people feel like when I use my telepathy powers? Rainier knows the most important pieces of my heart, and I've only been here a few seconds.

That's all it's been, right? Or has it been longer?

"When you died, I couldn't resist the opportunity to call you here," he says. "Not when I...*we* need her so badly."

He needs Harley?

Over my dead fucking body.

Oh, wait...I'm already dead. *Shit.*

Lilies and a roaring fire storm my senses, strong and angry.

"Surely you've figured it out by now," Rainier says, his expression almost pitying. "She's exactly what you hoped she's not."

My stomach bottoms out. There is only one thing he could mean—that she's what I've feared since the day I saw her black flames.

The Antichrist.

The Seven sent me to watch her, but I had Orders to kill her if she showed the true signs of the Antichrist.

She knows she's capable of dropping the veil between worlds, of opening gateways to Hell, but she has no idea...not a clue, the power she *truly* possesses.

Enough to eviscerate the world.

To bring forth the apocalypse.

All she had to do was want it badly enough.

And she's my *soul mate.*

Draven.

Harley's voice echoes inside my mind in time with the tugging on the chain between us. The connection grows as hot as the room around me.

Rainier's head snaps to the left, those glowing red eyes

following a trail as if he can *see* the invisible tether that binds Harley and me together. A slow, prideful grin makes him look striking and terrifying at the same time as he returns his attention to me.

"She's relentless," he says, almost a whisper. "We need that. We need *her*." He rises from his throne in a matter of blinks. "You must tell her," he says, his hand lashing out to grip my throat. "Tell her her people are in jeopardy. She's the key to freeing us all."

"I'm dead," I say through clenched teeth, flinching as I try to break his grasp. But I can't. My strength is all but gone, and the remaining pieces of me? They feel as if they're being called back. No, *demanded* back—

"She isn't standing for that notion, Judge," he says, power rolling in waves throughout the room, hitting my skin with an invisible flame that I feel along every inch of my body. The pain mounts. Is that him? Or is that coming from the other side?

The burning intensifies inside me, Harley's scent swarming everything that I am.

And I smile because I just can't fucking help it.

Stubborn, strong, *brilliant* Harley.

"Tell her, Draven," Rainier repeats, then considers. "Or better yet, *bring* her to me. I'll release your brother if you do."

I struggle against Rainier's grasp. Ever since he was taken from me, I've wanted to save my brother. Have tried to find him. I was prepared to kill for it. I'd planned to kill Harley to get him back…but that was before I knew her, knew what she was to the world, to me.

And, fuck. If she knew about this bargain? She would stop at nothing to get my brother back for me. I know it. That's who Harley is. She'd go through Hell to get him back for me. And I can't have that. Not with how badly Rainier obviously wants her. Not with whatever danger he's referring to. I will not let her be used for her power, for what she is. Not like I have been.

She hates secrets, I know that better than anyone.

But I can't let her sacrifice herself. Not for me.

Rainier's grip tightens. "Bring me the Antichrist, and I'll release him. If you don't, he will die."

I groan at the intensifying heat yanking on my insides, and Rainier releases his grip on my throat so fast I stumble backward. "She's vulnerable if she doesn't come to me." His tone is almost a plea. "Tell her there will be suffering the likes of which neither realm can imagine if she doesn't — "

Draven!

Harley's voice inside my head cuts off the last of what Rainier says, and the floor beneath me disappears, sending me plummeting down into a darkness laced with a lily-scented breeze.

CHAPTER ONE

HARLEY

*"It had seven heads and ten horns, with ten crowns on its horns…
the beast looked like a leopard, but it had the feet of a bear and
the mouth of a lion! And the dragon gave the beast his own power
and throne and great authority…"*

"Oh hell, I hope I don't grow horns." I shove the Bible back in its place on the giftshop shelf. I spin around, returning to the real reason I came in here in the first place—the selection of stuffed animals in a rainbow of colors.

Ray will be discharged in a couple of hours, and I want to give her *something*. Something that says, "Congrats on getting out of the hospital our abusive fake-father put you in, and guess what? You'll never have to see him again because you're being adopted by my boss, and oh yeah, I'm the Antichrist, don't hate me."

I close my eyes, willing the tightness in my lungs to ease.

Kai shoves the knife in my stomach.

His blood on my hands.

The look of betrayal before my dark flames engulf every inch of him—

I snap my eyes open, my chest aching from the memory. I've barely had a second to process what happened yesterday. I eye the stuffed animals but don't really see the shapes of fluff.

I see Draven, lifeless on the ground.

I see his amber-colored soul flickering around that internal chain between us as I haul him back.

I see his eyes, distant and worried over whatever he'd seen when he was dead.

A shiver skates across my skin as my mind jumps between worrying over Draven and that instinct telling me to reach for my phone and call Kai. To tell him about everything that happened, ask for his advice.

That urge has crept over my soul like a phantom wind more than once this morning already, and then my brain has to remind my heart that I killed my best friend—who I thought was my best friend. But Kai's betrayal hasn't fully caught up in my totally overridden system, so I keep short-circuiting every five seconds. Not my best look, for sure.

Draven passed out about ten minutes after he told me I was the Antichrist. Apparently, coming back from the dead takes a toll on the body, so I totally didn't blame him. I scribbled him a note, telling him to meet me at Nathan's later and assuring him I'd try to not ruin the world in the next few hours—the last being a joke, sort of. I mean, did I have the power to do that accidentally? If I stubbed my toe, would I burn a city down? I rub at my temples, wishing I had more answers, but I knew Draven needed rest. Tonight, we'd talk.

But the cold dread in his eyes before he'd passed out? The memories haunting me every time I reach for my phone to text Kai? *Those* two things have me doing totally, not-helpful-at-all, absolutely ridiculous things to distract myself—like Googling *antichrist* and flipping through the pages in a Bible while standing in a hospital giftshop that is the epitome of sad covered in rainbows.

I run my fingers through my hair, lingering on my scalp as I check for horns for the third time since Draven told me what I am.

Antichrist.

According to Google and the Bible, my powers come from the Devil himself, and I was created to bring forth the apocalypse to end the world. I shake my head, stopping my search for horns I know aren't there. I snatch a pink unicorn with a rainbow mane off the shelf and head to the register. I decline a bag, instead holding the fluffy thing against my chest as I weave through the hospital, taking the elevator up to Ray's floor.

A laugh bubbles up from my too-tight chest, and I get more than a few concerned looks from a couple of nurses in the elevator. But hey, can you blame me? The freaking *Antichrist* just bought a stuffed unicorn for her sister instead of bursting out of the ocean with seven heads to destroy the world. Take *that*, Revelations.

"You look like death," Nathan says by way of greeting outside Ray's door.

"You don't look much better," I fire back.

"Haven't slept?"

I shake my head. "You?"

"Couldn't," he says. "I think I dozed off for a second in that god-awful chair in there, but…" He sighs. "The nurse says the doc cleared her. We have some aftercare instructions to take with us, but we're just waiting on them to get copies of all the signatures and we can go home."

Emotion clogs my throat, and my nerves feel so frayed. After the last twenty-four hours—scratch that, the last *month*—I feel like I've taken a trip through the garbage disposal. I need a break. A long one, complete with a Marvel marathon and Nathan's brownies. Maybe since I closed the gates of Hell *and* stopped Marid and his cronies from wreaking havoc on earth, I'll get one.

That look in Draven's eyes, though—the one screaming there is more than he's willing to tell me right now—paired with his revelation about what I truly am, begs to fucking differ. But I ignore the doom and gloom threatening to rise up and consume me and focus on what really matters in this moment. Ray.

"Home," I repeat Nathan's sentiment, and for a second, he looks like he might get choked up or try to hug me. He must read something in my eyes, because instead of any of that, he turns toward the door and hurries through it.

I want to thank him. I want to tell him I'm sorry for lashing out at him when I found out he went behind my back to legally adopt Ray…but I can't. The wound is still too fresh, despite it being one of necessity. I'm grateful for him, more than he'll ever realize, but I'm still so tangled in my head that I can't possibly explain all the emotions racing through me at the moment.

Time.

I just need time. I don't know how much, but when I figure it out, he'll be the first to know.

I follow him through the door, my mood instantly lifting at the sight of Ray's smile.

"Harley!" she squeals from where she stands beside her bed. "They let me put on real clothes!" she says like it's the best news she's heard all day, but her excitement makes her little brow clench.

I'm there in two seconds flat, dropping to my knees beside her. "Take it easy," I say, my hands hovering over her but not touching. The nurse said she'd heal quickly from the cracked rib, but I don't want to do anything to slow that process—like crushing her in a hug, which is all I really want to do.

"I'm fine," she assures me, adding a little sass into the declaration. She takes the unicorn I offer her and lovingly holds it to her chest. "Thank you," she says, then adds, "I've been worried about you."

"I told you she was fine," Nathan says from behind us.

But Ray's blue eyes demand answers. And she deserves them.

Later, I mouth, and she reluctantly nods.

"I can't wait to go home," she says, and my heart swells. It's taken her absolutely zero time to adjust to the news that Nathan will be her legal parent in a matter of days, and his home will now be *hers*. Maybe ours, if I decide to take him up on his offer and break my lease on the apartment I just signed a contract on.

"Can we have waffles?" Her eyes look up and behind me, to Nathan, and I bite back a half laugh, half cry. Waffles weren't exactly a luxury we could afford at home with our father. Innocent questions like a simple breakfast request weren't, either.

As soon as the thought hits my brain, the kneejerk reaction for me to teach Ray to keep those desires to herself swarms over me like it has for the past seven years. I've always raised Ray to be cautious in revealing what she really wants to our father because he always found a way to ruin it.

But here? With Nathan? He'd never do that. He loves Ray unconditionally. He wants to make her happy while also keeping her safe.

How did an Antichrist like myself get lucky enough to have found someone like him? To have a sister like Ray? To have a... well, whatever Draven is to me? How can I be given any of that if I'm truly evil?

"Death Star shapes or regular?" Nathan asks, saving me from spiraling inside of myself.

Later.

I can panic and rage later.

Hopefully tonight, when Draven shows up rested and ready to cough up some answers.

"As long as you make them, I don't care," Ray says, smiling up at Nathan.

A nurse walks into the room and hands Nathan a folder thick with aftercare instructions. She grins at Ray, unable to resist the joyous effect she has on everyone, before telling us we're free to go. Nathan grabs the little backpack I left here yesterday with one hand, tucking the folder under his arm and reaching for Ray's hand with the other.

They head toward the door, an effortless display of trust as they walk hand-in-hand.

Something heavy and hopeful settles in me, but I can't help from shying away from the feeling. I've never been able to live in hope for too long, and even though things are looking better than they have in a long time, I can't stop the nagging sensation that if I look at a picture of happiness too long, it'll turn to ash.

CHAPTER TWO

I quietly shut Ray's bedroom door, sighing as I head down the hallway.

"She asleep?" Nathan asks from where he cleans up the dishes in the kitchen.

I nod. "She finally gave in to those pain pills."

Nathan nods toward his front door. "Draven is out there waiting for you."

My heart flutters in my chest. It's only been a day, and I feel like I haven't seen him in months. I try not to let the excitement show all over my face. "Thanks…"

I'm not sure what else to say. Sure, we've stayed at Nathan's before, but this is different. *Today* is different. I left my bag in the room right next to Ray's, but I still haven't decided if I'll be staying here permanently or not. The apartment I secured was meant for Ray and me…but now that she's here?

"Are you crashing here tonight?" Nathan asks, likely reading the dilemma on my face. I'm too exhausted to draw up the mask I normally hide under, but something inside me warms to his question as opposed to what he could've easily done, which is demand I stay.

He's not my father—who knows who the hell my biological parents are—but Nathan is more of a parent to me, to Ray, than anyone ever has been before. I respect him and trust him despite the secret he kept, but the fact that he treats me like an adult makes me love him all the more.

Love. I need to tell him. If almost dying has taught me anything, it's that life is too damn short. He deserves to know. Hell, he likely deserves to know the whole truth—as Ray so adamantly told me earlier after I'd told her everything that had happened while I was gone—but how would he handle that truth? How would he deal with what I am?

I don't even know how to deal with it.

There is still too much I don't understand, and that's what pushes me toward the front door, calling over my shoulder with a simple, "Probably."

I close the door behind me, and my heart races at the sight of Draven sitting on the porch swing to the right. Seeing him is like flipping on some spider-sense inside me, everything in my world narrowing to him.

His eyes are cast toward the quiet street, the sky clear and dark beyond the other houses. One arm stretches over the back of the swing as he slowly sways back and forth, his long legs covered in those black jeans he loves, a soft cotton T-shirt wrinkling slightly at his waist. I swallow hard, suddenly forgetting every single question I had before stepping out here—and there were like a hundred, at least.

Now all I can do is marvel at how damn gorgeous he is and how freaking worried he looks. He's staring at that street like he's watching a horror movie and can't tear his eyes away.

"You trying to rearrange the street signs with your mind or something?" I tease as I sit on the swing beside him. Shadows gather around his face, soft wisps that darken his eyes. "Draven?" I ask when he's barely blinked.

The shadows draw back, fading into the darkness of Nathan's porch. The darkness seems to shake off of Draven, too, and he finally meets my gaze, pinning me with a look that has my heart in knots.

"I'm glad to see you kept true to your word and didn't destroy the world while I slept." He says it like a tease, but there is a heaviness in his tone that prevents me from laughing.

"Are you so powerful that you know the state of the entire

world?" I try to tease back. "I mean, for all you know, I could've totally messed up Kansas."

A small half smile shapes his lips, but I was really hoping for a laugh. Hoping for him to be refreshed and totally ready to placate my worries, make this whole Antichrist thing seem like a bad dream.

From the look on his face, I know that's a ridiculous hope. He may have gotten some sleep after I yanked his fine ass back from Hell, but he certainly doesn't seem any less worried. If anything, he's worse than usual, and when he's the absolute king of broody on a *good* day, that doesn't bode well for me.

I rub my palms over my face, needing to soothe the headache building behind my eyes. When was the last time *I* slept? "I know I have no right to demand you let me in," I finally say, deciding to just dive right into the swimming pool of awkward. "We all know I'm the queen of wall-building over here, but I really would love to know what's going on with you."

"You mean besides coming back from the dead?" His tone is lighter than moments before, which gives me the courage to continue.

"Are you…" I work the words around the knot in my throat. "Are you upset that I brought you back? Was it wrong? I don't know the rules, but I couldn't…" I rub at the spot on my chest, the one that feels like an anvil will split the bone any second. "I couldn't lose you."

And that's bad, right? Like, really, really bad. Because what I did…bringing him back? Sure, I didn't exactly know what I was doing, but instinct has always been a hard thing for me to ignore. So whatever powers lie in my blood that allowed me to bring him back from the dead had me basically playing God, and I didn't care what rules I broke. Not when it came to Draven. And that kind of power? It terrifies me.

Draven shifts on the swing, stopping its easy swaying to turn and face me. "What you did for me," he says, his voice low and rough, "is more than anyone has ever done before." He shakes his head. "Half the people in my life would prefer it if I died. But you decided to fight for my life. I don't deserve you."

My pulse thrums beneath my skin from how close he sits, how intense his eyes are as he says those words. I swallow hard. "That line is getting pretty old," I say. "Plus, shouldn't the line be mine? You're the divine warrior of the Creator, after all. And I'm...I'm the *Antichrist.*" The title is sticky on my tongue, and his eyes go distant again.

"You haven't told me everything," I say, and that gets his attention. "I know we've been busy," I say, forcing the images of Kai stabbing me out of my mind, then glance toward the house where I know Ray is peacefully sleeping. "But you came back, and you told me you met the Devil. You told me I was the Antichrist, and I don't know how you figured that out or why you were even in Hell in the first place."

Draven is *good.* Why did he go to Hell when he died? Did the Creator hate him for his siphon powers that much? Or is it my fault? Because of that connection we share and because of what I am? Or did the Seven—who have always told him he's evil—ensure he'd go there just as sure as they snap their fingers and put him to sleep for decades at a time?

The questions spear my mind like chips of ice.

"I haven't told you everything because I'm not sure if I can trust what I saw." His brow furrows like he's trying to sort nightmare from reality.

"But you're *sure* I'm the Antichrist? Which makes me ten times worse and more in demon-demand than the Key you thought I was?"

He nods, his eyes regretful like he wishes he could give me a different answer.

"Did the..." God, I can't believe I'm about to say these words. "Did the Devil tell you what I was?"

"Yes and no," Draven says, and I give him a glare. He shrugs. "He didn't call himself the Devil, either," he says. "His name is Rainier."

He says the name, and something inside me twists tight, like I've heard it before.

"He claimed humans and people like me—Judges—created the Devil name."

"Okay," I say, deciding to unpack that one later. "And Hell? What was that like?" Maybe if I keep him talking about random details, he'll eventually want to open up to me. Let me in. Or it'll jog his memory enough for some real intel.

"I didn't see much," he says, leaning back against the swing. "I couldn't keep track of time, and before I knew what was happening, you were pulling me out."

I blow out a breath, nodding. I can't even begin to wrap my head around that one. Sure, I've thought of death before, but more in a…slipping away kind of idea. I never thought I'd be discussing it with someone who's actually come back from where you go after you die.

The sight of him broken and breathless on the ground chills my blood, but my mind travels farther back, to what Kai had said.

Draven came here to kill you. Use your blood to free his precious brother.

"Did you see anyone else?" I ask, my voice tight, wary. "Your brother?" He'd told me that Marid had taken his brother by mistake, thinking it was Draven he was taking back to Hell.

Draven closes his eyes, shaking his head before looking at me again. "No."

A sticky, gritty something slithers along my bones. "What Kai said…" I nearly choke over his name, over the phantom blood I can still feel clinging to my skin. I rub my palms like I can wipe it away. "About you coming here to kill me, to use my blood to open the gates and find your brother to set him free—was that true?" My voice is almost a whisper.

"Harley." He sighs my name, almost in apology.

"Tell me the truth," I say.

He nods, a defeated gesture, and the swing stops its motion, as if his admission has stopped my entire world. I swallow hard.

"There are many realms in Hell," he says. "And there are even more rules on where and how one can get to them. After my brother was taken from me, I tried to look for him any time I wasn't in the Divine Sleep. Judges have some access, but only to the places we're assigned. There is a gatekeeper at the entrance and he decides where you can and cannot go."

"As for what Kai said…" He looks to me. "I didn't know you," he says. "And maybe I'm a monster enough to say that if the Key had been anyone but you, maybe I would've gone through with it and killed them. Used their blood to slice through all those rules and find my brother. He's been there for a century because they thought he was me. I've lived with that guilt for so long, and I couldn't see past it."

I hate that I understand. Hate that I know I would do the same for Ray. And maybe that's why I'm not screaming and running the opposite direction.

"But then I saw you," he continues. "I saw your heart, your spirit, your unrelenting strength." He shrugs. "I knew after one day with you that I'd never be able to harm you. I didn't care what it cost me, didn't care what the Seven had ordered me to do, I'd die before I hurt you."

I blow out a breath, letting the truth sink into me and adjust around it, and quickly move on to the next issue. "So, the Seven really sent you here to watch me because they thought I might be the Key to opening the gates of Hell?"

"Yes."

"But that's not all," I say. "I can tell there is more. And while I'm not the Seven's biggest fan for treating you like their own version of the Winter Soldier, I need to know everything, Draven." I hold his gaze, noting the way the gold churns in his eyes. "Did *they* suspect I might be…the Antichrist?"

Draven's eyes darken the way they do when he's about to tell me something I absolutely don't want to hear. It's almost identical to the look he gives me when he's about to start a fight to push me away. The battle rages there, and a muscle in his jaw flexes.

"Yes," he finally admits.

"And the previous Keys you had to watch…" He'd told me he had to watch them die over and over again because they never ended up having the powers I do. "Did the Seven think they could've been what I am?"

Another nod.

I have the pieces of this little Seven puzzle, the one that brought Draven into my life, but I'm scared to death to put them together. My soul does it for me, though, my blood running cold before I can mentally form the question.

"There's that fear again," he says, hurt flashing behind his hard eyes. He leans back. "It's the correct reaction, Harley. You don't need to be ashamed of it."

"I'm not ashamed of it," I argue. "I'm *annoyed* by it."

He chokes out a dark laugh, glancing down at his hands as if a book lay open between them. "The Seven sent me to kill you," he says, and the words are like a blast of cold air clicking that last puzzle piece into place. "If you showed a hint of the powers and a penchant for the dark side."

The breath in my lungs grows tight. "And you wanted your brother back anyway, so win-win." He narrows his gaze at me, but I push on. "But you didn't kill me. You haven't." There is no denying what I am, what I can do with my powers. Kai and Marid's plans proved all of that, not to mention Draven's most recent trip to Hell.

"No," he says. "And I won't."

"Why?" I blurt the question. If Ray was in the position his brother is in now…what *wouldn't* I do for her? Would I kill Draven? My stomach recoils at the thought. No, but I'd rip apart the world to find another way to get her back.

"Why?" he repeats.

"Yeah," I say, shaking my head. "Look, I'm not signing up to throw myself on a pyre, but why? I am what the Seven fear. You're their divine soldier. What's stopping you—"

"We're back to this again?" He cuts me off with a frustrated glare. "You're playing the whole *the world is better off without me* card again?"

"No," I snap back. "I'm not playing any card. Not anymore. Not after…"

My voice trails off, the rage trickling out of me. I killed him. I killed my best friend. Even though our relationship was wholly fabricated, an utter violation of my mind, I can't seem to reconcile the betrayer with the boy I grew up with—thought I'd grown up with.

"No," I say again. "I want to live. I deserve to live. And according to my genius little sister, I decide what I am and what I do with these powers, not some old council."

Draven's mouth quirks into that wolfish grin that sends tendrils of heat spiraling down my middle despite all this talk of having orders to kill me. Maybe that makes me some undefined sort of twisted, but I'm well past caring.

I take a deep breath to steady myself. "*But* I'm guessing following Orders—like with the Divine Sleep—isn't really a choice thing in this gig, is it?" He'd told me himself he couldn't break the divine order of not revealing other Judges' identities. That's why he'd never been able to tell me about Kai.

"No," he says. "When you're Called, you come into a divine contract with the Seven. You are wielded at their will, for the good of the many." He says the words with so much sarcasm that I want to laugh, but I can't. It's no joke, and this is no game.

"The other potential Keys?" I ask. "The Seven—they forced you to kill them, even though they didn't show powers like mine, didn't they?"

His eyes snap to mine. "Yes."

The answer is ice from his lips, his eyes hardening so much I'm shocked I don't see cracks.

There has to be a way around this. Some way to keep everyone safe.

"Maybe I should send myself to Hell," I say. "Ray is safe with Nathan now. She's loved and cared for. And if I went there, found a way to get there and live there…" My voice trails off. His brother had been taken, not killed. At least, not that we know of. So it was possible. "Then I wouldn't be demon bait or a threat to the world. I'd be in a place no one could use me, right?"

Draven gapes at me. "And what the hell would you do there, Harley? Farm?"

I snort out a broken laugh. Farms in Hell? That idea is ridiculous. I picture stalks of corn growing from soil as red as blood or rows of Venus flytraps dripping acidic goop from their spindly openings.

"I have no idea," I admit, sighing. "At least if I was there, you wouldn't have to follow through with a command to kill me. And hey, maybe I'd be able to find your brother."

I wait for that fear to blast through me again, to send me into a panic or at least to conjure the dark flames to protect myself, but it doesn't come.

Because I don't have anything to fear from Draven.

I know that as easily as I know how devastated he feels. I can sense the bitter tang of it as it pulses down the chain between us.

"Don't," he growls, bolting off the swing so fast I jolt. He stomps to the other side of the porch, and I don't think, I'm *there*.

"Oh, we're back to this again?" I fire his earlier words right back at him. "*Stay away from me, Harley*," I say in my best Draven tone. "Let's not Edward Cullen this up, okay? I'm exhausted, I still have my best friend's blood under my fingernails, I'm contemplating buying a summer house in Hell, and apparently I'm the freaking Antichrist. Cut. Me. Some. Slack."

The tension goes out of Draven's shoulders, and he slowly spins around, a dark but amused look on his face.

"What?"

He cocks a brow at me. "*Don't Edward Cullen this up?*"

That's what he got out of that tirade? I shrug. "It's a book thing."

He takes a few steps closer to me, and air traces the line of my jaw. "A book thing," he whispers, and suddenly I'm having a hard time breathing for a whole new reason. "One I missed, apparently."

A shaky breath leaves me, and I nod. "I'll catch you up whenever we sort out this mess. But for now, it means don't shove me away for my own good. It's so two decades ago."

His hand drops, and I head back to the swing.

"I hate what the Seven does to you," I say when he finally takes a seat next to me. "I don't like how much power they have, and I double, no *triple*, hate that they use you like their own personal assassin. It's not fair to you, and it doesn't matter if the previous potential Keys were demons or not or whatever they were. You shouldn't have to live with that guilt—"

"Who says I feel guilty?" he asks, his voice low and raw.

"I can feel it." I don't have an answer for that chain between us. Maybe it's something the Seven concocted so he'd be able to kill me more easily, to find me no matter where I ran.

"I don't feel guilty about *all* of them," he admits, and I raise my brows at him. It's his turn to shrug. "Some of them weren't Keys, but they had power. Some of them decided to use that power to do very bad things." His eyes darken. "I didn't mind dispatching them. The others?" He shudders, and I reach across the swing, laying my palm over his.

"It's not your fault," I say. "But this brings us right back to my original question."

"What was it again? I forget."

Yeah, I doubt that. "Why haven't you killed me? If refusing Orders isn't really an option."

He sits back. "That is an incredibly complicated question."

"Aren't they all when it comes to us?"

He purses his lips as if to say touché. "Well, for starters, I haven't reported back to them what you are, so they haven't given me an official Order to kill you."

"I figured as much, or I wouldn't be here right now." But that gets me thinking about their ability to compel him to carry out their orders, which he is definitely not doing. "Is it easy for you to hide what you know from them?"

"It is not."

"Then why haven't you told them what I am?"

A muscle in his jaw ticks. "Why can I touch you and not drain you of power and life?" he asks, trailing the tip of his finger in light circles over my palm.

My breath catches. "You tell me."

"Why could you bring me back from the dead?" he asks instead, moving that finger up and over my wrist.

A warm shiver rushes beneath his touch. "I don't know."

His eyes meet mine, a depth there I don't understand. "When we figure that out, Harley," he says, smoothing that finger up my arm and over the line of my jaw, "maybe we'll have your answer."

I lean into his touch, but he's already dropping his hand, sending me right back to reality. "So, what you're saying is that I don't have to worry about you turning Winter Soldier on me at a moment's notice?"

"No," he says. "You don't need to worry about that."

"Would you feel it?" I ask. "If the Seven, like...flipped the switch on my kill order?"

A soft chuckle shakes his shoulders. "Yeah. I'd feel it."

"Enough to give me a warning?"

The laughter dies. "Enough to let you do what you need to do."

"Destroy the Seven for being power-hungry dicks?" I ask hopefully.

He shakes his head, not at all amused. "To kill me first."

CHAPTER THREE

O h.

"Hard pass." My body recoils, rejecting the idea completely. I'd killed Kai, but to be fair, he'd been trying to kill me and use my blood to unleash Hell on earth. And *that* still hurt. Hurting Draven? Regardless of the situation? I didn't think I'd survive that. "Well," I say, forcing my tone to stay even. "Now that we have all that cleared up…"

I search my racing mind for another important question. There are so many, but I'm so damn tired. You'd think being the Antichrist I'd have some kind of pass on the whole needing-sleep thing.

I absentmindedly run my fingers over my scalp again before smoothing my hands down my bare arms.

"Looking for something?" Draven asks, tipping my chin up to meet his eyes.

"Horns," I admit. "Or a mark. 666?"

He tilts his head.

"I may have Googled *antichrist* today," I say. "And looked at a Bible in the giftshop. My…*the person* who raised me was never religious. The only things I've heard about the Antichrist are from movies or books, and I *really* hope I didn't burst through some psychic twin's stomach at birth, but I wouldn't say no to Keanu showing me the ropes on how to kill demons." He cocks a brow, utterly confused, and I shrug. "*Constantine*. Movie about demons, Antichrist, the Devil."

"I'll have to fact check that one someday," he says. "And all this has you thinking you'll sprout horns any second?"

The lightness in his tone is such a relief that I laugh. "Well, yeah!" I say, flinging my arms in the air. "I know next to nothing about what I am." I snap my fingers, the black-and-silver flames sparking to life in an instant. Without the power-draining stone that had been on the wish-bracelet I'd worn all my life, my powers are now uninhibited and *tempting* with their need to be used. "I can manifest this, Draven. There is an entire well of power inside me I can feel now. Unrestrained and untested." I curl my fingers, extinguishing the flames. "Who's to say I won't grow horns or a 666 tattoo won't show up any second?"

Draven reaches for my hand, gently clutching my wrist where Ray's rainbow bracelet and Kazuki's tattoo rests. He shifts off the swing, settling on his knees before me so we're at eye level. The sight makes the breath in my lungs stall and my heart hiccup.

He gently separates my thighs as he slides between them, his eyes focusing on my arm in his hands. Slowly, he trails his fingertips over the tattoo and upward, over the crook of my elbow and up my shoulder until he pushes some of my hair back to expose my neck. He leans in closer, his hard chest grazing mine as he inches his lips over the line of my neck.

My entire body goes tight and loose at the same time, his scent filling the air between us, the warmth of his body radiating onto mine like a pulsing beacon of need. He drags his lips down, planting soft, searing kisses over my collarbone before he runs those fingers over the back of my neck and recreates the same path on my opposite arm.

"What are you doing?" I finally whisper.

"Looking for a mark." His grin is pure mischief as he brushes his lips over mine in the lightest of kisses.

My eyes automatically close, my mind and body narrowing to the feel of his lips on my skin, the way his warm breath sends delicious shivers shooting down my spine. He nips my bottom lip before grazing his teeth down the side of my neck, working his way back down my arm until I'm a tight string ready to snap. He kisses the tattoo, the leaf and flame now leeched of power and color but no less beautiful.

"This is the only mark you have, Harley," he says, rubbing his thumb over the tattoo. "The only one you're going to get."

"Are you sure?"

A wicked smirk shapes his lip. "Would you rather I look more in depth?"

His large hands fall to my thighs. The soft pressure there has me tightening my legs around him where he still kneels.

He draws closer, his lips an inch away from mine. "I don't mind. I'll spend the entire night going over *every* inch of your body if it makes you feel better."

My toes curl in my shoes, liquid heat replacing the blood in my veins. Flashes of what he's offering fill my mind so much I can't see around them, can't *feel* around the need to escape into Draven and never look back. I sway toward him—

He smiles a victorious grin like he's just won a competition.

Damn it. I smack his arm with my free hand. "Cheater!" I accuse, and he laughs, rubbing the spot on his arm as if I really hurt him. "Stop distracting me."

"Cruel, clever honey badger," he teases, but makes no move to get off of his knees. To separate us. Instead, he stays right where he is, his nose nearly grazing my own as he plays with a strand of my hair.

"I'm serious, Draven. I won't be distracted. We need to talk about everything." What happened, what it means for the future, what the next steps are—including me fleeing to Hell if that's the best viable option to protect the world from what I can do.

"I know," he says, his eyes flashing from my lips to my eyes and back again. "I can't help it, Harley." He visibly swallows and smooths a hand over my cheek. "When I gave you that power, when I woke up in that place…I thought I'd never see you again. Is it so awful to want to just *be* with you for a few moments before we have to deal with everything else?"

I lean my forehead against his, breathing in his scent, relishing that strong, powerful connection pulsing between us. "No. It's not awful to want that."

He takes that as an invitation—as he should—and brushes his lips over mine. I sigh at the too-light touch, fisting his shirt in my hand to draw him closer. He finally moves then, so fast and graceful I hadn't realized he'd taken me with him, shifting us until he's sitting on the swing and I have one knee on either side of his hips.

He cups my face in his hands, crushing his mouth over mine, and I open for him. His tongue teases the edges of my teeth, and electric sparks shoot to each of my nerve endings with his subtle claiming. This, here, with him...it's always been our escape. Our need for each other.

I whimper, the consuming desire rising up in me, demanding I give him all of me and take all of him in return. My body automatically rocks against his, and I *love* the way he feels beneath me, all corded muscle and roiling power, the epitome of danger and need.

Damn him, he's like the deep breath I've needed all day long, and here, in his arms, his mouth on mine? I'm not worrying about what happened last night. I'm not thinking about him laying lifeless on the ground. I'm not thinking about me murdering my best friend or the label Draven gave my powers or the fact that his brother is in Hell and his boss ordered him to kill me.

It's just Draven and me and the unflinching need between us.

Powerful.

Demanding.

"Harley," he sighs my name between my lips. "There is one thing"—he strokes the roof of my mouth with his tongue—"I have to tell you."

His fingers grip my hips, either to steady me so he can keep talking or to push me harder against him, I don't know and I don't care, because it feels so amazing that I rock over him again.

He groans. "Rainier said—"

The wooden porch creaks, and I jerk out of his embrace,

leaping off of Draven's lap like he's on fire. He's not, *thank you inner power control*. And I'm totally ready to yell at Nathan for not knocking, but, *hello*, we're outside on *his* porch...

But it's not Nathan standing in the opened doorway. It's Ray.

Her shoulders are hunched, her head tilted to the side.

"Ray?" I ask, hurrying over to her. "Did you have a nightmare?"

I kneel down so I can see her eyes, but her hair is in the way. I gently reach for her when she doesn't say anything, brushing away the slightly damp strands—

And scream.

CHAPTER FOUR

"What's the matter, *Harrr-lee*?"

Ray's mouth is moving, but that's not my sister's voice. Those aren't my sister's eyes, either.

Terror, sharp and icy, clangs through my body as I jolt back. Ray's eyes are yellow with blue veins spiderwebbing every which way across them. Her usually smooth skin is indented, a pattern of red and black like...

Like snake scales.

Marid.

Draven is at my side in an instant, jaw clenched as he helps me to my feet.

"Leave her alone!" I shout, tears gathering behind my eyes.

Ray's head tilts the other direction, the motion jerky and inhuman. "I don't think so."

Marid's voice is familiar and cold. Ray's body moves, the motions awkward and too fast. One second, she's in the open doorway, the next she's on the edge of the porch railing, her legs swinging back and forth, a cackled laugh echoing from her lips.

I whirl, nearly knocking Draven over to get to her. The fall from the porch wouldn't hurt her unless she went head first, but I'm not about to take the risk. "What do you want?"

My sister's legs stop swinging. "Who says I want anything, princess?" I edge closer, but Marid-Ray wags a finger at me. "Ah, ah. I'd hate to have to end our game so soon."

A slithering sound slides along the porch, and my eyes flare as a dozen black and tan snakes spiral around Ray's ankles, working their way up to coil lovingly around her neck.

Flames burst along my fingertips before I even think to summon them.

"What are you going to do with those?" Ray's lips peel back, baring a grin that is more teeth than anything. "*Burn* me?"

"What do you want?" Draven's turn to ask this time.

Her body does a little hop, and my heart leaps to my throat, but she balances perfectly on the railing, giving us another little cackle along with it. I smother my flames and reach for her, like if I can just touch her she'll come back to me.

"I used to want everything from you, princess," Marid says through my sister's voice, garbling it to a whispery hiss. "I used to think you were the real power. The one to change everything." Her body gives a shrug, those garter snakes flicking out fork tongues with the movement. "No more. I've found my plans lie elsewhere, with a power far greater than yours ever will be."

Rage rolls through me. "Leave her alone!"

He bares Ray's teeth again. "It doesn't work that way, *princess*. Not anymore. You saw to that." The words drag from her lips, the *S*'s going on forever. "This body is my tether. And I will use it to torment you for the rest of your existence for what you did to me. To my brethren."

"No," I whisper, cold panic clawing up my throat. "You can't—"

"Can't I?" Ray's head tilts, that vicious grin shaping her mouth and flexing the scales on her face.

Her body convulses so hard she loses her footing.

I gasp, reaching for her, but she's already hurling backward, off the porch—

Shadows catch her, a blanket of soft black laying her gently on the grass. I leap over the railing, hitting the ground beside her. I smooth my hands over her face, which is now free of scales, and watch as the dozen snakes slither back into the earth.

"Ray!" I scream, tears streaming down my face.

She opens her eyes, her little brow furrowing. "Whoa," she says, glancing around. "Why are we outside?"

I haul her to me, squeezing her in a hug before I remember her rib and loosen my hold. "Are you all right?" I ask, frantically scanning her body, her eyes. They're purely hers again—blue and confused.

"Did I sleepwalk?" she asks, eying behind me. I glance over my shoulder where Draven stands, eyes wide, that muscle in his jaw ticking.

"You..." Fucking hell, should I tell her? What would I do if someone told me a demon had just taken over my body? Not just any demon, either, but a Greater demon who's beyond pissed off that I ruined his plans to take over the world?

Shit, shit, *shit*.

Ray breaks my hold, rising to her own two feet. Her eyes jump from Draven to me and back again before she crosses her arms over her chest. "Harley," she says, and she sounds so much older than an almost eight-year-old. "Don't even *think* about lying to me."

I gape at her, and she raises one brow. I glance at Draven for help, but his eyes simply soften in support—whatever I decide.

He lied to me when he first met me. Kept me in the dark under the notion that it was saving me.

I can't do that to Ray.

She's stronger than that, deserves the truth.

So I tell her, and her blue eyes widen when I finish.

"There were *snakes* all over me! Yuck!" She does a little dance like there might still be one slithering under her clothes and hops onto the porch.

"*That's* what you say after what I just told you?" I follow her, shaking my head.

She swipes at her neck, her arms. "Right," she says, blinking a few times. "Okay, so, all those nightmares I've been having about Marid..."

"Were likely not nightmares," I finish for her.

Another shiver shakes her body. "What do I do to stop it?" She points the question at Draven, not me, and I try not to balk at how damn perceptive my little sister is.

Each second Draven is silent, my stomach drops another inch.

"There has to be a way to fix this," I say, almost begging him.

"I've never seen this before," he admits, and I shut my eyes, my head dropping. Draven is over five hundred years old—well, sort of. He wasn't technically awake for all of those years, but still, if he hasn't seen anything like this, who the hell has?

My eyes snap open, darting to the tattoo on my wrist. "Then we need to find someone who has," I say, and recognition clicks in Draven's eyes. "And checking in with an ancient warlock seems like a damn good place to start."

Draven nods, reaching into his pocket and pulling out his cell. His fingers fly over the screen, texting someone.

"Harley?" Ray says, and I draw my attention back to her.

"It's okay," I assure her. "We're going to figure this out." I drop to her level, gently clutching her shoulders. "I promise, Ray. I'll find a way to fix this."

"I know," she says without hesitation or doubt. "But if you're about to take me to some warlock, there is something you need to do first."

I tilt my head. "What could possibly be more important than—"

"You have to tell Nathan the truth."

CHAPTER FIVE

"No way." I shake my head, dropping my arms to stand and pace the length of the porch.

"You *have* to," she argues, and I halt my pacing.

"Ray," I groan. "He'll lose it." I know she told me earlier today I needed to eventually tell him, to not keep him in the dark about the world he is now inadvertently tangled in, but now? Too soon.

"So what if he does?" she fires back. "You can't expect him to just be fine with us running off in the middle of the night and not coming back until who knows when!"

I raise my brows at her determination but sigh. "You remember when I told you, Ray? About what I was? I gave you a choice on how much you wanted to know. This, telling him now before we have to go see Kazuki…it's taking away his choice."

"So is lying to him," she says, reaching for my hand. "It'll be okay, Harley. Nathan needs to know about our world." My heart snags on the way she says *our world* as if she's fully accepted her role in this as my sister. "If you don't tell him, you're basically saying you don't trust him, and I know that isn't true. Or you wouldn't let me live with him."

I swallow hard. Ray always has a knack for making the right thing seem like the easiest thing in the world. If she wasn't so endearing, it would be super annoying. "When did you get so grown up?" I ask, clearing the tension from my throat.

She shrugs. "I think I was born old," she says and squeezes my hand. "Come on. Nathan first. Warlock dude second."

Draven snorts and then reels it in when I glance back at him.

"What?" he asks. "If Kazuki knew she called him *warlock dude…*" he says, laughing again. "I just would love to see the look on his face."

I release a small laugh of my own, wondering how it's possible that I can go from unbridled terror moments ago to laughing now.

Ray.

Ray is how. She's the only one capable of staying so calm and hopeful in the face of overwhelming, dark odds. It's the reason she always stayed positive that our father would change. The reason she never once doubted me when I showed her what I can do.

She's the one to open the door, tugging me inside the house, urging me to wait in the living room while she gets Nathan.

"If he kicks me out, I'm blaming you," I call to her, and she just waves me off. Draven gives me a supportive glance as he takes up a good lean near the front door.

"What's going on, kiddo?" Nathan asks, rubbing his eyes like he accidentally dozed off while waiting for me to come back inside. His gaze clears and sharpens as he looks to Draven. Nathan takes a not-so-subtle move in front of me like he needs to protect me from him.

I laugh again, and Ray smiles up at me. I can't really blame Nathan—Draven *does* look particularly broody over there, and if Nathan has any sense at all, he can feel the power Draven has. He may not know what it is, but he feels it enough to put himself between me and Draven, which is such a sweet gesture I can't help but place my hand on his back. "I need to talk to you."

He slowly turns to face me, keeping one eye on Draven, and folds his arms over his chest. "What's up?"

"You might want to sit down," I say, motioning to the couch tucked against the wall of the living room. He visibly swallows but does as I suggest, eyes bouncing between Draven and me the whole time. Some battle rages across his face, but it quickly softens, and he nods a bit repeatedly. "Okay," he says before I can finish sitting down in the chair across from him. "Okay. This is fine. It's going to be *fine*, Harley. I'll support you in whatever decision you make. We can raise this baby together if he wants nothing to do with it—"

"*Ohmigod*," I cut him off, squeezing my eyes shut against the scenario he's painted. I mean, okay, it's not the worst thing, and yeah, I can totally see why his mind went there. With it being the middle of the night and Draven standing near the door looking like he's just been told life-altering news…but he's got it all wrong.

I glance over to Draven, his eyes locking with mine. We've only known each other a few weeks—despite it feeling like a lifetime. We haven't even had the "label" talk, let alone had a second to fantasize about a future—one I know for certain wouldn't involve children for like at least two decades. I'm only eighteen, for fuck's sake. And there's that whole *he was sent to kill me* dilemma we still need to sort out.

"That's not what's happening here," I finally manage to say, and Nathan's shoulders drop a fraction. I give him a rare smile. "But it means a lot to me that *that* was your reaction." I huff a laugh, shaking my head. "Now let's hope you're just as chill when it comes to the truth."

I swear I can feel the disbelief from Nathan as my story unfolds before him, including everything from my powers, to what we think I am, to what just happened with Ray. Something like pain flashes over his face as he glances at Ray, but she nods, and it only makes him look that much more conflicted. I can see it there, the doubt, the sadness at listening to someone you love tell you a story that simply can't be true. He probably thinks I've concocted the fantasy out of some defensive mechanism from the trauma I've suffered at my fake-father's hands. When I think about it that way, it scares even *me*.

"Before you say anything," I say when his lips part at the end of my story. I hold my hand up between us, my eyes glancing to Ray. She nods, and I sigh. A soft roaring sounds, and my dark flames engulf my hand.

Nathan scrambles back on the couch, throwing an arm across Ray's chest where she sits beside him, like he's bracing them both for impact. I let him stare at the flames for a few more seconds before I push my power further, creating little floating flowers and stars and moons, all to Ray's delight. All I have to do is picture it, and my flames create it. Without the stone on the wish-bracelet holding me back, the possibilities feel endless.

When I think he's seen enough, I draw my powers back, leaving my hands clean and bare.

Slowly, he drops the arm from Ray's chest, rubbing his palms over his face. "You knew about this?" he asks Ray.

"Not until recently," she says, flashing me a poignant look.

"Demons are real," he says, and I almost laugh at how similar he sounds to me when Draven told me about the real world. "And you're...you can create flames from your hands."

"Among other things, yes," I say.

"You're a Judge." He points to Draven, who nods. He turns to Ray. "And you're in danger." Ray gives him a little shrug.

"She is," I say, hating the way my voice cracks on the admission. "We need to take her to a...friend," I say, unsure what else to call Kazuki. He helped me for a price, but he seemed kind enough. I'll pay whatever he wants if he helps Ray. "He may know how to help her."

Nathan purses his lips, his fingers poised over them like he's stopping himself from asking a million questions. "Okay," he says, standing from the couch. "Let's go."

"*Let's?*" I echo him, shaking my head. "You can't go."

"Like hell I can't go," he argues. "This is Ray we're talking about."

I stand, too, looking up at him. "Yeah," I say. "That's why I just laid the truth out for you despite wanting to keep you in blissful ignorance."

"Well, thanks for that!" he fires back. "Now, where is this friend?"

"You're not coming with us," I say. I'm not going to drag Nathan deeper into my world than he already is, and taking him to The Bridge? A club drenched in demons and magic? Yeah, not going to happen.

"Harley—"

"Nathan," Draven cuts him off, stepping into the living room for the first time since we came inside. "It isn't safe for you."

"And it's safe for Ray?"

"She's not entirely human." Draven speaks the truth we've been thinking for a while now. With the way Ray sees things, with her connection to Marid, and me...there is no way she doesn't have power inside her. "And neither I nor Harley would *ever* let anything happen to her."

"Except for what happened tonight, right?" Nathan says and cringes like he instantly regrets it.

"Nathan," Ray says, her voice strong but sweet. "That's not their fault."

He blows out a breath, but I'm too busy telling those flames inside me to chill out. No way am I barbequing him for what he said, despite how tempting it might be.

"I know," Nathan says, flashing me an apologetic look. "I didn't mean it."

"I know," I echo him. "And you know me. Nothing matters more to me than Ray. I won't let her get hurt. But taking her to Kazuki is the only play I have right now. I don't want to waste a second, either, and give Marid a chance to come back for round two of traumatize Harley."

Nathan glances at each of us before looking solely at me. "You're expecting me to sit here and twiddle my thumbs until you come back with answers?"

"You could make yourself useful and cook some food for when we get back?" I give him a small smile, shrugging.

A grin lights his eyes, but he shakes his head. "You're asking a lot of me here, Harley."

"You think I don't know that?" I put all the weight of what's happened into the words, unable to shield the flood of emotions storming me anyway. "But after what happened to Ray? I don't care. I have to do this. We have to go. Whether you like it or not."

He's quiet for a long moment. "Can you check in?" he finally asks, and I don't answer. I just throw my arms around his neck. It's the first hug I've given him since he went behind my back to adopt Ray, and it mends some of those broken pieces inside me. I release him and glance down at Ray.

"You need to change," I say, eying her nightgown.

"Right," she says, looking down at herself. "Be right back." She walks a little slowly up the stairs, and I curse myself for having to put her through this when she's still healing. But I can't sit by and let Marid possess her again, either.

Nathan stares at the empty stairs, nothing but love and worry coating his eyes.

"I'll keep her safe," I say.

"She means the world to me," he says, not taking his eyes off the stairs.

"I know," I say, turning away from him to stand near Draven by the door as we wait. Ray is back in a few minutes, clad in galaxy leggings and a black, long-sleeve shirt.

"Ready," she says after hugging Nathan. "Let's go get exorcised," she jokes, and the three of us gape at her. "What?" she asks, reaching for my hand. "If anyone is allowed to joke about possession, it's me."

I snort laugh, shaking my head as Draven holds the door open for us. Nathan follows behind, lingering in the doorway as we step onto the porch.

"Kiddo," he calls after we've cleared the steps, and I turn around to look up at him. "You mean the world to me, too," he says, and a knot forms in my throat. "Stay safe."

I don't nod or bother to respond. Instead, I give him a look that says I'll do my best. Because with everything that has happened recently? *My* safety is the absolute last thing I can guarantee.

Ray's, though?

I'll burn the world to the ground before I let her get hurt.

I just really, *really* hope it doesn't come to that.

CHAPTER SIX

"No younglings."

The feminine voice is familiar as a pair of yellow cat eyes glances down at Ray through the slat in The Bridge's entrance.

The supernatural nightclub bouncer had no problems admitting me a couple weeks ago, and while I can understand the whole *we don't let almost eight-year-olds into our club* policy, I really don't have time for it.

Ray shifts on her feet before me, and I place my hands on her shoulders. "We need to see Kazuki," I say, trying like hell to keep my tone calm.

A cackling laugh is the only response before the female slides the slat shut.

"That went about as well as expected," Draven says, typing away on his cell again.

"Has he texted you back?" I ask, hopeful.

"Nope." Draven shakes his head. "He hasn't answered my dozen calls, either. I'm texting Cas now to see if he knows where the warlock is."

"Thanks," I say, appreciating his effort but unable to smother the anger ticking away inside me like a bomb on a countdown. I take a few steadying breaths, but as the minutes go by with no response from anyone, I'm just about done.

Those yellow and blue eyes, the scales on Ray's skin, the snakes slithering around her neck, all keep flashing in my mind. Each time ramps up my inner rage just a bit more, until I'm pounding on The Bridge's door again. When the bouncer doesn't bother to answer, I slam all my weight into it. The rose-gold insignia of a bridge shakes above the closed eye-slat.

"Harley," Draven says, almost as if he's trying to soothe the anger in me.

I ignore him.

"We don't have time for this," I practically growl. Any second, Marid could slip into Ray's mind again. I need answers.

I need fucking *help*.

"It's going to be okay," Ray says, her voice so strong and hopeful and mature for her age. All a product of the way we've grown up, and who knows? Maybe it has something to do with her own untapped power, too. Just another question to add to the growing list in my head.

I nod to her, then look to Draven. "Can you slip into your shadow self, slide under the door and open it for us?" I ask after I've tried the windows on the main street level that have apparently been spelled against entry.

"I would," he says, eyes apologetic. "But Kazuki has his establishments warded against all kinds of unwanted visitors."

"I'm not unwanted," I say and raise my voice to add, "I've got a bargain for you, warlock!"

Only the sound of bass thrumming through the closed door responds, the music inside enough to vibrate the brick of the building.

Another few minutes go by with no word from Kazuki or Cassiel.

And after everything that has happened in the last few weeks? After having to watch Ray get hurt by our father because he was so drunk he thought she was *me*? After not sleeping since before I had to battle my supposed best friend to the death? After shutting the gates to Hell in order to save the world and watching Draven die as a result?

I'm just so done.

After *all* that, getting into a club shouldn't be such a pain in the ass.

The rage rises inside me, sweeping over me like a wave of steaming water. I've always felt the sensation inside me, always thought it was a result of the abuse my father dealt out daily.

Maybe it has something to do with being the Antichrist.

Maybe I don't give a shit.

Not when Ray's life is at stake—and it *is* at stake. I will not have a Greater demon entering her mind and body whenever the fuck he feels like it.

Flames of glittering night engulf my hands, curling around my fists so fast Ray slips a foot away from me. "I'd never hurt you," I say, and she nods, silently telling me she knows that. "But this door?" I turn to face the steel monstrosity and dig my fire-covered fingers into it.

Power pushes back at me, something that feels older than time—Kazuki's magic, no doubt. But I push harder, driving every ounce of my rage into my dark flames, every ounce of pain and worry until the door swings open.

"This door is over three hundred years old!" The feline-female glares at me from the entryway, eying the door with those cunning cat eyes as if she's looking for scars. "Kaz will roast me on a spit if you damage it!"

I bare my teeth in a twisted smile. "What do you think *I'll* do to you if you don't let us in?"

She eyes my flames, fear turning her body rigid.

Ray gasps at my side, and in the back of my mind, I know I shouldn't be threatening anyone in front of my little sister. But all bets are off for me when she's at risk. Is it my fatal flaw? Maybe, but again, I'm beyond caring at this point.

The female's tail swishes behind her, an irritated motion as she shifts to the side, one arm extended.

I extinguish my flames, keeping Ray close to my side as we pass her.

"You're going to regret bringing her in here," she whispers. "There aren't rules for children because they aren't allowed inside. Bringing her here will only create a loophole for those who have a hard enough time playing by the rules as it is."

I glance over my shoulder, and she blanches at whatever she sees in my eyes. Likely the promise of death for anyone who even thinks about messing with Ray. It's been that way since she was born. Becoming the Antichrist and diving headfirst into a supernatural world hasn't changed that for me.

Draven follows close behind as we navigate the long hallway off the entrance. He scans the entirety of the club as we round the corner, the massive space packed with dancers. The giant square bar is lit up with neon green lights that twinkle along bottles of various liquors and other liquids I don't even want to know about. Ray's hand goes loose in mine as we reach the bar that rests in the middle of a sweeping dance floor.

I watch as she takes in the variety of creatures moving to the thrumming music—talons and hooves and feathers, scales and fur and glowing eyes of all colors. Some with horns, some with elongated ears, some with fangs, and others with too many appendages to count. Each moving in time to the music filtering from speakers hidden in the high ceiling above. Each one united in their love for the melody, despite their stark differences in appearance.

"Shoot," Ray says. "I should've brought my sketchbook."

I smile down at her as we reach a few empty spots at the center of the bar.

"It's beautiful. *They're* beautiful, aren't they, Harley?" She glances up at me, and it's the unflinching joy and awe in her eyes, the hope and love radiating from her that softens that anger inside me.

"It is," I say, scanning the area, hoping to lock eyes with a certain lavender-eyed warlock. "I remember thinking that the first time I came here." *Right before I was almost eaten by a Hypno demon.*

I leave that part out, though. Tonight is different. It's only been a little over a week since I first came to The Bridge, but so much has changed.

I've changed. I'm no longer a lost girl with no grasp of her powers—okay, maybe I'm still a little lost. But I do have better control of the powers. I may not know where they originate from or who my real parents are or why I was chosen to be this *Antichrist,* but I can defend myself all the same.

Draven leans on the bar next to me, calling over the bartender with a simple look.

The bartender hurries over to us, his bright orange eyes alight with the prospect of new customers. The fur on his head is the same color as his eyes, tapering off to a darker gray over his neck and bulging arms. A thick tail sways behind him, and if I had to guess, I'd bet his legs were like pillars behind the bar—he looks like a cross between a bear and a lion.

"What's your poison?" he asks, his orange eyes flaring when he peers over the bar to see Ray standing at my side. He returns his gaze to Draven, glancing between the two of us, wary.

"We need to speak to Kazuki," Draven says, sliding a crisp bill across the bar. "Can you call him?"

The bartender shakes his head, the fur on his head standing at attention. "I don't hit the summon button unless there is an emergency. Those are the rules, Judge."

I flinch at the way he sneers the word *Judge,* but Draven doesn't so much as blink.

"This *is* an emergency," he says, his voice low and cold. I wonder how many times Draven has had to shift into that icy role of Judge over the decades? Wonder how many times he's found himself on the receiving end of disgust and ridicule for being something he had no choice in?

"Doesn't look like it," the bartender says, leaning back to fold his bulky arms over his chest. "Looks to me like you're just breaking the rules to start trouble."

"If you *want* trouble," I say, seething, "you can have it—"

"We don't want any trouble," Ray's voice calls over mine, and she climbs onto the barstool so she can be eye level with the bartender. "We just really, really need to talk to Kazuki," she says. "Will you please help us do that…?" She lets the sentence hang there, and I'm about as shocked as Draven looks when the bartender softens his features, letting those massive arms, hands tipped with gleaming claws, fall loose at his sides.

"Crane," he says, filling in the blank she left.

Ray smiles at him, a beaming sort of grin that puts a knot in my throat. "Crane," she says. "I can tell you're a super nice person. You smell like apples and cinnamon." I blink at her declaration, but something about the words has Crane's eyes flaring. "Please help us."

I gape at my little sister, wondering how the hell we were ever matched together. She's the one in danger, but she's being all sweet and polite when all I've done is rage and threaten.

Crane leans on the bar, studying Ray a little too close for my comfort. Flames lick my fingertips as I watch him, but he *grins* at Ray before nodding. "Okay, tiny human," he says, his grin dropping the second he eyes Draven and me, but he turns around, reaching for a bright lavender cell phone resting on a shelf behind him.

"Look what we have here," a voice calls from behind us. I whirl around, almost in sync with Draven. "A murderer, a Judge, and a…" The Hypno—one of six—flares his nostrils at Ray. "A miniature seer."

"It's not murder when it's self-defense," I fire back, flames instantly on my fingertips as I step in front of Ray. Shadows gather around Draven's shoulders as he takes up the spot to my right.

"Doesn't matter," the Hypno says, eying his men on either side. "Blood for blood is due."

I groan, noting the way each one of the Hypnos is spreading out in a half circle around us. The four blue horns on each of their heads glitter in The Bridge's pulsing, colored lights.

I roll my eyes. "You guys are super repetitive. And I didn't do anything to you or your friends," I add. "If you turn around now, we can keep it that way."

The Hypno in the center laughs. "That's not the way the rules work—"

"I like your horns," Ray cuts him off, and I jolt, only now noticing she stands to my left, looking up at the Hypno. I'm so focused on the demons spreading out in an attack formation I didn't even hear her move.

"Ray," I whisper, urging her back.

She ignores me. "Cerulean is one of my absolute favorite shades of blue. It's the perfect example of a summer sky right before nightfall."

"*Ray*," I snap, the proximity to the Hypno too close.

The Hypno scrunches his brow, dismissing Ray and returning that lethal stare to me. "You die—"

"You have a choice," Ray says, interrupting him again. "You know that, right?" she asks, and Draven barely covers his laugh with his hand. "You can just walk away right now. You and your friends. Go find some pretty demons to dance with."

The Hypno gapes at her, and in this, we're the same.

"Don't give me choices, tiny seer," he says, baring his teeth at her. "It's been a long time since I've tasted the delicacy of your kind's blood."

She sighs, closing her eyes.

My flames roar, curling around both my fists as he takes a step toward her—

Something massive slams to the ground in front of Ray, the power rumbling the building so hard the ground trembles.

CHAPTER SEVEN

"About time," Draven mutters.

It takes me a few seconds to recognize the creature. The obsidian wings with thousands upon thousands of ink-colored feathers, the olive skin with hints of black ink beneath a thin white t-shirt, and the cold, silver eyes promising death.

Cassiel.

"I was *two states away*," he growls, his sharp eyes on the Hypnos as his wings expand, blocking Ray from sight. Even if he wasn't Draven's best friend, I'd like the angel of death for that protective stance alone.

The Hypno staggers back a step, his eyes widening at Cassiel. "You have no role in this, death striker."

Cassiel narrows his gaze, a ripple of power ruffling the inky feathers of his massive wings. "Try me," he says, his words like ice and smoke, sending shivers along my spine despite him clearly being on my side.

The other Hypnos in the half circle eye what is clearly the leader of their pack, some not even bothering to hide their looks of horror at Cassiel's appearance.

The leader stabs a thick finger in my direction. "Our fight is with her," he seethes.

"And me," Draven says.

"Then it is with me as well," Cassiel says.

I groan, shaking my head. "We *so* don't have time for this." Each second we waste with these guys is one more second we don't help my sister. I step around both Draven and Cassiel, putting myself within inches of the lead Hypno. My flames cast shadows upon the bare skin of his forearms, his shirtsleeves rolled to the elbows.

"You have five seconds," I say, letting all the rage pour into my voice as I raise my flaming fists between us. "It's been a day. No, a *week*." I glance at each Hypno before returning focus to the one before me. "Leave or become ash." And in that moment, I honestly don't care which path he chooses. He's lucky I'm giving him a choice at all after he threatened to drink my sister's blood.

"Five," I say, holding up my fiery fingers.

He growls.

"Four." I drop one finger.

"Three." Another finger. I shift my feet into a defensive stance.

"You have no authority here. You're just a weak little girl," the Hypno spits, baring his fangs.

Draven lets out a low chuckle. "Oh, shit."

"Two," I say, dropping another finger.

The Hypno sneers, laughing. "You honestly think you can take all six of us?"

"I know I can," I whisper and drop the last finger. A crowd has gathered around us now, forming one giant circle of onlookers near the bar. "One," I say and become a living, breathing flame of rage.

I lunge for him, lashing out faster than a snake strike. He doesn't have time to dodge my outstretched hand. I clamp my fingers around his throat, his eyes bulging. "Call my sister's blood a delicacy again," I say. "I fucking *dare* you."

"Language, darling," Kazuki's voice cuts through the air as if he's holding a megaphone to his lips, but when I turn to look at him, of course he isn't.

The ancient, powerful warlock doesn't need anything to magnify his voice. His presence does that just fine on his own. Honestly, he's gorgeous with his sleek midnight hair, high cheekbones, and neatly trimmed goatee along a strong jaw line. His lithe, defined muscles are displayed perfectly as he leans casually against that emerald-topped cane of his—and he knows it. Tonight, he dons a suit of rich royal blue, and his stark lavender eyes crackle with power.

"This is the second time you've broken the rules in my club," he says, voice like silk as he casts his gaze between myself and the half circle of Hypnos. "Both of you," he clarifies.

"I'm sorry, Kazuki," I say, snuffing out my flames in an instant. I need his help, and pissing him off is not the way to get it.

Kazuki notes the submissive move, then studies Draven and Cassiel and then Ray trying to peek from behind Cassiel's wings.

"She killed our kind—"

"Yes, we established that last week," Kazuki groans over the Hypno. He flicks his wrist at the group. "I ruled it self-defense. Do you wish to challenge *my* ruling? Thought not," he says after the Hypnos have said nothing. "Crane, dear?" Kazuki calls over his shoulder without turning to look at the bar.

"Yes, Kazuki?" Crane answers.

"Please see to it that all of these Hypnos' tabs are taken care of tonight," he says. "As a token for their best behavior."

After an intense stare-down that the leader ultimately loses, the Hypnos dip their heads to Kazuki, the leader flashing me a glare before they all saunter toward the bar. One look from Kazuki has the rest of the onlookers skittering back to the dance floor like they're afraid to become the object of the warlock's attention.

"Now," he says, turning to face the four of us. "This had better be interesting." He arches a brow at me. "I was summoned all the way from Rome, and let me tell you, I was having an *exquisite* time."

A blush creeps over my cheeks with the way he accentuates the word *exquisite*, but I press forward, ready to launch into my plea.

He raises one polished finger toward me. "Not here," is all he says before heading through the dancing crowd that naturally parts for him. He climbs a set of stairs, leading us down several hallways adorned with abstract paintings that look as old as the warlock himself, the art itself broken apart by little wooden tables with elaborate flower arrangements sitting atop them. Finally, we turn into a private room as big as an event hall.

Plush leather couches, chairs, and loveseats hug the walls in little groupings, slick stone tables resting between them. Crystal chandeliers with royal blue gemstones flicker in the light hanging from the high ceilings, and a long marble bar is situated on the opposite side of the room, glass pitchers and champagne glasses atop it filled with a sparkling pink liquid.

Kazuki snaps and one of the pitchers appears on the stone table in the center of the couches and chairs, and he sinks onto the couch, his arms outstretched to either side to take up all the space.

Ray plops down in one of the armchairs, me electing to sit on the arm of it, while Draven and Cassiel take the chairs on the other side.

"Drink?" Kazuki offers, but none of us move. Well, none of us except Ray, who smiles as she reaches for the sparkly pink drink. "Not that one, my sweet," he says, snapping his fingers again. A crystal glass appears in my sister's hand, a bright yellow liquid inside. "Lemonade," he explains when I sniff the drink. "Honestly, Harley, it's like you don't trust me," he teases.

I take a quick sip of the drink instead of answering. I trust very few people, though I'm trying my best to open up a little more now that I'm free of my father. Not that I've been free long enough to truly process what that means for my life or my sister's. But, seeing as how I've been fighting demons and closing the gates of Hell—and now dealing with a possession—I've been a little preoccupied.

Satisfied the drink is nothing but lemonade and not some potion that'll turn Ray into a cute little bunny, I hand it back to her. She sips and says, "Thank you."

Kazuki smiles at her, then looks to Cassiel. "So, what was so important you called me away from my favorite bathhouse, hmm? Got yourself in another pickle, angel?"

Cassiel shoots him a glare.

"It's me," I blurt before Cassiel has a chance to say anything. We need Kazuki in a good, *giving* mood, and having a battle of words with the angel of death doesn't seem like the best way to get him there.

Kazuki's cunning gaze slides to mine, eyes flickering to my tattoo and back again. "I'm happy to see you're alive," he says, and it sounds like the truth, but who can really tell? "What do you need this time, love? A tattoo that grants you the power to become invisible?"

I go to argue, manage to pull myself back, and instead smile. "Can you do that?"

Draven laughs under his breath, shifting in the chair next to me.

"What *can't* I do?" Kazuki replies, winking at Ray, who is still enjoying her drink.

"Right," I say, coming back to reality. "Your tattoo helped save my life," I say, burying all the emotions trying to storm me with images of Kai, of his betrayal, the knife sinking into my stomach. I clear my throat. "I don't have the right words to thank you—"

"While I appreciate the flattery, darling, I have a bathhouse and several delightful partners waiting for me. Get to the point."

"Marid possessed Ray tonight."

Kazuki stiffens as he gracefully slides to the edge of the couch, elbows at his knees, the cane gripped in one hand. "Say that again," he says, his voice lower and softer than I've ever heard it before.

"Marid possessed Ray tonight," I repeat, my hand sliding to Ray's back. She sets her drink on the stone table. "He said he no longer needs me to escape. That he's found real power to help him, and he simply wants to torture me through her for the rest of our lives."

Kazuki grips his cane a bit harder, leaning back slightly as if the words have finally registered in his mind.

"I'm here to beg for help. To sever whatever tether is between them allowing him to do this. We came straight here because I have no idea when he'll do it again."

When the warlock says nothing, his gaze distant as if he's seeing a hundred different scenarios play out at once, I try a different angle.

"I know you deal in favors," I say. "I'll pay whatever price you ask."

Cassiel sighs, and Draven clenches his eyes shut as if I've just offered up my soul as payment.

Maybe I have, because Kazuki's eyes clear, locking on mine as an almost feline grin shapes his mouth. "Anything I want?"

A shiver skates down my spine at the power washing through the room, my own climbing to match it as fear's icy laugh taunts me.

Maybe I should've played my hand closer to the chest?

But if it saves Ray, it'll be worth it.

"Anything."

CHAPTER EIGHT

Ray slips her hand over my leg, looking up at me. "Harley," she says, shaking her head.

Kazuki eyes the emerald atop his cane. "Coming from you, dark princess, that is offering quite a lot."

I frown at the use of the nickname *princess.*

"Be reasonable, Kazuki," Draven says in a low, warning tone. "She's new to this world, and all the rules haven't been explained to her yet."

Something warm slides through me at his primal, lethal tone. As if he has the power to go toe-to-toe with the warlock. Maybe, due to every power he's siphoned over his years serving the Seven, he does. But he can only use each power for a short amount of time before it drains him, and I sure as hell don't want to see that. I've seen Draven dead enough for one lifetime, thanks.

"Can you help us?" I ask.

Kazuki's eyes are still calculating. "Of course I can," he says, laying the cane flat over his long legs. "But tethers that act as open portals are rare. And why does he have one with you, little one?" He narrows his gaze on Ray, the look studying, not menacing.

"Is it because I drew him?" she asks, glancing from me to the warlock. "I dreamed of him first, then I started drawing him. I don't do that anymore."

"Draw him or dream of him?" Kazuki asks.

"Draw him," she answers. "It's been four days since I had a dream about him."

"Interesting," Kazuki says, leaning back against the couch.

His eyes trail to Cassiel, looking incredibly uncomfortable with his wings draped over the arms of the chair. "And you?" he asks. "What is your stake in this?"

Cassiel's silver gaze trails to Draven, then back to Kazuki. "Harley is Draven's—"

Draven coughs, cutting Cassiel off for a moment, and I quickly reach for a pink drink, handing it to Draven.

"*Friend*," Cassiel finishes, shooting Draven an irritated look. "And Ray is her sister. What is important to him is important to me."

Kazuki grins softly at this declaration, but his eyes are narrowed as they return to me. "Severing a tether is not as easy as snipping a thread with scissors."

"I figured that," I say, sighing.

"And I unfortunately can't do it myself," he finishes.

My stomach sinks. "You can't whip up some potion with your magic cane and make Marid's connection disappear?"

Lavender sparks seem to shoot from his eyes. "If I could do that, what would stop me from doing it to a million other beings with a million other connections?"

"But you know how." It's not a question—I can see the answer in his eyes. He knows. And the news must be grim, because he looks at Ray with the only show of sadness I've ever seen from him.

"Yes," he finally says. "I know how."

"Tell me what to do."

Kazuki tilts his head. "So determined," he says. "So eager, yet you know nothing of what the process entails."

"I don't care if I have to take a sacred ring to Mordor," I say. "Whatever it is, it has to be done." When Kazuki still seems hesitant to explain, I press on. "He entered her mind, Kazuki," I say, my voice cracking. "And unlike you or Draven, he didn't ask permission. He took control of her *body* without her knowing. I can't...I won't let that happen to her again."

Draven's hands clench into fists at his sides, his power radiating in an angry burst throughout the room.

Kazuki visibly swallows.

"Is there something I can do?" Ray asks before Kazuki can respond. "On my own?"

"You are not alone in this," I say, and she purses her lips at me.

"I know that," she says. "But if the tether is mine…is it up to me to cut it?"

"Such a clever little seer," Kazuki says, smiling at Ray. "Like I said, it's an involved process. I only know about it because a witch with a similar problem came to me four centuries ago, needing a powerful anchor to help facilitate the severing." A distant light glimmers in his eyes. "I have an endless supply of mugwart because of my assistance in the ritual."

I blink a few times, marveling at his casual reference to his vast and unknown age. "So, we need an anchor," I say, gathering one piece of the puzzle. "I can act as that, right?"

Kazuki raises his brows. "Are you trying to say you're as powerful as me, dark princess?"

I smirk back at him. "After what's happened in the last forty-eight hours?" I ask, leaning forward. "I know I am, *dark warlock*."

A booming laugh rips from his lips, and he nods. "I knew I liked you for a reason," he says. "Yes, your power will serve well as anchor, and if for some reason you fail, Draven's will suffice."

"Oh, sure," Cassiel says, his voice deep and sharp as steel. "Pretend like I don't have a wealth of power, too."

"Poor, sweet angel of death," Kazuki croons. "Are you feeling left out?"

Cassiel grunts.

"What else?" I ask.

"In order to sever the tether, you need four things."

Okay, that's not so bad. "Four is doable."

"Don't start celebrating yet, darling," Kazuki says. "You need a powerful anchor, like I mentioned, to wield and manage the second item on the list. Divinely blessed and concentrated phenacite."

I spare a glance to Draven, Cassiel, and then Ray. "Am I supposed to know what that is?"

"It's a crystal," Draven explains.

"But you simply can't hop on Etsy and order any old piece of phenacite," Kazuki argues. "Divinely blessed and highly concentrated phenacite is extremely rare and hard to find, yet it's the only crystal with enough power to sever ties and restore energy protection and clear internal pathways to and from the soul."

I pinch the bridge of my nose, my chest tightening at his use of the words *rare* and *hard to find.* Another task to throw on the list, but I want to hear the next requirements first. "What are the last two things we need?"

Kazuki purses his lips, pity shading those lavender eyes of his. "*If* you manage to get the phenacite, and your power is up for acting as an anchor for it, then you need to charge the crystal with a bolt of divine lightning."

Draven goes absolutely still next to me. The chain inside me tightens, frosting over with an ice so cold it burns.

"Divine lightning?"

Kazuki nods once. "It's the only power capable of liquifying the crystal. The one who is entering Marid's mind to cut the tether must drink it, and then…" His voice trails off, and my impatience stretches like a string about to snap.

"Just tell me, Kazuki."

I killed my supposed best friend less than forty-eight hours ago, watched Draven die, fought like hell to bring him back, and then he told me I was the freaking Antichrist. Whatever Kazuki is about to say can't be as bad as all that.

"Fine," he says. "If you manage to get the supplies you need and can buy, trick, or somehow command the help of a being who can conjure the divine light, then the two ends of the tether must be present."

"At the same time?" Cassiel asks. And judging by the hard glint in his eyes, he does not like the idea.

"Yes. Ray and Marid must physically be in the same space, not merely sharing a connection between planes."

I hold up a finger, asking for some grace while I slow my racing heart. "Let me get this straight," I say, wanting to make sure I haven't misunderstood anything. "I have to put my sister and Marid in a room together?"

Kazuki gives me a dip of his head.

I blink a few times, realizing the worst of it. "And I can't summon him here, right? Not without risking releasing him and his buddies into the world to wreak some major havoc."

"Precisely," Kazuki says.

I turn to look at Draven, whose expression is cold and hard and *angry*.

"I have to go to Hell," I say, the words thick in my throat as I turn back to Kazuki.

"And you have to take her with you."

CHAPTER NINE

Panic lashes at my insides.

I have to take my little sister to the same place I nearly *died* trying to close the gates to? The same place I've been considering exiling myself to so I don't end the world? I gape at Ray, apologetic and guilty. This is my fault. I brought her into this life, no doubt Marid targeting her just to get to me.

Draven and I both wear masks of barely restrained horror. How can *this* be our only option?

My mind runs wild with imaginings straight out of horror movies—fire and brimstone and demons snapping their teeth at every turn. But, to be fair, I'm not anything like what the media describes as the Antichrist, so maybe they got this wrong, too. Though a place like Hell probably won't be like a trip to Disneyland. If it was just me, I wouldn't care, but Ray...my sweet, innocent, optimistic sister...

Ray gives me a half smile and shrugs. "Road trip?"

Her hopeful expression, the confidence in her eyes, and her attempt at humor are just enough to stop me from sliding down another rung on the panic ladder. One step at a time.

"Where can we find this crystal?" I ask.

Cassiel clears his throat. "I may know someone who has access to it."

Kazuki's eyebrows raise. "Really?" he asks, grinning. "Please, *do* tell." Cassiel plants his lips in a firm line, and Kazuki waves him off. "You're no fun, angel."

"Okay," I say. "We get the crystal from your contact"—another favor I'll have to hand out, no doubt—"and then where can we find a creature with the power of divine lightning?" I glance at Cassiel, hopeful.

He looks at Draven.

Kazuki is unsarcastically quiet as he, too, looks to Draven.

I glance between the three males. What am I missing? If this is a power Draven has siphoned in the past, surely he'd speak up?

"I know someone who can do that," he finally says, his voice icy. "My brother. Ryder."

The air stalls in my lungs.

"Do you think that's wise—" Cassiel starts.

Draven cuts a glare at him. "Do you know of any others with this light?"

The angel doesn't flinch from his tone, as if he's used to Draven's guilt, his brooding.

Draven's fists uncurl, the golden skin shifting over the muscles rippling in his arms. "He can do it," he says, nodding a little too quickly. "He *has* to be the one to do it."

Something heavy settles in me, a steel box of questions, but I know better than to broach them with everyone in this room. Draven's brother—Ryder—is a sensitive topic, and I will not grill him about it here. So I turn back to Kazuki.

"All right, then. How exactly do we get to Hell?" I eye the tattoo on my wrist. "I know my blood can open the gates, but I don't really want to let anyone in behind us."

"I can transport in," Cassiel says. "But you know I can't carry anyone without a stamp."

"Transport…in?" I ask, brow scrunched.

His wings shift over the chair. "One of the many 'privileges' of being an angel of death," he says, voice like liquid steel. "Carrying demons or souls to different realms allows me to move between the veils separating them. I can't take anyone without a proper Order, though. Either from the Seven or the gatekeeper."

"You don't have to go at all, brother," Draven says, his voice much more steady now.

Cassiel rolls his eyes like Draven just suggested he tap dance on Kazuki's table. "You're venturing into the Ather. I'm going. End of discussion."

"Ather?" I ask, a familiar pain forming behind my eyes—the same one I associate with any amount of information I can't or don't understand. "Is that Hell?"

Cassiel's wings rustle as he looks to me. "What humans call Hell is actually called the Ather."

"Hell is a human term," Kazuki adds. "Rumors and legends handed and watered down throughout the ages have twisted what truth is behind the realm."

"And that is?"

Kazuki shrugs. "At its most basic definition, the Ather is a dimension that resides next to ours, housing all manner of demons, good *and* bad. It's not a type of 'hell' to them—it's home. There are good places, and there are very bad places. Some love it. Others want to escape. Same as anywhere here, really."

Okay, that sounded more promising than the images I'd conjured from movies and books. Maybe that meant I wasn't wholly good or evil, either. "And the Devil?" I ask, casting a quick look to Draven.

"Another human term," Kazuki says, crossing one leg over the other. "I only met him once, and it was ages ago."

"Rainier." I say the name Draven relayed to me...earlier? Damn, had that conversation been mere hours ago? Right before Marid possessed Ray?

"I called him Rain," Kazuki says, laughing. "He hated it. But his domain is the most heavily warded and is surrounded by the most dangerous realms in all the Ather. From what I know, Marid's realm is a few clicks west of Rainier's."

Demon realms. Clicks. Fucking hell. My head hurts, my body hurts. I can't remember the last time I slept—

"You should rest, Harley," Ray says as if reading my thoughts. "We can plan all this after you've gotten some sleep."

I shake my head. "No," I say. "I'm not wasting one second

sleeping when Marid could come back—"

"The little seer is right," Kazuki cuts in. "You will be no use to her on this journey if you're half dead."

"I'm *not* half dead."

Draven rises from his chair, sliding in front of me, a hand extended.

"Don't," I say.

"*Harley*," he says, and despite my anger, my terror, warmth glides over my skin. I take his hand, let him tug me gently to my feet. "I'm not going to fight you. You want to stay awake and spit fire while we gather what we need, then I'll stand behind you and clap while you do it." He smooths some of my hair back, his fingers lingering against my cheek. "But it will take Cassiel at least a few hours to get in touch with his contact for the phenacite. Right?" He glances over his shoulder at Cassiel.

"And maybe a few more for me to actually get my hands on it," the angel adds.

I groan. So long. So many hours where Ray could be overtaken.

Cassiel stands to his full height, his wings extending. "I'll work as fast as I can," he says before gliding out of the room so quickly my eyes can barely follow.

"I'm sure Kazuki will be happy to put us up for the night," Draven says. "And Ray will be safer here than anywhere else."

"Quite," Kazuki agrees, nodding. "The Bridge's wards may very well act as a magical buffer, deterring Marid or at least making it too difficult to attempt possession."

Hope blooms in my chest. "Thank you," I say. "For the information, for the safety."

Kazuki dips his head. "I'm certain you won't forget it, dark princess."

"Indeed, dark warlock," I tease and let my forehead slump against Draven's chest.

"See?" Ray says as I draw away from Draven, reaching for her hand. She takes mine as she stands up. "Everything is going to work out."

"I love her optimism," Kazuki says, winking at Ray, and I can't help but agree with him. Ray has never lost that unflinching hope or joy, not even when forced to live with the monster we called Dad.

But I'm too tired, too wrecked inside for her light to reach me this time. Not when I can do nothing but sit and wait while her life hangs in the balance.

CHAPTER TEN

"I'll show you to your rooms," Kazuki says, leading the way outside of the space we were in and down several more hallways, each twist and turn taking us farther away from the noise of the club and deeper into a comfortable, protected kind of silence.

Kazuki holds open a set of double doors, ushering Ray and us inside.

"Whoa," Ray says, and I echo her sentiment.

The room is slightly smaller than where we just were, but it is no less lavish. The walls are painted a rose gold, separated in sections by intricate woven tapestries of royal blue and white. A king-size bed hugs the left wall, bedecked in mountains of pillows and cream-colored comforters. A mahogany wooden table sits next to it, and a lamp that looks to be made from the remnants of some ancient tree illuminates the room in a soft golden light.

"This is one of my private quarters," Kazuki explains, pride rippling from the warlock. He points to a doorway tucked into the farther corner of the room. "An identical room is connected through that door. Both are heavily warded. It should do for the rest of the day."

Day. Because night has given way to dawn from the looks of dusky light peeking through the opened curtains draped around the bay windows on the farthest wall. Kazuki snaps, and the curtains fall shut, blocking out the light. "You should listen to the little seer," he says. "And get some rest. Both of you," he adds, eying Ray.

Ray nods, releasing my hand to hop on the bed. "This is the nicest bed I've ever sat on," she says, and I cringe at the truth. It's not like we were afforded sorcerer-level luxuries before.

Kazuki bows at the waist to her, smiling before he turns and lingers in the open doorway.

"I may never leave this bed," Ray half yawns from where she's already burrowing under the covers. Her eyes are already closed. I'm tempted to climb in with her, but with what Draven revealed about his brother, with what we're about to have to do...

I lean down and kiss her forehead. "I'll be just next door. I won't sleep long, I promise." A part of me shudders as I make it two steps away from her, and Kazuki must sense this because he waves a hand at me.

"I assure you, no one is getting through this door, let alone her mind. Do give me some credit, darling."

I flash him a silent thank-you. I know his help isn't free, that there will be a cost coming soon, but for now, I'm too tired to worry about it. He bows before closing the door behind him.

Draven is at the connecting door in the room, quietly opening it. I give Ray another worried glance, but she's already asleep, her little chest rising and falling easily. I just can't understand how she can look so peaceful after everything that has happened, but then again, she's always managed levels of hope I never could.

I walk through the doorway and sigh as Draven softly shuts the door behind him. The room is identical to the one we were just in, except the tables are made of an obsidian wood. Draven flicks on the lamp by the enormous bed, dimming it to where only a soft golden light illuminates the mostly dark room.

I sink onto the bed, feeling the exhaustion in my bones.

But Draven...he hovers near the foot of the bed.

"Tell me what you're thinking," I say.

He sighs, and the sound skitters along that connection between us. "I'm thinking that neither you nor Ray deserves any of this," he says, sliding his hands into his pockets as if he's afraid of what he might do with them if he lets them free. "I'm thinking that you two deserved very different, much brighter lives. And I'm wondering how much of a selfish bastard I am because I *know* this, and yet I'm happy you came into my life."

I huff a broken laugh. "Came into your life," I echo. "A divine soldier with a mission to kill." The words catch up in my heart, and it sinks. "Do you believe we'll find your brother?"

The question breaks something in him, because he finally sits down on the bed next to me. "We have to," he says. Something distant and dark and cold flashes in his eyes. A blink and it's gone. "Ryder has the power we need. I've seen it. Witnessed it several times in our training. He was always Aphian's favorite. That ability to control storms, to summon lightning that had the strength of the Creator's power made him a Judge to marvel at, not fear. Blessed." He says the last word like a curse.

I shift, folding one leg beneath me. "What's to say we get there and the gatekeeper turns us away like he has you all these years?"

"Ray's possession is certainly violating at least a dozen laws of the Ather. She's our reason for being there, and hopefully, righting that wrong will have to be enough to convince the gatekeeper."

Hopefully. That's not a lot to go on. "Okay," I say and smooth my hand over his hard jaw. "So we'll convince this gatekeeper, then we'll find Ryder. And we'll find a way to bring him back with us while we're at it."

Draven leans his forehead against mine. His strong hands slide over my thighs as he draws us closer. "I like this plan. But I'm also thinking something selfish."

My body melts as he tugs me into his lap, as our chests are flush, our noses grazing from how close we are. "What's that?" I whisper, my heart racing from his touch.

He smooths his hands over my hips, up my spine and back again, making me tremble. "That this is the first time we've been truly alone since I've returned," he whispers. "And that this may very well be the last moment of true safety we have before..."

I don't need him to finish that sentence, the task before us a daunting, terrifying thing.

"And you need sleep," he continues, grazing his lips along my neck. "But all I want to do is keep you up all night."

A tendril of heat coils inside me at his words, at the way his lips feel against my skin. I sink into that sensation, leaning closer to give him better access. "Sleep is overrated," I whisper, half sighing at the way he plants kisses along my collarbone. Those strong hands rub circles along my back, soothing my tight muscles.

"Tell me what to do, Harley," he says. "And I'll do it."

I tremble at the power he's given me, at the way he's so wholly supportive of what I want.

"Tell me you want me to hold you all night while you sleep, and I will," he continues. "Tell me you want me to stand guard at the door, and I will. Tell me—"

Slowly, I inch my lips to his, cutting off his words. My eyes close at the contact, at the warmth of his mouth, the taste of him. His scent swirls around me, and soon I'm not being gentle. I crave the bite, the hunger in our kiss, and he feels it, reacts to it as I press harder against him. I tangle my fingers in his dark hair, clinging to him like he's the last breath I have in the world to take.

I know what I should be doing—sleeping, strategizing, training with my power. Any would be smarter than this, but I don't care. He's right, we haven't had time, and we don't have time now, and we might not have time later. I don't have all answers, and I'm terrified for what is to come, but here? In his arms, his mouth on mine? All I can do is feel *whole*. Complete in a way I've never felt before. And when I've spent the last few days crumbling? Who am I to deny Draven putting me back together again?

"Harley," he groans between my lips as I rock against him. "You're impossible," he says, flicking his tongue over my bottom lip. "Beautiful, wonderful, impossible."

Heat bursts along my skin as he shifts beneath me, the move so swift and graceful I don't even realize until I'm on my back that he's moved our positions. He settles between my thighs, the solid weight of him sending warm shivers dancing along my spine. Our kiss barely breaks with the move, and he slides an arm beneath my lower back, hauling me against him as he deepens our kiss.

We're fully clothed, but I feel stripped bare, the heat searing between us and along that damn chain inside me so much I might combust. I mentally check my power, ensuring I don't roast us both. Luckily, it seems content to slumber while Draven steals my breath.

In another life, we could be two high school kids after their prom. A special night celebrated with a fancy hotel room and more than enough kissing. We could've danced all night and laughed with friends and then come back here to—

Draven breaks our kiss enough to hover over me, his eyes a churning gold as he cups my cheek with a gentleness that doesn't match the hunger of his kiss. "I *can't* be selfish with you, Harley," he whispers and plants soft kisses along my jaw, on both of my cheeks. "You haven't slept since you brought me back."

I drop my head against the pillow, knowing he's right. "But I don't want this to end," I admit, my fingers curling around his shirt as if I can hold him there forever. "I don't want *us* to end." And with what we have to face? What we've already faced? I know that wanting something to last is a fool's dream.

Draven shifts, rolling us so we're on our sides facing each other. His urgent touches turn to soft, sweeping strokes along my tired body. "That's not going to happen."

With each graze of his fingers over my arm, my hip, my thigh, and back up again, my eyes grow heavier and heavier. But still, I refuse to let them shut on this priceless moment of peace.

"What if where we're going…" I say, even my voice tired. "Separates us? What if I lose you while we search for Ryder, for Marid, for all of it?"

His touch slows for a moment before picking up again. "I will find you," he says. "You know I will. I *always* will."

"Promise?" My lids droop closed without me agreeing to it.

"Promise," he whispers, but he sounds so far away. His warmth settles over me as he tucks me into his arms, his strong chest rising and falling beneath my cheek.

Here, I submit.

Here, somehow despite everything, I know it's safe.

And so I sleep.

CHAPTER ELEVEN

A sharp pain slices into my side.

Kai holds the knife, plunging it into my belly to the hilt.

"You're too late," he says.

"Why, Kai? Why are you doing this?" I cry, my body slumping from the blood gushing down my side. "You were my friend. My only friend." The one who listened when I cried about what my father had done on any given night. The one who watched Ray for me when I had to work or train with Coach Hale. The one who held me when I needed some sort of physical contact beyond pain. The one—

Kai jerks the knife back, the sickening heat from the motion twisting my stomach, wobbling my vision. He poises the blade to strike again, but I lash out with what little strength I have left, snatching the knife from his hands.

I lunge, sinking the sharp blade into his chest.

His eyes go wide, the soothing green I used to look to when I was lost. Betrayal churns there, and he looks so much like he did when we met. Looks like that little boy in a Thor T-shirt who saw me at the park and asked me why I was crying.

"Harley?" he asks, and God, he sounds like that ten-year-old.

My friend.

My very best and only friend.

He slams to his knees before me, hands clutching the knife as blood stains that Thor T-shirt, the same one I asked him about to ignore his question about my tears all those years ago.

The knife is in my hands again, somehow, and without blinking or thinking or breathing, I plunge it into his chest again.

"No," he says, his voice weak. "Harley, please. No. No. We're friends. Why would you do this to me?"

Tears stream down my cheeks, but I don't stop sinking that blade into his flesh.

Over and over again until his cries cease and my hands are covered in blood—

I jolt upright in bed, gasping for breath that comes in razor-sharp gulps. Sweat clings to my skin, my hair plastered against my forehead. My neck and my cheeks are soaked with tears. Draven isn't in the bed, but I smooth my hand out over the sheets like he may suddenly appear.

I glance across the room, and silver eyes lock with mine through the darkness.

I'm off the bed in a second flat, flames licking my fingers as I lunge for the winged creature in the corner of my room—

Inky wings jolt out as the air crackles with cold. His power snaps against mine, and I throw a fiery punch. A strong, firm grip stops my fist from connecting, and icy shivers burst in my lungs.

"*Harley.*" Cassiel's voice is a whisper in the dark, his face finally coming into focus.

One heartbeat, then two.

My brain manages to reorient itself.

Kazuki's. I'm at Kazuki's.

I whirl around, frantic as I swing open the connecting door to our rooms, but Ray lays sleeping soundly on her bed. I shut the door, only partially, and turn back to Cassiel, extinguishing my flames as he drops his grip on my hand.

"Sorry about that," I say, swiping at the tears still coating my cheeks.

"It's cute," he says, smirking. "That you think you'd stand a chance against me." He lowers his hands, his wings relaxing behind him.

I huff out a laugh, thankful for the break in tension, and shrug. "I've danced near death's door all my life," I say. "Maybe I've got more of a shot than you think."

Cassiel arches a brow, but his silver eyes soften. "You had a nightmare."

Not a question. "Did I say anything in my sleep?" I ask, wondering—beyond the tears—if he knows more than he's letting on.

"No," he says, maybe a little too quickly, his gaze trailing to the side. "What was it about?"

I dart my eyes to his, all at once reliving the nightmare that had been truth mixed with fear and pain. "Snakes," I lie. "Always snakes." I try to shrug off the severity of the nightmare, unable to completely clear Kai's betrayed eyes from my mind. But he's the one who lied. He's the one who planted those memories in my head...him and Marid.

Something sticky clings to my insides, and I try like hell to shove it way down deep in a box, content to dig that shit up later. Much later.

"Where is Draven?" I ask, my brain catching up with my body, finally awakening.

"He woke only a short while ago and wanted to talk with Kazuki. He didn't want to wake you up but didn't want to leave you and Ray unguarded. I thought I heard something in here."

I nod, blinking the last of the sleep from my eyes. My nightmare. Right. "How long have we been out?"

"Almost five hours," he says, settling back into his chair.

I raise my brows, finally noting the strength in my muscles, the clarity slipping over my mind, helping to bury the nightmare and awake me to reality. "I didn't realize how much I needed sleep until I got it."

He nods. Quiet, calm, calculating.

"You can go now," I hurry to add. "If you want to. I mean, standing guard while we sleep has to be the most boring job you've ever been handed."

"I volunteered," he says. "There's a difference. You'd be surprised the kind of jobs I've been *handed*," he says, a wicked grin on his lips. "Trust me, guarding a pair of already heavily warded rooms is a blissful break."

I swallow around the knot in my throat, knowing he's right—I have *zero* clue what he has to deal with on a daily basis. And I kind of don't want to know, either. I mean, angel of death? How does someone even land that role?

How does someone land the Antichrist *role?*

"Since you're here, I'm guessing you connected with your contact?" I ask instead of giving in to my internal pity party. Later, when all this is finished, I'll have time to lament and whine and claw through my anger. But right now? I've got a little sister to save and a Greater demon to kill.

Funny, I never thought I'd sing the same tune over and over again, but shoving my mental crumbling away for later seems to be on repeat on my top-forty list.

"Yes," he says. "I flew in just as Draven was waking up. I have the crystal."

Anticipation and hope flares through me, but then reality sets in. "What did it cost you?" I fold my arms over my chest like the motion can protect me from his answer. Last time I needed help, Draven paid in blood. Cassiel barely knows me, but his devotion to Draven has made him accept me instantly.

Cassiel shrugs. "I collected a debt," he says.

"And I'm in yours now," I say. "Any ideas?"

He snorts, considering. "I wouldn't say no to any stories you may have or will collect about Draven. Stories he'd never want me to hear."

I laugh at that, at the totally human desire to have dirt on a friend, and nod. "I'll keep an eye out if..." If we ever get to have any kind of normal. Since I'm having a conversation with my sort-of-most-likely-boyfriend's angel of death best friend, I'm not banking on it.

My cell vibrates in my pocket, and I flash him an apologetic look as I glance at the screen, hoping like hell it's Draven texting me to tell me it's time to get this show on the road.

Coach Hale: Heard you're going on a road trip. We need

to talk. I'm at the bar.

I send a quick reply before glancing toward the partially closed door to Ray's room.

"I'm sorry. Coach—" I stop myself, rolling my eyes. She's not my coach anymore. "It sounds like Anka has information for me." Kazuki must've called her. I look back at that door, the internal struggle near bone-breaking to leave Ray totally alone for even a minute.

"I'll stay," Cassiel offers. "If you want me to."

"Thank you." I finally relent. I mean, if the worst did happen and Marid happened to claw his way through the wards, he'd be in for a brutal surprise to find the angel of death staring at him instead of me.

Cassiel nods as I head out the door, closing it behind me. It takes me a few tries, my sleep-deprived brain having forgotten to memorize the path from earlier, but I make it to the main level of the club. I spot Anka at the bar easily enough, her leathery indigo wings outstretched, her braids pulled back into an intricate crown, and that spiked tail swishing back and forth where she sits, forcing every other creature to give her a wide berth.

I can't help smiling as I make my way over to her—I like seeing her in her true form. Somehow, it's more fitting than the high school coach I knew her as before. And while the betrayal still stings in my chest from her keeping me in the dark for years about what I am or what I *could* be, it's lessened considerably in the scheme of things.

"Kazuki fill you in?" I ask by way of greeting, settling onto the open barstool next to her.

Crane takes one look at me and groans. I try to give him an innocent smile, but he merely growls and stomps to the other end of the bar. Guess I'm not ordering a coffee any time soon.

"He did," Anka says, flashing me a genuine smile. "You're really going through with it?" She lowers her voice. "You're going into the Ather?"

I nod, smoothing my hands over the slick black bar illuminated by neon rope lights. "I'm not letting Ray be used as a puppet for whenever Marid is feeling revengy."

"I figured you would say that," Anka says, nodding. "You're going to need a guide."

I raise my brows. "Are you offering?" I ask, knowing from our previous conversations she herself escaped from Hell—the Ather—a long time ago. Through one of those cracks in the world where the veil is thinnest.

Anka shakes her head, snorting. "Hell no," she says, but apology flickers in her dark eyes. "I...I can never go back there. The gatekeeper would take one look at me and send me right back where I don't want to be." She straightens, the motion clearing the shadows from her eyes. "There are good demons down there. But there are also demons who won't hesitate to try and slaughter you simply for sport. It's a mash of light and dark entities, all of which are clever. You'll need to be at your sharpest because you can't trust everything you see." She digs in her back pocket, retrieves a small business card yellowed with age, and hands it to me.

I scrunch my brows, flipping the card over and back, noting the near imperceptible, tiny bold lettering in the center of the card's face. One word, nothing more.

WALLACE

"Wallace?" I read the word aloud, and Anka taps the card.

"Keep that on you," she says. "She'll find you as soon as you enter the Ather."

"You know this Wallace?" I ask.

"Yep," Anka says, her lips popping on the word. "She's the absolute best guide in the business. She's one of the good ones, but don't be fooled—she's ruthless when she needs to be. She'll help you convince the gatekeeper to let you all at least inside, and then she'll take you wherever else you need to go."

I gape at Anka. "She can do that?" And here I was, thinking getting into the Ather was going to be the biggest hurdle. "Wait, there is a guide business for the Ather? How many people...

beings," I correct, trying like hell to make my mind adjust to be inclusive to all species, not just humans, "are looking for a tour?"

"You'd be surprised," Anka says, wrapping her fingers around the long-neck bottle Crane sits in front of her. Meanwhile, he's still ignoring me. She takes a fast drink before setting down the bottle. "She knows more about the Ather than anyone I've ever met. Tell her I sent you."

"Okay," I say, blinking away the thousand questions racing through my mind. "Thank you," I say. "For the help," I add, my voice thick. "I need all I can get."

"You've got that right," she says, not trying to sugarcoat anything, which I appreciate. "I dropped off some basic gear with Kazuki earlier," she continues. "Stuff you'll need to take with you, but Wallace has the real goods if you have any hope of getting through the Ather alive."

"I don't know what to say to that."

"You don't have to say anything," she says. "You just need to come back alive."

"I'll try?" I say, but it sounds like a question. I mean, how can I possibly assure her when I don't have the first clue about what I'm diving into?

"Good." She finishes off her drink, slamming the glass bottle a little too hard on the bar. The music blares around us, so many creatures dancing and drinking and laughing, going about their day without a care in the world.

My chest is heavy as I wonder when and *if* I'll ever be able to be that carefree. If there will ever be a time where I can simply come here to dance for the night, Draven's hands on my hips like the first night we met, moving and losing ourselves to the music. The memory of his mouth on mine, his body flush atop me, sends waves of heat crashing over me. When we're together, it feels like a dream. Everything with him does, and I want more of those dreams.

With the way the past few weeks have gone, and what we have to do next...

I'm leaning more toward nightmares heading my way.

"You're going to do *what*?" Nathan asks, shaking his head
again like that will somehow change the explanation I
just gave him. Shadows the color of bruises rest below his eyes,
indicating he hasn't slept much in the two days since we left for
The Bridge.

I flash Ray a look that screams, *Told you we should've come
up with a better story.*

Ray's blue eyes are determined and yelling, *He deserves the
truth.*

I rub my palms over my face. We have to meet Cassiel and
Kazuki back at The Bridge within the hour. Draven has slipped
into that stealthy quiet calm, adopting the stillness of a hunter
as he lingers outside on Nathan's porch. The demon hunt for my
blood has been quiet since I closed the gates—since I had to kill
my best friend—but we need to be prepared for anything.

A sticky, gritty something shifts beneath my skin, and I force
it down into the box I *swore* I locked after my nightmare.

"Nathan," I say, hating that this conversation is necessary.
Hating that I have to put him through this at all. He's not our
blood, he has no real obligation to us—or didn't, before he adopted
Ray—but still, putting him in this situation seems like handing
him a sack of shit when he signed up for a basket of roses. "I'm
being honest with you because I…" The words tangle in my throat.
"I love you, and I respect you. I know you didn't ask for this life.
Didn't ask for me to barge into your deli and beg for a job all
those years ago. I'll never be able to thank you for all you've done

for me and especially for Ray, and I probably should've lied to you about all this," I say, arching a brow at the huff Ray gives me. "But Ray convinced me not to. I wanted to lie to you under the guise of protecting you, but after what's happened in the last few weeks, I know that's a bullshit move. You deserve better. And I wish I could give you that, but Ray's life is at stake, and you know there isn't anything I won't do to keep her safe."

There. I somehow manage to force every word past all of my protective barriers and lay the truth at his feet. What he decides to do with it—

Nathan's arms encircle me in a tight bear hug, crushing me to his chest. "Kiddo," he says, no hint of releasing me.

Slowly, I fold my arms around his back, the hug almost awkward but at the same time not. Nathan, despite being only in his thirties, has been more of a dad to me than the fake piece of shit who raised me.

He takes a step back, clearing his throat. "I don't like this," he says, hands on his hips. His five o'clock shadow looks unkempt along his strong jaw as he shakes his head for the thirteenth time since we returned. "How will I know you're safe? How will I know you're fed?"

I swallow around the lump in my throat. "You won't," I say and shrug. "Not until we come back."

If *we come back*, some traitorous voice whispers in the back of my mind.

"And what the hell am I supposed to do in the meantime?"

"Work," I say. "You're pretty good at the whole deli-owner thing, you know?" I try to tease, but no humor reaches his eyes.

And I get it, I *really* do, but the last thing I need right now is the guilt trip. I can't focus on saving Ray and getting us home alive if I'm worrying about what a burden I've put on Nathan's life.

"Fine," he says, dropping his arms. "I'll work. I'll stock this place with everything you need so it's ready for when you two *come home*."

I bite the inside of my cheek to keep back the tears gathering behind my eyes. "Thank you," I say, wishing I had more words in my arsenal to fully express what an awesome human being he is. But I don't. And we're out of time.

Nathan hugs Ray, her little zombie unicorn backpack shifting on her shoulders from the motion. "We'll be back before you know it," she says with unflinching confidence. I shake my head, unable to hold back a soft smile. The girl is acting like we're heading off for a cross-country road trip complete with restaurant stops and plenty of souvenir shops—which I don't think we'll find where we're going.

But I've never been one to crush her joy, so I bite my tongue and guide her out Nathan's door, leaving him silent and tense as I shut it behind us. I cringe against the wilting sensation, the one whispering that that's the last time I'll ever see him.

CHAPTER THIRTEEN

Draven grabs a few black leather backpacks off the long marble bar in Kazuki's private event room and hands one to Cassiel, then me, then tucks one over his shoulder. "Now all we need is a portal. Cassiel," he says, turning to the angel. "You should conserve your powers and take the portal with us."

Cassiel cocks his head but then nods.

I look between them. The silent exchange has my anxiety ramping up. If they're worried enough that Cassiel has to save his energy and not simply teleport into the Ather himself, then I *definitely* need to be worried.

Draven looks at Kazuki expectantly.

"Hold on there, Judge. The past two days have been free," Kazuki says, the sorcerer lounging on the plush sofa across the room. "If you need me to open the nearest portal, there will be a price. You of all people should know that."

Draven glances at the ceiling as he turns to face Kazuki as if he's doing his best to not lash out. "Of *course*."

"How many times have you paid to use the portal?" I ask Draven.

"A few," he says, eyes still on Kazuki.

And he'd been turned away by the gatekeeper every time.

"You really have the power to open a portal to Hell—the Ather?" I ask, still shocked any of this can be true.

Kazuki nods.

I scrunch my brows. "If you can do that, then why aren't demons hunting you like they do me?" So many had tried to take a bite of me for a chance at my blood opening a gateway to Hell, and all this time Kazuki has had the power to do it himself?

"Because I can only open the portal for a blink of time, and it's a one-way trip," he says, and my stomach sinks. "You'll have to find your own way out, the same way those lucky enough to escape through where the veil is thinnest between our worlds."

"Lucky?" I echo.

"Some, like dear sweet Anka, flee here to live a different life," he explains. "Also, there are few creatures powerful enough to detect the portals as I do, even fewer who can open them. And the amount who know what *I* can do? Even fewer. I expect to keep it that way." His lavender gaze meets each of ours, and I nod.

Keep our mouths shut, got it.

"How did you get back the times you used it?" I ask silently, knowing Draven is listening.

"The gatekeeper always sent me back himself," he answers, his voice filling that spot in my mind just for him.

Well. Hopefully, with the help of Anka's connection, we'll get past the gatekeeper.

"What's the price this time, Kaz?" Draven asks coolly, his tone not lost on the warlock.

"It's about balance," he says to Draven, then glances to me. "I can't hand out favors to everyone. Could you imagine the requests I would get if my prices weren't steep?"

Ray shifts her weight at my side, readjusting her zombie unicorn backpack. Draven had transferred whatever contents Anka had packed for my sister into her preferred colorful one once we returned to The Bridge. I had somehow managed to stifle back a laugh. Only Ray would want to bring a rainbow to Hell.

"Don't look at me like that, Draven." Kazuki sighs. "We've done this before. And as much as I would love to play favorites, I can't." He twirls his emerald-topped cane in one hand, swiftly rising from the couch.

Draven's gaze narrows, studying the warlock like a hawk as his powerful gait eats up the room until he's standing right before us.

"Tell me the price," Draven grinds out.

It can't be money—Kazuki told me before he deals in favors. But the way Draven is talking, it looks like he's about to offer up whatever is needed. But it's not a trip for him this time, it's for *me*. For what I need to do to help Ray. "I'll pay it," I say before he can do such a thing.

Draven groans. "Harley—"

"I already said I would owe him a favor. We'll just add this to my tab."

"The toll for taking you to the portal isn't *just* a favor, darling," Kazuki says.

"Then what else do you want?" I ask, impatience edging my tone. I tell myself to chill, that Kazuki has already helped us more than he needs to. He could've kicked us out on our asses the moment we appeared in his club, but he didn't.

"You'll have to bind that favor as a sorcerer's bargain."

"Not a chance," Draven says. "The last time you sent me it was a blood payment."

"Sending you alone to the gatekeeper is much easier than sending four. You're a Judge. You have certain divine assistance that makes the passage easier. Not all in your group do. So, the price goes up."

I'm certainly not divine, not with what I am. And Ray? Who knows what is in her blood.

"What's a sorcerer's bargain?" I ask instead of lingering on those thoughts too long.

Kazuki's lips slip into a confident smirk. "It's an unbreakable contract between myself and the one who offers the favor," he explains, one perfectly polished hand splayed over his chest. He's wearing a rich emerald suit today, the dress shirt beneath his jacket a jet black, his nails a gleaming green.

I blink up at him, wondering what I'm missing. "Isn't that what I've already agreed to? Owing you a favor—"

"Not everyone is honest," he says. "Offering me a favor and actually following through on it are two totally separate things."

He glances at Draven before returning that bright gaze to me. "And having me reveal the location to the portal, along with opening it, isn't like asking for a mere protection spell."

Mere protection spell? I look down at my tattoo, the black ink creating flames and leaves over the underside of my wrist. The one Draven paid for with his blood. For *me*. It's tiny, no bigger than a couple inches, but it had given me *days* of safety from the one who hunted me—

Kai. His ghost pounds against that locked box, begging to be released, to consume me, drag me away from the present. I shove the lid closed, focusing on Kazuki.

"Okay," I say. "So this sorcerer's bargain ensures I somehow don't refuse your favor."

"Precisely," he says, hands moving to lean atop his cane. "If you try and refuse me, the magic of our agreement will take from you what it feels equates the favor I seek."

I swallow hard. "I hadn't planned on refusing you, anyway," I say honestly. "I don't ask for help often. If I say I'll owe you, then I owe you."

"I'll take the bargain," Draven says, and I glare at him.

"No," I argue. "You won't." Draven already paid for the protection spell, had already done so much for me...

"She's right," Kazuki says, holding up a hand to stop Draven from debating. "I want it with her."

A wave of power lazily tests the room, my own rising to match it. Kazuki likely knows infinitely more about my powers than I do—they're still so new to me, especially unrestrained by that damn ancient stone that had kept them on a leash. Had my mother known what that would do to me? She had to have known, right? What were the odds she accidentally came across a bracelet like that and made me swear never to take it off? But why? To what end? And where the hell had she disappeared to?

I shove those questions down, so not having time to play the woe-is-me-where-is-my-mommy tune. My powers are mine now, no longer hindered by the damn bracelet.

"I agree," I say, and Draven's eyes close.

Kazuki saunters to the marble bar, and I follow close behind. Ray, Draven, and Cassiel stay on the other side, watchful. I raise my brows to Kazuki when the marble remains clean. "Well?" I ask, eying him. "Don't I need to sign a contract? Where is the paper?"

"Who said anything about paper, darling?" Kazuki bares a grin, his teeth gleaming in the light above the bar. He snaps, and a blazing green bolt of light appears between his fingers. It's in the shape of a pen and humming with power.

He allows the pen of light to hover in the air between us, taking his time to shed his suit jacket and expertly roll up the shirt-sleeve of his left arm. His skin is smooth over significant muscles, and there are hints of faded tattoos freckled all over. He motions for me to do the same, so I mirror his movements with my left arm, this one free of a tattoo but donning plenty of scars of my own.

This time, though, Kazuki doesn't comment on it, merely plucks the green pen of light out of the air and presses the tip to my skin. "This is magic in its oldest form," he says, sweeping the heat of that buzzing power over and over again. My dark flames flicker beneath my skin, thrashing against the sting. "It cannot be broken without consequences, and it opens a doorway between us until the bargain has been called in by me."

The heat of the magic intensifies. Just when I'm certain my skin will start to curl backward, Kazuki draws the pen away.

There, in an almost shimmering black ink, lays a new tattoo, this one even smaller than my other. One thin line of black is hugged by two *C*'s, one backward and one forward, with tiny hooks on their tips. In the center of the connecting line, a half-complete infinity symbol holds it all together. It's no less beautiful than his flames and leaves had been. He extends the glowing green pen to me, and a wave of apprehension slides through me.

"I'm not an artist," I say, motioning to Ray. "She is."

"Oh, can I?" Ray's eyes are bright with excitement as she eyes the pen.

"Not today, little seer," Kazuki croons. "Harley must be the one to sign."

Sign. His *skin*. Binding bargain, indeed.

I take the pen from him, flinching slightly at the jolt of power that zings up my elbow. "I don't know what to draw," I say, and Kazuki shakes his head.

"You don't need to." He lays his arm across the bar. "The magic will flow through you to match mine."

Okay then. I set the tip of buzzing light to his skin, and in a blink, the pen is moving on its own. The power drawing from me radiates through it, a conduit that leaves me feeling vulnerable, drained—

Then it's over.

Kazuki snaps, and the pen disappears. He smiles down at our matching tattoos, holding it up for me to see. "Guess this makes us besties now," he teases, and I can't help it, a laugh bubbles out of me.

Because I'm an Antichrist with a divine siphon soldier boyfriend, an angel of death as his best friend, and a seer for a sister. Getting matching tattoos with an ancient sorcerer seems right up my alley.

CHAPTER FOURTEEN

"This is it?"

I gape at the simple—but beautiful—wooden door before us. A rose gold bridge insignia rests just above a pure golden door handle fastened dead-center in the thick wood. This hallway is filled with doors identical to this one, only the type of wood marking any indication of difference.

Kazuki clucks his tongue. "Harley," he chides. "You of all people should know outside appearances can be deceiving."

I clamp my lips shut, the words hitting their mark. He's not wrong—a lifetime of pain taught me the lesson a long time ago. Still, Kai's betrayal took all my lessons and blew them out of the water. My fingers tremble where my hands hang at my sides, and Draven grazes his over mine, the calluses on his fingers scraping against my skin, making my breath hitch for a different reason.

"But to answer your question, no," Kazuki continues. "This is merely a doorway to the location of the portal. Do you think I'd keep a portal to the Ather tucked into one of my establishments?" He scoffs.

"Okay," I say, waiting. After a few seconds, I shift on my feet. "Do we knock?" I ask when he's made no move toward it.

Draven laughs, Cassiel remains cool and stoic at his side, and Ray merely squeezes my other hand.

Kazuki rolls his eyes. "Teenagers," he grumbles, then grips the handle, tugging it open.

My gaze widens. There is nothing but pure, unflinching

darkness on the other side. Not a sliver of light to shed on what we're about to step into. "You're joking," I say.

"I would do no such thing," he says in mock affront, then jerks his head toward the darkness. "Who's first?"

"I'll go," Cassiel offers, stepping past me. He takes one step into the darkness and vanishes.

I gasp at the sight and feel something as soft as shadow brush against my mind. I turn to Draven, knowing the sensation from the few times he's silently asked permission to speak mind to mind.

"*I'm with you*," he says, his voice filling my head, the intimacy of the secret connection sending spiraling waves of heat to sweep away the tension clinging to my soul.

I give him a soft smile. "*And I'm with you. We'll find your brother, we'll free Ray. Together.*" It's an echo of the sentiment from days ago when we shut the gates together, nearly died together.

Something cold and fearful flashes over his eyes, but it's gone in a blink. He squeezes my hand before releasing it, motioning toward the darkness. I step forward, keeping my other hand in Ray's as she follows me.

"I'll be right behind you," Draven says out loud, and the words are solid, unflinching. There is something soothing in knowing he's with me, after all the dangers we've faced together.

Every warning bell chimes in my head about walking into a scenario I can't see. But Ray? She's practically bouncing on the balls of her feet, she's so excited. I make one move, and Kazuki leans down to whisper in my ear, "Be sure not to step on the dragon's tail," he says. "I'd hate for you to get eaten before I call in our bargain."

My eyes flare, and I haul Ray closer to my side.

Kazuki's laugh is booming as he throws his head back.

Never joke my ass.

"Kaz," Draven growls, and Kazuki reels it in.

"She started it," he says but gives me an encouraging wink.

The easy banter calms me, and my fingers stop trembling. Stepping through this doorway isn't even the hardest part of our mission, so I mentally high-five myself and make the final move into the darkness.

CHAPTER FIFTEEN

The darkness is a vacuum of space, heavy and thick like a weighted blanket. But it's over in a few steps, and a faint smell of fried food hits me as a bright fluorescent light illuminates the space we step into.

Cassiel is leaning against a simple white wall in what looks to be an industrial kitchen, no doubt where the lingering smell is coming from. Ray is still at my side, Draven and Kazuki shuffling in behind us. I turn, but the doorway from The Bridge is gone, nothing but that simple wall behind us.

"That was so cool," Ray says, hand still in mine. "Did you see all the different colors we walked through?"

"What?" I ask. "What colors? It was black —"

"Not just black," she says. "Purples and blues and even some grays!"

I glance up to Draven, a silent question. He shrugs, smiling down at Ray.

"We all see the doorways differently," Kazuki explains.

I scan the area around us. We could be anywhere — Chicago or Canada, I wouldn't know. Because, as I note a familiar logo on a box stacked in the corner of the kitchen, there are *thousands* of these places across the globe.

"Hold up," I say, glancing around the empty kitchen. "You're telling me a portal to" — I lower my voice to a whisper — "the Ather is in the back of a *McDonald's*?"

Kazuki grins, shrugging those elegant shoulders of his. "I don't control where the veils are thinnest," he explains. He motions a hand to the area we stand, surprisingly empty. It must be before opening hours, if the look of the light pink sky shining through the small window to the left is any indication. Dawn is just breaking. "Plus, the portal has been here far longer than the restaurant."

"Wow," I say, unable to articulate any other response.

I glance at Kazuki. "Okay then," I say. "Three tickets to Hell please, and a side of fries while you're at it."

"Oh, I need ranch if we're having fries!" Ray pipes in, and I laugh with her.

Draven and Cassiel share a look, and I shrug. If we can't joke about going to Hell, then what can we joke about?

The sorcerer swings that emerald cane of his in graceful circles before him. "Once the portal is open," Kazuki says, ignoring my sister and my teasing, "it'll only be a few moments before someone will sense it and try and come through. I can't assure your safety for long, so be quick." He keeps moving that cane in elegant circles, the motions practiced and calculated as he speaks.

I nod, shifting on my feet, all joking swallowed by the icy anticipation storming my senses. No more distracting kisses from Draven, no more jokes to make light of the situation.

Cassiel steps toward Kazuki first.

"Open," Kazuki says on a breath, holding his cane aloft, the air before him shimmering like a mirage. Cassiel shares a silent look with Draven before stepping through it, blinking out of sight.

"You're sure they can't open a gateway with my blood down there?" I ask Kazuki as Draven, Ray, and myself linger near his upraised cane.

"Certain, darling," he says, his voice slightly strained. "A Key only works from one side. You will have to find your own way out."

Okay, I can do that. Or, perhaps, I'll stay. If I can get Ray safely home, free of Marid's hold, and talk it all out with her. But that plan will only be viable if we survive.

A distant, terrifying scream echoes from those shimmering lines before us, and I swallow hard as I lock eyes with Draven. Even in the bright fluorescent lights, he looks devastatingly beautiful. His tan skin tenses over the muscles beneath, his black shirt straining under the way his body prepares for what's coming.

The scents of sulfur and smoke drift over the fried food smell, and the breath freezes in my lungs.

We're about to go to Hell.

I'm about to take my *little sister* to Hell.

Draven slides his hand into my free one, interlacing our fingers. "The Ather, overwhelming odds, plenty of obstacles to overcome," he says. "Sounds right up our alley for our official second date."

The statement catches me so off-guard that I laugh. "Okay, but I'm driving."

Kazuki sighs. "Before we're all eaten, if you please," he groans, and I blink out of Draven's gaze.

"Want me to bring you something back?" I tease. "Maybe a hellish paperweight? Or a suit made of scales?"

"I'm never one to say no to gifts." A smirk shapes Kazuki's lips. "Good luck, dark princess."

I give him a grateful nod and then check to see that Ray has nothing but excitement in her eyes. I squeeze her hand, then Draven's.

And as one, we step through the portal.

CHAPTER SIXTEEN

Some kind of force hooks my stomach, yanking me down, down, down.

Pressure mounts, grinding the joints of my bones together as I free fall through the darkness. I can't tell which way is up or down, but I cling to Ray's hand in mine like a lifeline. I can't tell if Draven is close by. I try to reach for the connection between us, but my mental fingers are slippery and frantic.

Seconds.

Minutes.

Hours.

Falling, falling, falling.

"You'll want to bend your knees, darling," Kazuki's voice purrs inside my mind, the shock of which is likely the only thing stopping the incessant adrenaline pumping and screaming at me to learn to fucking fly.

"What are you doing here?"

"I'm not there." I swear I can feel his eyes roll at my question.

"In my head," I snap, gasping as I tug Ray toward me with the effort of lifting a car. I manage to gather her in my arms. Acid replaces the marrow in my bones, the pain hotter than my dark flames.

"Our bargain," he says. *"I told you we'd be connected."*

Great. Just what I need, a cocky sorcerer traipsing around inside my head. *"I thought you said you always ask permission—"*

"Bend your knees!"

I react to the command in his voice, the annoyance and power roiling through it, and bend my damn knees as best I can. The movement aches, as if my bones and muscles weigh two tons, but I manage to do as he says—

My boots hit the ground, hard and solid, the pain zinging all the way up to my teeth.

"Now, imagine if that had been your pretty little head."

I push off the rock I land on, my vision wobbling as I manage to stand and set Ray on her feet. At least she didn't have to take that impact. I mentally flip Kazuki off but add, *"Thanks."*

"You're welcome," he says, and I can feel his mental retreat like he's pulled a rope from my mind.

I shake out my limbs. Each breath is labored as my mind reorients itself.

"Ugh," Ray groans beside me. She's holding her stomach. I immediately drop to her level.

"You okay?" I ask, which, to be fair, is a real ridiculous question seeing as we just fell through a portal to Hell.

"I don't feel so good," she says, her hand sliding over her stomach.

"Deep breaths," I say. "In through your nose and out through your mouth."

She nods, doing as I advise, and with each deep breath, she looks a little less green.

"Traveling between realms can have that effect." Draven's voice sounds behind me.

I whirl around, and relief barrels through me at the sight of him. He's there, just an arm's length away, standing steadily and looking as if he just stepped out of the shower, not out of a fall to Hell. "Are you okay?"

"Easy as a novice setting," Draven says. "You?" he asks Cassiel.

The angel walks up behind him, wings tucked in tight, and merely dips his head.

Ray finally looks steady, so I rise to my feet. My body is already adjusting, my powers working in sync to heal and strengthen me. I can feel it in my blood, the twin braids of earth and fire pulsing over every inch of my soul.

Cassiel hands Draven a tiny glass vial hanging from a gold chain. "Here." Inside the vial are glimmering metallic blue crystals, the blessed phenacite we need to sever the ties between Ray and Marid.

Draven grips the vial before sliding the long chain around his neck. He tucks it beneath his shirt. "I owe you."

Cassiel just shrugs.

I'd said as much back at Kazuki's, but that favor will have to come later. Right now? We need to figure out a plan.

I scan behind me—where Cassiel and Draven keep casting wary glances—and my eyes widen. The floor is a slick black rock, polished and gleaming in flickering red lights that cast everything in a hazy shade. The area spans the length of several football fields, an archway carved from the same rock with intricate details stretching above and over our heads higher than several skyscrapers.

In the center of the archway rests a large carved podium, a male presiding over it. Two long horns stretch and curl back from his head, gilded in gold with long white strands of hair slinking around them and down his shoulders. His cheeks are lined with glimmering swipes of gold the same shade as his horns. A black blazer jacket is the only thing covering his shoulders. His chest is bare beneath it, decorated with a variety of golden tattoos. I can't see anything beyond that behind the podium, but I wouldn't be surprised if he had a barbed tail or hooves for feet.

I blink a few times, following the demon's gaze to the mass of creatures and people that await his attention, the line zigzagging as far as my eyes can follow. And behind him? That's what freezes the breath in my lungs.

My feet move before I tell them to, one in front of the other like a magnet pulls at my core. I walk, awestruck, until Draven stops me with a gentle hand on my elbow.

Behind the podium, far past the archway, is an unfathomably large stretch of land, all manner of demons rushing about, their forms illuminated by a twinkling amethyst light. There are what look to be buildings etched from stone, but the realm is too far away to make out anything totally distinguishable.

Something tugs at the center of my chest, a whisper in the back of my mind urging me closer. I move, but Draven pulls me back and keeps me in place, pointing toward an edge near the archway I hadn't even noticed. A lip of stone that drops into the impenetrable darkness.

Was I being compelled to fall off the edge?

I swallow around the lump in my throat, the motion clearing the cotton in my ears. Chatter, pleas, and arguments swarm around us, and then there's the faint cries coming from somewhere in the darkness. I turn away from the edge, eyes locking with Draven's.

"So, this is Hell?" I ask.

"No," a sharp, feminine voice says from next to me. "This is just the archway."

I whirl around and look at her. She's gorgeous, no older than me if I had to guess, with smooth dark skin, her eyes a stunning, rich brown, and full, red-painted lips. Her hair hangs in long locks over her shoulders, each lock adorned with bands of gold or silver or smooth red stone. She's a dead ringer for Riele Downs—an actress from one of Ray's favorite superhero shows—right down to the hair adornments, but taller and with curves I'd die for.

She tips her chin and points a polished finger toward the demons we can just make out across the darkness.

"*That*," she says, "is the Ather."

CHAPTER
SEVENTEEN

"Who gave you my card?" the girl asks, arching a brow at me.

"How do you know I have your card?" I ask. I haven't even pulled it out of the zipper pocket of the leather backpack Anka had given me.

She takes a smooth step toward me. Tight leather pants cinch into black boots that lace all the way up to her knees, and her warrior look is completed with a cotton black shirt and leather jacket with all manner of pockets and zippers along the arms. Two holster straps peek from beneath the jacket, and two thigh straps show at least three sheathed knives on each leg.

"If this is going to work," she says, eyes locking with mine, "you're going to have to get good with the fact that I know infinitely more than you," she says, smirking. "All of you," she continues, eying Ray and Draven at my side, then Cassiel.

I step in front of her line of sight to Ray, my hackles instantly rising at the arrogance in her voice. "Wallace?"

"The one and only," she says. "Best guide this side of the Ather, and I don't come cheap. Hopefully, whoever gave you my card told you that."

"Anka," I say, and the sharpness in Wallace's eyes softens.

"How do you know her?"

"I train with her," I answer, not bothering to dredge up the full extent of our history. I don't know this girl, and we don't have time even if we *were* in the mood for a chat.

"Prove it," Wallace challenges, her dark eyes gleaming.

I reach for the backpack, ready to grab the card—

Her hand lashes out, her fingers curled and primed to grab my neck. I dodge, shifting my stance for balance, and grab her exposed wrist. I twist, sending her flying to her back. She clamps her hand over mine, though, tugging me right along with her, flipping until she's atop me. I pivot my legs beneath her, grabbing her left shoulder with my right hand at the same time, the motion freeing her hold so I can hop to my feet.

Wallace mimics my quick movements and grins. "She *did* teach you a thing or two," she says, her chest heaving like mine. "Then again, my aunt always did have a soft spot for charity cases."

Every inch of my pride ruffles at her tone. Wallace waves me off, jerking her head toward the line near the podium. "We can argue later," she says. "The line to the gatekeeper is only getting longer."

We follow her to the middle of the line, where all she has to do is *look* at the weathered soul standing there and it bows so deeply I can barely make out its face. She takes the now vacant spot, and not a whisper of a grumble emerges as we all follow suit.

I make some quick introductions while the line slowly inches toward the podium, and she notes all of our names with a casual dismissal that has my dark flames crackling near my fingertips.

"I love your hair," Ray says, eying the adornments in Wallace's locks.

Wallace flips some of them over her shoulder, winking at Ray. "I dig your braid, tiny human," she says. "Did you do that yourself?"

Ray shakes her head. "My sister." She motions up to me, and Wallace studies me with just a fraction of respect in those dark eyes.

"She likes Wonder Woman," I say, then cringe. "That's a superhero—"

"I know who Wonder Woman is." Wallace rolls her eyes as we gain more ground in the line. "Humans. They always think we don't know shit down here."

I arch a brow at her. "I'm not human. And forgive me if I didn't pick up the *Zagat Guide to the Ather* on my way here."

She laughs sharply, then swallows it like she didn't mean to let it slip. "Zagat Guide," she says, snapping her fingers. "Now *that's* a lucrative idea. But would it put me out of business?" She seems to be speaking more to herself, and I flash Draven a pleading look.

He's all sharp angles and glittering amber eyes as he studies not only Wallace, but everything around us—from the creatures standing in line to the demon at the podium.

Cassiel is cataloguing, too, the pair looking more like brothers in that moment than ever before. The thought has my stomach twisting.

I try to focus on the mission at hand. Draven's *actual* brother was taken by Marid, so we have to assume that is where he is still. Hopefully, Wallace can get us there. But what are the odds that we find him *and* convince him to help us, too?

"Realm 346,783B," the demon's voice carries from the spot just before us. From this distance, I can see his eyes are a blazing orange as he stares down at what looks almost like a human before him. Human…but *off.* His skin is almost translucent, the muscles and veins beneath visible, and what looks like mold spores pepper it in random places.

"What is that?" The voice is grainy, weak.

The demon flips the pages in a giant, totally *Book of the Dead* vibes book on the podium, then his orange eyes flare as his elongated fingers curl around the edges. "The Cages of the Drowned, in the reformatory realm," he says, lips pulling back to reveal rows of teeth filed to sharp points.

"No! Not there!" the demon shrieks before us, thrashing as two shadows in the shape of guards flank his sides. "No! I can't go there. I can't—"

"Then you shouldn't have escaped merely to prey on younglings in the Earth realm," the demon growls right over the creature's protest, and the hair on the back of my neck rises. He leans closer, baring those razor-sharp teeth. "You will be drowned over and over again until there is nothing left of the demon before me. There is no appeal for the crimes you committed in the Earth realm. If you're granted a next life, make better choices."

With a snap of his fingers, the shadow guards and the demon disappear.

I turn to Draven. "Is this where the demons you and other Judges catch are sent?"

Draven nods. "Yes. Upon vanquishing, they're returned to here where their crimes are judged a second time by the gatekeeper and punishment is enforced."

I reach out and softly squeeze his hand. I can see the battle in his eyes, the struggle to see things from this side. Sure, what this demon was accused of clearly sounds like the punishment is fitting, but what about the others? The ones Draven spoke of that he didn't feel needed vanquishing? The ones the Seven ordered him to send here against his will despite Draven trying to fight for them, to explain that they weren't malicious entities prowling Earth but simply creatures looking for a better life? Like Anka and who knew how many others?

The grittiness of all of it clings to my skin like a grime, however, and I resist the urge to swipe at it, instead focusing on what I can now see is a white rectangular sticker plastered on the side of the demon's blazer: Zion is scrawled in bold black lettering.

The gatekeeper of the Ather wears a nametag? What the hell kind of twisted front desk shit is this?

"Next," Zion says, not bothering to look up from his book.

Wallace saunters up to the podium. "Zion," she coos, "you're looking all kinds of delicious today."

The demon pauses his frantic page flipping, and a slow smirk shapes his lips. "Three times in one cycle?" He eyes the four of us standing behind her. "Larger group this time, too. Business is booming."

"Can't complain," she says as she moves to lean on the podium. "This one is more a favor to my aunt."

"*Anka.*" Zion drags out her name. "I often miss her."

"Careful or you'll make me jealous," Wallace teases, then perks up. "Speaking of, is your sister around?"

Zion laughs, the sound raspy. "Why? So you can beg us to join you for the night again?"

I roll my eyes. I'm all for consensually doing whatever and whoever makes you happy, but do we really have time for ménage talk?

"I'll never give up," she says, grinning at him. "I'd treat you both like the royalty you are."

Zion wets his lips, shaking his head. "I'll remind her of your offer."

"You always were my favorite."

Zion's gaze slides to Draven, something flickering there. "You again," he says, and Draven goes wholly still at my side. "How many times do I have to tell you that you don't belong here?"

"I'm not here for that this time," Draven says.

"We'll see." Zion studies him for a beat longer, then glances to Cassiel. "And you carry no traveler with you today," he says. "A pleasure trip, then?"

Cassiel shrugs. "More or less."

"Interesting," Zion says, those eyes of his too thoughtful, too watchful for my taste.

So I clear my throat, making sure the impatience is evident in my tone.

"Right," Wallace says, glancing over her shoulder as if she's forgotten we're there. "Where did you say you needed to go again?"

I hadn't. I step up to the podium, lowering my voice, not wanting to be overheard by anyone here who may have ties to Marid. "We need to find a Greater Demon."

Zion's orange eyes find mine for the first time since we approached him.

Wallace seems to note the reaction, her eyes darting between the two of us. "Which one?"

"Marid."

Zion blinks, then bursts out laughing at the same time Wallace groans, "You're fucking joking."

CHAPTER EIGHTEEN

"You didn't mention *him*," Wallace snaps.

"Oh, what, in the all of five minutes we've spoken?" I fire back. "Your aunt knew where we had to go, and she recommended you. So here we are."

"You're delusional if you think I'm taking you to the Isle of Snakes," she whispers. "That realm borders the King's palace."

"I don't care if it's next to the Devil's damn playground," I say, trying my best to not raise my voice. "That's where we need to go—"

Wallace's sharp laugh cuts across my words. "*Devil*," she says, shaking her head. She folds her arms over her chest. "The fact that you're still clinging to these human terms knocks down your chance of survival by at least a hundred points."

"Only a hundred? What did I start with?"

Wallace rolls her eyes. "It doesn't matter. You need to wake the fuck up—"

"Careful," I say with a lethal calm. Dark flames curl around the tips of my fingers, but I urge them back. We may have had a test sparring sesh, but I'm not about to threaten her to take me to Marid. "If you're too afraid, that's fine. Stop wasting our time." I'll plead my case to Zion on my own.

All humor vanishes from Wallace's eyes.

Draven and Cassiel share a look. Yep, I threw down the gauntlet. What are they going to do about it?

But it's Ray that shifts to step in front of me, glancing up at Wallace. "She's not scared," Ray says. "She's smart. She *lives* here,

Harley," she says, and I know she's right. I can't let my anger and trust issues get in the way of that, but still. Wallace seems hell-bent on knocking me down from pegs I never stood on in the first place.

"I like the tiny one," Wallace says.

"Enough," Zion snaps, his deep tenor offering no room for argument. He flips through the pages of his book, then lays his palm flat over one, a gold light rocketing from beneath his fingers. "This should be interesting and most certainly will result in your deaths, so I will grant you passage, if only to keep *him* out of my line." He glares at Draven. "I'm sending you to Kypsel—"

"*Zion,*" Wallace groans.

"You lot can argue about it there." His words slice through her protest. "I have creatures waiting their assignments. Go. Now." The gold light shooting from his hand intensifies, a pulsing beacon of light among the red and black tones of the archway.

Wallace sighs, and I think she's about to stomp her foot when the light splinters into five beams, shooting straight into our chests.

I don't even have time to scream before that familiar hook sinks into the bottom of my belly and jerks.

My vision blurs, a cascade of red and black and sparkling gray. A blink and I'm on my feet again, stumbling slightly into Draven to my right. I whirl around, heaving a sigh when I see Ray is right where she was by my side seconds ago, only now—

"Watch it!" someone grumbles, and Draven hauls us out of the way, closer to where Cassiel is standing, as a very cranky demon—one that has the body of a bear and the head of a lion—stomps past us, a pack tucked under his thick arm and a glowing red blade holstered to his side.

My jaw about comes unhinged as I take in the new area surrounding us. We're on a sidewalk of some kind, a slab of rock carved and tucked against buildings constructed from deep azure rock. Some are tall and wide with tons of openings that look like caves, and others are moderate sized and adorned with glimmering stones of every color. And there are demons everywhere, some with talons or claws, others with a simple spiked tail or rubbery wings like Anka's. Some look like Wallace—almost human. They all wear some variation of what looks like leather pants and shirts made of tough canvas-like material as they rush in and out of buildings, carrying things this way or that.

Some chat at iron tables across the way, taking bites of unfamiliar foods, the air tinted with wild smells that seem familiar but I can't place—spicy and sweet and rich.

"It's a city," I say, shocked.

"What were you expecting?" Wallace asks, shuffling to my side from wherever she'd landed by Zion's magic. "Fire and brimstone?" She mutters *humans* under her breath.

Well, yeah, kind of. But I'm too enamored with the inky, indigo sky high above to respond to the jab or correct her. There are three bright spots that look like stars but are strong enough to illuminate the entire area, the light giving everything and everyone a deep purple hue. And across the vast sky I can just barely make out shimmering lines, almost like the rainbows of soap bubbles that change depending on what angle you look at them from. I turn, and the lines disappear.

"Where are we?" Ray asks.

"Kypsel," Wallace answers, motioning for us to follow her. "The center city of the upper Ather," she continues as she leads us through more demon foot-traffic, the hurried pace almost the same as when I would walk down the crowded streets of Chicago. A pang of longing tugs at the center of my chest, but I shove the emotion away as Wallace stops in front of a garnet-colored doorway.

"My home," she says, pressing one of her adornments cinched around one of her long locks against the center of the door.

It flies open, and she ushers us inside, shutting it behind us. We follow her up a spiral set of stairs, the railing constructed of the same rough stone as the building. Cassiel grunts as he tucks his wings in tight to avoid the narrow railing, Draven keeping close behind me, Ray taking up the space just in front of me until the stairs level out, revealing a wide-open space with a view of the bustling city below.

The walls are made of the same deep azure stone, but they're covered in pictures—drawings of what look to be countless adventures, all with the point of view of a warrior's eye. Some are gruesome, depicting victories over monsters that lay in bloody piles at Wallace's feet. Others are soft, hopeful renderings of demons with kind eyes and laughing features.

A half-dozen lime green cushions span the length of one wall, a small table littered with empty food cartons right next to it. And the rest of what I can only call a badass flat? Its walls are lined with weapons. Some look pretty recognizable, knives and daggers and swords of all sizes, bows and arrows, crossbows, and even what look to be handguns. But the rest? There are entire sections of machinery, tools, and gear I've never seen before—things that look like futuristic hybrids of what I know: machine guns made of a sparkling crystal blue, crossbows with liquid vials of bright red fluid lining the top, orbs of smoky glass, corked and no bigger than the size of my hand.

A soft hissing sound breaks the silence, and we whirl toward it.

Wallace eyes us with arched brows, wiggling the bright red bottle in her hand. "Drink?" she offers, but we all shake our heads. She takes a long drink from the bottle, the liquid inside neon yellow and trickling down her chin.

"Are these yours?" Ray asks, pointing at the drawings on the wall.

"Yeah," Wallace says, slightly out of breath from finishing off the bottle.

"They're awesome," Ray says. "I love the shadowing technique you used in this one." Ray points to a drawing of a demon with floppy ears that hang down to her shoulders, wrinkles etched in the light blue grooves of her face. The smile the elderly female wears is toothy and filled with peace.

"Do you draw?" Wallace asks as she heads over to one of the walls of weapons.

"Yes," Ray answers proudly.

Wallace grabs a pair of goggles in each hand—the circular lenses thick and tinted with a thick blood red—and tosses a pair to Ray. "I knew I liked you," she says as Ray catches them to her chest. "Those should fit you." She throws a pair toward me, much harder than she did to Ray, but I catch them easily enough. She follows suit with Draven and Cassiel, who eyes the things like they might bite him.

"What are these for?" Draven asks.

"Just put them in your packs," she says, nodding to the matching backpacks we all wear —except for Ray's zombie unicorn one. "I'm sure my aunt packed what she could, but she's been gone a long time. You'll need those."

I unzip my bag, dropping the goggles inside.

"I'm guessing a guide like you has connections all across the Ather," Draven says after stuffing his own bag.

"You'd guess right, Judge," she says, barely taking her eyes off the weapons as she gathers more in a larger bag.

"Have you heard of any others of my kind being down here?"

"Sure," she answers but doesn't stop loading up her bag. "But never to where they don't belong. Why?"

"The Judge I'm referring to would've been here much longer than a quick drop-off session. He was taken long ago by Marid."

Wallace finally turns around to face him. "I don't make it a habit to stick my nose in Marid's business. Or any of the Twelve. Anyone who does is begging for pain."

Ray tugs on the hem of her tunic. "Please? Finding him is super important."

Wallace blinks down at my sister, her full lips pursed. With a heavy sigh, she plants her fists on her hips. "Fine. Okay, I'll bite, but only because the tiny human asked so nicely. Does this particular Judge have a name or…?"

"Ryder."

No recognition flashes in her eyes. "What's he look like?"

"Like me," Draven answers, motioning to himself. "But his eyes are blue-green."

She eyes him, her gaze sweeping his body, his face. "I haven't come across anyone that looks like you," she says, returning her attention to the weapons. "But if I find him along the way, I expect a bonus."

That sliver of hope is all I need to press for more. "So, you *are* taking us to Marid?"

"Nope," she says, sliding a few knives into empty sheaths I hadn't seen before in the interior of her leather jacket. She doesn't bother looking over her shoulder as she hurtles some of those smoky orbs our way. Luckily, none shatter at our feet, and I store them next to the goggles.

"Then why—"

"I'll take you as far as the Conilis realm," she says, her rich brown eyes going distant for a moment. She blinks, and her earlier confidence returns. "It neighbors the Isle of Snakes—Marid's realm. *If* you manage to survive the trip, then you lot should have no trouble getting to the Isle of Snakes yourselves."

CHAPTER NINETEEN

"Thank you," I manage, knowing I need to choose my battles. "Don't need to thank me," she says, shaking her head. "You need to pay me."

"Right," I say, glancing to Draven. "Anka didn't tell us what your price would be—"

"Depends on what you have to offer," she says. "I'm an inclusive female. All forms of income are accepted and welcome. Cash has no use in the Ather, but I've been known to slip through the cracks a time or two."

That's how she knows about Wonder Woman. She's been to earth before.

"I'm also a fan of jewels, rare stones, blessed crystals." She eyes the vial around Draven's neck, and he quickly tucks it beneath his shirt.

"This isn't on the table," he says, and she smirks.

"We'll see."

I cringe, biting my lip. I don't have any of the things she's listed, and I suddenly wonder why I've been ridiculous enough to come here empty-handed. I mean, yeah, I've been a little distracted with the whole possession and *you have to go to Hell, which isn't really Hell* quest thing, but still. I should've been smarter. Should've bartered with Kazuki for more—

"Did you ring, darling?"

I jolt at the sorcerer's voice in my head, and Draven furrows his brow at me.

"Seriously?" I chide him. *"I think your name and you show up?"*

"I live to serve, dark princess."

I roll my eyes, drawing in a breath when I feel Draven's slick-as-shadows presence slide into the spot in my mind I always leave open for him.

"We'll find a way to pay her. Don't worry, I can—"

"Not the issue," I cut him off.

"Then what—"

"She's referring to me, sweet Judge."

Draven's eyes flare at the sound of Kazuki's voice inside my head.

"Is there a reason why you're using the sorcerer's bargain doorway right this second, Kaz?" he asks, a growl to his tone.

"She was thinking about me."

Draven arches an amused brow, and I roll my eyes. *"Ohmigod, I was* not.*"*

"Lies. The doorway flings wide open between us when you think my name."

I clench my eyes shut, my power rising at the multiple intrusions inside my mind. *"I was only thinking that I should've conned you out of some of your precious jewels to pay our guide,"* I explain as I meet Draven's eyes again. *"That's all."*

Draven's gaze flickers with light, a challenging primal promise of *that better be all* dancing in his eyes. And damn it, it makes my breath catch, that claiming look. The way his body shifts toward mine, even as we stand among our friends and Wallace, as if we might be the only two people in the room. I can't help but want to reach for him, want to curl my fingers around his neck and draw his lips to mine, allow him to siphon every thought from my head with his tongue—

I suddenly remember I'm not alone in my mind and clamp down my thoughts.

"But it was just getting good, darling. Cruel of you to cut it off there."

I groan out loud, and Cassiel raises his brows. Ray is too distracted by the art on the walls to care, and Wallace is studying me like I'm about to grow another head.

But Draven? A shudder racks his body as if he felt and saw every inch of my desire. And if *that* wasn't awkward enough, Kazuki played audience to it, too.

"Tell Wallace to put it on my tab," Kazuki offers.

I straighten. *"What?"*

"You heard me," he says, a bit apologetically. The sensation slides over my mind. *"I'm not a voyeur,"* he chides. *"Not unless I'm asked to a watch party. Honestly, Harley."* I can almost see him shaking his head and clucking his tongue. *"Try to remember I'm not a monster the next time you think about needing my help."*

"I won't," I quickly respond but add, *"What will this cost me when we return?"*

"Nothing," he says. *"What good is a sorcerer's bargain if I don't hold up my end?"* I hesitate, gratitude and wariness slipping into my chest. *"Ta ta,"* he says, and I feel his mental retreat, feel the cold shiver at his exit, as I glance to Draven.

"That wasn't creepy at all," he grumbles.

"Hey," I say. *"I didn't ask for either of you to be inside my head."*

He flashes me a faux-pout. *"And yet you keep that spot open for me* all *the time."*

I wet my lips as he steps into my space, the entire room around us forgotten. *"How often do you check to see if it's open?"*

With his telepathy powers, he can enter my mind whenever he wants, when all I can do is leave a space open for him so we can talk. Sometimes, I wish I had his power, especially when he's being hard as hell to read.

Draven smooths a finger down my cheek, sliding some of my hair behind my ear. *"As often as your mind wanders to using me for distraction."*

"I don't mean…I wouldn't use—"

"It's all right," he says, and that connection between us blazes with heat, like the links on the chain are being held over hot coals. *"I'll be whatever you need me to be, Harley. Always."*

Something swells in my chest, an almost painful sort of

expansion. I reach up on my tiptoes, my lips inching for his because I can think of nothing else to say or do in that moment. Nothing I can say to match his words, to make him understand that he means so much more to me than a distraction. My mouth barely grazes his, but electric shocks fly in warm tendrils down my spine—

"You know we're standing here, right?" Wallace says, and I'm jolted back to reality. "Like *right* exactly here." She points to where she stands for emphasis. "If you're going to stink up my flat with your lust-starved scents, the *least* you could do is give a girl an invite."

Her words are teasing, but that quickly, dark flames spring from my fingertips, curling around my wrists.

Wallace smirks, eyes on my glittering black flames. "Relax. It was a joke," she says, waving me off. "No need to go all apocalyptic on me."

I quickly tamp down my anger and my instant jealousy, and over what? Because she made a joke? I coax my dark flames beneath my skin, hating the way it glares at me for reining it in. I need to do better. I glance at Ray, who is looking at me with nothing but support in her eyes. She may not be concerned, but what kind of example am I setting for her if I instantly set to kill-mode when someone makes a joke at my expense?

I breathe in, once, twice, then shake off the adrenaline vibrating under my skin.

"Sorry," I mutter.

Wallace laughs. She *laughs*. "It's funny," she says. "Because that little jealous reaction is totally normal for—"

"When do we leave?" Draven cuts across her words, likely saving me from being the target of another joke. Which either means he doesn't want to hear it or he doesn't want me exploding into a living torch. Either way, I'm grateful for it.

Wallace arches a brow. "We leave when we settle the payment."

"Right," I say, an ache wrenching in my skull. It's either from the dimensional travel, the oh-so-fun attitude of Wallace's, or the two males who'd been in my head moments ago, and I'm trying like hell to talk past it. "Kazuki says to put it on his tab."

She studies me for a second. "You're friends with Kazuki, too?"

I nod, though I'm not sure if *friends* is the right term. More like *powerful sorcerer I'm indebted to.* I roll up the sleeve of my simple black top, showing her the warlock's tattoo.

"Interesting company you keep," she says.

I raise my brows at the way she says it. She's not wrong, but still.

"If Kaz is offering to pay the debt," she muses, "then I'm ready when you are."

"Good," I say. "Now. We don't have a lot of time." I have no idea when Marid will become privy to our plans, and I would really, really like to have the element of surprise on our hands when we kick his fucking door in.

Wallace gathers a few more things, tossing more weapons, several bottles of the neon-yellow drink, and some packaged food our way. Our bags are fully stuffed by the time we head down the spiral stairs where Wallace holds the door for us.

Draven walks as close to Ray as he can without touching her, and I'm once again struck with how shitty his life has been. To be a human only to get Called by the Creator to be a divine Judge, ruled by the Seven. To get a power that makes him a threat to anyone he touches—beyond me, for reasons we still don't understand. I know he will protect Ray with his life, and yet he can't even hold her hand without being a threat to her himself. It makes my chest ache in all sorts of ways, but I force myself to move past it.

Cassiel follows them, leaving me to linger by Wallace.

"You never asked why we need to find Marid," I say.

Dread fills her eyes before vanishing. "I don't need to know," she says, a bit too harshly to be believable. "I'm only here to get paid."

CHAPTER TWENTY

"Blasters, acid bombs, flame throwers…" Wallace mutters the name of each item as she loads it into the back of her vehicle, and I can do nothing but gape at it.

"Is that…an old fire truck?" I ask, eying the vehicle that's lifted, with near monster truck–sized tires filling the wide wheel wells. The tread on them are massive and thick, looking like razor-sharp teeth eager to chew up the ground. Parts of the original red paint flicker beneath the thick, haphazard coats of rich navy blue, likely to help camouflage the thing. A vehicle of this size would be hard to miss, though, and that's not mentioning the gear attached to it, because *that* is extensive. Two large, claw-like metal contraptions jut out just beneath the front grill, the rear of the truck outfitted with welded iron storage—the same place Wallace is tying weapons to now.

"Yep," Wallace says, not taking her eyes off the duffle bags she hauls into the back. "Nineteen eighty-seven, if we're talking about the frame. The tires I scored on my last trip up."

"You built this yourself?" I ask, impressed.

"'Course I did," she says, heaving what looks like a rolled-up life raft into the back. "I'm not really one of those walking-tour-type guides." She glances at Cassiel. "You think four string strobes will be enough?"

Cassiel cocks a brow at her, then me before returning her gaze.

"You're right," she says, though Cassiel has said nothing. "Better bring one more." She grabs a spool the size of a barrel, a chain with glass bulbs between each link coiled around it, and slides it into the back. She nods at her work.

"Do you normally take this much firepower on your tours?" I ask.

She laughs. "Firepower. That's funny, coming from you." She shakes her head, securing the back of the vehicle closed. "No," she finally answers, eying the loot. "I don't get many requests to go as far as you and your tribe are demanding."

Something serious steals over her gaze. "There are a ton of peaceful realms in the Ather, but for every realm we manage to find balance in, another crops up that is as vile as all the legends from Earth talk about. Thanks to those assholes who have more power than the rest of us taking over and ensuring they only leave us with the barest scraps to get by, more and more realms turn to violence to survive. *Those* are the realms your Hell stories come from, not the Ather as a whole."

I nod, swallowing hard. So power here is like money on earth— you either have it and thrive or you don't. I immediately feel a pang of sympathy for those who don't, just as the anger rises for those finding it acceptable to exploit them. I've always been poor and hungry and worked my butt off to make sure my sister is fed, clothed. How many creatures here are just trying to do the same?

"*But*," she continues, "in order to get to Conilis, we'll have to go through some of those realms that give the Ather a bad name. Plus, my contacts in those certain realms have more connections than I do. You can ask them about Ryder as we go, if you want, but not all are friendlies. Hence, the firepower. And if all that fails?" She reaches into an interior pocket of her leather jacket and pulls out a tiny red vial the size of her palm, the cork sealed with black wax. "I've got confetti here as a get-out-of-jail-free card."

"Confetti?" I ask.

Ray perks up. "Like glitter?"

Wallace nods, slipping the vial carefully into the pocket near her breast. "Kind of," she says. "I really, *really* hope I don't have to use it, though." She rounds the vehicle, where Draven is eying the lettering scrawled across the back passenger side. "You like?"

He huffs a laugh. "Emergency and Ass-Kicking Rig?" The first two and last word are in what was likely the vehicle's original white script, but the middle *ass-kicking* phrase is written in painted, jagged, bright blue letters.

Wallace bounds for the driver's side door. She hauls it open, using the welded-on side step to heave herself inside. She shuts the door, hanging her leather-clad elbow out of the opened window. "This baby has saved my skin at least a dozen times," she says, affectionally patting it as if it's some giant pet of hers. "Ass-kicking isn't the only thing it can do, but it seemed pretty damn fitting." She jerks her head, motioning for us to climb inside. I help Ray up and into the back passenger seat, Draven following in behind me, as Cassiel climbs into the front passenger seat, his silver eyes glowing in the darkening light.

"What else can it do?" Ray asks after I've figured out the harness to strap her between Draven and myself.

Wallace adjusts the rearview mirror so she can meet Ray's eyes. "Hold onto something," she says, and the engine roars to life, the sound like some beast's hungry awakening. "And I'll show you."

CHAPTER
TWENTY-ONE

The truck—or *Easkr* as Wallace so lovingly calls her emergency ass-kicking rig—is surprisingly quiet as its giant wheels tear through the terrain. We fall silent, Wallace focusing on navigating the busy city streets of Kypsel, Cassiel eying the area like a hawk. Ray's head slumps against my shoulder, her little body and mind finally succumbing to the exhaustion this trip has squeezed from us.

The city's beautifully constructed buildings give way to a more rural terrain, stone roads melting into dark dirt pathways bordered by trees with gnarly trunks of royal blue, their glossy leaves wide and floppy and gray like an elephant's ears. I tear my eyes away from the animals I see prowling beyond the trees—birds as big as mountain lions, with glistening talons and green eyes. Lizards that look like dinosaurs, and even a few Lagartis demons. I shudder as I see one slip into the red pool of water we pass, a small lake drifting and winding between the trees until it's out of sight.

The memory of those snapping teeth, the albino alligator-like demons desperate to tear into my and Draven's flesh, turns my stomach. I turn and find Draven's eyes on mine, severe and slightly ashamed, as if he's remembering the night, remembering the moment he absorbed the demon's power and became half beast, half boy. His intense look quickly fades into the distant stare he's kept slipping into since I brought him back to life.

"Do you think your brother will help us?" I ask, knowing he's listening through that doorway I leave open for him—the same piece of my mind that pulses with a warmth that reminds me of his eyes right before he claims my mouth.

"He has to," he says. *"I don't know if there will be any part of my brother that remains, but…"*

"I know." He doesn't need to finish the statement. He needs his brother to be okay, to make amends to him, to try and reconnect, if such a thing is possible after one hundred years of separation. And one hundred years in the Ather? As Marid's prisoner? What kind of life has he lived here?

Wallace looks to be thriving, despite what she said about some of the realms and the power here. Could I do the same thing?

I study Draven, noting the wall over his gaze, the one I haven't seen up since we'd successfully torn each other's down days ago.

"We haven't really had time to finish talking about what happened." My throat tightens, and I shift in my seat, doing my best not to wake Ray. *"When you died."*

The mental image flashes through my mind, the sight of his body lifeless on the ground. I hope like hell he can't see it, can't feel my terror, my pain. Hope that the larger portions of my mind outside this little pocket of space I've cleared just for him are private.

From the smooth look on his face, it seems to work that way.

"Draven," I beg. *"You saw the freaking* Devil. *He told you things about me. About what I am. And I stole you back. Don't you think he's pissed? Don't you think we should talk about it, plan for something in case this Rainier decides to get revenge on me—"*

"I think we've had enough on our plate." His arm stretches across the back of the seat. *"We can't strategize for every possible attack. If we did that, we'd never stop. With what you are, with the power you hold, there is no end to what may come after you. Finding Ryder is top priority so we can sever the tether between Ray and Marid. After that?"* The voice in my head goes quiet for a moment before he continues. *"We'll figure out everything else."*

And isn't that always the case recently? Focus on the big bad problem and push the other little bad problems to the side. *"Like me staying in the Ather."*

I can almost *feel* the argument rising in Draven, but he's calm and gentle as he says, *"Yes, that will be a conversation for after… everything. Have you brought it up to Ray yet?"* He glances to her, asleep against my shoulder.

"No," I admit, guilt eating at my insides. I need to talk to her about it, get her take on it. The last thing in the world I want to do is leave my sister's side, but if it keeps her safe? Keeps the world she belongs in safe? Then I'll do it.

"Let's take it one step at a time," Draven says, tracing soft, teasing circles on the back of my hand, sliding around my wrist and back again. *"We survive this and figuring everything else out should be a breeze."*

He's not wrong, but I can't ignore the pit in my stomach. The instinct roaring at me that nothing will ever be easy again.

Draven keeps up that too-light touch on my hand. Each pass sends jolts of heat down my spine. *"We have to stay sharp here. Just because you can't open a gate from this side doesn't mean you won't be hunted. Your powers are the same, maybe even magnified down here. Some will see it as a threat to their existence. Others will see it as a challenge to prove themselves against."*

"Great. With the way people keep calling me princess, you'd think I could command a little more serve and pamper and a little less kill-now, ask-questions-later," I tease, and Draven's touch pauses for a moment. *"That was a joke,"* I clarify, bracing myself after Wallace drives over a particularly large bump in the road.

A slow, wicked smile shapes his lips, clearing the weight from his eyes. He picks up that teasing touch, that stare of his burning right to the center of me.

"What?" I ask when I can't stand his silence anymore.

That grin deepens. *"I've always loved your dark sense of humor,"* he says, adding a graze of his nails to the underside of my wrist. *"And even here, in the Ather, demons and monsters alike at every turn, you find a way to laugh."*

"If I can't find humor in the twisted life I've been handed, then…" My voice trails off, and memories flood my mind: a boot sinking into my stomach, a gold rock paperweight crunching against my

temple, a candle flame held against my bare skin. Minions and Cannis demons and Lagartis demons and everything in between trying to kill me.

Kai.

The blade in his hand, the way it sank into my stomach like a warm knife through butter. The way his eyes had lit up at the blood splashing the ground.

That…that I haven't been able to find anything funny about yet.

"It would be a very sad life," I finally finish, and Draven lays his hand flat over mine, as if he can see where my thoughts took me. I know he didn't *read* them, not when I keep them in the dark portion of my mind where I know he can't reach, *won't* reach unless I tell him to. Which I won't. No one needs to see this kind of darkness, feel this kind of pain, betrayal.

"Tell me what you're thinking, Draven," I manage to say—like I had at The Bridge—after our connection has fallen silent for too long. After that distant, sad look overtakes his eyes once again.

He blinks the look away, pulling his hand away and leaning against the back of the seat. *"I keep getting flashes,"* he admits, and I can hear the strain in his voice, feel it in my bones. *"Of Rainier, what he was saying to me while I was…gone. Only parts of it, though."*

I swallow hard, grateful he didn't use the word *dead.* "And what you did see, you said you didn't know if you could trust it all."

"Right," he says, closing his eyes for a moment. *"I don't like it,"* he admits. *"It's like a dream I can't reach, but it's so close. And something in my gut tells me not to look too close. But then being here, searching for Ryder…"*

I bite my lip, waiting. When he doesn't continue, I decide to switch tactics, hoping to steer him away from the heavy. *"Tell me something about him,"* I say. *"From when you were both human."*

A slow, broken smile shapes his lips, his eyes opening. *"We were inseparable as children, even though we were as different as two people could be. I loved piano, he preferred violin. He loved* cats, while I much preferred dogs. He used to be so persuasive. He could talk me into anything, including sneaking him treats after bedtime." He laughs softly, shaking his head. "Mother doted on him, while I took the blame for most things." He sighs. "It's no wonder he loved being a Judge while I resented it. I just wish it hadn't cleaved us apart like it did. Wish it would've been me who Marid took, and not him."

"Do you think there is a chance he got away?" I ask, trying to be optimistic for once. Though searching the whole Ather for him doesn't sound like a picnic.

"I doubt it," he says. "But I'll certainly ask Wallace's contacts just in case. A hundred years is a long time." His head lowers. "I have no idea what he's endured while surviving here or who I'll see when I look in his eyes."

Longing and fear radiates down the chain connecting us, and I have to blink back tears.

"Maybe he'll still be that boy begging for you to sneak him treats," I say. "Maybe he'll be happy to see you."

"Or maybe he'll hate me for what he's endured."

And knowing Draven like I do, I know he thinks he deserves it. It's so unfair. All of this is just so damn unfair. So instead of patronizing him or placating him, I let him have his worries, his memories, and simply reach for his hand, silently holding it in support. Because in all reality? We don't have a clue who or what we're going to find when we find Draven's brother.

When, not if. Because as much as I want to find him for Draven's sake, I need him, too. Selfishly, I need his power to save my sister. And there is nothing that can stand in the way of that—even a tainted history between the brothers.

After we've driven for what feels like forever, I rub my palms over my face, forcing my mind to focus on one impossible task at a time.

First, find Ryder.

Second, we need to somehow find and detain Marid to break the tether between him and my sister.

Third, we need to escape the Ather with all our lives intact.

"That's a stone wall," Cassiel says, his cool yet concerned voice cutting into my thoughts.

"Sure is," Wallace says, the engine revving as she pushes on the gas.

My spine straightens as she speeds straight toward the massive wall of slick black rock. "What the hell are you doing?" I gasp, holding Ray to me, the motion shaking her awake. She's still blinking the sleep out of her eyes when Wallace lets out a whooping laugh. "You're going to kill us!"

Shadows gather in the backseat, curling around Draven, then me and Ray, as if he's fully prepared to fly us out the window. Already, he's reaching to drop down the glass.

Wallace snorts, shifting gears before she slams her booted foot against the pedal as far as it can go. I squint through the growing shadows and gasp. She's *glowing*. Literally. A beautiful violet light illuminates her brown skin.

What the fuck?

But we have other problems. The wall is so close I can't see up it or around it.

And nothing but that dark rock fills the windshield as Wallace crashes the truck right into it.

CHAPTER TWENTY-TWO

I clench my eyes shut and brace for the impact, the quick slice of pain, and then the descent into death.

Simultaneously, I'm plotting to haunt Wallace for all eternity as well as praying to whatever Creator or King will hear me to somehow perform a miracle and spare Ray.

But the pain doesn't come.

Nothing but cool shadows caress my skin, the scent of amber and citrus filling the air. That, and a little zap of electricity that is a literal shock—not a reaction to Draven's shadows on my skin.

"Harley," Ray groans, shoving against my hold. "You're going to re-crack my rib."

I instantly release her, my eyes adjusting as Draven peels his shadows away from the protective orb he's encompassed Ray and myself inside.

Wallace's laugh echoes in the vehicle—a vehicle that is *still* moving. The violet glow under her skin flickers, sending little waves through her emergency ass-kicking rig.

"Works every time," she says, careening the wheel to the right.

The rig makes the sharp turn with ease, but Cassiel lets out a warning growl. She ignores him, spinning the vehicle, expertly navigating it to a spot squished between two other equally geared-out vehicles that look even more suited to the Ather than the truck Wallace rebuilt.

My fingers melt into the leather base of the seat where I've dug in my flames.

Wallace sniffs once, twice, then whirls around, glaring at the scorched leather. "That's going to cost you extra."

I level her with a glare of my own. "No way. I thought you were about to crash into a freaking *wall*. I can't be liable for damage I do under that kind of stress."

She rolls her eyes, which are transitioning back to their stunning brown. "Please," she says. "I've never lost a client due to *my* actions, and I don't intend to now."

"Then you should've told us you could..." My voice trails off as I struggle for the right word to describe what she'd just done.

"Leap?" she fills in for me. "Where the hell is the fun in that?"

"Fun?" I gape at her as she opens her door and hops down from the rig. I'm out my own door and rounding to the front in two seconds flat, stepping right into her space. "Maybe you didn't realize this about me," I say, my tone low and lethal, "but risking my sister's life, or *joking* about it, doesn't sit well with me. I will gladly destroy the fucking *world* if it means protecting her. What do you think I'll do to *you* if you unnecessarily put her in danger again?"

Wallace's brow arches higher, stark violet light flooding her eyes and pulsing in the palms of her hands. She steps toward me, and I don't back away an inch. I don't even blink, even when she's close enough to kiss. "How about I teleport your ass to another realm? Then we'll see how your threat stands—"

"That purple is beautiful." Ray's voice cuts through Wallace's as Cassiel helps her down from the rig and she walks over to us. Her eyes are wide as she notes the colored energy in Wallace's eyes and hands. "It's the same shade as these sea stars we saw in school last year," she continues, wrinkling her forehead as if she's recalling information. She smiles after a moment, nodding to herself. "The purple sea stars are important."

I frown. Why is she giving us a marine biology lesson? But then I notice Wallace's eyes are firmly on hers.

"They get rid of things that threaten to overrun the place," my sister continues. "And they're always upgrading their bodies to survive. Kind of like how you're able to move through walls meant to keep everyone in place."

Wallace's hands lower, her eyes shifting back to rich brown, her hands absorbing the violet light. "Sea star, huh?" she says, a genuine smile shaping her lips. "That's one I've never been compared to before." Her smile quickly falls to a more serious look, and she clears her throat. "Thanks, tiny seer."

Leave it to Ray to be able to defuse a bomb with a few perceptive and kind words. I'm breathing easier, my dark flames relaxing easily beneath my skin.

"Wait," I say, making sure I keep my tone even so I don't start another fight. "If you can teleport me to another realm, why not just do that for us in the first place? Why the journey through all of these realms?"

Wallace heads to the back of the rig, grabbing her own leather backpack and slinging it over her shoulders before ensuring all the doors are locked. She places her hand over the dark hood, violet light sliding over it like a sweeping wave until it surrounds the vehicle. "That would drain me," she says, and from the way her eyes twitch, she *really* didn't like admitting that. "And no one can afford to be drained here, no matter what realm you're in. That leap between the wall was a blink in time. Trying to teleport four of you to one of the farthest realms in the Ather? I don't even know if I *could* do it, let alone survive it."

Ray nudges my side with her elbow, and I blink a few times. "Thank you," I say, and Wallace scrunches her brow.

"For what?"

"For taking us," I say. "And for being honest. I know admitting that isn't easy," I say, then hurry to add, "admitting weakness isn't easy for me, either."

Maybe I have more in common with the guide than I think. Maybe there is hope for a common ground between us—

"Don't thank me," she snaps, slicing off my thoughts like she's lopping off the end of a carrot. "I do this for the currency. Nothing more."

I clench my teeth. Fine, then.

"Speaking of payments," she says, jerking her head toward a gold-paved road a few yards away from where she's parked, "the next realm we have to go through requires a pass. I'll need to buy them from the demon who runs this place."

Great. "Wait. There are *passes*?"

"Most travel in the Ather is through the connecting archways. Some cost, and others are free. This one is not."

"Like toll roads?"

She snorts. "Something like that."

Cassiel tucks his wings in tight, positioning himself directly behind where she leads, and I urge Ray behind him, then me, then Draven. As far as protective lines go, this would be a hell of a one to get through. Not that I see a single demon as we walk for what feels like forever down a gold stone road, the sky a deep cobalt above us. Valleys of more gold stretch beyond the road, vast and rolling like silk.

"Not much to this realm," I say.

Wallace shakes her head as we come to the top of the road where it starts to slope downward. "You just really don't know anything, do you?"

I clamp down on my response, the sharp words swallowed by the sight rippling out before us.

Down the slope of the golden road is an enormous hub—silk tents of every color house what look like market booths selling trinkets and food and drinks and other things I can't see. Music pulses and ebbs, even up here, and flickering lights bounce back and forth, some demons dancing in the pathways that line the tents. Others fight in big brawls of five or more, all teeth and growls and claws.

"Welcome to Xses."

CHAPTER
TWENTY-THREE

There's a tendril of wariness in her tone, but she blinks out of the stare before I can question it, then ushers us to follow her. "Not a bad place to find a weapon or a drink, but watch your gear. There are no rules here except for one—no one leaves without a pass from the ruler."

I tighten my hold on the straps of my backpack as we move down the road. "You can't just leap the rig through the next wall?"

Wallace stops, her eyes on the dark blue sky for a few moments. "If I could do that, don't you think I would have?"

"I don't know you that well."

"Fine, fair enough," she says, turning to face me. "One thing you *should* know, I don't do things the hard way for funsies. If there is an easy way? An easy out? I fucking take it. Every. Single. Time. So, if I'm saying we need to get a pass in order for me to haul your asses to the next realm"—she eyes each of us—"then I need one. M'kay?" Her eyes fall to Ray at my side. "Does she always have this many trust issues? Or do I just bring it out in her?"

Ray shakes her head. "She has reasons," she answers. "Believe me."

Wallace nods, glancing at me with a much softer gaze, and I nearly snap at her pity. "Don't," I say, low and cold.

Draven intertwines his fingers in mine, a silent show of support as Wallace and I stare each other down.

"We're wasting time," Cassiel says, his wings stretching as if being inside the vehicle for that long made them ache.

"The fine-as-hell angel of death is right." Wallace snaps her fingers. "Let's roll."

The music swells as we reach the heart of Xses, sweeping over us in sensual, rhythmic notes that I can feel all the way in my bones. The urge to dance, to grab Draven and move to the beat, is overwhelming, as if the notes are laced with thrall enchantments that would rival the Hypno's powers. So many demons writhe against their partners in any open spaces they can find, drinks in one hand sloshing liquid over the lip, soaking clothes or fur or scales, their partners content to lick up the spilled contents. All while thrashing and lashing at each other, grinding and moving to the music as if their lives depend on it.

But they all look happy. Blissfully, drunkenly happy as they dance and eat and drink.

The memory of stumbling into a tall, muscled boy on a dance floor races through my mind. The first night I met Draven at the Bishop Briggs concert. He'd danced with me, carefree and confident, teasing me with his light touches.

That was before I'd known anything about who I was or what I was. Before I'd been thrown into a world I never knew existed. And while there is a small part of me that would love to go back to that moment and live in blissful ignorance forever, there is a bigger part of me that is grateful for every moment after. Draven and I haven't had a relationship status talk or anything, but despite every danger, he hasn't left my side. And that speaks more volumes than any label ever could.

Smells of rich spices, smoked meats, and candied nuts tint the air, the earth-like smells shocking me out of the memory that seems years old, not weeks. My stomach rumbles, but I'm no stranger to hunger. Hopefully, after this stop, we can eat some of the food Wallace packed in our bags for us.

"Tullgon is usually at the Den this time of night," Wallace calls over her shoulder to be heard over the music then fixes a pointed look on me. "Let me do all the talking."

I raise my hands innocently.

She weaves through tents and pathways, each one more

elaborate than the next. Many of the tent's owners try to entice each of us—even Ray—to partake in their wares. To buy food and drinks or sheer clothes or any manner of jewelry.

"Stay sharp," Wallace mutters as she turns into the largest tent we've seen so far, this one a stretched white silk that is clear enough to see the sky high above.

A thickly muscled demon with four bulging arms and one long horn atop its head takes one look at Wallace and waves us through the entrance. The place is more packed than even The Bridge, with demons so closely crammed together we have to literally shove our way through the dancing crowd. The music is so loud there is no chance of hearing each other unless we speak directly into an ear.

Ray stumbles, and I reach to steady her, but Cassiel's wings flare outward, the movement sharp and strong enough to stun half the crowd, urging them backward. His eyes glow a stark silver in the muted lights of the tent, and gasps of *Cassiel* or *Death Striker* sound from several of the demons near us. Many seem to know or at least *sense* who he is. None are brave or brash enough to even graze one of those inky feathers.

He nods at us, urging me and Ray to step in front of him, his wings clearing the path.

"Show off," Draven mutters from close behind me.

Cassiel rolls his eyes.

I flash Cassiel a thankful look, and we hurry to catch up to Wallace. She's made it to the back of the tent and another roped-off section, curtains of velvet enclosing whatever lay behind it.

Two more bouncer-like demons stand before this rope, but this time, they don't wave Wallace through. She motions one of the hulking beasts down to her level, whispering something in its ear. Thick, caterpillar-like eyebrows raise high as its solid black eyes survey us.

The hair on the back of my neck stands on end, my flames spiraling up to just beneath my skin as the bouncer continues to stare and stare at us while Wallace talks. What is she saying to him? For all I know, she could be selling us out, getting help to auction us off to the highest bidder.

Which is precisely why I've never told Wallace exactly who or *what* I am. I hoped my flames weren't so uncommon down here that she wouldn't put two and two together, and her aloofness seems like she hasn't, but...

The bouncer nods, jerking his head to the side. His partner moves the rope, waving us in. Wallace blows the bouncer a kiss as we shuffle through the velvet curtains.

Somehow, the music is muffled by the curtains, no doubt some form of magic quieting the room. The space is as large as a ballroom, with red velvet cushions sitting atop rock benches that line the silk walls, and slick wooden tables sit before each, topped with every manner of food and drink imaginable, most of which look just a tad different than what I'm used to. Purple apples, black potatoes, golden vegetables, pink breads, and pitchers of the neon yellow drink Wallace had at her place.

"Wallace," a deep, almost gurgley voice calls out from the center of the room. "It's been too many cycles," he says before chomping into what looks like some kind of animal leg, but it's much bigger than anything I've ever seen before.

"Been busy," she says, smiling at the demon who I assume is Tullgon.

His body is almost as wide as the bench he sits on, a suit of gold straining against it. His body is human looking despite the size, his fingers like sausages as he reaches for one of those purple apples and bites into it with wide, flat teeth. His nose is elongated, his face covered in fine brown fur, the top of his head flattening out with two long, pointed ears. Gold earrings hook in each ear, weighing it down slightly.

"Business is good, I see," he says, chunks of the apple flying onto the table. He doesn't seem to care or notice, and there are no plates to speak of. Just a large glass filled with that neon drink, and platters upon platters of food. I eye the table, noting there are no other chairs and no sign of guests joining him.

All for him, then—a feast that could feed at least twenty people.

"And why I'm here," she says, keeping her voice respectful. "I need five passes."

"Five?" His black eyes spark, trails of his drink dribbling down his fur. "That'll cost you."

Wallace shifts, crossing her arms over her chest. "How much?"

He considers, chewing on another hunk of the animal leg. "Sixty."

"Sixty?" She gapes at him. "Last time it was ten."

Tullgon shrugs, one of his ears twitching. "Inflation."

"That's damn near robbery, Tull," she says, softening her voice. "I'm a frequent customer."

"It costs keeping the other realms from spilling into this one. To keep Marid from gouging my realm for all it's worth."

I try not to jolt at his casual mention of Marid.

"I get it," Wallace says.

"Where are you passing to?"

Wallace doesn't miss a beat, curling her lips into a wicked smile. "Lusro." She lets the word slide off her tongue in such a way that I have the urge to look away, as if we're all intruding on some private moment.

"A group thing?" He smirks as he glances at each of us. "Quite the spread."

It's only then I realize Ray is hidden beneath Cassiel's wing, the length of it easily concealing her from head to toe. I don't know how I'll ever repay Cassiel for his offer to help, to come with us, but it's apparent he takes his job seriously. Protecting Ray will be worth any amount of debt the angel of death will call in later.

"You know I have unlimited tastes," she says, and he laughs, more food flying from his mouth.

"Forty," he says, and Wallace bows deeply at the waist.

"Forty," she says, reaching into her pocket and sliding a small rectangular piece of shimmering gold his way. It's thin as a credit card and no bigger. The stamp on the top is an intricate set of symbols I don't recognize, but the sweeping lines and sharp edges remind me of the sorcerer's bargain tattoo I have on my arm.

Tullgon snatches up the gold piece so fast I almost jump back, but he pockets it just as quickly, returning to his food. He gives a grunt, and one of his bouncers comes into the room. Tullgon says, "Five," and the bouncer exits the room again.

"I'm searching for someone," Draven says, his voice a mask of light and casual.

Tullgon cuts his eyes to Draven, intrigue glimmering there. No doubt wondering how he can squeeze more out of us. "Who's that…" He sniffs in Draven's direction. "Judge."

"Has another Judge passed through here? One who looks almost identical to me and goes by Ryder?" I hear the hope in Draven's voice, just a small hint of it. Hope that Ryder escaped Marid's realm and made it to one of the more peaceful places Wallace spoke of. Even this place would be better than what I'm imagining Marid's realm to be like.

Tullgon continues eating. "Doesn't sound familiar."

Draven dips his head. I hate the look of defeat in his eyes.

"Five," the bouncer says, returning to the room holding a carved wooden box. He pries open the lid, revealing a smooth black silk cushion, five dice resting on top. Each one is a different shape— from a basic cube to an intricate pentagonal trapezohedron—but they all share the same colors of emerald green and sparkling gold. Each face has a different symbol etched atop, the lines hair thin and blazing gold.

Wallace grabs all in one swipe of her hand and bows again to Tullgon. "Until next time."

He waves her off with a fresh animal leg in his hand. "I'd hurry if I were you," he says once we've reached the curtain door of his room. "You know how badly everyone wants one of those passes, and I won't be the one to stop them from trying."

"Thanks for the tip," Wallace says, then urges us out of the room.

Once the velvet curtains close behind us, I release the breath

I've been holding.

"We need to get back to Easkr," Wallace says, all teasing gone from her voice.

She doesn't have to tell me twice.

Draven's shadows are at his back as we weave through the still-dancing crowd, and a knot forms in my throat once we make it back to the main marketplace. The demons I noted as looking blissfully happy are still doing the same things—eating, drinking, dancing.

The *exact* same things, over and over again.

It's only when I look a little closer that I notice the desperation in their eyes, the exhaustion in the lines of their faces.

A cool shadow tickles the back of my neck, urging me to focus.

I do, my breath heaving we walk so fast. "They're stuck here, aren't they?" I ask as we make it to the road we need to get back to the rig.

"Some," Wallace answers as we continue power-walking.

"Why?"

"You remember Zion passing a sentence on that demon earlier? There are all kinds of punishments in the Ather for the demons who are sent here from the Earth realm, those captured by Judges. Zion decides their sentence and where they should go based off their crimes. If it's an internal Ather matter, it's usually one of those in power who decide. Marid or one of the other Twelve Greater Demons. And then some of those here are simply fool creatures who came here looking for a good time and fell prey to its temptations. There are bets here no one can win." She motions to the dancers. "Hence, their predicament."

"Damn," I say, my stomach sinking. I'd brought Ray to this place. Big sister of the year award is totally *not* going to me.

"Yeah," she says. "Those sentenced here or trapped here by their own bargains are stuck here unless one of them gets their hands on—"

"A pass," a gravely voice says, a scaled demon stepping onto the road to block our path. Five of his friends follow, each one looking more bulked up than the next.

"Shit," Wallace says.

"Toss them over," the scaled demon says, flicking a clawed hand toward Wallace. He stretches his thin lips, showing off three rows of needle-sharp teeth. "And no one gets eaten."

CHAPTER
TWENTY-FOUR

"W ow," I whisper, shifting into a defensive stance. "Tullgon didn't waste *any* time selling you out."

"He didn't sell me out," Wallace whispers back, sliding back a step to stand at my left. "They can smell them."

"Sure."

"Let's table your trust issues for later," she says. "Right now, we need to team up to survive."

"These guys don't scare me."

She snorts. "I'm starting to get that. Is there anything that scares you?"

My sister being hurt or killed. Draven dying... "I'm not a huge fan of wind chimes."

"Wind chimes?" Cassiel asks from behind me. I glance over at him to make sure Ray is safe. Sure enough, she's a safe distance behind him and Wallace.

"They make noise even when there is barely a breeze," I explain, turning back to face the demons. "And the sound grates on my nerves."

The demons are getting pissed, clearly not fans of us carrying on a conversation like they aren't standing there all menacing and threatening to eat us. Which, from Draven and my fights in the past, has always worked to our advantage in throwing them off-balance.

"What are these things?" I ask him.

"A sub-species of minions," he answers. *"Drakels."*

I nod, noting the scaled skin that looks as hard as armor, the reflective eyes likely giving them perfect vision in the dark, the three rows of sharp teeth set into a scaled but humanoid face. They totally look like intelligent, upright komodo dragons, their legs like pillars, their clawed hands slick and dripping with black liquid.

"Enough," the leader says. "You have five breaths to give us the passes."

"And you have three," I reply casually. "Move aside, and I won't kill you where you stand."

Ray gasps at my words. I may have told her every detail of every demon attack I encountered, but hearing about it and seeing it for yourself are two totally different things. In that moment, I wish I could slip into her mind, assure her that I don't *want* to slaughter them, but I can't let them put her at risk, either. Put any of us at risk.

But that's a lie, even as I think it.

I *want* to fight.

I want to burn and sear and brawl.

Anyone who threatens her threatens me. Isn't that what's kept me alive this whole time? When so many fucking things keep trying to kill me?

The leader cackles a slithering laugh, his forked tongue flashing behind those rows of teeth. "The human thinks she's a match—"

"Bad idea," Draven drones over the demon's words.

"What? Tell them, guide." He nods toward Wallace. "You know what we can do to you. Smash some sense into the mouthy one."

"Mouthy?" I snap.

"She's not the easiest to talk to," Wallace says with a shrug.

"Three breaths," the leader warns.

"And that means you're down to one," I say.

"Fine," the leader says. "I like it the hard way." One step, and his five friends converge, herding us into a tight circle. My back touches the rest of my friends, plus Wallace's. The drakel closest to me slashes a clawed hand toward me, and I dodge it enough that it pushes everyone back, closer to the leader.

"Cassiel, get Ray out of here," I demand, dark flames surging from my fingertips.

Cassiel hesitates, his hands in fists, his eyes a searing silver as he stares down the demons, more than ready for a fight.

"Please," I beg. "I need her safe."

The plea in my voice must break something in him, because a cold wind *whooshes* from behind me.

I spare a glance upward. There, in the cobalt sky, Cassiel flaps those glorious wings, rushing Ray away from harm.

Something hot and slick sinks into my forearm, the drakel's claws tearing away skin. I groan against the pain, lifting my knee and landing a solid kick to its thick stomach. It hurtles backward, scrambling on its feet.

Draven is already a sheet of smoky shadow at my right, weaving in and out of the claws and teeth. He fights two in this form, a third snapping close behind.

Wallace is all bursts of violet energy, her leaping power allowing her to fade in and out of focus. In a blink, she appears behind the one lunging for her, unsheathing those knives at her thighs. She spins them expertly in her hands, and in that moment, I'm wicked jealous.

The drakel I kicked races toward me, snarling, his remaining buddy not too far behind. My powers rise up like an uncorked bottle, and glittering black flames shoot from my hands in the shape of an axe. I will the dark fire to lop off the head of the drakel before it even registers what happened.

Wallace grunts, and I spin around. Her drakel is close to knocking her off her feet.

I send my axe soaring. It splits the drakel in two before it can get a hold of Wallace. The pieces fall on either side at her feet.

Wallace gapes up at me, her eyes darting from my axe to my face and back again. "Damn, Firestarter."

I note—and fully ignore—the look of shocked respect on Wallace's face. It's clear she underestimated my power, my strength.

A hard, heavy something slams into my stomach. The other drakel, damn it. I slam my bleeding forearm into its throat before it can rip my head off. "Last warning," I say through clenched teeth. This thing weighs at least a ton, I swear. It's like trying to push off a car. "Leave now and live. Unlike your buddies."

A screech followed by a loud *thunk* sounds to my right. Draven stands above two of the fallen drakels. One is leached of color and twitching as it scrambles away.

"You're dead," the drakel above me snarls.

"So, that's a no?" I ask as it struggles to break through my defenses.

"That's a fuck no," it says. "I bet you taste sweet as candy." He snaps his teeth, the sound reverberating down my bones, awakening the rage I've kept bottled for Ray's benefit.

The bottle cracks open. *Wide* open. Dark flames twist and writhe and shoot from my fingers. No shapes this time, no flaming weapons. Just pure, undiluted dark flames.

The drakel yelps as my fire funnels into its mouth and glides back out from its eye sockets. He's not dead, but he probably wishes he is. Shrieking, it hauls ass off of me, and I leap to my feet, gulping sweet lungfuls of air as I steady myself. It claws at itself, trying to smother those dark flames, but only succeeds in tearing away hunks of its own flesh.

It falls to the ground—

A foot away from where Draven is thrashing against his body's shift.

Oh shit.

I skid to a stop in front of him, my blood running cold. His skin is now covered in scales, his face contorting as his lips form around the razor-sharp teeth replacing his normal ones.

Fuck. The drakel must've gained an upper hand if Draven had to result to touching it, siphoning its power in order to defeat it.

"Draven." I say his name, and his head snaps my direction.

I jolt backward, unable to not be shocked by the look in his eyes—eyes that are no longer a brilliant gold, but *green* and with slit pupils.

CHAPTER
TWENTY-FIVE

"What the ever-loving *fuck*?" Wallace asks, breathless as she heads toward me. I wave her away. For once, she listens, backing up slowly, leaving just Draven and me.

"Draven?" I lift a hand toward him. My fingers are still crackling with flames.

He bares those new teeth at me, a growl ripping from his chest as those green eyes focus on my fire.

"No, wait—"

Draven leaps the distance between us, his movements all wrong. He's clunky and aggressive where he's usually graceful and slick. But he's strong and fast, and before I know it, I'm on my back and his teeth are snapping at my neck.

Adrenaline shoots through my blood, locking my muscles for precious seconds before I manage to work an arm between him and me. I shove him up, and he fights against my defense, his massive body pinning me to the ground. I hook my leg around one of his, trying to twist beneath him, but he's just so damn strong.

"Draven," I groan beneath his weight, my flames begging to be set free. And yeah, I probably should burn his ass right now to snap him out of it, but this is Draven, and I'm not really into barbequing my maybe-boyfriend. Regardless if he's trying to kill me. "This. Isn't. You."

Scuffling sounds right next to me, but I shout, "No!" to either Wallace or Cassiel, I don't know. "I've got this," I say, though I'm sure it totally looks like I don't. "You can't touch him." It would only result in him siphoning their powers, too, and we *so* don't need that right now.

"Draven," I say his name inside that pocket of space between our minds, and his movements jerk to a halt. Those sharp green eyes are on mine, but he makes no move to get off of me. *"This isn't you."* I repeat the words. *"You are stronger than your power. Stronger than what the Seven label you. Stronger than Orders or destiny or any of that bullshit. You decide who you are, remember? No one else."*

His body tenses against me, his muscles trembling like something deep inside him is ripping open. He clenches those eyes shut, the shaking ramping up so much I have to hold onto him. A deep growl rumbles his chest.

"Draven," I whisper, my heart racing as I watch his eyes change from green to gold, the first sign he's shifting back to the boy I know. I relax a fraction, dropping my hands as the shaking stops, as those eyes flash with recognition—

Right before he draws back a clawed fist and slams it toward my face.

CHAPTER TWENTY-SIX

I clench my eyes shut, waiting for the impact. I've been punched plenty of times in my life, but never by a boyfriend and certainly not when he's amped up on demon powers.

The hit never comes.

I open my eyes and breathe out a sigh at the sight of his claws sinking into the ground right next to my cheek.

He yanks his fist back, watching as the claws turn back into his long, elegant fingers.

He looks down at me, his face fully shifting back to his own in the span of a blink, and his golden eyes churn. Devastation colors his features, and shame.

"Harley." He says my name like both a prayer and a plea. "I almost...I almost killed you."

"I'm fine," I say, my voice a whisper as I reach a trembling hand up to his cheek. "I'm okay." Sure, he's fully Draven again, but the adrenaline is still rushing through my body like it's trying to decide if we need to fight or—

His mouth slants over mine before I can say or think one more thing. I sigh at the contact, at the way he crushes his lips against mine, parting them with his tongue in a claiming, primal way. "I'm sorry," he growls against my mouth. "I'm so fucking sorry."

I wrap my legs around him when he tries to draw away, holding him in place. I forget everything outside of the feel of his body against mine, the way he tastes, the way his kiss ignites something inside of me so much I feel unstoppable.

There is nothing but *this*.

The danger in this boy I can't get enough of.

The devastation in the powers he's been given.

The agony of how many people have pushed him away or damned him for what he never asked for.

But not me.

Never me.

Instead, I pull him closer.

"I hurt you," he says, pulling back enough to look down at me. "I almost—"

"I'm fine," I assure him, holding his face in my flameless hands.

"Next time, kill me," he says, and the pain in his eyes, the agony, is enough to crack open my chest. "If I hurt you, I wouldn't be able to live with myself."

"You didn't," I say, pressing my forehead against his. He closes his eyes, his breathing ragged. "*You didn't.*"

"I'm sorry," he whispers against my face before kissing me again, faster, harder, and with a ferocity I match.

Heat unfurls deep in my belly, shooting to each of my nerve endings with the hunger in his kiss.

"As delicious as this all is, now that he's not about to devour you whole, we really need to get the hell out of here."

Wallace's voice shatters the suspended bubble we'd fallen into, and I pull out of our kiss to blink stars out of my eyes.

Draven helps haul me to my feet, and I flash Wallace an apologetic look.

"Where is the last one?" I ask.

"It ran," Cassiel says, landing behind me with such force I whirl around. "That way." He points toward the busy market in the distance.

"No doubt to get more," Wallace says, her breathing heavy. "Let's go."

"You're hurt," Ray says, hurrying to my side, eyes on my forearm, the blood welling from the three claw gashes.

"I'm fine," I say again. "Come on."

We follow Wallace's lead, running up the road toward where

the rig is parked.

Shrieks rip through the night behind us, loud and angry as hell.

I glance over my shoulder, keeping my pace as I note at least a dozen more drakels rushing behind us. "Faster!"

Cassiel scoops up Ray and leaps into the sky.

Wallace lights up the path ahead of us, flashing violet before she disappears.

"Damn." I will my muscles to move faster. "Everyone can basically fly but me? What kind of bullshit is that?"

"Really?" Draven laughs from my side, and the sound is so *him* that my panic eases. "You've got jokes at a time like this?"

"Always. And twice as many when people are trying to kill me."

I spin around, running backward, aiming my hands at the road, hoping like hell I can demolish it. *Please let my second power work here...*

To my surprise, it connects with the ground, feeling wholly different than the nature of earth. This is more like connecting with a cool, smoke-like substance, one crackling with pain and a sense of forgottenness I can't explain and totally don't have time to. I sink my mental hooks into it, willing it to rise —

The shrieks get louder, swallowing the sounds of crumbling stone as the road behind us shifts, jutting upward, sending the chasing drakels soaring backward.

"You always have to one-up me." Draven winks, then shifts wholly into smoke, the swirls of it surrounding me so fast I don't even have time to breathe before he sweeps me off my feet. I settle into the sensation, so damn happy he's back to himself. Knowing him, though? There will be much brooding and self-deprecation later.

After a few breaths, my feet touch the ground next to the rig, and Draven shifts back into himself next to me.

Wallace is already behind the wheel, revving the engine to life. Ray is in her middle backseat, Cassiel in the passenger. Draven and I hurry in on opposite doors, slamming them behind us.

And yet the Easkr doesn't move.

"Why aren't you driving?" I ask.

"Oh, I don't know," Wallace snaps. "Maybe because you just destroyed the road I need to get to?"

"What did you want me to do? Let the horde of drakels reach us?"

"Um, ladies?" Draven hedges.

"What?" we ask in unison.

He points through the windshield at the drakels in question, scrambling over the thick chunks of shattered road.

Wallace hits the gas. "I'm going to need a full night's rest after this," she groans, her skin and eyes glowing violet.

One second, we're careening toward the huge gap I created in the road, the one big enough to swallow the rig whole, and the next? We're slamming against the road on the other side, wheels screeching at full speed as Wallace takes a sharp right down a side road, navigating us away from the busy market.

"Death boy," she says. "Reach into my pocket and get the passes," she demands, hands firmly on the wheel as we sail down the road, the back end of the rig fishtailing from the speed.

Cassiel grunts and pulls the dice from the interior pocket of her leather jacket. "Don't *ever* call me *death boy* again."

"If we live, I'll think about it," she says, jerking the wheel to the left. After another right, she snatches the dice out of his hand and jabs a button to her left with her fist. The window drops, and she slows the rig just a fraction as she comes up to a stone archway gilded with gemstones the size of my fist. Two demons, almost as tall as the archway itself, are draped in golden robes with red and blue details along the trim. The one on the left holds a giant stone bucket, while the one on the right holds a giant scythe.

Wallace slows almost to a stop and tosses the dice into the bucket. The demon gives her a slow nod, and the empty darkness between the giant archway shimmers like a mirage in a desert. She gives the demon a wink, then presses the gas, the sounds of angry shrieks hollering behind us. I turn in my seat, noting even more drakels are now racing down the road behind us, six hanging out of the back of their own vehicles that roar in the darkness.

"Nice work, soul sucker," Wallace says, hitting the gas hard enough that I turn back around and hold my breath as she pushes the rig through the glowing, wavy lines pulsing in the archway.

The growl Cassiel releases isn't funny—it's downright lethal—but still...

I *laugh*.

I can't help it. The laugh shakes my whole body as we pass under the archway, and Draven softly chuckles to my side, shaking his head at my reaction.

Wallace tries to hide her grin by biting her lip, but I see it there, too. See it, and file it away as we're sucked through another vacuum of darkness, only to drop out onto a quiet expanse of road. She pulls off to the right, coming to a dead stop next to an outcropping of baby blue trees once we've cleared the archway.

I reel in my laughter the second Cassiel turns and arches a smooth brow at me. I flash him an apologetic look, and maybe it's the gashes from the drakel's claws that has my head suddenly giddy, or maybe it's the fact that we weren't killed, but I offer him a real smile. One that shows my gratitude. He nods, then focuses a glare on Wallace, who kills the ignition.

"Where are we?" he asks.

"A pocket between realms," she says. "I need a minute before I can get us into the next." She opens her door, hopping out of the rig. "We camp here for the night."

CHAPTER
TWENTY-SEVEN

"Firestarter," Wallace calls to me after we've hiked deeper into the baby blue trees that rustle slightly in the wind. She tosses her pack to the ground when we've reached a small clearing among an outcropping of the trees. "After that epic showdown—which will absolutely have everyone talking—you think you can manage to warm the space?"

My vision fuzzes a bit at the edges.

Shit, I'm tired.

I don't let any of them see that as I gather some fallen blue branches and pile them up in the center of the clearing. Draven grabs some stones and makes a quick circle of them around the wood. I snap once, twice, and finally my flames make an appearance. Almost sluggishly, as if they're as tired as I am...which makes no sense because they *are* me. I am them.

They?

Wait.

The branches flicker to life with obsidian and silver, crackling with warmth but keeping our location concealed, though Wallace doesn't seem worried about that at all. In fact, she's staring at me like she's asked me a question. I glance around, noting Draven's eyes look similarly concerned.

"Her cuts," Ray says, the only voice clear in the cobwebs of my mind. "They're green." She rushes to my side, and somehow, I'm sitting on the ground. When did that happen?

"Cas," Draven says. "I need the pink vial." Draven gently grabs my shoulders when I slump, almost tipping over. Cassiel digs in his bag, then tosses something to Draven. He catches it, sliding one leg on either side of me, situating himself behind me. I lean back against his chest. "You smell so good," I say, my tongue feeling like it's caked in sand.

Draven clears his throat, laughing softly as he uncorks a tiny bottle with his teeth, spitting the cork on the ground. "You smell quite delicious yourself," he whispers in my ear, then his voice drops even lower. "Almost as delectable as you *taste*."

Warm shivers dance over my skin, and I'm suddenly wondering why I'm not kissing him right this second.

"What does it feel like?" Wallace asks.

Does she want me to explain how Draven makes me feel? Because, boundaries much?

"I've heard drakel poison is almost euphoric," she explains while Draven is shifting my arm back and forth.

I laugh.

Again, I'm not sure what's funny.

Draven's grip on me suddenly tightens, sobering my mind a few degrees. "Draven?" I ask, but his hold on me only grows stronger. Shit, is he shifting again? That would be a whole bag of crap he doesn't need.

My legs and arms tingle, and not in a way that makes me a puddle of warm liquid, but more in the I-fell-asleep-at-a-really-bad-angle type way. My mind is an ocean current sweeping in and out with no end in sight. "I can't move my legs," I say, and it has nothing to do with Draven's hold, one I only now realize I can no longer feel.

"Yeah, that's their whole thing," Wallace says, her voice sounding off somehow, almost as if she's speaking super slow. "They claw you so if you get away, you won't get far. They can prey on your body later. You're awake the whole time, too."

"Brutal," Cassiel says, his wings outstretched behind him from where he gazes down at us. "But effective."

Cold washes over my insides.

"Right?" Wallace says. "I've heard of people lacing their knives with it. But drakel venom is hard to get."

"Is she going to be okay, Draven?" Ray asks from my side, her tone laced with worry and fear.

"Yes," Draven says, but he doesn't sound as convinced as I'd like.

Somehow, I get my eyes to work and lock onto Ray's baby blue eyes that have given me hope my whole life.

"You're the most beautiful thing I've ever seen," I say, my words slurred. "I thought that the moment Dad put you in my arms." I try to lift my hand to smooth it over her cheek, but I can't feel it.

A million memories race through my mind, a strobe light of joy and pain: holding her, giving her a bottle as I hum my favorite songs, rocking my body back and forth on my paper-thin mattress because we don't have a rocking chair. Watching her two-year-old self toddle around the trailer, following her like a hawk, ensuring she doesn't fall into anything sharp.

Then me, laying on the floor, unable to get up from a hit Dad just delivered. The tears streaming down her cheeks, her eyes unable to understand what just happened. I manage to contort my face, to make a silly raspberry noise even though the simple motion hurts every nerve I have. I manage to wink at her, make her little toddler self believe it's all just a silly game. Anything to make those tears stop, to steal the worry from her eyes.

"Go hide," I say to her, keeping that smile on my face. Dad's gone outside to smoke a cigarette, but he'll be back. I don't know what I did to set him off this time, but I can't get up to get Ray in our room myself. *"Go hide, baby,"* I say again, my mind flashing from the memory to the present and back. *"Hide and seek, 'member?"* I coo, forcing that smile not to break.

Her face smooths a little, tears no longer in her eyes as she gives me a proud grin and a nod. *"'kay, Har."* She runs, her diaper scuffing against her little legs fading as she runs to her favorite hiding place, the one I always take forever to find because it's the smartest one—the closet in our room. The front door swings open and Dad towers over me, rolls me to my back with his boot—

"Harley." Draven says my name with such intensity I crash back to the present.

Ray is crying next to me, and Wallace urges her away, her face grave, fear and pity shaping her features.

I look at Ray again. Did I say those things aloud?

"Harley. Look at *me*." Draven's voice is pure command, and I turn my head as best I can, locking onto those amber eyes, the way they churn. "Don't look down."

The insistence in his voice clicks in my brain. I disobey him.

I look down at my arm in his hands anyway...

And I *scream*.

CHAPTER
TWENTY-EIGHT

"Harley!" Draven yells, frustration lacing every inch of his tone.

But it's not enough to tear my eyes off what I'm seeing.

What *used* to be my arm is now covered in scales, dripping with black ooze in every linked crevice. Claws grow from beneath my nails, splitting the fingernails as my bones twist and crack. It's like I've somehow switched powers with Draven, and *ohmigod* if this is what he goes through every time, then holy fucking hell, he got the shittiest power in existence.

I thrash, but his strong arm clamps over my chest, holding me to him.

"Just a little longer…"

"She needs to keep it down, Judge," Wallace says from where she stands by the fire, Ray behind her. "She's going to call every predator within a fifty-foot radius right to us."

"Listen to me." Draven's voice slices into my mind, heeding Wallace's warning. *"You need to listen. Be still. Be silent. We're hiding, Harley. We're hiding."*

The words silence me in an instant.

Hiding is important.

So vitally important for me—if Ray doesn't hide, she'll get hurt.

But wait, that's not true anymore. Ray is safe, Ray is—

Hot liquid slides over my arm, a heat that rivals my flames as it seeps into the wounds in my scaled arm.

"Almost done, Harley. Just a little more." His words are

encouraging as he somehow manages to hold me tight while still dropping the liquid on my wounds.

I can't respond, can't *think* around anything other than the need to be still and quiet. How many times have I told Ray to do that in her lifetime? How many times was it vital to not draw attention to herself? To keep her safe? If I expect it from her, then I can endure any amount of pain in order to do it myself.

Slowly, *finally*, the fiery pain gives way to a cooling sensation that tingles over my arm. Each deep breath soothes another aching part of my body, waking the dead limbs up with a pins and needles feeling I relish.

"*Good,*" he says. "*Keep it up.*"

"Impressive work," Wallace says.

Ray is giving me an encouraging look from where she sits next to Wallace by the fire, but her eyes are glazed with tears.

The feel of Draven's gentle yet strong touch on my arm clears the sticky webs over my mind, some mental barrier shattering. I blink fog out of my eyes and jolt a little when I see my arm.

It's mine again, and the three claw marks are sealing beneath the pink liquid Draven has expertly spread over them. He moves then, maneuvering me to lean against the fallen log behind us. The vial lies at his feet, now corked and half full as he wraps some black cloth around the wound, smiling down at me.

My stomach twists as I look at Ray, those tears still fresh on her cheeks.

"Did I hurt you?" I ask, shame coating my body in a layer of grime at the question.

"Of course not," she says. "What did you see?"

I shake my head, unable to tell her.

"Why were you crying?" I ask, needing to know.

"No big deal," she says with a shaky smile. "You're better now?"

I nod. "I think so." Thanks to Draven, who finishes tying off the fabric.

Wallace sits down next to Ray, eying the sketchbook in Ray's zombie unicorn bag, and nods to it.

"Can I see?" she asks.

Ray turns to her, nodding eagerly, and soon, the two are lost to her drawings, chatting about colors and shading techniques. All thoughts of me and whatever just happened forgotten, those tears dry on Ray's cheeks as if they were never there in the first place. And a piece of me warms toward Wallace for that alone, the way she somehow knew how to distract my little sister in the midst of all this chaos.

"You told her to hide," Draven says into my mind as he reclaims his spot behind me, and I shift in his embrace to face him, my entire body celebrating being wholly mine again. *"You called her* baby."

"Fuck." I rub my palms over my face, the memory hitting me like a ton of bricks. I shake my head, a cold shudder jerking my body. *"The poison had my mind whirling,"* I admit. *"I didn't know I said it out loud."*

"You played hide and seek with her as a baby?" It's an innocent, purely interested question.

"Yes," I admit. *"It's the first game I taught her. Because it was the most useful one. She knew what hide and seek meant before she could even say my name properly. She used to call me Har."* I shake my head. *"It's the only safe way I knew to get her out of the danger zone when my dad…when that man I called Father decided to beat on me for fun."*

A boiling anger ripples down that connection Draven and I share, and I can't tell if it's mine or his or both of ours combining.

"That's why she cried, beyond the sight of you in so much pain."

I swallow around the knot in my throat, the tension easing the longer she sits and laughs and grins pridefully as Wallace dotes on her work.

She's safe. She's even laughing. It's okay. It's okay.

I keep telling myself this until my muscles unlock.

Until Draven and I settle into an easy—if not weighted—sort of silence.

Until the fire I created dies down to a soft glow, Wallace

asleep on her pack a few feet away, Ray softly snoring next to her. Cassiel is a couple yards past them, eyes closed in sleep despite him sitting straight up against a tree, as if he's used to needing to leap to his feet at a moment's notice.

"You should sleep," Draven whispers, and hearing his voice outside my head almost jars me. We've been using our secret way of communicating a lot lately.

"I'm having a hard time," I say. We've shifted to laying with our heads on our packs, facing each other with only an inch of space between us.

"Have you ever camped before?"

I try to soften the grim laugh that escapes my lips. "Tons of times. Family tradition of ours."

"Sorry. I thought Nathan might've taken you."

"No," I whisper, not wanting our voices to wake the others. "We never have."

Draven reaches across the small space between us, trailing his fingers down my healed arm. "Another first, then," he says with a smile. His eyes glow gold in the darkness here, and I truly believe I can stare at them all night and be more rested than if I turn over and let my mind wander.

Wander to the demon who sank its claws into me. To the poison that almost took over my mind. Wander to what I would've done if that had happened to Ray instead of me. Wander to the knowledge that I've brought my sister a world of darkness and pain by simply being what I am. Because I know, I *know*, that she wouldn't have been targeted by Marid if she wasn't the most important thing in the world to me. If she had a normal sister not fated to ruin the world.

"Harley," Draven whispers, his fingers trailing to the spot between my eyes I haven't realized I've scrunched until he smooths it out. "I'm sorry—"

I shake my head. "You don't need to apologize for something you can't control."

Anguish ripples over his features. "I could've killed you."

"You're seriously underestimating my ass-kicking abilities if you believe that," I say, and he sighs. "Plus, you just saved my life with that magic liquid trick. I'd say we're even."

"I know how powerful you are," he says. "I've always known. And there is no way we're even. You brought me back from the dead."

"And you kept me from becoming dead," I argue. "Let's just stop keeping track."

"Still. It shouldn't have happened," he says. "If I wasn't what I am. If you were with someone normal—"

"Normal doesn't exist," I say, arching a brow at him. "And you know I've always said your darkness matches mine, Draven. We're the same. Who knows when it'll be my turn to almost kill you because I can't control what's inside *me*? Can't control what I am…" Weight sinks onto my chest. "Unless you're saying you'd see me, every broken inch of my soul, and turn away?"

He smooths his hand over my cheek, shaking his head. "Never."

"Then don't ask me to. And don't apologize for things you can't control."

He looks like he wants to argue, but he seems to get lost studying my face. I can't imagine what I look like after the fight, the poison, all of it, but it feels like he's looking past all that and seeing right to the heart of what is eating at me. All the things *I* can't control and how much me just being me is putting my friends in harm's way.

"Tell me how to help you," he says, the concern in his eyes punching me right in the chest.

"Reading me?" I ask, needing to know if he's slipped into my mind deeper than I've allowed.

"You're basically shouting at me," he says, face apologetic. "I'm trying to block it out, to push you out of that space between us. But you're very stubborn, even when you don't realize it."

Another soft laugh. Another piece of tension sliding down the mountain of it inside me.

I spare a glance at Ray and the others, content to find them restfully sleeping. "Distract me?" I mean it as a statement, but it comes out a question.

"How?" he asks, giving me a mischievous grin. His fingers slide down my nose, brush over my bottom lip, over my collarbone, and lower. His hand settles on my hip. "You like so many different ways of distraction," he says. "Do you want me to tell you a story? Or do you want to have another fight?" He smirks, and I press my lips together to keep from laughing.

"I *do* love to spar," I whisper, inching closer to him until our bodies are flush. "You know what I want."

"Tell me, Harley," he says, grazing his lips over mine in a featherlight touch that makes my toes curl in my shoes. I lean in, but he draws back, his grin half wolfish, half desperate with need. "I want to hear you say it."

Heat that has nothing to do with my flames licks up my spine at the demand in his words.

"I want your mouth," I say, my cheeks flushing at the admission. "I want your hands on me."

A triumphant grin replaces the hungry one, his eyes blazing as he crushes his lips against mine. Whatever leash he held on himself has completely snapped.

I arch into his body as he smooths his hand around my hip and to the small of my back, drawing me to him as close as possible. He slants his mouth over mine, his tongue teasing my bottom lip before sliding in.

A whimper escapes my throat at the taste of him, all citrus and heat and everything Draven. I meet him tease for tease and flick for flick, grazing the edges of his teeth with my tongue. I fist his shirt in my hands, slipping my fingers beneath the fabric to touch his skin.

A low, throaty groan rumbles against my mouth as my fingertips tease the tight muscles of his abdomen. The sound sends warm shivers dancing along my skin, and I instantly decide I want to hear him make that sound over and over again.

His free hand slides under my head, his fingers tangling in

my hair. He tugs slightly, dipping my head back to kiss me deeper, harder, unrestrained and hungry, matching me on every level of need.

Every touch is a wave of heat crashing against all the worries, the doubts, the fear, consuming them until there is nothing but me and him and the electricity between us. Until there is nothing I want more than to sink into his kiss, sink into this boy and never look back. Here, I'm not on a slim-odds-of-survival mission to the Ather. I'm not someone demons want to sink their teeth into. I'm not the Antichrist. I'm just Harley, a girl totally enamored and consumed by *him*.

Draven nips at my bottom lip, and the slight hurt sends tendrils of crackling heat straight through the center of me. I arch against him, needing more.

More distraction.

More hope.

More Draven.

"Harley," he whispers.

I open my eyes and smile at the sight of him, eyes glazed and needy, the look softening his usual broody demeanor. He grazes his lips to my neck, flicking his tongue there, and I tremble against him. He softly sucks at the sensitive skin. "*Harley.*" He draws back to look down at me.

"What is it?" I ask him, our breaths matched in ragged need. "Tell me, Draven." I can see it there, in the intensity of those amber eyes. In the way his lips tremble just a fraction as if the words are battling to be set free.

"I...We..."

"Y'all *need* to go to sleep," Wallace whispers, jarring us both out of the moment. I roll away from Draven, focusing a glare at Wallace, who has her brows raised at us from where I thought she'd been asleep moments ago.

She shakes her head. "If you two are this bad, I can't imagine what the hell you're going to do in the next realm."

"What is that supposed to mean?"

"We're going to *Lusro*." She says the name like that explains everything, which of course, it so doesn't. She laughs softly, settling back against her pack. "Just go to sleep, please," she almost begs, shutting her eyes. "There will be plenty of time for *that* in the next realm."

"When you said *plenty of time for that...*" I say after Wallace has parked the rig in the next realm.

Lusro, as she called it yesterday.

Sand stretches outward in every direction, beautiful, sparkling red sand that meets a pinkish sky on the horizon. There are giant mounds of it far in the distance, shooting upward toward the sky like sand stalagmites.

A palace of slick white stone—the same one Wallace is leading Draven and me into now—rumbles with laughter and delicate music. The smell of rich incense fills the room, accompanied by a floral scent coming from the exotic flowers spilling out of huge vases settled on every shelf built into the palace walls.

I've never been more grateful that Wallace convinced me to leave Ray with Cassiel in the safety of Easkr. Not because this place is terrifying and crawling with threats—on the contrary, Wallace informed me this is one of the more peaceful realms in the Ather—but for reasons I can't explain.

Since we stepped foot inside the realm, all I've wanted—all I've been able to *think* about—is Draven. His touch. His taste. The way he made me forget everything outside of us last night, before Wallace brought us back to reality.

And, don't get me wrong, wanting Draven has pretty much lived rent-free in my mind since he crashed into my life, but this? This is taking the need to an entirely new level. I shouldn't be thinking about that right now. Shouldn't be thinking about the way his mouth feels against that spot on my neck when he grazes his teeth—

"Yeah," Wallace says, snapping her fingers in front of my face.

It's only then that I realize I'm in a staring competition with Draven. The way he's looking at me only shows his mind is in sync with mine—which is *so* not good for my thought process.

"Focus," Wallace says, and I blink a few times.

"What kind of realm is Lusro?" I ask.

"You know exactly what kind," she says, arching a brow at me. "You can feel it."

Lust.

It's totally, a thousand percent *lust.*

"The realm isn't *only* about that," Wallace says. "And lust isn't always sexual," she whispers. "It's for anything your heart wants most. Lusro is one of the most proficient producers of luxury fabrics and adornments in all of the Ather. These beings are a peaceful kind. A great deal of their product is donated to realms in need of warm clothes or medical fabrics. They are often bullied by the larger realms, like Marid's, or even powers from above because of their generous, compassionate nature." She grinds her teeth, navigating the hallways. "But their culture can be a little… *intense* for those not accustomed to it."

The information grounds me enough in the present that for about two seconds I don't think about the way Draven's fingers make my body feel. The way he unraveled me days ago in his bed with just a few touches. How he'd kissed and explored my body, those fingers dipping between my thighs with a gentle claiming that made me see stars. How badly I want to lose myself in him again—

"Harley," Draven groans inside my head. *"If you don't stop thinking such things, I'm going to give you absolutely everything you want right now. And that will* gravely *deter us from the mission at hand."*

"Right," I say. *"Sorry."*

I force myself to focus incredibly hard on Wallace, on her boots, how badass she looks in them. Force myself to count the number of diamond shapes in the colored tile floor. When I make it to forty-three, I feel like I've grabbed some form of control. "Why are *we* here again?"

"They don't normally demand payment for passage, but their lands stretch wide, and there are a shit ton of obstacles standing between us and the next realm. It's considered a courtesy to let them know you're traveling through. I brought you two in order to be transparent with the rulers about the clients I'm guiding across the realms. And, if you happen to get ensnared by their *pull* for any length of time..." She shrugs. "Then you've done them a favor."

"How?" I ask as we weave through hallways adorned with art—paintings in gold frames depicting sweeping, sandy landscapes under every color of light, couples embracing, dances and parties and so many more joyful illustrations of life in Lusro.

"This realm pretty much runs off lust," she explains. "Consider it like their electricity. You two could power this place for a few cycles. Maybe more." Heat blazes across my cheeks, but she waves me off. "Don't worry about it. What you two have? I can think of at least a dozen beings who would *kill* for it. Wear it proudly."

"Wallace," a masculine voice calls as we round a corner. "I haven't seen you in some time."

"Gareth," she says and smiles as she walks toward the demon who stands before an open doorway. He has a flat face of hunter green, with four eyes of solid black. An elegant blue silk tunic covers his body, tighter fabric covering his legs—all six of them. He brings his hands together, bowing slightly, and Wallace mimics the gesture. "I'm on my way to see Lux and Ore. How are you?"

"I'm working in Lusro," he says, his eyes twinkling. "I'm practically divine."

She laughs. "It's definitely a better place to work than Machis."

"Don't get me started." He shakes his head. "All they want from me there are horrid, dull fighting uniforms."

"The audacity," Wallace says.

Gareth glances at Draven and me for a moment before returning to Wallace. "You *must* see what the rulers have me working on. Come," he says, waving those hands—and the eight long dexterous fingers on each one—for us to follow him into the room.

We so don't have time for this, but then we enter the room, and I stumble to a stop.

"Whoa."

CHAPTER THIRTY

The room is a dream—all golden walls, marble tables, and panels upon panels of the most luxurious fabrics I've ever seen. Every color of the rainbow is in this room, some wrapped around makeshift mannequins that have the shapes and sizes of all creatures imaginable.

"Gareth is one of the finest clothes makers in all of the Ather," Wallace explains. "So renowned that every ruler in the Ather has granted him access to their realms so they can hire him at will. Some beings even sell their blood just to purchase his clothes."

"You've always been my favorite guide," Gareth says, beaming at her as he motions to a mannequin with a wide torso, four legs, and a tail. A stunning dress made of iridescent fabric flatters the shape. "Do you like?"

"Gorgeous," Wallace answers.

"Are you here for business or pleasure?"

"Business this time," she says. "Hence the need to introduce my new clients to Lux and Ore, but you know I can never resist seeing your work."

Gareth smiles at that, fussing those many fingers over a piece of the dress on the mannequin. "Interesting that a Judge would need a guide, even if he did pick the best one," he says, turning to Draven.

"I know when I'm out of my element," Draven says, an easy grin on his face. "Have you seen many Judges pass through here?" The question seems innocent enough, but I know he's hunting. Hoping for any information on Ryder that will lead us in any direction other than Marid's realm.

I hate that I hold my breath. That I don't want to see the disappointment in his eyes again.

"I work all over the Ather," he says. "Like Wallace said. I've met several Judges before."

My heart climbs into my throat.

"Any recently?" Wallace asks.

Gareth nods. "Quite, actually." Those fingers flare the skirts on another mannequin. "In Machis."

Wallace gives a low whistle. "In the pits?"

"Yes," he says. "Quite the fighter." Gareth considers Draven for a moment. "He looked like you. Longer hair, though."

I'm barely able to contain my gasp.

"Did he…" Draven swallows, as if his mouth has gone dry. "Did he have blue-green eyes?"

"He did. Angry, Judge, that one. Why do you ask?" He looks to Wallace. "You're not taking them there, are you?"

"Not sure," she says. "There are a few different routes for where we're going."

Her tone is casual, calm, but my heart is thundering.

Ryder. We may know where he is.

Draven looks to be barely breathing.

"Gareth," someone says from the opened doorway. "Are you giving these creatures a tour *and* a story for free?"

Gareth straightens, bowing more deeply toward the creature in the doorway than he did to Wallace moments ago. "Yes. Wallace is a friend—"

"Be that as it may," the creature cuts him off. "You know the rules here. Balance. Trade. Appreciation—"

"Relax, Roux," Wallace cuts in. "This was a pitstop on the way to see Lux and Ore."

The creature grins. "Then by all means, let me escort you."

Roux ushers us out of the room, down the hallway, and toward a set of massive double doors, which glide open effortlessly at Roux's touch.

We're led into a massive, elegant room. Three red crystal chandeliers hang from the vaulted ceiling, the floor a polished stone of the same color. The walls are slick white marble, the entire space dancing in red light from the flickering sconces on the wall.

Ethereal demons with long limbs and smooth, baby blue skin lay atop thick velvet cushions scattered about the sides of the room. They grip bubbling drinks and pluck delicacies from trays of fuzzy green fruit sprawled next to them, all of which look far nicer than the quick breakfast we'd scarfed from our packs earlier. The food Wallace had packed had been simple yet vastly different from what I'm used to—bread, but heartier and packed with so many herbs it made it taste like a full-course dinner.

Some of the creatures are laughing, some are embracing multiple partners, and some are dancing on the wide expanse of floor resting before a raised dais. Two throne-like chairs sit atop the thick cut of stone, but only one seat is occupied.

Roux leaves us standing before two demons, their skin a dusty blue, with long, swishing tails and eyes the color of some tropical ocean. They sit together in one throne, one draped over the other. Smiles shape their lips between kisses, their sheer robes covering only the barest details of their bodies.

They're not doing anything other than kissing. Still, it *feels* like we've caught them in a much more intimate moment, despite the doors opening to welcome us inside.

"That's a great color on you, Lux," Wallace says.

The demon atop the other swivels their head around, still resting on the other's lap, arm draped over the other's neck.

Lux runs elongated fingers over the sheer material, laughing. Their voice and stunning creature looks neither male nor female, but rather a fluid combination that radiates nothing but power and joy and freedom. "Wallace," Lux says, drawing out her name. "It's been ages, my sweet. Are you here for tea?"

"No," Wallace says a bit quickly.

And I get it. After what we just learned? I'm dying to get out of here and get to Machis as fast as possible.

Roux leans down to whisper something in Lux's ear, and they nod.

"Are you sure?" Lux bats a long set of royal blue lashes before sliding those fingers over the other demon's chin. "Ore and I would be honored if you joined us for *tea*."

Wallace lays a hand over the center of her chest. "I will take you up on that offer one day," she says. "It would be my honor." Something wicked twinkles in her eyes, and I swallow hard, suddenly feeling like I'm intruding on *her* moment.

I look away, but that only means I'm looking at Draven now, and *shit*, he's gorgeous. All carved muscles, strong jaw, and dark hair unkempt. I want to run my fingers through it. I want to yank on it, draw him down to my level, and crush my mouth on his—

Draven's eyes meet mine, and they're almost animalistic. He reaches for me, interlacing our fingers like he's prepared to haul me into a private room and give in to everything our bodies are demanding right this second. And I'll let him. I know I will. I'll let him do whatever the hell he wants to me as long as he's touching me—

Focus! Some inner voice rages at me, and I jerk my hand from his touch.

Holy hell, we need to get out of here. It seems being in this room has only magnified the realm's effects.

He's not offended by my sudden need to *not* be touching him. In fact, he takes a step away from me, adopting that attitude he had when we first met, and he believed he would drain me dry with one simple graze of his skin against mine.

His skin, the way it's warm and strong and—nope! Not going there.

"Roux tells us Gareth was entertaining you with a story and a showing. Who are your friends?" Ore asks, drawing me to the present. "They look fun."

I shudder under the gazes zeroing in on Draven and me but manage not to dip my chin.

"He caught me on my way to you two," Wallace explains.

"They're why I can't stay for tea. But I wanted to show you the party I'm guiding across the realm."

"Pity," Lux says, still casually running those fingers over Ore's body.

"I didn't want to pass through your realm without letting you know," Wallace says. "Especially since you know my track record with the sand ants."

I scrunch my brow, letting my mind wander to thoughts of what kind of demon that is. Anything to stop me from thinking about Draven. I picture some tiny insect that's camouflaged by the sand with a penchant for burrowing under people's skin and feasting on their muscles.

Well, if that isn't sobering, then nothing in this place will be.

"Of course," Lux says. "We thank you for making us aware."

Wallace turns on her heel as if that is that.

"But," Lux says, and Wallace's entire body freezes, "Lusro has been under a tremendous amount of strain as of late. The power players constantly demand more and more from us, beyond what we have means to do."

Wallace dips her head, but a muscle in her jaw flexes. Her anxiousness has every instinct in my body roaring past the lust-haze trying to sink its claws in me. My flames flicker beneath my skin.

"Surely, you would agree in times such as these, we need to be compensated for passage through our homeland," Lux continues, arching back slightly against Ore. "*Especially* after already partaking in company with Gareth and with your track record with our sand ants. Plus, more travelers means we're more likely to lose a great deal in the transport, and you know their venom is crucial to the production of some of our most in-demand lines."

My mind fills with questions, but I clamp my mouth shut. I make note of every demon in the room carrying on about their business like they have *no* interest in us. Draven is doing the same thing, his eyes snagging on the rulers. They are stunningly beautiful, there is no question there, but I'm more worried about the payment they're about to demand of us.

"What compensation would you like?" Wallace asks, seemingly unruffled, even as she grinds her teeth slightly.

Lux takes a few moments, stretching out the tension so tightly I'm about to say fuck it and set the floor on fire as a distraction so we can bolt. Dark flames curl around my hands, waiting for the command.

But then Lux and Ore point those elongated fingers toward me and Draven, their dark blue lips curling into matched feline smiles. "We want them," Lux says, "to *dance*."

Wait, *what*?

CHAPTER
THIRTY-ONE

I draw back my flames.

They want us to dance? Like some sort of *sing for my supper* shit?

My muscles uncoil from their defensive stance. I can dance if it means we avoid any issues in passing to the next realm. I glance to Wallace, shrugging in a silent *how bad can it be?*

But she wears a pitying, almost mortified look.

Which tells me it can be pretty fucking bad.

"If you don't agree to these terms, we can easily find a monetary payment," Ore offers, those tropical sea eyes fixated on me.

I lower my voice to a whisper. "I'm guessing we won't have enough to pay them?"

"Not unless you want to beg another favor from—"

"Don't say his name," I cut her off. The last thing I need is for the warlock to kick the door open inside my mind right now. He'd have a field day with how my blood is pumping, every thump of my heart begging for *Draven, Draven, Draven.*

"We just have to dance?" I ask, addressing Lux and Ore for the first time.

They nod in unison. "A show," Lux says. "For our guests."

I swallow around the knot in my throat. I've always loved to dance, whenever I had the freedom to, which was rare. But the music and movements always consume me in a way that quiets my mind. And Draven and I danced the first night I met him, but the butterflies in my gut are telling me we won't be doing a *simple* dance for this crowd.

"Do you agree?" Ore asks.

I glance at Wallace.

"We're passing through their realm, and we got information we clearly wanted from Gareth, even if we didn't intentionally seek it. They can sense that. If we don't offer them compensation, they can easily use other means to demand it," she whispers.

"I thought this was a peaceful realm?"

"It is," she says. "But you heard them. Even the most peaceful societies can resort to extreme measures when put under enough pressure."

I wonder who, beyond Marid and his Twelve, exactly is demanding more than they should from this realm. The king of the Ather? Or those powers above that Wallace mentioned? Both? How deep does the power-hungry trail run? I make a mental note to ask her about it later, because right now, I can't solve that problem.

"Draven?" I ask, doing my best to only look at him from the corner of my eye. If I look at him directly, I'm going to lose myself to that desperate need pulsing inside of me.

"Whatever we need to do," he says, and there is a determination in his voice that I cling to. He's right. We had to go *through* the drakels in the last realm in order to get what we needed, him losing himself momentarily in the process only for me to yank him back again, so if we have to dance like puppets in some twisted show? Then so be it. Anything to get us back on the road, the one that, thanks to Gareth, suddenly leads to Ryder. Then to Marid and severing his ties with Ray for good.

"We agree," I say, and Lux claps.

"Marvelous," Lux says. "Roux, darling, will you be a dear and assist our performers to their respective dressing rooms?"

Dressing rooms? What the hell? Lux must read the confusion on my face, because they say, "You can't possibly dance in those clothes."

Roux bows deeply at the waist before gliding toward us.

Draven and I can do nothing but follow as the demon guides us from the main room and through a side door, twisting down another hallway before opening a door for Draven and ushering him inside. "Someone will come with your clothes soon," Roux says, and I offer Draven a confused and almost panicked wave before Roux closes the door.

Wallace sticks close by my side as Roux leads us to another room not far away, saying something similar before shutting the door behind us. The room is bedroom sized, with two chaise lounges, an elaborate vanity, and a changing curtain with beautiful floral details.

"Tell me the risks, quick," I say to Wallace, who's plopped onto one of the velvet chaises, crossing one booted foot over the other. "Before whoever comes back."

"Dances in Lusro aren't like the ones you know from above," she says, her eyes gleaming. "They can last for days if you're not careful."

My eyes widen. "We don't have days."

"I know," she says, shaking her head. "They've never demanded compensation before. They must really be suffering on energy if they're subjecting passersby to donations."

"This isn't a donation. It's a payment," I counter. "Who is doing this to them? Making them resort to this kind of desperation? Is it the king?"

Wallace flashes me a pitying look. "You know Marid. Know how diabolical he is. His friends are just as bad. And the king? Legend says he once wanted balance for the peaceful realms in the Ather. But that was ages ago, and rumors are just rumors. No one has seen him in…" She shakes her head. "There are those even more powerful than him who are determined to exploit the realms for every commodity they have, leaving nothing for the beings who produce it."

"Who could be more powerful than— You know what? Never mind." I shake my head. "Tell me later. For now, how do I ensure Draven and I don't end up losing ourselves to this *dance-for-days* bit?"

"That's the really hard part," she says. "You have to make sure you produce enough lust to pass for the compensation, but not so much that you both lose yourselves entirely and forget why you came here in the first place…which, from what I've heard, is incredibly easy to do."

I wave my hands in circles, urging her to get to the real answer.

"The dance, the pull this realm has, it's seductive and enthralling. To escape into something that's pure pleasure? For long enough to erase any memory of trauma or pain? That's tempting to even the tamest of creatures." Wallace eyes me. "You'll have to find the power to stop."

I nod. I can do that. I *have* to do that.

I mean, yes, Draven is irresistible on a good day, and this place is making it ten times worse, but I *know* why we're here. I know what is at stake if I fail: my sister. And there isn't anything I won't do for her.

"Is there a specific dance we're expected to do?" It's not like I've ever learned an actual, choreographed dance before like in some popular rom-com movie. And I know next to nothing about this culture beyond the bare details Wallace has told me.

"The music and magic this place has is going to take care of that for you," she says. "Your job is to walk that line between giving them what they need and stopping before it consumes you."

"Great," I say, shaking my head.

Footsteps echo outside the door.

She stands before me, her mouth tight. "Just remember why you're here, Firestarter," she says. "Don't lose yourself in that boy or in this place."

"I won't," I assure her.

"Good," she says. "Because if you do? I'm still taking Ray and Cassiel where they need to go."

Fear bolts icy cold down my spine. The idea of me not being by Ray's side as she travels through the Ather is sobering enough to have my fingers shaking.

"Remember *that* feeling when it gets to be too much," she says, just as the door swings open.

CHAPTER THIRTY-TWO

I've never felt so naked or nervous in my entire life. I'd rather face a horde of lagartis or drakels than *this*. At least with the battles, I know where I stand. I know I can wield my flames or coax the earth. But this? How am I going to survive *this*?

"They're ready for you," Roux says. The demon's fingers are like silk against my skin, pushing me back into the main room.

Heat floods my cheeks as I stumble into the room. As all the beings' eyes are now fixated on me. On what I'm wearing.

It's not that the garment Roux dressed me in is awful—it's just that there is so *little* of it, and when I'm used to wearing covering clothes to hide all my scars? It feels like my dark past is on display for all to see.

If I get past that, I can admit how beautiful the outfit is. The stunning fabric is sheer royal blue, a mixture of silk and gauzy materials that feel buttery-soft against my skin. A flowing skirt hugs my hips, the seams decorated in sparkling jewels and gold thread that leaves my stomach fully exposed. The top spreads over my chest and down my arms, leaving my shoulders and neck bare, the cuffs of the sleeves velvet and cinched around my wrists.

Roux swept my hair half up and away from my face with some intricate beaded headpiece, the rest of my red hair falling free and over my shoulders. My lips are painted red, my eyes decorated in smoky black. Wallace had given me a two-syllable *day-amn* before I was led here, but while I appreciate her sentiment, I feel more exposed than I had when I was bleeding on the ground and opening the gates of Hell.

I try not to think about my scars being on display for everyone to see. But when I've spent my life choosing clothes to hide them? This goes against every instinct I've ever had to hide what's been done to me.

Even now, as I make my way to the middle of the room and stand before the thrones, I wrap my arms around my stomach, hating the shiny bits of raised skin that pepper across it—scars from broken glass or cigarettes or steel toe boots.

There is a collective gasp, and I'm not sure if the demons in the room are shocked by the number of scars I have and I'm still standing or if it's the beauty of the fabric. Likely the latter, because it *is* stunning. In another life, maybe, I'd wear it confidently and proudly. An honored guest of Lusro, happy to help with their realm's needs.

But I'm not that girl, and this isn't that time.

Whispers echo around me, and I swear I hear one of them ask, *"Is that the one with the dark flame?"* but Lux says, "You look stunning."

Heat blooms across my cheeks, but I can't meet their eyes because Draven just walked in from the other side of the room and...

Hot damn.

CHAPTER THIRTY-THREE

Draven is fucking *gorgeous*.

They've dressed him in a similar royal blue, his fabric thick and iridescent as it fits snugly over his broad chest. The shirt is more of a tunic, hanging down past his hips with a slit up the front to expose the black cotton pants that cinch at his ankles. His eyes are rimmed in black, which make their amber color blaze.

He looks at me like there is no one else in the room, and his confident gait eats up the space between us, each movement both predatory and graceful.

Damn. I wish I could look so sure of myself, be as certain in my own body as he is when he stops an arm's length away from me.

I swallow hard and gaze up at him, my mouth suddenly dry. His lingering gaze is like a brand, and I feel it *everywhere*.

"Beautiful," he whispers.

Warmth dances over my skin. He's not cringing at the scars, not turning his nose up at what my body has suffered. He's looking at me like I'm...majestic. Someone that hasn't suffered, but *survived*.

A wide expanse of floor immediately clears for us. "Music," Ore demands softly, leaning back in the throne. Lux sprawls over the demon's lap, eyes fixated on us.

"Harley." Draven says my name with a sort of reverence that has me trembling. "May I have this dance?"

I dart my tongue out to wet my lips and nod because there's no way I'm going to be able to make my voice work. I'm stretched so tight I'm about to snap.

The music swells, consuming and rhythmic, a melody that

glides around us and between us like some ethereal creature demanding attention. Draven's hand slides to my hip, his callused fingers warm and strong over the bare skin just above it. I gasp at the contact, grip his other hand with mine...

And then we're moving.

I hold his gaze, note that wicked smirk as we spin and soar around the dance floor. Every spin, every step, sinks me deeper into this warm, bubbly sort of sensation that leaves no room for doubts or fear or insecurities. There is only Draven and me and the way his strong body moves, the way his eyes are glazed as he watches me watch him.

The melody shifts, a slow, seamless transition to something wild and pulsing. Without missing a beat, Draven hauls me against his body.

Energy jolts through me. My hands move on their own, my body entirely at the will of how this *feels*. I dig my fingers into his wide shoulders, arching into his hands at the small of my back. The music beckons me to roll my hips against his, the sensation flooding me with heat and life until all I want is more, more, *more*.

A low groan rumbles from Draven as I spin in his embrace, pressing my back against his chest, swaying and rolling my hips left and right as I grab his hands and put them on my body. I guide them over the bare expanse of my stomach, no longer ashamed of those scars as his fingers glide over them. How can I be, when his touch feels *so damn good*? Like molten heat and iron-clad strength.

Consuming, electric, mine.

Draven is *mine*.

Here, with the music swelling around us, his breath at my ear, I know that without any shred of doubt. His tortured soul matches my broken one, and somehow, despite the odds and every fucking thing that keeps trying to kill us — including each other — we *fit*.

What can be more important than that?

I whirl around, needing to see him, needing to drink in the strong planes of his face, needing to see those lips that have the power to free me from my own mind. His amber eyes are almost pure gold as he gazes down at me, an endless well of *something* churning there as his hands find my hips again. I wrap my arms around his neck, submitting to the music, to the steady rise and pulsing ebb of the notes, each one a demand to rock against Draven's body, each hard angle meeting every soft part of mine in the most delicious way.

The music turns sharp and demanding. I'm a breathless, wild, *free* thing in his arms. I tangle my fingers in his hair, rolling against him in long, teasing waves that have his grip tightening on my hips. The bite of pain only fuels that building heat inside me. My breaths go ragged as I arch against him, and then Draven's hands are beneath my knees, hauling me up until I have to lock my ankles around his back.

Nose to nose, I inch my mouth toward his.

That connection between us pulses and aches, tightening with each heartbeat.

Draven holds me to him with one arm, freeing his other to cup my cheek. The look in his eyes is so tender but so damn possessive. Like I'm his and fuck anyone who tries to take me from him. I don't know how to think or breathe or feel. Just that this, here, with him, is where I've always been meant to be.

I crush my lips against his just as the music reaches a crescendo of notes that swirl and cascade around us in brilliant sparks of light.

Something tugs on the back of my mind, some soft whisper to stop this. But why would I ever want to stop kissing Draven? Stop him from looking at me like that? Because when he does? I feel like I can do anything. Literally *anything*.

Like defeat Marid.

Marid.

Ryder.

Ray.

The tether.

The mission.

The thoughts are like ice-cold daggers, yanking me to the real world.

I tear my lips away from Draven's with a gasp. *"We have to stop."*

He goes still, clarity slipping past the haziness in his eyes. Slowly, he slides me down his body, each touch a match to a rough strip, desperate to ignite.

I groan. *Focus, damn it.* Tamping down the desire coursing through me, I concentrate on my breathing.

In and out.

Fuck, it's filled with his scent. How can anyone smell that damn good?

"Very soon, honey badger," he says into my mind, all the lust and desire evident in the rawness of his tone. *"I will make good on every promise made between us here today."*

"Swear to me?" I ask, not totally recognizing the confident girl who's asking...no, demanding it.

He steps back but keeps our hands linked. *"On my life,"* he says, then gives me a wink that feels like a signature on a contract between us.

Applause erupts around us, the music giving way to the sound, and I blink, once, twice, until I've returned to myself enough to dip my head to the rulers of Lusro.

They're standing before their thrones, clapping and whistling.

CHAPTER THIRTY-FOUR

I've slipped back into my own clothes, but I still feel totally exposed. And not in a bad way—more like a layer has been peeled back to expose sensations I didn't know existed. Draven and I danced for longer than either of us realized. Luckily, that was all it had been, because I certainly could've seen myself doing that for…

Well, much longer than that.

Silky tendrils of need coil deep inside me, and I wonder how much of this feeling is the realm and how much is just me and the connection that strings tight between us.

I need a distraction. At least until we get out of Lusro.

"What were you guys doing that took you so long?" Ray asks as we climb into the rig.

Yeah, that's totally not the distraction I was looking for.

"Nothing," Draven and I say at the same time.

Wallace lets out a stark laugh as she slides behind the wheel. "Right."

Cassiel arches a brow at Draven, who shakes his head.

Is that a blush on my Judge's face?

"We got a lead on Ryder," Draven says, switching to mission-mode. "In the Machis realm."

Wallace starts the engine.

I settle into my seat. The tiny flicker of hope that's been growing with every step that brings us closer to finding Ryder and breaking the tether flares a little brighter. Ray hasn't been possessed again, either, so maybe time really does work differently here. Or maybe Marid's been too busy oppressing the peaceful realms of the Ather to give me another heart attack.

That's a depressing thought.

"Are you all right?" I ask Ray.

"Yeah," she says, nodding toward Cassiel. "I taught him how to draw an eye."

"I'm terrible at it," he grumbles.

"You are *not*."

As we navigate the sandy pathways, my sister chatters away about trying to teach the Angel of Death how to draw. It's funny, but nowhere near distracting enough to keep dangerous thoughts out of my head. The faster we get out of this realm, the better. Somehow, this place has become more of a threat to me than any of the more deadly ones. Because I'm starting to want things I didn't think I could have. Seeing a future I never thought possible. One where I'm not used to ruin the world or wielded like a damn weapon of mass destruction.

If we survive this, and I know Ray would be safe…Lusro might not be a bad place to stay. It'd be fun, that's for sure. Would Draven stay with me? We haven't even defined what we are to each other, but with him at my side, I could easily lose myself in this realm, worrying about nothing but doing my part to contribute to the culture's energy source. Totally not a hardship with Draven around.

But life isn't easy. I know that better than anyone. And I have a Greater Demon to kill.

CHAPTER THIRTY-FIVE

We've been driving for hours when my sister gasps and bursts into giggles. "Harley was in a *skirt*?"

Apparently, Wallace took up the responsibility of telling my sister that story while I spiraled into my own thoughts. The pink sky has given way to an inky dark blue, forcing Wallace to turn on Easkr's lights.

"A really pretty blue one," Wallace answers.

"I wish I could've seen it," my sister says, and Wallace snorts. Over the course of the drive, the two have adapted an easy sort of back and forth, much easier than I have with the guide, but that's Ray. Always breaking down anyone's defenses with a simple smile and an open sort of understanding that is just super hard to explain or replicate.

"You really don't," I say.

"And you danced? That's so great. I know you love to dance."

Draven coughs, shifting in the seat on the other side of Ray, and I press my lips together. Fortunately, Wallace didn't tell her the reason behind the dance or how…intimate it was.

"I can't wait until I'm old enough to go dancing," Ray says.

I wrap an arm around her, a lump forming in my throat and killing all other emotions other than the hope that I can grant her that. A *long* life where she gets to experience everything she deserves. Happiness and joy and the space to change the world for the better. Because I have no doubt that's what she'll do.

If I can manage to somehow break the tether between her and Marid.

If I can't? I know he'll slowly eat her alive from the inside out, just to destroy me.

The thought leaves a bitter taste in my mouth.

"There is a spot in Paris where people dance under the stars," Cassiel says, and my brows raise at the angel of death.

Ray's wistful expression shifts to excitement. "You've been to Paris?"

"Of course I have," he says.

"That is so cool. Did you dance there a lot?"

Draven barely covers his laugh.

Cassiel glares over his shoulder at Draven. "No," he answers Ray. "I don't dance."

"Well, you should," she says firmly.

I love the way she sees things, how she hasn't pointed out the reason for Cassiel's likely being in Paris—to collect souls and usher them into whatever beyond they deserve. She only sees a friend, a protector, someone she wants to help find joy in any way possible.

I wish I could be more like her, but I'm not.

I see the Calling on Cassiel's shoulders. See his glorious obsidian wings not as freedom, but chains binding him into an eternal profession at the beck and call of the Seven. Any moment, him or Draven can be placed in the Divine Sleep against their will, but it seems here in the Ather, the Seven can't reach them. Or maybe they don't want to.

Draven and Cassiel are traveling with the Antichrist, after all. That was Draven's mission in the beginning—to watch me and kill me if I became a threat. Maybe as long as either of them are near me, the Seven will assume they're doing their jobs and leave them alone.

"Shit," Wallace says, slowing the rig as we reach the giant mounds I'd seen from the palace. Now they tower above us, just a mere thirty yards away. They're more solid than I originally thought, their tips more like rock formations than sand.

"What is it?" I ask.

"Sand ants," she says, sliding her goggles over her eyes.

How the hell can she see out of those when it's already so dark outside?

"I hoped the darkness would've shrouded us."

I scan the area outside the rig, noting nothing but the structures and miles upon miles of red sand that looks almost purple in the darkness.

"I don't see anything," I finally say. Are there tiny insects crawling up the hood of the rig or something?

Wallace spares me a glance, then huffs. "Put your goggles on!"

I jolt at the intensity in her voice but comply, digging the things out of my pack. Ray, Draven, and Cassiel do the same.

I slide the circular things over my eyes—

"*Shit.*"

Ray gasps as she slides her goggles into place.

Because now we can see what Wallace does, and the sand ants are *so* not what I pictured. They aren't anything close to the pesky, *tiny* insects I imagined.

They're as big as tigers, and there are thousands of them swarming out of the tips of those giant structures.

And they have *wings*.

CHAPTER THIRTY-SIX

"Any chance they'll leave us alone and let us drive through?" I ask even though I highly doubt it. Not with the way they're flying down those mounds, their massive see-through wings propelling them toward us like some intense military formation hell bent on seeking and destroying.

"Not even slightly," Wallace says, irritation coloring her tone.

"Can the rig outrun them?"

Wallace is already killing the ignition. "Nope. They'll swarm it in seconds. They must smell us." She hops out of the rig and stomps toward the back. "I've never traveled with more than two before, and usually it's only a handful of them. That's the entire colony," she says, grabbing the crystal blue machine-gun-looking weapon.

I hurry out of my door. "I thought Lux said these things are vital to their production."

"They are." Wallace snaps something on the gun, and it flares with lights and a whirring sound. "But they don't take kindly to anyone other than the chosen handlers nearing their colony. Unfortunately for me, the colony stands in the way of the archway to the next realm." She blows out a breath. "They can't be reasoned with. They're natural predators. Kill or be killed time, Firestarter." She tosses a gun toward me, and I catch it against my chest.

Adrenaline races through my veins so fast it hurts. I race back around to my open door, instincts kicking in. "Stay in the rig," I order Ray.

"Stop telling me to hide!" she snaps. "I want to help, too!"

The sound of thousands of wings flapping fill the prior peaceful silence with an ominous machine-gun-like *buzz*.

"You *do* help," I fire back. "By staying safe!" I turn to Cassiel. "Start the engine," I say.

"Hey!" Wallace shouts. "No one drives this rig but me!"

"Then give Cassiel a weapon and we'll clear the way while you drive!"

She looks to Cassiel. "Have you ever shot a blaster before?"

He gives her an incredulous look. "When would I have *ever* needed to shoot a blaster?"

Wallace groans, then throws her keys at him. "If you get one scratch on this—"

"No time," I cut her off as Cassiel slides behind the wheel.

Draven is already out of the car and grabbing his own blaster.

"Harley!" Ray argues from the backseat, lunging for the door.

"Please. Stay in here," I say, letting the bone-deep need to protect her edge my voice. "I have to keep you safe."

"Then who keeps *you* safe?"

I smile at her. "I do."

Then I turn my back on her, hating her angry protests as Cassiel locks the doors and slowly creeps the rig behind us. Draven, Wallace, and I race to the front, running as fast as we can through the sand toward the approaching swarm.

"Lux is going to *skin* me for this," Wallace says, aiming her blaster toward the giant flying ants that are blotting out the dark sky behind them.

"What are our other options?" Draven asks, barely out of breath where I feel like I'm breathing razors as we gain several feet away from the rig.

"Let the ants take us back to their colony where they'll poison us and bury us alive until they decide to use us as a family feast."

Fuck that. I'll die before I let them touch my sister. "Blasters it is," I say, sliding to a stop at Wallace's side and mimicking her stance.

"Squeeze the trigger," she says. "Don't pull."

The ants are closer now. So close I can see their prism-shaped, reflective eyes, all nine of them on one giant head. Their wings flap rapidly, and six long, sticky-looking legs hang down as they descend toward us.

"Brace for it," she says. "They've got a hell of a kick."

Then she fires, an eruption of blue light zaps through the air, hitting its mark and incinerating a dozen ants in the light's wake. The force of power from the blaster barely throws her back an inch, and that's all the time I have to marvel at her before I feel the wind from beating wings on my face.

I aim my blaster at the swarm diving straight for me, then squeeze the trigger—

The butt of the gun kicks hard into my shoulder, and I stumble back a few feet. My ears ring from the sound of the blast, but I work my jaw to clear it as I manage to get my feet steady beneath me. The cluster I shot leaves a pocket of empty space, but it's quickly replaced by another wave of the beasts.

Draven grunts, firing his blaster without so much as blinking from the kick. Instead, he manages to shift positions, his feet graceful and strong as he aims and fires, aims and fires, lighting up the sky in streaks of bright blue. The ashes of the ants fall like twisted snowflakes into the sand beneath.

Wallace does the same, over and over again, all of us working together to clear a path for the rig rumbling along behind us. I lose myself to the adrenaline, to the sole focus of getting us through this swarm and getting the hell out of this realm.

But they just. Keep. Coming.

"We're almost through!" Wallace shouts over the sound of screeching wings.

We've almost made it past the towering mounds. I can see another archway shimmering in the distance.

Wallace waves an arm behind her, urging Cassiel to stay on our heels. "Keep pushing!"

The blasters haven't made the ants think twice, nor has their fallen companions. They're relentless, and my arms ache from holding the weight of the blaster so long. But we're close to the archway. Close enough that we may not even have to kill any more if we can just—

Ray's harrowing scream shakes every bone in my body.

CHAPTER THIRTY-SEVEN

"Ray!" I scream, my entire being narrowing to the sight of her being dragged out of the rig's open window and upward, the sand ant's wings working overtime to haul her up and up and up—

Cassiel skids the rig to a stop so sudden it nearly tips the thing, but all four tires manage to settle on the ground as he throws it in park and bolts toward the sky.

He's as fast as lightning, and Draven is a mass of swirling shadows by his side, hurtling toward the sky. Toward my little sister.

She's fighting, her little body flailing against the thing's hold, her hands punching and scratching at the legs that grip her. I race toward her while the sounds of Wallace's blaster still rattle the world behind me.

"Let me go!" she shouts at the thing as if she says it sternly enough it will listen and gently drop her back to the ground.

But the thing does nothing but tighten its grip, curling those long, spindly legs closer to its body, the motion squeezing a pained cry from Ray.

All at once, I see her hitting the wall of our trailer, our father tossing her against it like she's nothing more than a bag of trash. She screams, and I see the blood on the wall. I hear my father call her *my* name.

Me.

My fault.

Seconds ago, I wanted to spare some of these creatures. Wanted to make it through the archway and leave as many alive as possible. Wanted to respect the Lusro realm's needs. We're in their territory, after all.

Not anymore.

Ray's pained cry shakes loose the rage I've barely kept bottled since the second Marid invaded her body, her mind.

And I'm fucking *done*.

"Catch her!" I yell to the guys.

The lid on my rage cracks open, and every ounce of anger, pain, and betrayal unleashes. My dark flames jerk to attention, answering my call with half a thought. They coil around my fingers, my arms, my neck. Hell, I can feel their soft caress over my cheeks, over my entire body as I become one with the flame.

Monstrous.

I must look monstrous as I raise my flaming hands above my head, because the creatures are no longer aiming for Wallace and her blaster. All of them shift toward me — the biggest threat — save for the one dragging Ray toward its colony.

Good.

They all should know the monster I'm capable of becoming.

I *erupt*.

The power storms out of me like a tidal wave. A solid stream of black and silver, my flames shooting straight at the creature with its hooks in my sister.

Instantly its ash, and Ray's cry, is swallowed by her sudden free fall —

Straight into Cassiel's open arms. He banks and weaves in and out of the sand ants filling the sky.

A scream wrenches from my throat, a call for blood and retribution for what they almost took from me. The sound rocks through my body, my muscles trembling from the rage unleashing and pulsing inside my flames.

Draven's shadow-self jerks to a halt, looping and diving right for me.

To stop me or help me, I don't know, and I don't care.

There is no tamping down the power roiling in my blood.

There is only Ray's scream sounding on repeat in my head.

There is only the mass of creatures now swarming toward me, their movements in sync, a hive-like mind made up of thousands of horrific pieces.

My eyes flicker beneath the goggles, my flames reflecting on the surface. I mentally will my dark fire into thousands of sand ant–seeking missiles and launch them all at once. Pops of black and silver flame soar through the air, following each sand ant as it tries to dodge the fire.

None can.

My flames too strong, my power too great.

As each flame hits its mark, the rage inside me ebbs a degree, until the buzzing is gone and the land around us descends into silence. I settle into a satisfied sort of cold calm as ash falls from the sky, little flakes of gray smothering the fire below.

CHAPTER THIRTY-EIGHT

Ray races to me the second Cassiel sets her feet on the sand. I drop to my knees before her, catching her against me as she throws her arms around my neck.

I cradle her head, holding her tight, my body still shaking from the power.

"Are you okay?" she asks, cheek pressed against mine.

"Me?" I ask. "Are *you* okay?"

"I'm fine," she assures me. "But you just went all dark princess on us. Does your head hurt?" She pats my head like she can check for damage.

A choked laugh escapes my lips. "I'm great now that I know you're safe."

She tucks her chin over my shoulder, squeezing me back.

Draven's form slips from the shadows on the ground next to me, his eyes wide. Wallace wears a look of absolute horror, and Cassiel's silver eyes scan me like he's trying to determine if I'm safe enough to be that close to Ray.

"I didn't know you could do that," Ray says, her hold loosening only a fraction. She keeps her head pressed against mine.

I close my eyes, reveling in the feel of her safe and unharmed in my arms. "I didn't, either," I admit, not even sure what I'd done. How I splintered my power and yet gave it direction at the same time. And it *listened* to me, heeded my every request.

And because of that, because of what I'd done, Cassiel and Wallace are looking at me like I might turn on them any second. A dog they considered a friend before it turned rabid and feral in a blink.

But that thing had *taken* Ray.

Didn't they know I would always be the monster protecting the real princess? Didn't they know I would raze everything to the ground to keep her safe?

Draven knew, which is why he isn't looking at me with judgment, only support, and maybe a little concern.

But I'm fine. I feel fine, despite the retreating adrenaline threatening to crash my body here on the sand.

Ray's hold on my neck tightens, almost to the point of pain, and I run my fingers over her hair. "Hey," I say, softening my tone. "It's okay, Ray." Her hold only tightens, and I have to swallow hard around it. I shift, barely able to break her grip, urging her backward so I can look into her eyes and assure her we're safe—

But those aren't Ray's baby blues staring at me.

They're yellow with blue veins spiderwebbing outward from the slit pupil.

Marid.

"Shadows!" I mentally scream to Draven, and he instantly shifts, encircling Ray, Cassiel, and myself in a cocoon of darkness to hide our surroundings and Wallace, who Marid has likely seen before.

"I'm scared, Harley," Ray says, but it's not her voice. A sickening sucking sound flexes between us as her cheeks sink, the red imprints of scales puckering across her skin. "*Hold* me," the grainy, hissing voice says, and she throws her arms around my neck again.

Only this time, I can't breathe around the grip.

CHAPTER THIRTY-NINE

I send a ball of fire to our right, willing it to keep the space lit as I try to be as gentle as possible, prying my possessed sister off my neck.

Draven keeps up his spiraling, and somewhere in the back of my mind, I worry about the power he's draining by concealing our location. We spoke about it before coming to the Ather, what we'd do if Marid showed himself before we'd made it to his realm. But, fuck, right now? Ray had barely escaped the sand ants, and now this? Is that why he came? Could he sense her fear, her vulnerability?

"Did our little Ray have another nightmare?" Marid's voice says through my sister's lips as I manage to shove her off of me.

"Why are you hiding from me?" Ray's body moves in jerking motions that look painful as she stomps around the shadow circle. "You didn't honestly think the Judge's little shadows could keep her safe from me, did you?"

I swallow hard, giving away nothing on my face.

"You did!" Marid-Ray cackles, and the sound, the sight of her—all scales and yellow veiny eyes—sends shivers of ice down my spine. "You fools."

"Release the girl," Cassiel says, his voice cold as ice and sharp as steel. His wings are fully extended, his eyes a shocking silver in the cocoon of Draven's shadows. Ever the vision of the angel of death, my instincts balk at the sight of him, at the terror rolling off him in waves.

Ray's body whirls toward the voice, craning her little head

up and up. Her feral grin is nothing like the one she always gives Cassiel. "Ah, angel of death, what are *you* going to do?" Ray's arms jolt outward. "I don't have a soul to take. Unless you want hers."

Cassiel crouches in front of Marid-Ray, the move wholly lethal as he focuses on her eyes. "I see you," he rumbles. "Earth doesn't hold me, Marid. I'm not chained here. I will come for you."

Ray bares her teeth at him.

"You don't need a soul for me to steal your *life*."

Ray's hand lashes out, almost making connection with Cassiel's face, but I grab her wrist, whirling her to face me. I don't need Cassiel's threats—though valid—setting off Marid, triggering him to do something worse than invade my sister's mind and body. He could kill her. He could hold her forever.

I *can't*.

"Ray," I say. "Please. Come back. *Fight* him. Come back."

"She can't hear you," Marid sing songs, tilting Ray's head at an awkward angle. She slides her hand over her chest. "She's buried. Screaming for you to help her but you're not listening. Have you ever listened to her? *Truly* listened? Or have you merely kept her caged in a bubble of safety that only made her weak?"

My blood chills at his words, and the ball of fire I have lighting the shadows flares brighter, stronger.

"What are you going to do? Kill me?"

A knife of cold terror slides into my chest.

That's what he wants.

That's what Marid plans to push me to.

Kill her to spare her this pain. This torture.

"Never," I whisper, my voice choked with fear.

"*Never* say never."

Her body heaves, convulsing as a scream wrenches out of her mouth, one that sounds more like Ray than Marid. Her knees hit the ground as her body crumples, her eyelids falling closed as that scream dies.

"Ray?" I smooth back her hair, noting the scales are gone. She opens her eyes, smiling up at me but looking like even that effort exhausts her.

"I fought him," she says as I haul her into my lap.

Fresh air hits our skin as Draven sinks to his knees by my side, his own chest rising and falling too rapidly. "What do you mean you fought him?" he asks.

Cassiel stalks over, crouching by Draven's side.

Ray's forehead crinkles. "There was a ladder. I climbed and climbed even though it stung to grab each rung. And then he was there, standing at the top of the ladder. I hit him over and over again until he fell off."

"You're so brave," I say, not sure what else to say. My instincts are screaming, worrying about her putting herself at risk like that. What if he fought back? What if he decided to get rid of that piece of her for good?

But I don't say any of those things. Because she asked me, *begged* me to stop forcing her to hide. And as I gaze down at my amazing little sister, at how strong and brave and hopeful she is, I can do nothing but wonder how she got so damn fierce.

"I'm tired now," she says, her voice weak.

I stand, hefting her into my arms as I do. "Let's go find Wallace. You can sleep in the rig—"

"The fuck you say."

I freeze at the sight of Wallace's terrified stare. The one that is no longer about me, about what I'd done to the entire colony.

No, her eyes are on Ray.

CHAPTER FORTY

"You didn't tell me Marid was *possessing* Ray," Wallace hisses as she stomps toward me, glancing at Ray, half asleep in my arms.

"How—"

She scowls at me. "I have *ears*. Shadows may block sight, but not sound. And Marid's voice is one you never forget."

A lead weight sinks in my stomach. I move around her, heading toward the rig.

"You should've told me." She follows me step for step, Cassiel and Draven only a beat behind her.

I stop, exhaustion hitting me like a bat to the head. I have nothing left inside me but the bitter taste of terror and the unflinching need to get Ray away from here.

"Are you still taking us or not?" I ask, the fight leaving my voice. When Wallace doesn't answer, I sigh. "Fine. That's fine. I'll walk through the damn archway if I have to, but there is no way in hell I'm sticking around for the next wave of sand ants or Lusro guards or Marid to come back. I'm moving. Now." I start to walk past the rig, fully prepared to do as I said. Footsteps hustle behind me, and I know Draven is jogging to catch up.

"Wait," Wallace says, and I stop and turn. Ray's weight in my arms is a comfort, despite my muscles feeling wrecked. She's here. I've got her.

"Get in the rig." She hauls open the driver's-side door as she climbs in.

And for now, that's all I needed her to say. I tuck Ray into her seat in the middle of me and Draven, Cassiel settling heavily in the passenger seat.

Ray fully slumps against me, and as Wallace starts the vehicle, I wonder what the hell the cost will be when we find Draven's brother.

CHAPTER
FORTY-ONE

Wallace and I lean against a log same as we did the night before, needing to camp in the safety of another pocket space between realms after the attack and possession.

Sleep will be a long time coming, if I get there at all. Every time I close my eyes, I can't see anything but that ant taking her into the sky.

Draven is passed out a foot away from Ray, both of them needing to recharge after everything that had happened. Cassiel stands guard not five feet away from them, those silver eyes so contemplative they're almost painful to look at.

"You told me you didn't want to know," I say as I watch the small fire I've made. "In the beginning," I clarify. "You never wanted to know the reasons why we were here. That's why I didn't tell you about Ray." I curl my fingers, and the flames lazily sway and pulse with my movements.

Wallace glances at my sister asleep on her pack. "I broke my number one rule."

"And what's that? Never wipe out more than you can afford to pay back?"

She flinches. "I deserve that. You're not exactly a picnic to be around, either, Firestarter."

"And *I* deserve *that*." We share a similarly broken smile. "What's your rule?"

"Never like the clients," she admits, leaning back against the log. "I've lost more than I'd like to admit. Not by any fault of my own, but because some clients"—she aims a pointed look at me—"think they know better than me. Don't listen. End up getting themselves killed or, worse, trapped in the wrong fucking realm."

"I don't think I know better than you," I say. "I know you have way more knowledge of this place than I do. But, as you can tell, I don't think clearly when Ray is in danger."

"I get that. I like the tiny seer. You, not so much," she says, a slight tease in her voice. "But her? I can't help it."

I chuckle. "She has that effect on people."

"You need to get to Marid's realm to break his hold?"

I nod.

"And his brother," Wallace says, nodding to where Draven sleeps by Ray. "Ryder. What's his role in all this?"

"He has power we need," I say, unsure how to properly explain it the way Kazuki had. "A divine lightning strike, basically. Ryder can do that. We go to the Machis realm to find him and then convince him to help."

"Fuck," she whispers. "I've seen power like that before. There are a handful of creatures that can do it. It's terrifying."

I furrow my brow, wondering if she was mistaking the power for something else. I mean, Draven made it seem like his brother was the only one capable of it. If there was someone easier, faster to get to, he would've said. We wouldn't be dragging Ray through all these realms, putting her at risk, trying to find him.

Right?

My gaze falls to where he sleeps, and I shake the nagging thoughts away. He nearly drained himself of power just now to conceal our location from Marid. He'd exhausted his powers so many times to save me or Ray. There is no way he'd delay severing the tether just because he wants to find his brother.

"Well," Wallace says, drawing me out of myself. "Let's hope Ryder really is in the Machis realm."

"Let's hope," I say, not bothering to voice my concerns out loud. If we're lucky enough to find him, how hard will it be to convince him to help? Being that he's Draven's brother, I'm really hoping I don't have to use my flames as an incentive, but again, I'll do what I have to. "Then it's on to Marid's realm."

"You do realize his realm is one of the most dangerous in all of the Ather?" Wallace asks. "It'll be a brutal battle, even if you somehow manage to sneak past his guards."

"Don't care."

"You should—"

"I *don't*. I don't care how much blood I have to spill, don't care if that blood is red or green or yellow or blue. Whatever amount I have to shed, I'll do it. To save her, to spare her this assault? I'll pay any price."

Wallace raises her brows, studying my gaze more intently. She must read something there because she digs into her pack, retrieves two bottles of neon yellow liquid, and hands one to me. "This coming from a girl who says she's afraid of wind chimes."

The tease hits its mark, and a hoarse laugh rips out of me as I take the bottle from her.

Wallace joins in, the tension broken between us as we crack open the bottles. "What's up with that, anyway?"

I take a sip of the bubbly drink. It's not sweet or bitter but has more of a sharp taste I can't place—almost like lime but harsher. I'm growing oddly used to all the new flavors here in the Ather.

I go back to watching the flames. It may be exhaustion or it may be her admission of concern for Ray's well-being, but I find myself saying, "My mother put one up outside our trailer. A wind chime." My chest clenches as the memory consumes me. "I'm not sure if she was my biological mother or not, but it's one of the few memories I have of her. I couldn't have been more than four because that's the year she left."

I shake my head. "She hung up this ridiculous contraption that tinkled and chimed every time the wind even *breathed* in our direction. Dad beat her for it because it would wake him up when he was sleeping off a hangover. Not my real dad," I say, sending the flames swirling with a small flick of my fingers. "I don't actually know who he is, either. Anyway, she tried to take it down, but he wouldn't let her. Said she needed a reminder for what happens when she did things without asking."

I remember the bruises on her face, remember wondering why she was packing her bag when he'd gone out drinking one night shortly after. That's the same night she put the bracelet on me and left, never once looking back. Never once stopping to think about *who* she was leaving me with.

"Even after she left, he left the thing hanging there. And every time it chimed, every time it made enough noise to wake him up, *I* got punished for it because she wasn't around to take it." I clear my throat, coaxing the rising flames of the fire to calm. "I managed to break the thing when I was fourteen. My friend Kai helped me knock it down with rocks—"

The words choke me. I can still see him in the memory, his youthful face, those light green eyes, as he handed me rock after rock until I managed to shatter the thing to pieces.

Not real. Not real.

He hadn't been there, cheering me on, giving me the courage to do what I needed to. Marid had created that memory, that relationship...

I'd been alone.

Totally, utterly alone.

"Did he punish you?" Wallace asks when I don't continue.

I blink out of my spiraling emotions. I hate that I'm still paralyzed over the loss of someone who never really existed in the first place. Not in the way it mattered, anyway. "My dad punished me for everything," I say by way of answer. I glance at Ray's sleeping body, the steady rise and fall of her chest. "But as long as it kept his eyes off of her? I didn't care."

"Whatever price," Wallace whispers, echoing my earlier words as she looks to Ray, then me. There is a softness to her gaze she's never showed me, a sense of support and understanding and even the hint of companionship flickering there. Maybe even pity, but I'm trying like hell not to notice it.

Then she rolls her eyes.

"Well, *boohoo*," she says, leaning back and folding her arms behind her head. "What a tragic fucking sob story. You think you're special? Everyone has pain, Firestarter. Everyone has problems. Doesn't mean you *wallow* in it."

I gape at her, the flames in our campfire flickering. That...*bitch*.

But before I send those flames to incinerate her on the spot, she winks and clinks her half-drunk bottle against mine.

Oh.

I laugh, returning her gesture. Maybe she knows me better than I've given her credit for. She's not reaching out to hug me, not offering to braid my hair while we cry into each other's ice cream—*fuck*, double fudge brownie ice cream sounds *so* good right now. She's pushing my buttons, showing me she doesn't pity me for one second. But for the record, "I am not *wallowing*."

She arches a brow. "Oh, you're not?"

"*You* asked."

"And I'm so sorry I did," she says, a smirk shaping her lips. "Shit, I bet all your stories are that sad. Poor little Harley grew up with a monster."

Ugh. I'm regretting this whole conversation. *This* is why I never open up.

"There are a million beings here suffering the same or worse just because of the realm they were born in," she says, shifting the conversation from teasing to something more solid and harrowing. "So many, because those in power deemed it so."

"Who are all these *power players* you keep talking about? You said it's not the king, so beyond Marid and his Twelve, who?"

Wallace tosses a strip of blue bark into my flames. They snap and devour it instantly. "Whoever he's working for."

"Why doesn't the king do anything about it?"

"He tries," she says. "Or, at least, that's the rumor. Supposedly his power is trapped. Some ancient bullshit, I don't know. There are groups, though, beings who try to right the wrongs. Working under the hope that we can free every peaceful realm that is oppressed."

Guilt settles in my gut. "I wish I could help you."

But what can *I* do to help? What power do I have to help her in this? Especially when I have one goal right now. The same goal I've had since I was thirteen years old—protect Ray so that she has the life she deserves.

And I can't help but hate that cold, whispering voice at the back of my head, saying the life she deserves is one without me in it. And maybe the Ather is the answer to that question, but I have to kill Marid before I can even think about it.

Wallace studies me for a few moments as if she's waiting to see if I'll say more. Then she settles back against her pack, closing her eyes as she folds her hands over her chest. "You can't save us, Firestarter," she says. "Not when you haven't even figured out how to save yourself."

CHAPTER FORTY-TWO

My cheek stings as I fly backward. The air rushes from my lungs as my spine hits the ground.

"Kai." I say his name, unable to get my feet underneath me. "Please!"

He's relentless, steadily chasing after me with that knife in his hands.

"You're my friend!" Damn it, why won't my legs work? It's like they're made of jelly. I can't move, can barely speak loud enough for him to hear me.

"You deserve to die," he says, standing over me with the knife. "You're evil. Pure. Evil."

Tears slide down my cheeks as he raises the knife. He jerks it down, and I barely dodge as it snicks into the ground next to my face. Kai roars, angry and seething as he tears the blade from the ground.

I grapple for it, my hands slick and wet and heavy.

Warmth floods my hands as I look down.

Kai stabbed me.

He legit stabbed me.

I hold the knife in my side, the heat spiraling out of me from the wound.

"Weak," he says, shaking his head. "Worthless."

"Kai."

I pull the knife from my side, nearly heaving from the pain, and plunge it into his chest.

He doesn't flinch.

Doesn't scream or cry.

He smirks at me, eyes on the knife buried to the hilt in his chest.

I stumble backward, terror raining over me in icy sheets.

"You really shouldn't have done that," he says, ripping the blade out and brandishing the bloody thing in his hand.

And then he's chasing me again.

I run because there is no way to beat him. I know this now. Know he's stronger than me, better than me. He always has been.

"Harley." He sings my name just like he did when we were kids playing hide and seek. "Harley..."

I trip, landing face first in a pool of blood.

So. Much. Blood.

It soaks the grass, painting the green in red.

I scream, trying to get up, but my feet slide in the slickness.

"Harley—"

I jerk upright, a blade firm in my hand as I tackle him to the ground and press the knife to his throat.

"Harley," Draven whispers, hands held palm up.

Gold eyes meet mine, not green.

But the nightmare still clings to me, my arms shaking with adrenaline as I pin Draven to the ground, that blade kissing his neck. The hilt is warm in my hand, as if I'd fallen asleep with it. A dagger Wallace gave me for my pack. When had I reached for it?

I look down, tears still rolling down my cheeks as I lean closer to him. "I killed him," I whisper. "I killed him."

"I know," Draven says, his voice soft, understanding despite the dagger at his throat.

"I'm a monster." The confession slips past my lips, my fear and doubt coiling from the nightmare. From having to relive what I did to Kai over and over again despite what he'd done to me.

"You're not," he says, still unmoving beneath the knife.

"I am," I snap, frozen in my panic.

"Then do your worst, Antichrist," he says, his hands moving to my hips. The touch is searing, his eyes golden and churning, hot enough to slice through that panic coating me and bring me back to reality.

A reality where I hold a blade to his throat.

The dagger instantly clatters to the ground, and I collapse against his chest, my lips crushing his in an instant.

"Draven," I sigh between our kisses, all at once my mind and soul snapping into place. I'm here, with *him*. Not with Kai, not with the boy who helped violate my mind and alter my memories.

Draven.

My siphon.

My friend.

Mine.

He doesn't hold himself back, instead sensing I *need* his relentless hunger, need the kiss to border on pain to wake me the fuck up. His fingers tangle in my hair as he arches beneath me, sending jolts of electricity and heat rushing through my body.

I meet him move for move, breath for breath, until I'm falling into his kiss and leaving the rest behind me.

And I don't ever want to look back.

CHAPTER
FORTY-THREE

"Stay alert," Wallace says over the shouting that echoes off the walls of the enormous building that is dead-center of the Machis realm hub.

The place reeks of something similar to stale beer, bodily fluids, and wet sand. Other things try to penetrate the air—the food and drinks being sold in small stations lining the walls—but they're quickly swallowed. Other booths selling weapons and tonics scatter about the space, which is wide and expansive, all circled around an interior structure walled off by wood. Cheers echo through the wood as if it holds some great arena.

"What's in there?" I ask Draven, who scans the wooden structure in the center, the one people are lining up to get inside.

"The fighting pits," he answers. "Remember the one I took you to in Chicago?"

I nod. We'd been searching for the Second—for Kai.

"This is the *original* fighting pit," he says. "Rumored to be more brutal and unfair than all the ones that stemmed from it."

That isn't hard to picture. Not with the agonized cries and wails that leak through those wooden planks. A chill races across my skin.

Ray's eyes are wide as we try to blend in with the crowd of ruthless-looking demons, many wearing all manner of battle scars, some still fresh and dripping blood.

"Gareth said Ryder was in the pits," I say. "Do we start asking around or…"

"I can talk to the Pit Master," Wallace says. "But she's not a fan of outsiders. I'll have to do it alone."

"I'll check out the arena," Draven says. "If what Gareth said is true, Ryder may still be a fighter."

"I'll ask around the market," Cassiel offers.

The market is so vast and expansive there is no way Cassiel can cover all the ground on his own. "I can, too."

Ray sticks close to my side because staying with the rig wasn't an option, not when demon promoters started hassling us the second we arrived, shoving their questionable weapons in our faces or the tonics that looked like anything but, their eyes hopeful of us parting with any and all currency we may have on us. I'd bet one of Wallace's blasters that they deal in gold like the Xses realm.

"I don't like the idea of you and Ray going it solo," Draven says. "Maybe you should stick with Cassiel."

I arch a brow at him. "Doubting my powers?"

He sighs. "No."

"We'll be fine," I assure him. "We'll cover more ground if we split up."

He hesitates, the battle clear in his eyes.

"It'll be quick," I say. "You check the arena. Wallace talks to the boss. And Cassiel and I will ask around. We'll meet right back here in an hour." When he still seems conflicted, I sigh. "You know what I can do. I can handle it."

He relents. "Meet me right back here." He points to where we stand, and I note the booth selling drinks.

"We will," I say, already hustling Ray in the opposite direction. It's cute that he worries, but I'm glad he didn't put up too huge a fight. We really don't have time for macho-hero stuff, and I have plenty up my sleeve if someone attacks us.

We weave through the crowd, Ray keeping up without a hitch as we move booth to booth, asking about Ryder as we go. After several without any luck, I'm starting to worry that Gareth might've been mistaken. Maybe Ryder is still stuck in Marid's realm.

I can only hope Draven is having more luck than we are.

After we've made it to the end of one long row of vendors without any luck, I turn to tell Ray we'll have to start heading back to the meeting spot, but she's not where I left her.

"Ray?" I catch a peek of her blond braid as she hurries over to a booth across the aisle. I go after her, having to shove my way through a thick crowd of demons to do it.

I clear the crowd, finding her as she hands a youngling with fuzzy blue fur and three eyes a basket of food that the little demon had been reaching for. The youngling cradles it to its chest, hurrying off to disappear into the crowd.

"She said she was starving," Ray says in way of answer to my gaping stare.

"You can't run off like that, Ray."

"I'm fine," she says. "Did you see her? She was crying. I had to—"

"You owe me a power boost for that," a gruff voice says. "Eighteen vials of blood."

I look up. *Way* up. The voice belongs to a giant demon. His thick legs are covered in scales and shake the booth he walks around. His eyes are solid green with a thin strip of black down the center.

Ray takes a small step back. "I don't, I can't..."

I step in front of her. "I don't have that form of payment," I say as calmly as I can. Already, my flames are gathering beneath my skin, but turning him to ash will only cause a scene we don't need. Plus, he's only demanding to be paid for his goods, which really isn't out of the question—

"Then it's to the fighting pits," he growls. "She'll represent me in the ring. If she wins"—he glances at her then rolls his eyes—"scratch that. I'll bet on her to lose. That will suffice as payment."

A tiny gasp comes from behind me, but I don't dare turn around to reassure her.

"I have other forms of payment," I say, reaching for my bag for some of the medicinal vials we have.

The demon shakes his head. "Only forms of currency I deal

in are power boosts and blood. She goes to the pits."

"She doesn't," I say, then tip my chin. "I'll go in her place."

"Harley, no!" Ray gasps.

I usher her back behind me. A crowd is starting to gather, eyes greedy with the prospect of a scene.

The demon's eyes rove over me, studying the length of my body, lingering in areas that make me suddenly want a shower. I snap my fingers, revealing the barest hint of my dark flames.

A sickening smile shapes his too-wide mouth, exposing dripping, flat teeth. "Yes," he says. "Finally, I'll have a contender."

I crane my neck, trying to see around the gathering crowd, and spot a pair of familiar obsidian wings an aisle over.

"Cassiel!"

His head snaps up, and he shoves his way over in a hurry. Not that it takes much once the crowd gets a look at him in all his dark, brooding glory. He glances at the demons gathering around us. "Trouble?"

"Can you take Ray, please? I have to go…handle something."

Cassiel looks from me to the demon, those silver eyes clearly contemplating fighting his way out of what I got myself into.

"Don't," I say and raise my hands. "I've got this. Just please, take her. I'll be in and out in no time."

Of course, I don't know that, but the longer we stand here, the more likely this demon is to change his mind, and I really, really don't want to set the whole place on fire because of a misunderstanding.

"Draven is going to kill me," Cassiel grumbles, nodding as he silently guides Ray away, despite her glaring protests at me.

The demon grabs me by the arm, hauling me toward the wooden structure.

The sounds of the crowd erupt around me as we pass through the doorway, bypassing the line of awaiting spectators as the demon shakes me toward another demon guarding the door.

"My contender," he announces, and the other demon waves us through. My captor smacks my arm with a stamp he's pulled from one of his many pockets, the ink the same shade of green as his eyes. It's a symbol of some sort, a sick brand to show I belong to him. Like I'm no more than a piece of property.

Thousands of demons pack the stadium seating, all raised and looking down at the main event fifteen feet below them. The demon drags me toward the edge, a smooth drop-off to the pit below, and acid bubbles up the back of my throat.

The floor of the pit is sand, stained with various colors of blood, and it's split in half by a chain of fence. Both sides are empty for the moment, but cold dread fills my bones at the sheer size of it.

It's not an arena. Not like I initially thought.

It's a fucking superdome.

And at the sound of a gong, he shoves me right into it.

CHAPTER
FORTY-FOUR

I barely get my feet under me before I hit the sandy pit, my muscle memory remembering to tuck and roll to soften the impact. The air *whooshes* out of my lungs, but I scramble quickly to stand.

"Watch out for the beasties!" the demon shouts from where he stands on the lip high above me. I eye the fence splitting the pit into two. It only comes up to my shoulder — not enough to keep things out or in. Its silver chains are stained in red and blue and green liquid. And they *smell*.

I breathe through my mouth, shifting on my feet to gain balance on the sandy floor. It's a giant circle, the walls solid concrete except for two rectangular doors — one on either side of the fence splitting the pit — all the way across from me.

The spectators above shout and laugh and fight while they wait for something, and my blood floods with adrenaline as each second passes and I'm left alone in the pit. The demon said *beasties*, and while I'm confident in my survival skills and my powers, I wasn't given a set of rules on how to beat this game. Has Draven made his way into the pits, or is he still trying to get in?

Suddenly, the crowd goes dead silent. A red-tinted light illuminates a spot high above the crowd, a box carved above the stadium seats.

"We have a new batch of contenders," a feminine voice says loud enough to fill the giant room. "One of whom already so *graciously* volunteered to go first." The green-skinned demon points down to me, and I roll my eyes. Volunteered my ass. "The betting booths will be open for ten more minutes. You know the players. Bet quickly, for in mere moments, the matches will begin. You know the rules—last contender standing after three rounds takes the loot!"

The crowd erupts in cheers, the sound echoing off the walls and rumbling my bones.

Three rounds. Okay, I can handle three rounds. How many times have I survived multiple beatings in one night? And that was *before* I had my powers. Before I rid myself of the ancient stone holding them back, making me weak.

A succession of howls resonates through the door on the other side of the fence, and my mind empties of everything beyond the shock.

Wolves, or what *look* like wolves, race through the door. Two of them snarl, fangs snapping at each other as they scramble through the small space. The second one is the biggest animal I've ever seen—its black-and-gray fur is curly and matted along its muscular frame. A chunk is missing from one ear, and gray scars zigzag along its flank. Its eyes are wholly black as it paces in the sand, almost calm and calculating while the other hound is already biting at the air in front of him. Not the big one, though. It watches patiently, those intelligent eyes missing nothing.

The ground vibrates on my side of the arena as a demon the size of a giant steps through the doorway across from me. He wears some sort of white uniform of cotton, half his belly exposed beneath the fabric.

He holds up a fist the size of my head, and the crowd cheers and chants some name I can't recognize or pronounce. The giant is someone they've seen and rooted for before.

The giant's four bulging eyes narrow on me as he approaches me.

A gun cracks, and one of the beasts yelps and barks. I risk a quick glance—

White-hot pain splits my cheek, and I go sailing through the air, crashing against the solid wall behind me.

Stars glitter along the edge of my vision as I hurry to my feet.

I've been backhanded before—several times. I hate it now just as much as I did then. There's just something *so* disrespectful in a backhand. The person wielding it has no respect for the person receiving it, not even giving them the honor of a full punch.

I shake off the thought and focus. I can't let myself get distracted by anything, not my past, not our mission, and not the snarling wolves across the fence.

Three opponents.

Three rounds.

And I assume each one ends when one of us is unconscious or dead.

That's all I have to get through. Then I can get back to Ray.

I feed off that anger, let it fill the very marrow of my bones as the giant demon launches at me.

I dodge another hit, tucking my knees under me to roll to his unprotected side.

Anka's training flares to life inside me, my instincts roaring. My powers are no longer in a cage, and my muscles remember everything she's ever drilled into me.

Size doesn't matter, she always told me.

Strategy does.

Reading the moves. All it takes is one well-placed hit, and I can buy myself time enough to get away.

But not today.

Today I have to take him down.

Take them *all* down.

He didn't expect the move and swings again, propelling his massive arms toward me. Frustration ebbs from him as I continue to dance around the room, dodging without attacking. Wearing him down. He's huge, after all, and it takes a ton of energy to swing those meaty fists my way.

"Stop being a coward and fight!" he yells, and the crowd shouts its agreement.

"I *am* fighting," I snap. "Not my fault you can't catch me!"

A deafening yell rumbles from his chest, and the hounds

fighting behind me howl at it. The close proximity of the sound draws my focus no matter how hard I try to ignore it. I'm terrified of those beasts climbing the fence and adding a new obstacle to this fight, but another quick look I can't help but take is all the giant needs.

He moves faster than I anticipate, bounding the distance between us in one massive leap. His meaty fist wraps around my body and slams me into the fence, smashing my face against the chain links. Blood trickles from my split cheek over the metal and down my jaw.

The white hound instantly smells it, paws digging into the sand as it launches toward the fence. It nips and bites, the edges of its sharp teeth catching my skin between the wiring.

The black hound jumps on the opportunity, clamping its massive jaw on the white hound's tail, hauling it back and back—

The giant squeezes, the crowd cheering at the prospect of my death.

But fuck *that*.

I didn't survive sand ants and drakels and my monster of a father and killing my supposed best friend to make it easy for *this* demon.

I grip the fist holding my neck, drawing my dark flames to my palms.

He drops me, wailing as he stumbles backward, waving his singed hands in the air.

I eye the crowd, then tap my fists together, both instantly engulfed in black and silver flames.

They *cheer*.

I turn my focus back to the giant, who glares at me, and motion for him to do his worst.

He rushes at me full speed, like a bull hell-bent on trampling the taunting fighter. Can't really blame him, but since he just tried to kill me—

I call on my second power, willing and shaping the sand beneath my feet, the element propelling me up and up like I'm riding the tip of a tidal wave. The giant's momentum is too fast to stop, though he tries and fails, and he skids into my wave of sand. I flip to land on his back, snake one arm around his neck. Drawing the flames on my other hand down to a smolder, I cover his nose and mouth with it.

He thrashes back and forth, trying to shake me off, but I squeeze every muscle in my body to hold tight.

He attempts to break my hold as he heaves in breaths of smoke and fire, and then—

We crash to the ground, the giant going limp beneath me.

I hurry off of him, noting the rise and fall of his chest. Alive, but unconscious.

"Finish him!"

"Kill him!"

"Waste him!"

The brutal calls ring out from the crowd above.

I glare up at them, but the door in the wall swings open. A demon with a black, blood-stained apron grabs the giant's ankle and hauls him out.

Through the copper fencing, the white hound is covered in bites, and spatters of blood stain its fur. A handler comes through its door, muzzling the panting animal and jerking it out of sight, leaving the black hound alone.

It looks at me with those dark eyes, its chest puffing as it limps and paces the length of its cage.

A sadness hits me at the sight, a deep sort of understanding as the pair of us stand on either side of the cage. Trapped and forced to fight against our will. All for the pleasure of the blood-thirsty crowd high above.

I sizzle with the hate of it, the hate of such *senseless* violence.

The doors swing open again, and a red-furred hound, smaller than the black one, comes out. It looks defeated before it's stepped two paws onto the sand.

And for me, another demon, smaller than the giant but twice my size, growling like a wild animal. Metal winks in the flickering lights from above, and he spins two blades in his hands.

I suppose it's only fair, since I have earth and flame on my side.

He snarls at me, a twisted sort of smirk that screams my death song.

I shift my stance, preparing to block his first attack—

But he hurls a knife through the holes in the copper wiring. A loud yelp echoes throughout the room, the blade slicing across the red hound's leg, leaving a deep gash.

I gape at him, my hands shaking as the crowd cheers their approval.

And he *laughs*, spinning the remaining blade in his hand like he only needs one to kill me.

The black hound snarls at the fence, clawing at it. Like it might tear through and rip the demon to pieces for wounding its opponent.

Undiluted rage storms through me. The animal is innocent in this, forced to do the will of its captors. Just like me. And he hurt it for *sport*.

"You're next, little girl," he growls, pointing the blade in my direction.

Little girl.

The hound whimpering in the sand not five feet away as that handler comes in and hauls it to who knows where.

The way the demon's eyes have the same sheen of unremorseful hatred as my father always did.

I see nothing but red.

The demon rushes me, his blade held out horizontally.

I drop to my knees, twin daggers of fire manifesting in my hands.

And they cut through his belly like a hot knife through butter.

I feel them sink into his flesh. His cry of pain rattles my mind, filling with visions of another battle.

Flames sinking into Kai's flesh. Smothering him, consuming him. His blood on my hands.

Rage and hate and anger fills me until I choke on it.

He falls as easily as the hound he injured.

My chest heaves, and the crowd quiets as they watch me and finally *see*.

I'm not a little girl.

I'm not someone to be put in a cage and toyed with.

I flick my wrists, the fire daggers disappearing, and I step toward the copper fence, crouching.

The black hound sits, yet it's as tall as me in that position. It doesn't try to claw at the fence, doesn't snap its teeth in my direction.

It sits and stares at me with those dark eyes.

"One more to go," I whisper. One last opponent, then we can regroup.

It ducks its head in what feels like acknowledgment.

The door to its cage clangs open, and a gray hound of equal size pads out.

I turn on my heel, standing as I wait for my door to open.

I raise my fists, covering them in flames as I shift to an attack position. I won't kill this one if I don't have to, but given the malice of the last opponent, I'm not holding my breath. Don't they always save the best for last?

The door on my side opens.

A dark blue uniform clings to a muscled body...

And Draven steps into the ring.

CHAPTER FORTY-FIVE

No, can't be.

I focus on the smirking, angry boy in front of me. The one that looks eerily identical to Draven, but this boy's eyes are a shining turquoise where Draven's are golden amber.

Ryder.

He stares me down with a jagged look in his eyes, like he wants to rip my throat out.

"No," I whisper, unable to hold the word back as I snuff out my flames and drop my hands.

Those turquoise eyes are edged in hunger, desperation. Blue-white lightning crackles between his fingers as he curls them into fists. Just a flicker of the power I've been told he has, the power I *need*.

Damn it, where is Draven when I need him?

But I *did* find him, so…mission accomplished?

The crowd cheers and hollers, stomping their feet or hooves or talons on the seats above.

Ryder strikes faster than a snake, his fist cracking against my jaw with a sparking jolt. I'm on my knees before I know what happened, my muscles twitching from the electricity jolting through each nerve ending.

I groan, shoving to my feet—

The wind whips past my face from another hit I manage to dodge.

"I don't want to hurt you," I say.

Ryder's cocky yet confused look is so like Draven in that

moment. "You're in the wrong realm, then."

I glare at him, arching back to miss another swing. Frustration swarms me in hot waves as I dance out of the way, keeping my flames firmly beneath my skin. Because he may be trying to kill me, but this is Draven's freaking *twin*, and I need him to save Ray.

"Listen to me, Ry—"

A swing near my face cuts me off.

Okay, he's wicked *fast*. A machine in his movements yet graceful and deadly like a gathering storm. He feints right but hits left, clipping me in the stomach so hard I topple over. My body zings with those sparks again, the ones locking my legs despite me trying like hell to leap to my feet.

"Damn it," I groan through clenched teeth, willing my muscles to obey me.

Ryder crouches, a taunting smirk on his face as he studies me. His hair is dark like Draven's but hangs in messy waves to his shoulders, the strands straight where Draven's is more curly.

"You think because you're female, I'll go easy on you? You came into the pits for a reason. No rules in here." Those turquoise eyes spark with tiny bolts of white lightning. "Get up. I want to see how much you can handle before I kill you."

His words, the way he underestimates me, break something inside me. Because *fuck*. I know you're supposed to be forgiving of your boyfriend's family, but Ryder is being a real asshole. Though, to be fair, he has no clue who I am.

Still, assholes are kind of a trigger for me.

I jump up faster than he can blink, my flaming fist connecting beneath that strong jaw. His feet lift off the ground, and he lands on his back in a sprawling heap a few feet away from me.

Whoops.

I raise my hands in defense as he's on his feet in seconds. He swipes at the blood trickling from the corner of his lip, then smiles. And it's a terrifying smile, one filled with rage and hate and just the hint of pleasure. Like he hasn't met a real challenge in a long time. And from the power in his punch? I can totally see that.

"Please listen," I practically beg over the roaring of the crowd.

"This isn't the place to chat," he fires back, crackling fists raised. I dodge two hits before he lands one and I'm on my ass again. He lashes faster this time, all rueful taunting gone as he grabs my shoulders and hauls me to his eye level, my feet dangling above the sand.

The crowd cheers. Seriously, this is *no* way to have a conversation.

"Ryder," I grind his name out through my shaking body, his electricity rolling through me, threatening my consciousness with black sparkles ebbing my vision.

His eyes flare wide, recognition and confusion churning. He drops me, and my feet hit the ground, my knees almost buckling, but I manage to stay upright.

"How do you know that name?" he demands. "Who told you!"

I flick my fingers. Ropes of sand ensnare his ankles, hauling him up and up into the air. I flip back to my feet, eying him as he dangles there, upside-down, his blue shirt drifting up to his neck, revealing his chest—

Scars.

There are *so* many scars. Enough to rival my own count.

The crowd hollers, screaming at me to finish him. To kill him.

He thrashes like a rabid animal, bolts of lightning shooting at me so fast I can barely dodge them all.

And from the cage next to me, the gray hound lays whimpering on the ground. Alive, but subdued. The black hound hangs its massive head as it limps toward the fence.

The handler on the other side comes out, dragging the gray dog behind the door—

And releases *six* more hounds. Each one snarls and barks at the black hound, who lifts its head high as it faces down the pack.

Six against one.

The injustice in it sets my blood on fire.

Like pitting me against a giant, against monsters. Like forcing anyone to fight at all. Forcing anyone to do something against their will at all.

I move without thinking, stepping into Ryder's space, holding his flailing hands with ropes of sand now, too. "So I'm totally sorry about this," I say, hoping like hell he believes me. "But I'm with your brother. And I *really* can't have you trying to kill me right now."

His thrashing stills at my words, and I cup my hand over his nose and mouth, filling it with smoke until his eyes roll back in his head.

"Again, wicked sorry," I say as his body goes pliant in my sand ropes.

A door that wasn't there a second ago opens to my left — this one a black so dark it looks solid.

The way out.

The way I'd *earned* by beating all my opponents.

I grab Ryder's arm, maneuvering my sand ropes to drape him over my shoulder and drag him toward the door.

A yelp and snarl echoes on the other side of the fence, and I freeze.

The hounds have descended upon the black one, nipping and biting, tearing and thrashing.

And yet the black dog still fights. Still manages to stay on its paws. It will not go down easily. Will not give the crowd what they want — a bloody massacre.

Before I can blink, I leave Ryder on the ground by the door. I make floating stairs out of sand, bounding up and up until I leap over the fence...

And land before a pack of wild hounds so large they look like lions.

Maybe this is the worst idea I've ever had.

Because the six hounds look at me like I'm the most delicious meal they've ever seen. They lick their chops, growling as they bound toward me —

And meet a wall of fire.

They yelp and draw back, scattering away from the fire, only to be met by another one. And another. Until I've trapped them inside a new cage.

The crowd cries its distaste, but the handlers don't come to stop me. Likely hoping the black hound will tear my throat out since I've left it uncontained.

I turn toward it, and it stands on steady paws, eyes level with mine. Terrifying and beautiful and tortured.

It doesn't growl when I approach it with an upturned hand. It sniffs my palm, once, twice.

I flick the wrist of my free hand, sandy steps manifesting at the silver fence.

"You coming?" I ask, jerking my head toward those sand stairs.

It doesn't need to be asked twice.

It bounds up the steps, its massive legs and paws propelling it easily up and over the fence until we're both on the sand before the open doorway.

I shove my shoulder under Ryder's arm again, hating how limp he is against me.

My fault. I did that. I hurt him. Hurt Draven's brother.

Not now. Later. I can crumble over everything later.

I keep clinging to that hope. To that notion that there is always time to completely break down another day.

The hound nudges me with its nose, and I whirl to see what it's looking at.

The demon in the apron is enraged, and the handler behind him. Both are rushing toward us.

"Let's go!"

The hound waits until I've taken the first step into the darkness, its teeth bared at the approaching demons as if it'll tear them apart before ever letting them get to us. But I reach back after getting Ryder halfway through the door and gently grip the hound's fur.

I tug, urging the beast to follow me.

The darkness swallows us up, the door slamming shut behind us as we clear it. My ears pop with the change in pressure, but at least the sounds of the crowd have dulled to a soft murmur.

The hound shifts against my free hand, and I lightly touch the coarse hair on its head. After a few tense strokes, the hound leans into my touch, a low rumble escaping its chest as my eyes adjust to see where the hell the door led us.

"Thanks for not tearing out my throat…" I whisper. "What do I call you?" The hound looks at me with those black eyes, too intelligent for a mere animal. I chew on my lip. "Nice to meet you…Wrath."

"Interesting friend of yours," a feminine voice says from somewhere in the room as it floods with light.

Wallace is sitting back in a black leather chair, one long leg crossed over the other, her brow arched in impressed respect. Beside her sits the apparent ruler of the Machis realm. Her skin is covered in slick, pink scales, her eyes a stark, solid lilac. A spiked tail drapes over one of the armrests.

It takes a lot to squash the urge to turn her to ash where she stands. I know nothing about her, but getting one taste of her fighting pits has left a bad fucking taste in my mouth. And the demon who dragged me there? He'd wanted *Ray* to go in.

My legs shake from the weight of the unconscious Ryder still draped over my shoulder. I glance behind me at the one-way glass wall that shows the fighting pit, now empty of everything but blood as the rowdy crowd above it files out. I whirl back around, eyes on the female demon sitting next to Wallace.

Yep. I still want to ash her.

"I told you she was tough," Wallace says, her voice all casual and easy, but her eyes are screaming about a dozen things— warnings?—at me.

What does she want me to do? Run? Fight? Grovel? I'm going to need a hell of a lot more information than whatever she's trying to give me.

"So, you're my new victor." The female demon tips her chin. "What prize do you claim? Choose wisely."

CHAPTER FORTY-SIX

Oh.

Well, crap. What am I supposed to choose? And how the hell did Wallace think I'd be able to figure that out without an actual discussion?

Wallace pushes out of her chair, confidently striding to me, but her expression is no less serious. She takes up Ryder's other arm, helping hold some of his weight.

Wrath growls low and steady at my side, black eyes on that swishing tail of hers.

"Sage," Wallace says, shifting beneath Ryder's weight. "I told you she's new to the Ather. She has no idea what she can claim."

Sage springs from her chair, and Wrath bounds in front of me. The female demon tilts her head, a wholly animal movement. "I've never seen an Ather-Hound behave like this," she muses.

"Maybe that's because you force them into pits to fight their own kind," I snap, and Wallace sighs. Clearly, I'm not following some Machis realm etiquette, but I'm so far past caring. I found Ryder, if by sheer luck, and even if he does want to kill me, I'm going to convince him to help me first.

"You're bold," Sage says, running her smooth fingers along her chin. "I could use a contender like you long-term. Interested? I'll pay you well."

I shake my head. "Not interested in being someone's puppet, thanks." I glance at Wallace. "What prizes can I ask for?" I whisper.

"I can hear you," Sage drones.

I roll my eyes. "Perfect. Then you can answer."

Wallace holds her breath as I stare Sage down.

"Whatever you wish," she says. "The rules of the pits are binding, even if you didn't read them before. A true victor can claim whatever prize they wish, though there hasn't been one for many cycles. Usually, contenders opt for power boosts or finer accommodations." She glides toward me, stopping only far enough away that Wrath can't reach her. "Some beings like their cages. They feel safer in them than facing what's out there." Her eyes fall to the unconscious Ryder, and my hackles raise.

"No one deserves to be trapped like that," I say, glancing to Wrath. "Animal *or* being."

Sage shrugs.

"I want Ryder's freedom," I say. "And Wrath's. I also want our safety guaranteed any time me or my...tribe travels through this realm."

Sage's tail twitches, but she says nothing as I list off the names of Draven, Cassiel, Ray, and Wallace.

"And I want you to stop using the hounds," I add for good measure. "Demons that volunteer for your pits are in full awareness of what they're signing up for. The animals have no choice."

A cackling laugh rips from Sage's lips, and Wrath tenses, his massive body urging me backward and away from her.

"Such a specific little bleeding heart." She shakes her head. "What a shame. You would've brought demons in from all the realms to watch you fight."

She flicks her fingers, sighing. "He's free to go," she says, eying Ryder. "But don't be surprised if he tries to run back to his cage. He's grown to love it, and he's quite known for always returning to his masters."

She glances at Wrath. "As for that one? Good riddance." She turns her back on us, padded feet soft against the floor. "I don't expect to see you here for a great many cycles, Wallace. You bring nothing but bad luck."

"One time I brought you a crate of smoke orbs," Wallace says, then urges me toward a door to our right. "But noted."

I nearly cry with relief when Draven and Cassiel and Ray are waiting just outside the door that leads to the building's market. Word must've spread, alerting them to what I'd done. The second we clear it, the door disappears into the wood completely as if it had never been there in the first place.

"Fuck," Cassiel whispers at the sight of Ryder, his silver eyes wide as he glances between him and Draven.

"Language," Ray chides the angel of death, who fastens her with a look that would've made grown men cower. But not Ray, she merely folds her arms over her chest until he blinks an apology at her.

"I can't believe it," Draven whispers. Almost all the color has leeched from his face, leaving a sickly, muted glow. He parts his lips like he's going to say more, but I groan under the weight of his brother. He blinks a few times, reaching for him then darting his hands back. "I can't — "

"I know," I say. *Of course* I know he can't touch his brother. I'm the one and only person immune to his siphon power, and even that is still a mystery as to *why*. More than likely some Antichrist loophole.

"Here," Cassiel says, offering his hands, but I shake my head.

"I've got him," I say. "I don't want you trying to fly with him and then he wakes up only to electrocute you."

"Would he?" Ray asks.

"Probably," I say. "And trust me, it hurts like a — " I cut myself off. "It hurts really bad," I amend before I curse again.

"Are you hurt?" my sister asks, and it's the first time I wonder what I look like.

"I'm fine — "

Her gasp cuts off my words as Wrath takes that moment to step from behind me.

"Don't worry," I say. "He's nice…" At least I *think* he's nice. He's very protective of me, which is obvious in the way he sniffs the air toward everyone as if he's smelling their intentions. "This is Wrath," I say to my friends. "He's coming with us. Wrath, these are my friends. My sister," I say, pointing to Ray. "They're important."

I turn back to my friends, who are all looking at me like I've grown another head. I mean, yeah, I'm talking to a giant hound that looks straight out of a horror movie like he can understand me, but from the way he dips his head? It's almost like he can. Stranger things have happened.

"What?" I ask when Draven's stare widens.

And then he laughs, a sharp sound that brings some of the color back into his cheeks. "Fucking hell, Harley," he says. "Only *you* would adopt a pet from Hell."

CHAPTER
FORTY-SEVEN

"Should we be worried that he's not waking up?" I ask an hour later, eyes firmly on Ryder's sleeping body. His breathing is even with the rise and fall of his chest as he lays, bound by thick ropes, in the third-row seating of Wallace's rig.

"How much smoke did you make him inhale?" Wallace asks from behind the wheel.

"I wasn't exactly using a measuring cup. He wouldn't stop electrocuting me."

Wallace snorts, but I glance at Draven across the seat. I've apologized about a dozen times, all of which he said were unnecessary.

"I would've killed him if I'd seen it," Draven whispers, his eyes distant as he stares down at his twin. "I would've siphoned off every ounce of power and life he has."

Cassiel whistles from the passenger seat while Ray says, "Draven, you can't do that to your *brother*."

"I know," he says, blinking out of his stare to reassure Ray with a soft smile. "I wouldn't have. I just can't stand your sister being hurt."

"Cassiel wouldn't let me come to you," Ray pouts, and the angel of death merely grunts.

"Good," I say. "You didn't need to see any of that." The ick of that place clings to my skin. And the realm we're heading toward? It'll be a thousand times worse. The truth of that thought sends exhaustion through my bones.

Ray crosses her arms over her chest. "You have to stop

treating me like a baby."

"You're not a baby," I say. "I wouldn't even want Draven seeing that, and he's like a thousand years old."

"I'm *so* not that old," Draven argues. "Cassiel, on the other hand—"

"Easy, brother," Cassiel warns. "You forget every time you've been awake, I have been, too. Want me to dredge up some stories—"

"Never mind," Draven says, but there is a lightness to his tone that hasn't been there since we loaded into the rig.

Wallace makes a sharp right, slowing to a stop in an area packed with tangled webs of blue trees, so thick it's hard to see through them. They hug a cropping of stone that kisses the sky.

"Why are you stopping?" I ask Wallace.

Wallace throws the rig in park, then turns around to look at us. Her eyes linger on Ryder, unconscious, in the back. "You sure he's going to agree to help you?"

"I'll convince him," I say. I told her this before. I'll do anything, make any bargain—

"He didn't seem like he was in an agreeable mood before," she says.

"Well, yeah, we were in a pit and he was trying to kill me—"

"And you knocked him out. You think he's going to wake up and say yes to whatever you ask?"

I rub my palms against my face. "It doesn't matter. I need his power. I'll find a way to convince him."

"He'll help us," Draven says. "I'll talk to him—"

"There had to have been at least a dozen demons in that market who wield the power you need," she says. "They tend to flock toward the fighting pits. With enough incentive, you can hire one to do the job. Better than taking your chances on someone who looked more than happy to kill you."

My heart stutters in my chest as I gape at Draven.

Waiting for him to argue.

To say she's mistaken.

He doesn't.

Cassiel sighs from the front seat.

"Draven?" I ask. "Is that true? Could we have hired someone and gone straight to Marid's?"

Something breaks in him because he finally looks at me. "Technically, yes, but—"

"Ohmigod," I say, shaking my head.

"His divine light is stronger than any other creature in *existence*," Draven counters. "I've seen it. I didn't want to risk hiring someone we don't know or trust only to have their power fail in the end."

A knot forms in my throat. We've wasted days. Days in which Marid could've been poking around in Ray's head, just waiting for an opportunity to torture her—and me—like he did after the sand ants. "You should have told me."

"Harley—"

I shake my head, holding back tears. "You *kept* it from me," I whisper. "Again. Even when you know me. You know I would've searched the entire Ather for your brother for as long as you wanted. After we save Ray—"

"I'm sorry," he says, and I know he means it. I can see it in his eyes, the way he believes no one else will be good enough to break the tether. I know he's regretting not telling me, not mentioning the other options, but after everything? I'm just too tired to care.

I swing open my door, hopping out of the rig. I need air. I need time to sort all this out.

Wallace kills the ignition, quietly climbing out.

"Wait," Draven begs as he rounds the rig, and normally I'd fall into that plea. I'd succumb and listen and talk it out. But I just can't right now, and the look I give him conveys as much.

Ray and Cassiel remain silent as they lean against the vehicle, my sister absently toying with one of his feathers, as if they're afraid if they say something it'll only add to the hurt filling the space. Wrath is at my side, his giant paws eating up the distance

I've put between me and my friends in an instant.

"*Harley,*" Draven tries again, this time in my mind. "*I messed up. I didn't think. And there's more—*"

I shut that space in my mind and seal it with mental dark flames that stop his voice from sounding in my head. I need space, and he needs to give it to me.

CHAPTER FORTY-EIGHT

W rath barely leaves my side, even when I'm pacing outside the rig. He follows me, step for step, always sticking to my left, those black eyes sharp and aware despite being the only ones this close to the archway.

There are no guards to this archway because it leads straight to a peaceful realm that hugs Marid's.

I've caught my breath, at least, and have cooled off slightly, but I still don't know what to say. Draven waits, silent and patient near Cassiel, who seems content to keep watching the still-passed-out Ryder through the rig's window.

What. A. Mess.

I catch Draven's gaze, open my mouth, then shut it. I think I've done this at least fourteen times in the past ten minutes.

"You two," Wallace says, and I jump at her sudden nearness.

"You've got to stop doing that," I say, catching my breath.

She laughs, nodding toward the tangle of trees behind us. "You two should go take a walk," she says, glancing behind her to where Ray is drawing in her sketchbook. "I've got her. We're going to chat art for as long as we can." She looks toward the rig, where Ryder lays sleeping. "And he was clearly overdue on his sleep. Go. Talk. Sort your shit out, because when you *do* get to Marid's realm?" Her eyes turn serious. "There won't be any time for that."

I glance at Ray, then back at Wallace, hesitant.

"I said I've got her. And we have the hulking death boy and scary Ather-Hound. We're safe, for now. We'll head to Conilis once you two have figured out what you want to do."

Right. Because I have to decide if I want to hire someone from this realm, someone with the power of lightning to charge our crystal, or I have to trust Draven's instincts that Ryder is the only one we need.

"Go."

I head toward the cover of the trees, knowing Draven will follow. A few seconds, and I can feel him behind me, that chain between us aching as if there is a weight on it.

Once I slip between a clearing in the branches, the leaves block out the light, leaving only the barest visibility. I snap my fingers, my silver and black flames illuminating a small pathway. We follow it, silent, the nerves tangling in my chest as we go farther away from our friends and their prying ears, until it's just the two of us.

"This place looks cozy," I say, noting a small cavern in the rock that the trees hug. "You think a beast lives in there?"

Draven closes his eyes for a moment, as if he's happy I'm at least speaking to him again. "It's empty," he says. "Which begs the question—is this where you finally kill me?"

CHAPTER FORTY-NINE

I can't help it. I *laugh*.

"Doubtful," I say. "Even when I want to strangle you for keeping things from me, I can never stay mad at you long enough." Even now, I can feel my anger ebbing. "You should've told me, though. You should have talked it out with me. You keep saying we're in this together, and then you don't let me see the full picture."

"I'm sorry," he says. "I truly am. There may be some other demon that has a similar power, Harley, but I *know* Ryder's. How strong it is. How pure. And I don't want to take risks with Ray's life."

As far as explanations go, it's a damn good one. There is so much to him that is good and supportive and makes me feel alive.

And he deserves to know all those things. Especially with all the things we have to face.

"I know," I say finally, the teasing gone. I swallow hard, my heart racing. You'd think this would be easy, talking to him, admitting things to him. I've faced demons with less fear, but here? In this private space with him, this stolen moment in time…I'm terrified.

Because this boy, this siphon, divine, tortured boy has somehow claimed every broken piece of my heart. And I've never let anyone have that power over me so thoroughly.

"But," I continue, my eyes cast down at the slick cave floor, because I simply can't look at him, "if we're going to…stay together, Draven, you have to start trusting me. You have to let me in. I know I don't have any experience with relationships, but you can't keep shutting me out. Even when you think you're protecting me. I think I've proven I can handle it."

"Of course you can handle it," he says, but I still can't look up at him. "I know that. But, Harley, you deserve *choice*. You deserve to discover things on your own and *then* make decisions instead of having things thrust upon you and you forced to make a rash decision."

I can't argue with that, and my heart swells at his words.

"Okay, fair enough." I kick some loose rock with my boot, finally drawing my gaze up to his. "But when two people are... dating," I nearly stumble over the word, "there should be some line of trust."

He grins. "Dating?" He laughs around the word, and my cheeks flare.

Oh God. Are we not dating? Is what we're doing—facing life and death obstacles and making out every chance we get—just a regular thing for him? Something in my chest curls in on itself, wilting like dying flower petals.

"I know we've never had the label talk," I say, miserably trying to recover. I shrug, as if to show that either way, it doesn't matter to me.

But it does.

It really, really does.

His fingers are warm and strong as he tips my chin up, making me meet that golden gaze of his. "Harley, if you want to say we're dating, then we're dating." His brow furrows. "But what you are to me is so much more than a girlfriend. That word simply doesn't encompass what we are...what I *feel* for you."

My breath catches at the declaration, at the intensity in his eyes.

"You are my match, Harley. In every way a person can be," he says. "But while I'm done pushing you away, I still know in my heart you deserve someone so much better than me. Someone who isn't a threat to your life. Someone who can't be Ordered to do such heinous things."

Tears bite the backs of my eyes, my heart breaking for how

little he thinks of himself.

"I make plans by myself because I'm not used to having anyone who cares enough to stand with me," he continues. "I keep things to myself because I've so often been betrayed. It's an automatic setting in my twisted soul, and I'm sorry. I've nearly killed you so many times, have hurt you, and have subjected you to the dark side of my world." He drops his hand from my chin, backs away. "If I were you, I wouldn't choose that life."

"Draven," I whisper his name. "You have done all those things, but you've also saved me so many times, and not just from outside threats. From myself. From my own mind."

I close the space between us, reaching for his hand and interlacing it with my own.

"You came into my life and woke me up. And we're in the Ather, about to willingly walk into Marid's realm and start a fight. One we aren't slated to win. And even knowing that, feeling that in my bones…" I lift his hand to the center of my chest, right over my racing heart. "I would still choose you."

Draven's eyes shudder closed.

"Even if you're activated by the Seven and Ordered to kill me, I'll still choose you. If you're shifting into the worst demon imaginable, I will still choose you," I continue, willing him to open his eyes and look at me. To see the truth right in front of him. "And even as we face the odds of horrible death, there is *no one* else I would choose to be by my side."

Draven opens his eyes, and they glimmer as he looks down at me.

"I choose you," I say again, because somehow those words hold more weight, more value than saying love. Because his whole life, he's only been chosen for what he can do, not who he *is*.

"Harley." He says my name, his hand slipping from my chest to cup my cheek as he leans his forehead against mine. "You are…" He stops, his other hand on my hip, drawing our bodies flush.

"Yours," I say when he hasn't finished, and he crushes his mouth on mine.

CHAPTER FIFTY

His tongue slides between my lips, and I open for him, relishing his taste, the way he slants his mouth over mine. There is nothing slow or easy about this kiss as he grips the back of my neck, tilting my head to stroke my mouth deeper.

A whimper escapes the back of my throat, and he moves to pull away, but I shake my head, kissing him harder, needing more. The hand on my hip grips me harder, yanking me against every strong angle of his body, and the move sends shocks of heat zipping up my body.

"*Harley*," Draven groans against my mouth, shuddering slightly when I nip at his bottom lip.

The hunger in the way he says my name has my heart racing, has my body going tight and loose at the same time. I pull back from our kiss and find his eyes glazed and churning as he looks down at me. And in that moment? There is nothing more I want than him.

Than this boy who has made me come alive in so many ways.

The one who has seen all my scars, seen my darkness, and never once turned away in fear.

My fingers tremble as I reach for the end of his shirt, and he raises his arms to help me slip it over his head. I toss it to the cave floor, never taking my eyes off of him. He's so damn beautiful, all golden skin over carved muscle. There are faint scars on his chest, his abdomen, evidence of the life he's lived when allowed to live it.

I run my fingers over a shiny bit of raised skin near his hip, the wound long-since healed, and he sighs under that touch. I smooth my other hand over his abdomen and up over that strong chest, enjoying the feel of his muscles reacting to my touch.

Then, slowly, not entirely sure I'm breathing, I reach for the band of his jeans.

"Fuck," Draven groans as I flip the button and plunge my hand in, gripping him. He moves then, walking us backward until his strong arms are on either side of my head, caging me against that cave wall. I squeeze him a bit harder, exploring, teasing, touching. Learning what makes that muscle in his jaw pop and what makes his hips pump toward me.

"Does this mean you forgive me?" he whispers.

"Maybe," I tease. "Kiss me," I say when he seems to be holding himself back. "Touch me, Draven."

His eyes are molten pools of gold. "If I start touching, Harley," he says, his voice low, raw, "I won't be able to *stop* touching you."

Something hot washes over me, anticipation curling low in my stomach.

"Then don't stop," I say, and his eyes flare.

Slowly, he shifts, until my hand slides out of his jeans, and his hands are snaking underneath me until he lifts me up to his eye level. I lock my ankles around his back and plant a teasing kiss on his lips.

Nose to nose, eye to eye, he draws back an inch. "Say it, Harley," he says, demanding.

"I choose you," I say, my arms wrapped around his neck. "And I know we don't have time, that we're selfish in taking this moment, but we never have time. And with what is to come?" I tangle my fingers in the hair at the base of his neck, squeezing my thighs around his waist. "I may never get another chance with you."

"Don't say that," he practically growls. He steals my breath with another kiss, then pulls back. "I'll make sure we have all the chances in the world. We don't have to—"

"Please, Draven," I beg, rocking against him, the motion sending all kinds of heat rippling over my body. "Unless you don't want to?"

He teases my lip with his teeth, and the slight bit of pain has me arching in his embrace. "I want you. Always," he says. "It hurts with how much I want you. You're my...*Harley*, you're my..." Something flashes in his eyes, something deep and more than I can understand.

But what I can understand?

He wants me.

He loves me.

And I choose him.

The rest? We can figure out as we go, as we've always done.

"Then I'm yours," I say, sealing those words with a kiss.

He holds me to him, meeting my kiss with a hunger of his own, and then we're spinning, and I'm falling backward.

I squeal and clench my eyes shut, bracing for the impact of the cave floor, but nothing but soft, wispy shadow meets my back.

I dart a look to the side, noting the thin layer of shadow holding us above the floor as Draven grins above me. His weight is a comforting, intoxicating thing between my legs, and he moves, shifting so he can reach for my shirt.

I don't hesitate as he slides it up and over my head, tossing it to join his. And then his fingers are at my pants, eyes glancing up from where he kneels there. I lift my hips, nodding, and the smile he gives me as he slides them over my legs? It's enough to make my heart stutter.

I put that there, that look on his face, one of such hunger and love and need.

Me.

His shadow is a soft, smoky caress against my now bare back, and my breath stalls as he slowly stalks up my body, planting a kiss over every single scar I have.

"Will this..." I can hardly speak from the feel of his breath on my skin, his lips and tongue teasing my scars. "Drain you?" I manage.

He draws up, shaking his head as he finishes what I started moments ago and rids himself of his jeans. "Not a chance," he says, and I can do nothing but marvel at him as he slides his boxer-briefs off, baring himself to me while I'm still covered in my underwear.

And I realize, looking at him, my mouth going dry at the gorgeous sight of him, that I don't want him to be the only one. So I move then, before he can reach to do it himself, giving him this piece of me. This part of myself I've never shared with anyone.

In seconds, I'm naked, my body delicately and almost lovingly supported by those soft shadows, the scent of him storming everything that I am.

Draven takes his time looking me over, those golden eyes of his glazed, and I swear I feel every look like a touch. "You're so beautiful," he says and leans over me, planting kisses over my collarbone, my breasts, and down my stomach.

I gasp as his strong, callused hand grips one of my thighs, his lips grazing there before he works his way back up, grinning down at me. The sight has me tangled and searching for breath that seems too fast in my lungs.

"Tell me again," he says, and the warmth of him washes over me.

"Yes," I say, unable to articulate everything we've already discussed.

"I need to hear it one more time," he says. "Need to know without a doubt you want this. You want *me*, Harley. Because if you say so, I'll stop right now. It's your choice, always your choice."

"Yes, Draven. I want this. I want you."

He settles himself between my thighs, and suddenly, a wave of apprehension washes over me. Not from anything he's done, but because I realize how little I really know about any of this.

"I…I don't know what to do," I admit, my cheeks flushing deeper with the truth. "I've never—"

"I haven't, either," he says and, well, obviously he hasn't. He can't, not without draining whoever he touches. But not me. And for one brief second, I wonder if that is what everything between us comes down to—him being able to touch me. A convenience. And I hate that voice of doubt in my head and slap the bitch away. I know my body, and I know my heart, and both belong to Draven in this instant.

"Together," I say, what is quickly becoming our mantra, despite the differences we've had, the struggles. Together, we can face anything. I reach up, cupping his face in my hands as I kiss him, as I put all the love and trust I possess into it.

"Tell me if I hurt you," he whispers, and I nod, sliding my hands to those strong, broad shoulders. And then he's moving, so slowly, so gently.

I gasp at the unfamiliar tightness. He pauses, waiting, his eyes watching my every reaction as I adjust to this newness.

After a few moments, that pain turns to heat. A building, consuming heat that rivals my flames as it crashes over me in waves. My grip on his shoulders loosens, and I give over to pure instinct as I start to move.

"Harley," he whispers, his muscles flexed and tight as he holds himself so damn still. He plants kisses over my neck, my jawline, as I explore the sensations, as I seek out what makes him groan, what makes me dizzy.

"Move, Draven," I practically demand. Now is not the time for gentle or those eyes filled with concern over hurting me.

The command in my voice has him arching an eyebrow, a purely mischievous smirk shaping his lips. The shadows at my back curl around my shoulder, gently tugging my hair so that my chin tips up, and he slants his mouth over mine at that angle at the same time he moves his hips—

I gasp between his lips, the sensation unraveling everything. My powers glitter inside me, threatening to burst from my skin with how much he makes me burn.

"Easy," he warns as he moves above me. "If you turn me to ash, I'll never be able to do this to you again."

My heart is in my throat, my mind a spiraling thing I can't possibly catch. "You're strong enough to take my flames."

"God, I love you," he groans, and his lips crash into mine.

"I love you," I manage to gasp between kisses. I cling to him, my fingers digging into his back as he increases his pace. Longer, deeper strokes that has every thought emptying from my head. There's nothing but the way he feels moving inside me. I arch into the sensation, chasing some tight, coiled thing inside me.

I've seen everything that he is—darkness and all—and still chose him.

Whatever leash he's had on himself comes undone, and even his shadows grip me tighter as he loses himself in me and me in him. He takes me to an edge I've never experienced, an entirely new cliff to fall over.

He kisses me, as if he can devour the sounds coming from my mouth with each stroke of his body against mine. The shadows around us swirl.

That chain of connection between us goes taut, so much so that I'm afraid it will snap.

But it burns in the most delicious way, and the taste of him, the feel of him, has my body unraveling until there is no part of me that doesn't belong to him.

CHAPTER FIFTY-ONE

"So, you're not going to kill me, then," Draven teases as we start slipping back into our clothes.

"You didn't seem to mind when I held a dagger to your throat," I fire back.

"As long as you're the one holding the knife," he says, taking one careful step toward me, "I'll die a happy man."

I laugh. "Okay, but are you *sure* that didn't drain you?" The absolute last thing we need going into these final realms is Draven not at his strongest.

My skin is still flushed, my heart still trying to make room for everything that just happened between us.

Draven finishes sliding his shirt over his head, adjusting it as he walks over to me. There is something lighter in his steps, in his eyes, than I've ever seen before, as if a weight has been lifted from his shoulders.

He gently grips my chin, softly kissing me again before smiling down at me. "You know it didn't," he says, releasing me to finish putting on my boots. "In fact, I think you might be the answer to charging my powers. I feel stronger than I ever have before."

I laugh, but I know what he means. I feel as refreshed as if I had a full, peaceful night's sleep. And that definitely isn't what we just did.

"What now?" I ask when we're both dressed.

He cocks a brow at me, that one look telling me exactly what he'd like to do now. Again.

And I can't blame him. I didn't want to stop. Didn't want it to end. If things were different, I could stay here forever, exploring him, loving him, but…

Marid.

His brother.

Ray.

Draven pushes off the wall and closes the distance between us. "With where we're going, with what could happen…" His voice trails off, and all his confident teasing leaves his eyes, replaced with something close to agony. "I have to tell you—"

"Draven!" A menacing call sounds outside of the cave, beyond the trees.

My eyes widen, and in seconds, we're both sprinting out of the cave.

Because we know that voice.

Ryder.

He's awake, and he doesn't sound happy about it at all.

CHAPTER FIFTY-TWO

I clear the trees moments after Draven, skidding to a halt as he's shifting from his shadow form back to himself in front of the rig.

Flames burst over my hands as I stop at his side.

"Ah, ah," Ryder says, his turquoise eyes on me as he points behind him.

To where Cassiel is bound by that crackling white electricity, on his knees as he struggles against it. Wrath, too, with the same light keeping him subdued. Ray and Wallace are tied back-to-back with the rope we secured Ryder with before we left.

"Let them go," I demand, my dark flames writhing up my forearms.

"You found yourself a *murderous* little girlfriend, brother," Ryder says, eyes on Draven.

"Ryder, wait—"

Draven goes rigid, then falls, his knees cracking against the ground, blue-white sparks dancing over his body.

"Stop!" I shout, moving toward him.

Every muscle in my body clenches as Ryder's power hits me. I drop like a bag of bricks, convulsing as he amps that power up. My heart slams against my chest, an erratic beat begging me to stop the pain. Fire and earth churn in my blood, writhing against the white-hot lightning shaking my body. Bursts of the ground shoots up in random places, my flames flying this way and that, never landing where they need to. Never coming close to Ryder as he continues to hit us with that power.

"Stop!" Ray begs from where she and Wallace are tied.

But he doesn't, merely walking over to Draven, glaring down at him, his eyes distant as if he's seeing something else. As if he's not entirely sure where he is or if it's real.

Draven manages to move, to shift into a darkness that swarms Ryder. Their powers clash in an intense shadow of light.

But the electricity stops, the blue-white light extinguishing.

Ryder groans, dropping to his knees in a heap as Draven shifts back into his normal form.

The pain slowly ebbs from my body, my flames washing over every internal inch to revive my muscles until I can stand again.

Cassiel is on his feet, instantly untying Wallace and Ray.

Wrath bounds to my side in a heartbeat.

"Dick," Ryder groans, rolling to prop himself up against the rig.

"You started it," Draven fires back.

I gape between them before looking to where Wallace is rubbing at her wrists. "He got us before we even knew he was up," she says, breathless. "I couldn't leap with the risk that he'd attack me and hit Ray. I'm sorry."

Cassiel looses a low, menacing growl.

I wave them both off, putting the blame where it belongs. Ryder.

Or me. I'm the one who left to go…be with Draven. Hello, guilt, thanks for staying gone for thirty whole minutes.

Wrath pads over to the rig, stopping only an inch away from Ryder's face.

"Wrath," I say softly, hugging Ray as she comes to my side. "If he tries to electrocute us again, bite him but don't kill him."

Draven whirls on me, but I merely shrug, releasing Ray and lowering to a crouch in front of Ryder. I hold his gaze, raising my brows. "Are you ready to listen to me now?"

A slow, jagged smile shapes Ryder's lips as he raises his hands in innocence. "I've been listening this whole time," he says and then laughs as he glances at Draven. "You sure know how to pick them, brother. Isn't there some kind of saying for what's going on here?" Those eyes twinkle with arrogance. "Oh, right, love is a poison. Love will get you killed. Because that's all that will happen if you follow her into Marid's realm. *Death.* It's a promise the second you step foot in that place—"

"*You* managed to escape," I point out. "*You* survived."

"Who says?" Ryder tilts his head, the look half predator, half prey.

Anything else I might've said dies in my throat.

"Ryder," Draven says, his voice low and calm. "We need your help."

"Oh, *now* you need my help, brother?" He glares at him. "You were fine without me for so long, but the second you need something, you decide to come looking?"

"He's been trying to get you back since you were taken," I snap. "Are you not happy to see him at all?"

Ryder visibly swallows, glancing at Draven. "I've been down here for…" He blinks, like he suddenly can't remember.

"A century," I offer softly.

He huffs. "A century in *your* time," he says, but his tone has lowered. "Not here. Time moves differently here."

"And I can't imagine what you've been through," I offer, focusing only on him. Not on Draven, jaw hard at my side. Not on Wrath, watchful and wound tight like a spring. Not on Ray's breathing, which is erratic, or the feel of Cassiel's wings moving behind me. Wallace is stone silent, but I let all that fade as if it's just the two of us. "What you've suffered, no one deserves."

Ryder looks at me a long moment, really looks. "Let me go back to my realm."

I gape at him. "Your realm? Machis? Where you, what—live each day to fight and kill?"

He scoffs, but not before I see the crack in his facade. "Live," he says. "I live there. Because that sure as hell wasn't what I was doing when trapped with Marid. At least in Machis, the pain lets me know I'm awake. I'm real. I'm *alive.*"

My heart breaks at his words, at the way my soul flinches with understanding. The fearful look he's trying to hide in those deep eyes shouts volumes about what he's endured. Torture, likely mental and physical, knowing Marid. Who knows what he saw while there? Who knows what he suffered?

"No one deserves to live in a cage," I say. "And we've all got pain. We've all got history. So don't pretend like you're the most damaged one here. We're all in line for that prize, Ryder."

He laughs, but this time it isn't so malicious.

Draven edges closer. "How did you escape?"

The laughter dies on his lips. "I didn't," he says. "Marid gave me to Sage as a pet. She pulls me out to use me when she's bored."

Acid burns my chest. *Gave* him. Like he was a piece of fucking property.

"And you want to go back to that life?"

He shrugs.

"Ryder," Draven tries again. "Whatever differences are between us, whatever you think I have or haven't been doing, I'm here to make a bargain with you."

"You have nothing I want," he fires back. "And if you think letting your murderous little girlfriend drag me back to the one place I hate—"

"I'm not dragging you anywhere," I say. "You're a *person*, Ryder. You have choices. I thought I was handing you choices when I asked for your freedom from the pits. It's up to *you* what you decide to do. You can go back to the pits and be someone's puppet, you can sit here and rot, or you can help us—help *me*—and take part in vengeance well deserved. As you heard, he's possessed my sister. You saw what I did to you when you threatened *me*." I flash him a smirk and climb to my feet. "I was holding back because of who you are. *Imagine* what I'll do to Marid."

"Brother," Draven says, and my heart breaks for the sadness in his tone. So different from moments ago. He points to Ray standing behind me with Wallace and Cassiel. "Marid has taken possession of Ray. She's an innocent."

Ryder flinches, eyes darting from Ray to Draven.

"You know how rare that is," Draven continues. "We need you.

We can't break this tether without you. Your light is the only thing that can charge the crystal."

Ryder shakes his head. "After all this time, you show up and expect me to be the hero?"

"I expect you to be my brother," Draven says, almost too quietly for the rest of us to hear. "I haven't stopped trying to get to you since you were taken, Ryder. But the Seven, they put me in sleep so many times, the gatekeeper rejected me at every chance, and then I couldn't find the key."

A cold shiver races over my skin as Ryder studies Draven, the silence between them stretching tight.

There has to be some of the brother Draven remembers in there, right? The twin who loved his brother so much they were even called to be Judges together. They were inseparable, until they weren't.

Draven remains silent, his eyes going internal in the way I've seen too many times recently. So much brewing in his mind, so much turmoil. I want to help him, to soothe his worries, but what can I say?

"Maybe we should find someone else," Wallace says. "Take him back—"

"I will not be a prisoner again," Ryder snaps.

"And Sage was what?" I ask. "Your chosen partner?"

He slams his lips shut.

"What's it going to be, Ryder?" I ask, offering him a hand, an olive branch. "Wallace is guiding us through one more realm before we're on our own."

"Conilis," Wallace says.

Ryder glares at Wallace. "You're not going with them to the Isle?"

She shakes her head. "I made a vow a long time ago to never travel to the lowest realms. It's how I've survived this long."

There's that sinking feeling in my stomach again, but I toss it to the side.

"Do you want to come with and help us? Join with your *brother* while we finish Marid once and for all?" I ask. "If you accept this deal, I'll owe you. A favor from me is apparently worth a lot. Even an ancient sorcerer leaped at the opportunity to make a bargain with me."

Ryder considers that for a moment.

"You really think you can stop him? End him?" he finally asks, studying me, my open hand before him.

"Yes," I say, and I hope like hell it's believable. Because deep down, I know the odds. I know who we're going up against. But it's my little sister's life at stake, so the odds can fuck right off.

Ryder must read the determination in my eyes because he slides his hand into mine. His skin is rough with calluses but free of electricity as he pulls himself to stand. He's as tall as Draven and bearing a whole hell of a lot more scars beneath the bloody shirt he wears.

"It's not like I have a choice, do I?"

I can't tell if he says it because it's a child at risk, if it's because he thinks I'll force him to do it, or if he just doesn't want to look too agreeable, but I keep my mouth shut.

"You know the right choice to make," Draven says, giving his brother a look I've never seen before, an old look, one likely harkening back to some memory between them.

"Fine," Ryder relents. "I'll help you. But I want your word, when I ask you for something, you deliver. If you don't?" He glances to Draven, then Wrath at my side, and my sister behind me. "I'll ruin you all."

CHAPTER FIFTY-THREE

"How much farther?"

"Seriously?" Wallace asks Draven from the driver's seat. "We're going to play the *are-we-there-yet* game?"

"Time *is* of the essence," Draven fires back. "If we're speaking in clichés."

Wallace snorts, tossing some of her locks over her shoulder.

Draven eyes me from across the backseat, and I tremble from the memory of his mouth on mine, his shadows on my bare back, the way he filled me so completely.

So not what I should be thinking about right now.

The road we're on cuts between mountains of stones, some bigger than skyscrapers, the masses only separated sparsely by little camps of dozens of black structures that look like tiny, minimalist homes. The demons in this realm all wear a similar canvas fabric jumpsuit, regardless if they have six legs or two, tails or wings, and every single one of them is covered from head to foot in gray dust. It clings to feathers or fur or scales as some push large iron carts packed to the brim with the rocks, others drive monstrous-looking vehicles, toting enormous amounts of the stones beyond where I can see.

"What's this realm called again?" I ask, my eyes snagging on the endless piles of gray rocks that create hills bigger than skyscrapers.

"Conilis," she answers, her voice dropping all teasing from moments before.

"They better have food," Ryder grumbles from the passenger

seat. Cassiel elected to sit in the very back with Wrath, Draven wanting to be able to keep both eyes on his brother by sitting directly behind him.

Ryder hasn't said much since we piled into the rig and headed through the archway. Hopefully, that's a good thing. He agreed to help us, anyway, though I'm still not sure if it was because of Ray, Draven, or my threats. But hey, it's something. With this being the realm that hugs Marid's, we're so close to finishing this.

Ray gasps as we round the sharp turn, the piles upon piles of rocks giving way to a wide, mountainous expanse dripping in tones of gray and silver. The highest peaks seem to touch the periwinkle sky, their craggy crests stark against the pastel color. Evenly spaced plumes of dark smoke are rising in columns at the farthest mountain base. From our raised position on the road, we can easily see thousands upon thousands of tiny structures scattered about the valleys between the mountains, each one separated by piles of the same rocks we saw on our way in.

"Where are they taking all these stones?" Ray asks as Wallace navigates us around several semi-sized trucks hauling the rocks toward where the smoke churns.

"To the transforming stations," she answers, and I note the way her throat bobs up and down as she swallows.

"To do what?" Ray asks, all pure, innocent curiosity.

"The primary commodity in the Conilis realm is *Colis*," Wallace says.

Ray's confused blue eyes meet Wallace's as she glances in the rearview mirror, and the guide's gaze softens.

"You know how you have silicon above? How when it's properly treated it can be used to help build your electronics, your cars?"

When Ray and I do nothing but blink at her, Wallace spares a look over her shoulder. "Seriously?" she asks, returning her focus to the road. "What *are* they teaching you in those schools they force you to go to?"

"Math," Ray answers sweetly. "Reading."

Wallace huffs. "Okay, well, quick lesson—"

"God, why didn't you just let the murderous girl kill me?" Ryder groans.

Wallace ignores him. "Silicon is one of the earth's...*your* world's most powerful and lucrative commodities. It's an element that can be broken down and transformed to do so many incredible things."

"Like electronics and cars," Ray says, ever the good student. I smile down at her.

"Exactly," Wallace says, then frees one hand from the wheel to point at the piles upon piles of the stones around us. "Colis has the exact same properties as silicon, but it's about a thousand times more powerful. Not only that, because it originates in the Ather, it's susceptible to magic, meaning it can absorb it if directed to."

Something sinks into the pit of my stomach as I eye the demons we pass—covered in grime, the uniforms, the way they look haggard from the work. If Colis is such a valuable commodity, capable of magic and power far beyond what Earth has, then why isn't this realm flourishing?

Ray must be thinking the same thing, because she asks, "Why aren't they using it to power this place? I don't see any electricity anywhere."

The rocky pathways smooth out to flatlands, the sides of the pathways bordered by royal blue trees, the same ones that have sheltered us in the pockets between realms.

"For endless cycles, Conilis was the wealthiest and most peaceful realm in the Ather. But that was before Marid and the rest of the Twelve took over. Each realm has to pay their dues, some more than others according to whatever bullshit rule they spout. They claim they're charging realms for the right to continue working and living unbothered, but we all know it comes down to power."

Wallace slows the Easkr to a stop, near the largest gathering of small homes, all hugging an expanse of what I can only describe as farmland spanning and bordering the base of the mountains.

Stone fences house creatures that look like bulls crossed with jungle cats, and birds the size of dogs that peck the ground with their neon-green beaks. Rows and rows of crops sit behind the homes—stalks of red plants that look similar to wheat sprouting out of the blackest soil I've ever seen. Variations of the plants stretch as far as I can see, ranging in color and size.

Huh. Apparently there actually *are* farms in the Ather.

Robed figures move gracefully around the crops and along the structures, younglings darting in and out wearing the jumpsuits we'd seen before. Several wave, not at all bothered by our sudden appearance.

Wallace hops out of the rig and doesn't bother reaching for any of the blasters or weapons in the back. Instead, she grabs four large duffle bags, tossing one to me, Cassiel, and Draven as we round the rig to meet her. Wrath sticks close to Ryder, who doesn't offer to carry anything. Naturally.

"It's beautiful," Draven says, his eyes taking in every detail from where we stand.

I can't help but agree. Far to our left, on the opposite side of the towering mountains under the soft periwinkle sky rests a rushing river of bright pink, contrasting against the obsidian soil that hugs it.

"Are they forced to grow food for the other realms, too?" I ask.

Wallace shakes her head. "They learned to get what they could from the land because food became so scarce after their resources were strained." She sighs. "Over seventy percent of their product is taken as payment for their supposed protection."

She motions to a road in the distance, where I can just barely make out an archway on the edge of the horizon. Giant trucks haul thousands of wooden crates toward it, looking like insects they're so far away.

Ray reaches for Wallace's hand. "Could they fight back?"

"Sure. But at the cost of more than half their lives. These people are peaceful, not warriors, and even a dozen combined don't have power to match Marid's or his Twelve."

Something white hot blisters beneath my skin. "He can demand that kind of payment? Is he really that powerful?"

Ryder scoffs, folding his arms over his chest. "This coming from the girl who's ready to spit in his face?"

Wallace spares a glance to Ryder, then back to me. "You know how powerful he is."

"And the king? He can't stop it, either?" Is this Rainier guy such a sadistic asshole that he'd let his people suffer?

Wallace purses her lips. "I told you, legend says he's as trapped as any of us." She spins on her heel, and Draven flashes me a confused glance before we follow her through the camp.

Each home is alike, simple and only big enough for one or two demons, but some spaces have crammed four or more inside. Several demons cluster around small fires, stirring something in pots hoisted above the crackling flames, a spicy aroma that reminds me of the three-day chili Nathan would make at the first snap of winter.

A pang of longing hits me dead center in the chest.

The demons note our presence but don't attack or question, merely dip their heads in a peaceful, friendly greeting. Ray smiles and waves at each of them as we walk by.

"Wallace?" a feminine voice calls as Wallace leads us into the center of the main section. Wallace bows, then rushes to hug the creature who spoke.

The demon wears the same jumpsuit most of them wear, her purple skin streaked with gray dust. Her eyes are a stunning shade of pink with lightning bolts of blue shooting from the center pupil. There are two of them, but they are three times wider than a human's, the gorgeous orbs tilting toward her nose. Her long hair, the color of sapphires, is fashioned in locks with similar adornments to the ones Wallace wears. Her fingers are long and tapered and end in claws that she wipes on a strip of dirty cloth. Behind her, three demons in robes of blue that cover every inch of their bodies, their hoods hiked up so high I can only see a sliver of their faces, shuffle to and from the place. Their rich, smooth, hunter-green skin reminds me of Gareth's.

"What brings you to Conilis?" the female asks, releasing Wallace from their embrace.

"Business," Wallace answers, then nods to us patiently waiting behind her. "Figured I'd drop off some supplies while I'm here." She sets the duffle bag on a long wooden table to the left, and Cassiel, Draven, and I follow suit.

"This is too much," the female says, her pink eyes widening as Wallace unzips each bag.

"It's not enough," Wallace says. "But you know I would've brought more if I could have."

"Your generosity knows no depths." The demon dips her head to Wallace, then makes a soft chittering noise. Three of the robed individuals glide toward the bags, their movements silent. The female finally takes notice of us standing behind Wallace. "Who are your friends?"

"Clients," Wallace corrects but introduces us, saving me for last.

"Harley," the demon says, dragging out my name as she sways up to me. Her movements are fluid and graceful, as if she came from a world of water, not one of stone and dust and crops. "You smell..." She inhales deeply.

Oh, great, this again. How many demons have pointed out that I smell differently to them? Was she about to sink those claws into my throat? I shift into a defensive stance. Regardless of Wallace saying they're a peaceful realm, I have no real proof of that.

"Familiar," she finally finishes, and my tense muscles loosen a fraction.

"Familiar," I repeat. "That's a lot better than what I thought you'd say."

"What did you think I'd say?"

"That I smelled like dinner."

A tinkling laugh flies from her lips, and she whirls, grinning at the robed figures now sorting through Wallace's supplies—food and medicine and fabric from the looks of it. The robed figures don't join her laughter, instead remaining quiet but smiling at her all the same.

"Apologies," she says, reeling it in. "But you would taste awful."

That earns a laugh from Wallace and Ray, but Draven whispers into my mind, *"Speak for yourself."*

A warm shiver glides over my skin at his words, at the tease in them, and I relax even more. I tell myself it's okay since this is the last moment of peace we see before we go to Marid's realm.

"My name is Delta," the demon says to our group. "You will stay for dinner, yes?" More a demand than a request.

Wallace looks to me. "Do we have time? I'd like to help them distribute the supplies and check their stock to see what I can bring next time."

"Yes. Please, food," Ryder pipes up from where he stands with Wrath on one side of him, Cassiel on the other, both watching him like a hawk.

I glance at Draven. His eyes are as conflicted as I imagine mine are.

I know we should move on. I know we shouldn't waste a second of our time, but for reasons I can't explain, I *want* to stay here. Something about this place, these beings, seems...familiar, like Delta had said about me. Lusro felt similar, and even when I lingered outside in Zion's line, something about the Ather called to me. A curiosity I can't quell; I want to know more, see more, experience more. And yet I know Marid's realm won't offer any warm fuzzies. Maybe it's just the exhaustion from the fighting pits, what Draven and I did, and the fight with Ryder after, or maybe it's just fear, plain and simple.

Fear of what is to come and if I'll be able to survive it.

And the fact that Draven somehow understands that, or gleans that from my eyes...well, it makes me want to shout *I love you* all over again.

Instead, I find myself nodding. "We'd be honored," I say, then glance to Wallace. "Show us how we can help."

CHAPTER
FIFTY-FOUR

I lose track of time, my mind fully abandoning all thoughts other than the tasks Delta and her tribe hand down to me. Sorting supplies into small, chipped wooden crates, then distributing those supplies throughout the village. Ray meets a demon youngling, the two instantly best friends, as is Ray's way. They chatter on each trip we take down the smooth pathways.

Each family is more in need than the next, despite the community farms ensuring they all stay fed. Bitterness takes up residence in my chest with each malnourished youngling I see, each grown demon whose dirty gray jumpsuit hangs off its bones.

"It's hard, isn't it?" Wallace asks me when we've returned to Delta's home. "Seeing what those in power do to those without it, just because they can." She sighs. "Marid and the Twelve have so much power they could help each realm thrive, help the Ather grow into something to marvel at. A place to be proud to be born in."

"I see it on earth, too, though not this close. So many people are suffering, but when they reach out for help, the wealthy look at them like they're garbage. Less than. Even if they have enough money to feed someone for an entire year, they'd rather spend their fortunes on yachts and trips around the world."

Not that people didn't deserve to do those kinds of things, but shouldn't there be a balance of help for those who needed it and fun for those that can afford it?

Delta and her robed guests will be back any moment from their own supply runs. Draven and Cassiel and Ryder are helping a group of elder demons mend some damaged homes across the way, and Ray and her new friend chatter endlessly just outside. I'm surprised at Ryder's willingness to help, but he assures everyone that there isn't much he won't do for food.

If I'd known that, maybe I could've convinced him to help us with a simple meal, but I guess him calling in his bargain whenever he wants will have to do.

"Will you hate me even more if I say I'm surprised how much this all bothers me?" I ask, not really sure why I care what Wallace thinks. But I do. After everything we've been through so far on this journey through the Ather…I do.

"I don't hate you, Firestarter," she says. "I don't like you all that much, but I don't hate you. Why are you surprised by this place not being easy for you to see?"

I sink onto one of the hard benches near the table. "When Kazuki told me what I needed to do to break the tether between Ray and Marid…where we had to go…" I run my fingers over the hard wooden table, dropping my eyes to trace the grooves. "I imagined everything I've ever learned or heard about Hell."

"You rang, dark princess?" Kazuki's voice shocks me like a bucket of cold water over my head.

Damn it. Why did I say his name out loud?

"No, I didn't."

"Could've sworn I heard my name," he says.

"You did. But I don't need you right now. Thank you for showing up, though." I guess. I mean, what if I *had* needed his help? At least he's consistent.

"Where are you?"

"The Conilis," I say. *"We found Ryder. He's being…almost agreeable."*

"You've been busy," he says.

"You have no idea." Or does he? I didn't think this bargain acted as a constantly open door between us, more like a walkie-talkie with really great range. When I pushed the right button, he showed up.

"You're close to finishing this. I'll start thinking on that favor I'm owed."

"Thanks for the encouragement." He thinks we'll survive, which is a nice comfort from someone as powerful as him.

"Anytime," he says. *"Say hello to Delta for me."*

I feel his retreat, and I blink a few times as I come back to the present.

"And she's back," Wallace says, throwing a leg over the other end of the bench, eyes on me. "You know your eyes turn lavender when you're talking to the sorcerer with the weird little mind trick?"

I raise my brows. I had no idea.

"Anyway, back to *our* conversation before I was so rudely interrupted," she teases. "You pictured fire and brimstone, right? Malicious entities clawing at each other?"

"Monsters," I say. "I pictured a place full of things like Marid. But...the *sorcerer*," I say instead of saying his name out loud again, "and Anka told me that wasn't the case. Told me there were good places here, it's just...it's hard to shake what books and movies shoved into my head. Plus, all the things that have tried to kill me in the last few weeks."

Wallace whistles. "I suppose if the only experience I ever had with beings from the Ather were the ones trying to kill me, I might think that, too."

"But it wasn't," I say, not letting her give me any slack. "I knew Anka, even though I only recently learned what she truly was. And she's never once tried to harm me. She made me stronger." I shake my head, laying my palm flat on the table. "I saw demons at The Bridge, carefree and laughing and enjoying themselves. Sure, I met some who wanted to kill me there, too, but it wasn't all of them."

"And now?" she asks when I've grown quiet. "What do you think of the Ather now?"

"It's not Hell," I say with a shrug.

"There are malicious realms," Wallace hedges. "You've seen a glimpse of them. And where you're going is worse. You will see *beyond* what you imagined first."

"But you've shown me there is no black and white to this world," I argue, waving a hand toward the entrance. "This place? These beings? The Lusro realm and their people? Your home in Kypsel? How many more like those are in the Ather?"

"Many," Wallace says, her shoulders sinking. "Too many to keep fed, to keep healthy. Not when the larger, deeper realms are doing everything they can to squeeze all the worth out of them. Not every realm is as lucky with their land as they are here. At least Conilis can grow food, though even that isn't enough."

Dark flames flicker on my fingertips. I know that helpless feeling all too well. Know what it was like to merely *survive*. It's no way to live. But what can I do? Do I have any real power here? In a world full of incredible beings with just as incredible powers, does me being the Antichrist mean I have *any* pull? Enough to change things?

Something shifts in Wallace's eyes, an emotion I've never seen before and can't place. She blinks, drawing up her usual confident exterior to cover it. "We have legends, too, you know," she says. "Legends that the Ather was once peaceful, each realm working in unison to better the Ather as a whole."

"Then what happened?"

"The Fracture happened," Delta's smooth voice cuts in from the entryway.

"The Fracture?" I ask.

Her wide pink eyes close as she dips her head. "Come," she says. "We will sit and drink, and I will tell you the story of how our world was ripped apart."

CHAPTER
FIFTY-FIVE

We follow Delta outside, and I skid to a halt so fast at what's waiting for us that Wallace stumbles into my back. "Walk much?" she whispers behind me, giving me a not-so-gentle nudge...and stops in her tracks. "Holy shit."

A crowd has gathered around a large sitting circle that's been constructed of fallen blue logs. Ray and her new friend already perch on one, and to my utter shock, *Ryder* is next to them.

In fact, a whole group of younglings has gathered around Ryder, laughing as he makes little animals out of electricity dance before them.

Cassiel stands like a sentinel near Ryder, who quickly stops the animal show when he sees Wallace and me gaping at him.

Draven, who sits on the other side of the group of younglings, raises his shoulders, flashing me a crooked grin.

I weave my way over to him, trying like hell not to notice how every being's eyes are on me, despite Delta walking ahead of us. I sink next to Draven, and he smooths his hand over my thigh, helping ease some of the nervous energy bubbling through me. There are at least a hundred demons here and more funneling in. They fill in the empty spaces left on the surrounding logs, the ones closest to us giving me the widest berth, and the rest elect to stand in waves behind them, all quiet and waiting as if this was a planned event.

"I may have spread the word that you came to visit us today, Harley," Delta explains, likely noting my confused-as-hell look.

I try to smooth my features. "Me, but why—"

"It's not every cycle we are honored with visitors," she says, her eyes on Draven for a moment before looking to Wallace, who has plopped down on my left. "Any friends of Wallace, especially those that bring gifts, are honored guests for my tribe." She lays her hand over the middle of her chest, her smooth purple skin now cleared of the gray dust that clings to so many of her kind surrounding us. "Though word of your arrival in the Ather had already spread, Harley, even here. There are stories of a girl with dark flames silencing those who seek only to harm."

My cheeks flush as too many eyes look to me, whispers of *drakels* and *sand ants* murmuring through the crowd.

I try my best to think of something to say, anything that would match the kindness she's shown, but apparently, I left my ability to speak back in Delta's.

"And it would be our honor," she continues, sparing me from making an absolute fool of myself, "to share the tale of the Fracture with you and *your* tribe."

The word *tribe* clangs through me, my eyes darting to each of my friends. And yes, I consider Wallace a friend, despite us arguing at every turn. Because she's gotten us this far and managed to teach me a few things along the way. Ryder I'm not even remotely sure about yet, but he *is* Draven's brother. So that makes him important to me, despite his constant state of snark. Cassiel, Draven, and Ray are a given.

Maybe we really are a tribe of our own.

"The Ather, in the beginning, was created before the Earth realm," Delta begins. "Millenia ago, we were a peaceful place, filled with numerous cultures and creatures and ways of life, yet we all worked together. As it goes, greed and malice slipped into our utopia, spreading like a disease until even our savior was betrayed. The one being who protected us from the dangers no longer could, and the Ather was ravaged by evil."

Chills burst along my skin, and Draven slides an arm around me, tucking me into his warmth.

"So the Creator decided to make a much larger realm, one

that would be opposite of the Ather, and saw fit to fold our worlds together. We existed not collectively, but next to each other. Where they had shades of greens and yellows, we had tones of purples and blues. Where they had no magic, we had endless wells of it. Where they had countries and states, we had realms. Our similarities lay in the types of people we had—both good and bad and all those in between, as all worlds do. But for the majority, our worlds worked similarly—each of us a community of beings trying to better our individual worlds as a whole."

The periwinkle sky faded to a deep lilac while she spoke. She gestures to a pile of logs surrounded by stones in the center of our circle.

"Harley," she says. "Would you do us the honor of igniting these?"

I swallow hard. Aiming my fingers toward the pile, I send gentle flames swirling around the logs until they catch. They flicker cheerfully, earning a gasp and a few mutters from the crowd.

Delta smiles. "There were barriers," she continues, "even in the beginning, between our world and the Earth realm, but not like there are now. Beings from either world were once allowed to cross into the other, with passes and proof of no ill intent."

I can't even imagine this. The demons I've run into on Earth were the definition of "ill intent." I glance at Draven, but he seems as surprised by the story as I am. Ryder, on the other hand, clenches his hands into fists that rest on his knees. There is recognition in his eyes, and pain.

"But there were those who became jealous of our magic," she says, her features growing grave, the dark flames casting an eerie glow over her purple skin. "Or those who feared it because they didn't understand it. And when the Creator sent a new power to the Earth realm, they sought council with the king of the Ather.

"With the growing age of both the worlds, new problems had arisen. More fighting between the beings, magic and non-magic alike. And there were those who did evil in both. So the king and the powers on Earth agreed to designate some of the Ather's many magically warded realms to be prisons for any demons or creatures who were solely malicious and wanted nothing but to hurt, to destroy. The realms were spelled to deliver the punishment most befitting to their crimes, and only when they were rehabilitated would the realms set them free."

We'd seen as much in the Xses realm. How long would those creatures have to dance?

"The king and the powers on Earth agreed upon this, as it seemed the most productive and just solution for the crimes committed in both realms."

She stares into my fire for a long moment, and her features sadden.

"But the damned mounted in numbers. Realms were overrun with maliciousness. Soon, that maliciousness threatened the many peaceful realms still working to keep Ather whole. One by one, they began to fall. The king begged for a meeting with the powers on Earth. It had been millennia since they'd made their last terms, and the king believed it time to update them. He suggested that Earth bear some of the burden of rehabilitating or permanently confining those who would do either world nothing but harm, as well as bring the Ather back into the light for the humans who had long forgotten we existed. To bring our worlds together again, open and honest and free."

Wallace's head drops as she studies her hands.

"The powers on Earth had no intention of sharing their world with the likes of the prisoners they sent here. They felt the Ather—with its endless magic and variety of species—was the only place for the evil that threatened the world. When the king disagreed, when he threatened to use his considerable powers to plead his case to the one who created *all* beings, they trapped him in his own realm. That was their sole intention for entertaining his meeting in the first place. The whole time he'd been presenting the needs of his people, of the Ather, they'd been spelling his great realm to contain *him*. They wove their great magic, allowing only those creatures with divine blood—*their* blood—into and out of the realm, so that they would always hold that power over him."

Gritty anger slips beneath my skin.

"The powers above did not stop there. They dropped a veil over the Earth realm, ensuring few beings from the Ather ever return and that those clever enough to find the weak spots and slip through can't be seen as who or what they are by humans."

Anka. I hadn't been able to see her true self until I had my powers.

"It is no life for any of us, here or on Earth. The Ather's people can do nothing but stay and watch as our realms grow and grow with each being sentenced here, while those in power continue to steal our livelihoods."

Draven goes still next to me, and it's my turn to stroke his hand, my turn to interlace our fingers and squeeze. He's one of those people who sentenced beings here, demons, by Orders from the Seven. And maybe most of them deserved the punishment they received, but I can tell from the broken look in his eyes that he's seeing things from the other side now. And it's not at all what he wants to see.

"The legend of the Fracture has been passed down throughout each generation," Delta continues. "With each generation, we lose more and more believers of the one thread of hope we have left."

The silence grows thick.

"What is it?" I ask, unable to take the weighted tension slithering through the crowd. "What's the thread of hope?"

Delta gives me an almost pitying smile. "That one day, a being of both worlds who possesses the king's power will come to the Ather. A being with enough power to stand against those who seek to keep the Ather under their control."

Dread spirals through me, and I look to Draven.

Because what Delta's just said sounds a whole lot like an Antichrist—a person destined to destroy the world. Only, from this angle, from *this* side of the story, it sounds more like I'd be freeing a world, not destroying it.

But that can't be right. They can't possibly think that's me. I don't have the king's power and I certainly don't have enough of my own power to stop everyone — Marid and the Twelve and beyond. And that thought has me speaking without realizing it.

"Who are the powers on Earth?" I ask, my throat dry. I have a hunch, one I can feel like a solidness in my bones, but I don't want to be right. "The ones from the legends?"

A low grumbling rumbles from the crowd, but they calm when Delta raises her hands. The dark flames dance in her pink eyes as she looks to me, then Draven. "I believe they call themselves—"

"The Seven," Ryder cuts her off. "Obviously."

CHAPTER FIFTY-SIX

"That's correct," Delta says, nodding to Ryder. "Now you know the legend of the Fracture," Delta continues like Ryder didn't just drop a bomb on top of us.

An expected bomb, because I've had my suspicions about the Seven from the get go, but an explosion nonetheless. And from the casual way she transitions into a call for music and food, maybe she has no idea that she's just accused the Seven—the ancient beings supposedly chosen by the Creator—the same beings that deliver orders to Draven and Cassiel and Ryder and so many like them…as the catalysts to the destruction of their world.

Several of the demons move and gather, grabbing makeshift instruments and slowly aligning the notes together to create joyful, lively tunes. Ryder returns to his electric animals, and I wonder if Ray—who is captivated by the show—didn't somehow rope him into doing it. The other younglings, and even some of the demons, watch in delight, too.

And how? How are they capable of laughing and singing and playing music? Capable of telling jokes and sharing what little food they have while paying dues to the likes of Marid and his Twelve for false protection? When they're bullied by a being who certainly has more than enough wealth to go around?

I turn to Wallace. "Does Marid show up here often?" It's the first question that flies out of the tornado of thoughts in my head. And let's be honest—thinking about the one demon who has fucked with us all is easier than letting myself obsess over legends that may just be fairytales masquerading as history.

"No," she answers, looking as if she's trying to shake off the mood the story left on her. "After the Fracture, when the Twelve took it upon themselves to play kings and queens of the Ather, they set their terms with each section of the Ather they took over. Marid got this one, Xses, Machis, Agrotimas, and a few more. He raises the fees for his protection each cycle, despite each realm already giving him all they can spare."

What he's done to these realms, what his buddies have done to the rest of the Ather...it's abhorrent. A headache starts to bloom behind my eyes. The need to do something is overwhelming to the point of pain. The legend, Ryder casually tossing the Seven under a bus I didn't know existed, and the looming threat of Marid possessing Ray again, not to mention totally robbing all these people, is about to boil my brain.

"Do all the Twelve simply collect the wealth from each realm and count it in palaces? Or is there an ulterior motive?" I wonder aloud. "I know Marid, and he doesn't do anything without a reason." He convinced Kai—a divine Judge—to manipulate my mind, to pretend to be my best friend, all with the hopes of using me to break *free* from the Ather. Why would he go to all that trouble if he has such a sweet setup here?

"He could be amassing it to create weapons," Wallace muses.

Cassiel sits on the other side of Draven. "Would the weapons be powerful enough to shatter the veil and set him free?"

"No," Wallace says. "They can do some damage. Especially if he got them to Earth. They'd be a thousand times more powerful there. *All* of our powers are."

"So, what is his angle?" Draven asks.

"Maybe you can ask him," Wallace says. "When you kick his door in."

And there goes my headache again. This is our last stop before Wallace leaves us to go on our own. I rub my temples and try not to let myself think about this as the music swells around us and the people of Conilis enjoy the supplies Wallace brought them.

Ray's laughter rings out over the music as she dances with her new friend. I manage to smile. The fact that she can find joy and friends no matter where she goes is one of her superpowers.

"When do we leave?" Cassiel asks, his silver eyes scanning the demons as if he's waiting for one of them to fall out of line.

"I'll take you to the archway after you rest," Wallace answers, shoving to her feet. "You'll need it before you make the last transport into Marid's realm."

I knew the words were coming. She'd already told us several times, but I hoped after everything she might decide to join us. She'd be an asset, that's for sure, but I can't—*won't*—ask her. She has more people depending on her than I know, and it's selfish of me to want the added layer of protection for our group.

That's not the only reason.

No, if I'm being honest, her skills aren't the only reason why I want her to stay with us. I've never had a girlfriend before, not that we were about to stay up all night munching on snacks, painting our nails, and gossiping about our favorite superheroes, but she's been the closest thing to it. And when friends are few and far between in my world…

I cut the thought off before I can launch into a woe-is-me party. I've survived fine without girlfriends before, and I'll be just fine after she leaves us. Besides, in the grand scheme of things, making new friends is the least of my concerns.

"Dance with me?" Draven's words slice through my thoughts. He's standing above me, a hand outstretched between us.

I instantly take it. After how we started? With the walls he threw between us because he thought one touch would kill me? I'll never *not* take his outstretched hand—whether it's his or some variation of demon he's absorbed.

"You want to dance again?" I tease, hiding the more serious worries in my tone. "I don't know. That didn't go so well last time."

He flashes me that smirk I can't resist. "Oh, I think it went *very* well."

I laugh as he guides me to a few feet beyond where Ray and

her demon friends dance.

Draven tugs me to him with one simple move, our bodies flush as he rocks back and forth to the melody. It's a soft, hopeful tune, one that cascades over the crowd in a sweet, drifting kind of way. And while it doesn't hold the rhythmic drumming of the Lusro music, it's beautiful, reaching a part of me deep inside that I've never felt before.

"What's going on up there?" Draven asks, smoothing a fingertip over my forehead.

I release the tension there, sighing at his touch. He drops the hand to my hip, gently holding me against him as we sway back and forth. "Promise you won't laugh?"

"You know I can't promise anything like that," he admits. "What if you say something like 'Cassiel would look wonderful if he tattooed smiley face emojis all over his wings'?"

I laugh again, I can't help it, and drop my forehead against his chest.

"See?" He tucks his chin over my head. "How can you demand such impossible things of me?"

"I guess I like challenging you."

"Delightful, addictive, Antichrist."

Warmth floods my body at his words, at the way his voice lowers between us into a tone he's always reserved just for me. The way he rolls my newest title over his tongue has me dangerously close to accepting it without the fear I originally felt. It's like he's turning the term into one of endearment, and I know he's doing it on purpose. I close my eyes, keeping my head against his chest as we move.

"I was thinking," I finally say, long after we've danced for a while. "That something…" I struggle with the right words. "Something about the Ather feels familiar. Like a dream I can't quite remember. And…"

Draven draws me away from his chest, just enough to meet my eyes after I've let the sentence hang there too long. "And what, Harley?"

"It feels more like a home than I ever felt in the trailer I was raised in."

Something flickers in his eyes, a sense of sadness and hope and distance I can't fully explain. But there is no judgment, and he doesn't laugh. Instead, he smiles, that distance in his eyes disappearing as he pulls me back against him. "Jumping realms, dodging ferocious demons, battling me in a monstrous form, blowing up an entire colony of vicious sand ants," he says, swaying us back and forth. "Truly, there is no other home like it."

I bite back a smile. "Yeah, when you say it like that, I sound ridiculous."

"Not ridiculous," he says, tucking me in tight against him. I wrap my arms around his neck, wishing like hell I had the ability to stretch time. To live in this moment with him, in his arms for a little longer. "Hopeful," he says, smiling down at me. "It's a beautiful look on you," he continues. "Though I love your murderous looks, too. And your playful ones."

"Oh, really?" I grin up at him. "You love the murderous ones?"

He nods. "And the rage-fueled ones. Those are a particular favorite of mine."

Heat blooms beneath my cheeks. "What does that say about you?"

Draven's eyes are like molten pools of gold as he stares down at me. "It means I'm a sucker for you."

I grin. "Did you just steal a line from the Jonas Brothers?" The notion is so ridiculous and *human* that a pang of longing hits me for home. My home—the one with Nathan blaring Jonas Brothers' playlists at the deli during closing because Ray loves them so much.

"Maybe," he says. "It made you smile, did it not?"

I grin even wider. "*Did it not?*" I mimic his sometimes-elegant voice. "Okay, wise and ancient one."

He groans. "Are you ever going to let that go?"

"Nope."

One dance transitions into another, the new song even

more relaxed than the last. I rest my head on his chest. "Are you worried?"

"You're going to have to be more specific," he answers. "I worry about a great deal of things. Survival, the Divine Sleep, whether or not I'll ever be able to finish *Game of Thrones*."

"I mean about your brother. Taking him to Marid's realm. Trusting him to actually help us when we need him. Surviving it all."

Draven slows our pace, clinging to me a bit tighter, as if the upcoming battles are playing like a movie in his mind.

"You found him," he says. "Against all odds, you found my brother. Someone I've tried to reach for a century. And while I can't say I fully trust him yet, I do trust his power. And his desire to have that bargain with you. I'll go into Marid's mind, you'll be the anchor, and I'll cut the tether. We'll save Ray together. And then? We'll worry about Ryder's intentions." He looks down at me. "There is nothing we can't face when we're together."

I lean into him, let that confidence slide over my body as we sway to the beat. He falls silent, no doubt his mind wandering to the exact same place as mine. Marid took his brother. Marid tried to kill me and open the gates to the Ather. He's robbed too many realms of their worth. *And* he possessed Ray.

"I'm going to kill him," I say after counting up all of Marid's grievances.

Draven looks down at me, not needing me to explain who I mean as he flashes me a challenging smirk. "Not if I get there first."

CHAPTER FIFTY-SEVEN

"Thank you again," I say to Wallace, my throat tight as we stand before the archway hugging the mountains of Conilis.

"I don't like it when you're nice," she says, but I hear the tease in her voice.

Ray stands next to me, still a little sad after this morning. It was hard for her to say goodbye to her new friend, and now she's having to say goodbye to Wallace, too. While I love and admire her huge heart, I wish I could build a wall around it, because things are about to get a whole lot harder.

"You ready for this?" I ask the question to Ryder, knowing everyone else here has been prepared for this moment since we came to the Ather.

His arms cross as we stand outside that archway. "I didn't run off in the middle of the night."

That's not an answer. "Wrath wouldn't have let you," I say, petting the hound that stands on my other side. He huffs at Ryder like he's agreeing with my statement.

Ryder hisses back like a cat.

"You understand what we need you to do?" Draven asks.

"You need my light," Ryder answers, rolling his eyes. "You need me to make a fun potion so you can cruise the mind of the most malicious greater demon I've ever known. It's a stellar plan."

"I *will* kill him," I say, almost as if I need to convince myself. "You don't have to know me or trust me, Ryder. You just have to trust my anger."

"That murderous part of you is the only thing I do trust," he says. "I saw it in your eyes at the pits. You learn a lot, fighting for your life all the time. Learn to smell fear and rage and desire. All are different. And your rage? It's what has me standing right here." His facade slips again, only for a second, but I see the same fear I saw when he woke up.

"I would've remained a pet for as long as they wanted me to in those pits," he says, "and while I lived for the fight, I've plotted Marid's demise for longer than you've been breathing." He looks to Draven, then back to me. "So, if anyone is going to kill Marid, it's *me*."

I nod once. "Fine with me. He just needs to die."

He studies me for a long beat, then sighs. "I still think you're all ridiculous for even attempting this. Anger or not. Warranted or not."

"With that glowing endorsement…sure you don't want to join the party?" I ask Wallace.

She shakes her head, but her eyes look glossy. "Hell no," she says. "Try not to get killed." She glances at Ray, swallows hard, then stomps back toward the rig.

Well, goodbye to you, too, then.

I glance at the darkness in the archway, study the energy swirling there, and grip Ray's hand in mine. "Ready?"

Draven nods, then Cassiel.

Ray squeezes my hand back.

Wrath noses the archway like *what are we waiting for?*

I steel my spine and step into the dark.

And just before we're wholly consumed by the darkness, I hear Ryder whisper, "We're all going to fucking die."

CHAPTER FIFTY-EIGHT

"What the—"

Draven gently clamps his hand over my mouth from behind, my back against his chest as he silences my words.

My ears pop, and my eyes adjust, our surroundings illuminated by a soft gray light. Thick vegetation lays before us, hunter green and purple and blue branches twisting and winding through leaves so wide it's almost impossible to see through the jungle before us.

We stand in the middle of some long-forgotten ruin—broken bits of crumbling rock that likely once resembled a building of some sort, but nothing structurally sound remains beyond the archway behind us. The ground beneath my feet is wet and dark like mud, and the air is so humid and hot it feels like I'm drinking my breath.

But that's not what freezes my blood. It's the area just beyond us, the bit of mud and purple overgrowth that lays before the jungle of trees...

It's moving.

Writhing and wriggling.

At first glance, they look like twisting vines reaching out from the trees that consume the space. But they're not vines.

They're *snakes*.

Thousands of them hang from the trees, some coiled in spirals atop the thick branches, others slowly slithering over one another.

Draven peels his fingers from my mouth, and I don't say a fucking word, even as terror slices through me. I hold my breath, waiting for Marid to gather from those piles of snakes, waiting for him to strike us down the second we've stepped foot into his realm.

"He's not here," Ryder says, the loudness of his voice making each of us jolt. He steps past Draven, careful not to bump any part of his body, and stops in front of me. "He has his own twisted palace, of course." A shudder shakes his body, but he locks his muscles and cracks his neck. Blue-white sparks buzz over his skin.

"And I'm guessing we have to go through all that," I say, pointing to the dark jungle, "to get to it?"

Ryder grins a jagged sort of smile.

"Great," I say, hating that the mere sight of those snakes turns my bones to jelly.

Not Marid.

They're not Marid.

But they could report to him. They could slither away and warn him about our arrival.

"We need to move quickly," I say.

Draven's eyes are fixed on his brother, studying him like he's a bomb about to explode. Maybe he is, but at the moment, he's the least of our concerns.

"Try not to touch anything," I say to Ray, who nods. She mimics my movements, staying behind me and in front of Cassiel, who protects the back of our line.

"Well, damn," Ryder says. "I planned on grabbing a few snakes for breakfast. The purple ones taste like tacos." My eyes widen, and he laughs. "*Kidding.*"

The air grows thicker as we slip beneath the winding branches until a clearing appears. Okay, clearing might be an overstatement, but it's big enough to walk through without hunching the whole time and shoving branches out of the way. The canopy above us yields little light, though, so I fashion a small orb of black and silver flames, holding it in my palm as I lead the way.

My friends and Ryder follow quietly behind, Wrath sticking close to my side. We duck beneath the handful of low-hanging branches, some leaves thin and shredded while others are fat and pointed. All look deadly, as do the snakes curled up where the branches meet the trunks of the trees.

Some hiss as we pass, others lower their middles from the branches like they want to snag us in a trap, but none coil to strike. Wrath's low rumble seems to work as a warning, because the snakes recoil from the hound's presence.

I run my fingers through his coarse fur in a thank-you. I've always wanted a dog, but for obvious asshole father reasons, I never thought I'd have one. Not that Wrath *belongs* to me, but there is something about the way he sticks close to my side that makes him feel like mine. And yeah, he's not a dog, but I'm not exactly human, either, so maybe we fit in some twisted sort of way.

There is only one clear path through the thick, humid-as-hell jungle, so I stick to it. If Marid has a palace he resides in, but travels to other realms through the archway, then this path is the most likely one he takes.

"So," Ryder says, his voice too loud in the chittering jungle. "What kind of demon are you?"

I scrunch my brow, gaping at him. "What?"

He eyes the trees around us. "We have a walk ahead of us, and thanks to your super-cute puppy, the wildlife is giving us a wide berth. I'm bored."

I blink a few times, then remind myself he's been here for more time than I can even fathom.

"Don't tell him," Draven warns, only furthering my confusion.

"Why not?"

"Beyond the idea that there are ears around us, I don't trust him."

"He's your brother."

"He was *my brother when he entered this place. After Marid's torture and the pits and the years between? I don't recognize the person standing before me enough for you to trust him with that."*

"I don't know what kind of demon I am," I say, and it's half the truth. Sure, I may have the title of Antichrist stamped on my forehead, but there is still so much I don't know about what that means. Where I and my powers come from.

"How can you not know what kind of demon you are?" Ryder asks.

"I was raised on Earth," I answer. "I thought I was human for most of my life. Then I turned eighteen…" And my entire world changed. Everything I thought I knew turned on its head.

"You discovered your powers once you came of age?" he asks, then glances at Draven.

"Yes," I answer, dipping under a low-hanging branch.

"And how did you meet my brother?"

"We met at a concert."

"And you just happened to be enjoying yourself, brother? Or was there another reason you were there?"

"So many questions," Draven says.

"I haven't seen you in a span of many lifetimes," he says, and Draven flinches, his hard gaze softening.

"I'm here now, Ryder," he says. "I want to make up for that time lost."

I try like hell to focus on the path in front of me, try not to eavesdrop, but it's kind of hard when we're all packed together in a tight-knit unit.

"There's no such thing," Ryder says, shaking his head. "That time is gone. Poof. Dust."

"Do you remember anything of our life together?" Draven's tone is raised, sharp, as he steps into Ryder's path, forcing him to look him in the eye.

Cassiel slows, his expression dark as he watches them.

"Do you remember Mother?" Draven pushes. "The way she forced me to play piano and you the violin? Do you remember when she tried to separate us and you would sneak into my room every night, unable to sleep alone?" Draven's voice is heavy with memories. I can feel his pain lashing against the connection between us.

"I remember being Called. I remember being trained by the Seven and you…" His eyes flare. "*You* were a terror to behold. Everyone feared you. But not me. You never scared me."

"Because I would never hurt you," Draven answers.

"And yet, you *did*."

Utter confusion laces Draven's face. "I had nothing to do with you being taken. You're my brother. My *twin*. I can't change what happened, but we've been offered a second chance to live as brothers. Don't you want that? Does that give you any hope?"

Ryder's face goes blank. "Hope doesn't exist here," he says and then continues walking. "You may get to Marid, but you all *will* die here. And I did not sign up to watch."

CHAPTER FIFTY-NINE

"You've arrived," Ryder whispers in my ear what feels like hours later, and I flinch from the way he draws out the words. He nods to the palace resting several yards away, our location concealed by a giant turquoise tree.

Marid's palace is made of smooth brown stone, a collection of columns supporting an intricately carved stone roof that peaks at the top. The vegetation hugs the edges of the grand estate, purple and blue roots twisting up a few of the columns like giant snakes. Flames flicker from the inside, a trail of black candles illuminating the interior. Blue moss floats on top of the murky water that ripples against the stairs leading to the columned entryway.

It'll take only minutes to clear the water, dash up the steps, and enter his palace. A few minutes and we can catch Marid unaware, finish what he started.

"Congratulations on reaching the finish line of your life," Ryder says, and I turn to glare at him.

"Hey," I snap. "I'm really fucking sorry you're the one with the power we need and sorry if I thought you might want a hand in executing your previous captor, or god forbid, reconnecting with your *brother*." Anger rises until my hands shake. "But you can cut the *we're all going to die* bullshit, okay? Not one of us here is unaware of the odds. It's been a hell of a time getting here, and I know you've suffered. I get it. I'm doing my best to offer you a place to heal from it, but you keep spitting on my hand and I'm going to end up slapping you with it."

Draven covers a dark laugh with a cough, and Cassiel, well…

the angel of death just grins.

Ryder frowns, his gaze intense. His turquoise eyes shift to chips of ice. "Who the hell *are* you?"

"You know who I am. I'm Harley—"

"No," Ryder cuts me off, stepping within an inch of my space. "You're much more than that." He cracks his neck as he studies me. I don't flinch from his stare, but dark flames gather in my palms when I see those blue-white sparks of electricity on his skin. "You're more than my brother's soul mate, and you're *much* more than what you've told me. Something about your scent…"

His voice trails off as he inhales, but I'm not sure I'm moving. *Soul mate?*

Beside me, Draven's gone still as a statue.

"Draven?" I say his name, but it sounds like a choked plea.

"Wait. You didn't know?" Ryder asks, his eyes wide. "Truly? How could you not? You two *reek* of the scent." He looks at Draven. "Why didn't you tell her?"

Draven swallows. Hard. "Harley—"

"Wait, it's *true*?" I gape at him, seeing the recognition in his eyes. "I'm your…" I can't say the word. Can't wrap my head around it.

"I didn't want to tell you—"

He cringes, because yeah, that sounded really bad. But really, I know exactly why he wouldn't want to tell me. Who would want to be mated to me? The Antichrist? Something born to ruin the world?

"No, Harley, it's not like that," he says, either reading my thoughts or my eyes, I don't know.

You're my…Harley, you're my…

The words from the other night, the way he was struggling to get them out, echo in my mind.

"It's fine," I say, straightening. Once again, I totally don't have time to crumble. Don't have time to think about what Ryder has just revealed, though I suppose, in a sick way, it makes sense. The reason I could bring Draven back to life, the reason he can touch me and not drain me. The chain of connection pulsing between us.

Guess that isn't something the Seven concocted after all. Nope, it's something deeper, ancient, binding.

But he didn't tell me.

Didn't *want* to tell me.

"Harley, please listen," he begs, but I shake my head.

"We don't have time for explanations," I say, my voice a little too cold. "We never do, right? *Too busy*." I throw that in his face, hating the way he flinches, but I can't get past the fact that he's kept another thing from me. That his brother laid it out there like it was the most obvious thing in the world, and I didn't have a fucking clue. Once again, I feel so in the dark about my own life that I want to scream.

After what we'd done...I'd *chosen* him. I'd given myself to him completely. And maybe he'd been trying to tell me then, but how damn hard was it to say it?

It was only hard because he didn't want to say it. Because being mated to an Antichrist had to just royally suck. I mean, we're always being attacked and I'm legit contemplating staying in the Ather simply so no one uses me as a weapon. Who would want that life?

I pin him with a hurt, accusing glance. *What else are you keeping from me?*

He reaches for me, like he'll lay his soul bare right there.

But I turn back to face the estate.

"Cassiel," I say, hating the way my voice cracks. "Please keep an eye on Ray. She needs to be close to me, but I don't want her near a battle if it happens," I say. "I'll be the one to trap Marid. And then we'll get the ritual over with." I'll use every ounce of fire and earth I possess to make sure of it.

The angel of death dips his head.

"Let's go."

I step into the water, hating the fact that I can't see where I'm stepping. Can't see what kind of creatures no doubt prowl beneath the murky surface. I keep my steps long and smooth, not wanting to create too much sound.

To my relief, Ryder follows suit, then Cassiel carrying Ray with a swirl of shadows above the water, and finally Draven. Wrath is at my side, his snout tipped toward the air as if the water smells horrid to him. I sigh when my boot hits the first step, and I climb upward. Wrath shakes out his fur as we clear the last step, the black candles illuminating the path inside the mansion. It looks like a trap—even I can see that with the easy way the candles trail inside a thrown-open doorway—but we have no choice.

"He's definitely in there," Ray whispers, her eyes closed. "I can feel him."

Cold crystalizes in my stomach, but I nod. "Can you feel where?"

She nods, her eyes still closed, her grip on Cassiel's neck so tight. "Up. To the right."

I waste no time following the trail of candles inside, the humid air magnifying in here and sticking to my skin. A set of grand, winding stairs half covered in the same thick vines from the jungle leads to the upper levels. I hurry up the stairs, keeping my footsteps quiet, willing them to be as silent as Wrath's paws beside me.

Cassiel flies softly behind us, no need to make a noise at all.

Ryder and Draven are right behind me, and while my chest is tight with everything unsaid between us, I stop once we reach the landing and look at Draven. His eyes are unflinching, his shadows already gathering around his broad shoulders.

I'm not alone.

Regardless of everything, I'm not alone.

I remind myself of this as I find a partially cracked open door to my right and check Ray for confirmation. She nods, fear crackling in her blue eyes. I try to reassure her that this is almost over. That we've made it this far. That I'm not going to let anything happen to her.

I push the door open far enough for Wrath and me to step through, and the hound's hackles rise. A large wingback chair faces a giant hearth, roaring flames inside it.

Slithering is the only other sound in the room beyond the flames, and I gather my own around my fists as I edge closer.

My fingers tremble as I grab the back of the chair, then yank and bring the whole thing tumbling down.

Snakes, *hundreds* of them, hiss and coil and slither at my feet, but their scales are blue and yellow. Not Marid's black.

The door slams, and I whirl around.

"You brought my possession to me," Marid whispers, his horde of snakes in constant motion to make up his form beneath a black cloak. Ryder struggles in his grip as Marid tightens it around his throat. "How thoughtful of you, dark princess."

CHAPTER SIXTY

"I've always been a people pleaser," I say, stepping casually to my left, making sure I don't step on any of the snakes slithering around the room.

I cast a quick glance around. Cassiel and Ray hover in the farthest corner of the room, but Draven is nowhere to be seen.

"Couldn't stay away, could you?" Marid says to Ryder, who is struggling in his grasp, his blue-white shocks barely flickering. "Or did the princess *order* you to come back?" Marid turns his black gaze on me, those sunken pits in his face hollow. "Not very fair of you."

"You never play fair," I say, stopping to stand in front of Cassiel and Ray.

"Sure, I do," he says, then throws Ryder across the room. His body flies through the air, his back smacking hard against the wall near the hearth. He crumples in a heap on the floor.

Dark flames surge around my fists.

Marid folds his arms behind his back. "I must admit," he says, "coming here yourself is a bold choice."

I mimic his steps, keeping myself between him and Ray no matter where he moves. "You practically handed me an invitation when you slipped into my sister's mind."

"Now, *why* would I do that?" Marid's snake mouth shifts into a grin.

Dread spirals through my body. And panic. He *meant* for us to come to him. The whole time, he knew I wouldn't stand for his possession of Ray. But why? Why would he want me here? I can't open the gates from this side…

Shadows snap from the corners of the room, swirling in a tornado of smoke and shadow, lashing at Marid.

Draven.

I suck in a deep breath and try to pull myself together. Because it doesn't matter why Marid wants me here. It doesn't change anything. This ends right here, right now.

I rush Marid, who thrashes against Draven's hold, and dig my flaming fingers into his neck. He screeches, and I draw the flames back just a little. I can't kill him. Not when whatever powers him — soul or pure evil — could survive and cling to the tether. We have to perform the ritual or Ray will never be free.

"We need to get him tied—"

White-hot pain bursts across my cheek, and I sail backward until I hit the wall. Marid has one arm free of Draven's shadow hold. Wrath growls loud enough to shake the room and launches at Marid's throat.

"We need him alive!" I yell to the hound, my mind shaking from the hit as I scramble to my feet.

Wrath stops before sinking his teeth into the array of snakes creating Marid's form.

Marid laughs, and a surge of power pulses through the room. "You are no match for me."

Draven's roar rattles inside my head, the sound like a knife to my chest as I see his form gather from his shadows, writhing on the floor.

I don't think, don't *breathe* before I sprint toward Marid. Dark flames gather over my fists and up my arms as I land a punch to his face. Hard enough that his head jerks to the left.

Come on, come on. I just need him subdued. Unconscious so I can break—

Something strong yanks at my ankles, and my chest hits the floor. I struggle against the hold, flipping to my back as dozens of fangs pierce my calves.

Snakes.

So many damn snakes. They coil around my ankles and haul me back, back, back.

Cassiel flies across the room, those giant obsidian wings outstretched, his eyes a pure, terrifying silver. He sinks his fingers into Marid's neck, gripping so hard he lifts him off his feet, his long black cloak swaying above the floor.

"Sleep," he commands, his entire body trembling as he holds Marid in the air. "Sleep!"

Marid laughs a horrifying laugh that sends waves of ice over my skin. "I have no soul to sing to, angel of death," Marid spits, releasing some of his snakes onto Cassiel's wings. "You have no power here!"

Cassiel drops him and hits the floor, the snakes striking and ripping at his feathers.

Marid walks toward Ray, that sinister grin on his face. I dart between them, covering Ray's body with my own even though my muscles feel like Jell-O. The snakes, whatever venom they possess, it's sliding into my veins like warm honey, thick and hot and tugging me down. Coaxing me to the darkness.

The flames on my fists, my arms, flicker in and out, just like my vision. I will myself to stay awake, my chest tightening at the sight beyond Marid. At Draven, grabbing his hair and clenching his eyes shut as if he's seeing something horrible, living out his worst fears. And Cassiel, ripping snake after snake out of those glorious wings. Ryder, lying unconscious near the fire. Wrath, tearing the heads off every snake he can reach, but there are so many, *too* many. They swarm his paws, coil up his long legs, snap onto his bushy tail.

"I thought you'd be more of a challenge," Marid says, and the words hit every single mark I have. Kai...*Kai* had said those same words to me before he demanded my blood, demanded my death.

And I killed him.

Where is that power now?

Another wave of stinging rolls over my body, and I drop to my knees before my sister. The snakes keep striking, adding a hundred new scars before I die.

I glare up at Marid, who towers over me. He whispers something in a language I can't understand, and the snakes slide off my body. I sigh with relief and use what little strength I have to push my back into Ray, try to make her one with the wall behind her.

Marid crouches down to my level. "Can't have you dying too quickly, now can I? Not when there are so many uses for that blood of yours."

My blood. Even now, I can feel the power surging, the dark flames and crackling earth inside me swirling and spiraling over every wound, every hurt. Mending and binding, but it's not fast enough.

I'm not fast enough.

Black sparkles around the edge of my vision.

"Ray," I whisper, an apology and a prayer.

Marid reaches for me, a blow to knock me out of the way of what he wants—

A crashing piece of glass cracks over Marid's head.

His form goes rigid, snakes and all, as sparks of pulsing light every color of the rainbow fills the room. With a final rattling shriek, he falls to the floor.

Wallace grins from where she stands behind his now-limp body. "Told you confetti would come in handy."

CHAPTER SIXTY-ONE

"I leave you alone for *five* minutes," Wallace grumbles, hurrying to my side. She digs through a pack that's been tossed near the wall, grabbing the pink vial from the pocket. She slathers the goop over every wound I have, each pass bringing me back to myself.

"He knew we were coming," I say through clenched teeth.

"Give Draven the green vial," Wallace barks at Ray, who immediately launches into action.

Wrath growls, his massive chest heaving as he destroys the last slithering snake in the room. I reach my hand out to him, and he drops his snout into it. The poor animal is exhausted but standing.

My sister empties the last of the contents into Draven's mouth. He stills, slumping to the floor, his eyes closing peacefully. "Ohmigod, did I kill him?"

"No," Wallace says, stepping back as I manage to finally haul myself to my feet. The healing potion has cleared the poison from my blood, from my mind, but I still feel a little unsteady. "It just stopped Marid's visions," she explains. "He'll need a minute to wake up."

"You followed us," I say, slumping into the chair near the hearth. "Why? I thought—"

"I told you I broke my rule," she cuts me off. "And clearly, you needed my help."

I glare at her, opting for that angry banter between us. "I had it handled," I say, because if I said the truth? If I told her how much it meant to me that she came for us, that she saved us…it would only piss her off. I knew that much about her but gave her a silent, thankful look regardless.

Wallace waves me off, walking over to Cassiel, checking if he needs anything. The wounds on his wings are already healing as he moves toward where Draven lays, and then Ryder, who looks like he is struggling awake.

"What did you do to him?" I ask, eying Marid's motionless form on the ground.

"Confetti," Wallace says. "It's a one-shot weapon of the rarest kind. A specially concocted powder with properties and magic from realms across the Ather. It subdues a victim regardless of power. Giving you time to get away or…"

"Perform a ritual," I say, already bounding over to Draven's resting body. "Sorry," I say, grabbing the vial from around his neck. "I can't wait for you." I look at Wallace, kneeling next to Ryder, smacking his cheek to wake him up.

He blinks a few times, jerking to standing in the span of a breath. Blue-white sparks shoot across the room, but I manage to dodge them. Ryder's eyes fall to Marid, then meet mine, noting the crystal in my hand.

"It's time?" he asks, his voice hoarse.

I nod, then glance to Wallace. "How long will Marid be out?"

She shrugs. "With his amount of power? You have minutes."

Then that will have to be enough.

CHAPTER
SIXTY-TWO

I settle next to Marid, bile clawing up my throat as I slip my free hand in his limp one. The scales brush against my skin, the snake bodies shivering at my touch.

"I will be your anchor," Cassiel says, breathing ragged as he drops to his knees on my left.

"Kazuki," I say, summoning him like we agreed upon.

"You're there, darling," he says, something like relief in his tone.

"Yes, we have no time. Tell me what to do."

"The anchor needs to hold the crystal."

I hand the vial to Cassiel. I'm going to owe the angel of death a hell of a lot after this trip.

"Tell Ryder to charge it. It has to be done in one shot to liquify it."

"Ryder," I say, pointing to the vial in Cassiel's hands. "Kazuki says you have to hit this with your most powerful blast to charge it. One shot."

He cracks his neck, nodding as he draws his hands together, the muscles in his arms bunching as blue-white light gathers between his palms. He shapes those searing sparks with each move of his hands until it looks like he's crafted a spear of the purest light I've ever seen. It fills the entire room so much I feel it on my skin, the hairs on the back of my neck standing on end.

He aims that spear at the vial and sends it soaring. A loud crack cleaves the air.

The room goes dark. Ryder slumps on the floor but otherwise looks fine.

Meanwhile, the liquid inside the vial in Cassiel's hands starts to glow.

"*Done,*" I say to Kazuki. "*Now what do I have to do?*"

"*Draven is meant to be the one to break the tether,*" he argues. "*He has the mind power experience. You're meant to be an anchor.*"

"*He's out of commission. Cassiel is the anchor. Tell me!*"

"*Gods damn it, Harley,*" he snaps. "*To enter into Marid's mind, you have to swallow the liquid,*" he hurries to say. "*Make sure Cassiel is linked to you. He'll be able to see everything but not interfere unless you're near death. And even then, he may not be able to pull you back.*"

That's a risk I'll have to take.

"*Make sure you touch Marid and Ray at the same time. You will be the conduit between them both. He will fight you, Harley. Extensively. He will do anything in his power to hide the tether from you. Do not trust what you see. Only when you find the tether and shatter it will Ray be free.*"

"*Okay,*" I say. "*Thank you.*"

"*Trust nothing but your own heart.*"

I nod, then wave Ray over to me.

Cassiel uncorks the vial, handing it to me. I swallow the hot liquid, the substance thick like molten ore. I toss the bottle over my shoulder and grab Ray's hand.

"I love you," I say.

And then I'm falling.

CHAPTER SIXTY-THREE

I drop into a wasteland made of jagged black rocks. Gaping holes crisscross the ground, opening up to pits of darkness so deep I can't see the bottom. Spheres glowing with iridescent swirls of blue and red and orange line the edges of what little ground is intact. They illuminate the massive area, showing the way to a skinny, crumbling bridge that ends at the base of a golden door glowing with white light.

"You will not survive my mind." Marid's voice seems to come from everywhere at once, but there is no sign of him.

A cold shiver races over my body.

Wait.

I'm inside Marid's mind.

This wasteland is his attempt to keep me from finding the tether.

Fuck. *That.*

I scan the area, listening. The only sound is my breathing. No breeze or hint of creatures slithering toward me. It's obvious I have to get to that door on the other side of the ramshackle bridge hanging over the darkness. Even though the terrain is dangerous enough that one wrong move will send me falling over the edge, it still looks too easy.

There has to be a catch. One I'm not seeing.

But I can't stand here and puzzle it out. Not when every second I wait, I run the risk of Marid's power gathering and him waking up. And I for *sure* don't want to know what happens if he wakes up and I'm still in his mind.

I take one step forward, trying my best to place my foot on the narrow path between those perfect glowing spheres, but just the tip of my shoe grazes the edge of one and—

It *bursts*.

Acid sprays across my legs, and I jerk back, stumbling into another sphere and then another, all of which spray me with the foul liquid. The pain...it's unbearable. Enough to make me see stars.

Worse, with each sphere that shatters, a dozen new spheres appear in its place, covering what little clear ground there'd been between me and the bridge.

I force my muscles to lock, to block out the pain, and suck in a sharp breath through clamped teeth. "Okay. This is a test of cunning, not chaos. It'll be fine—"

The sound of chittering and the clacking of claws cut off my pathetic little pep talk. Ice chills my blood as I watch the wall before me tremble. No, not tremble—it *moves* with a hundred tiny creatures that look like some demented combination of rats and Yoda. All of them screech a war cry as they clamber down the walls, heading straight for me. They crush those spheres as they go, completely immune to the liquid's effects.

But *I'm* not.

I can barely contain my cry as all that acid rains down on me.

The need to fight or run thrashes inside me with each second. Technically, both are *totally* needed right now.

The smell of burned hair and flesh fill my nose.

Me. My hair. My skin. *Ick*.

Yep, time to run.

There is no other exit except for that door across the bridge, and the creepy creatures are only getting closer. I cringe against the pain of the acid rain and say fuck it, hauling ass through the ground littered with those godforsaken spheres.

The creatures screech like nails on a chalkboard. My brain rattles inside my skull, accompanying the onslaught of pain from each broken sphere, but I manage to reach the lip of the bridge.

It's narrower than I originally thought. The bridge is at least two hundred yards long and only big enough for me to put one foot in front of the other. Almost like a damn tightrope. And on either side? An endless fall to the pitch black below. I dare a chance, and gently maneuver one of the glowing spheres over the lip of the bridge, and watch its iridescent light get swallowed up by the darkness.

I never hear it shatter.

That is *so* not the way I want to die.

The demons are close now. Too close for me to waste any more time thinking.

I take one step. Heel to toe, heel to toe. Over and over again. I stretch my arms out to the sides for balance, the bridge wobbling with every step I take. Some bits of the rock bridge are jagged, like tiny spears jutting up from the surface, threatening to tip me this way or that. But I make progress, steady and slow and agonizing to the middle of the bridge—

No bigger than house cats, the demons land on the bridge behind me. Those tiny rubbery wings have glistening talons on their tips, propelling them toward me. Their clawed feet *click-clack* against the rocks, their tiny maws revealing rows upon rows of serrated teeth.

I draw power from the depths of my exhausted body and try to form some sort of shield around myself. A dozen of the creatures leap into the air, straight for my neck…and run into a wall of fire. Their ashes hit my chest and flutter away to the blackness below.

High-pitched wails mount, and the bridge trembles as they all descend at once. Their frantic, enraged movements shatter more of those glowing spheres, acid flying like I'm stuck in a hurricane of it.

More and more creatures fly toward me, so close I can feel the heat from their wings flapping. I just have to get to that damn door.

I close my eyes and search inward, slipping deep down into the power that rumbles next to my fire. I call to whatever stone and dirt and rocks lay around me, and I fashion a new bridge, braiding both earth and flame together right alongside this one.

And I run.

As fast as my weakened body will take me. I make the new bridge into a tunnel, forming a roof of earth and fire over my head and closing up the end as I go. I hear the angry thwacks of demons as they try to break the earth I've constructed to shield all around me.

The door gets closer and closer with each pounding step until I finally jerk to a stop in front of it. I push with all my might against the door, shoving the thing open.

Instantly, I stumble through it, the floor on the other side cushioned and soft. The creatures are still screeching, still trying to break through my tunnel with their claws and teeth. But I shut the door behind me, latching it.

Silence fills the space around me.

I turn, steeling my spine to see what new hell Marid's mind will bring.

CHAPTER SIXTY-FOUR

L ush, royal blue carpet stretches out in the moderate-size room. A four-poster bed tucks up against one wall, which is papered with floral designs of pink and green. A mahogany wardrobe rests on the other side of the wall with beautiful lion's-head finishings of bronze that glisten underneath the light twinkling from a chandelier above.

A *bedroom*.

No windows.

Only a picture—a painting of an old woman who is screaming so hard her wrinkled skin looks like it might split open. Captured forever in a moment of horror and fashioned with a gilded golden frame for all eternity. I tear my eyes away from the painting, every instinct in my body roaring at me to get as far away from it as I can.

I open the wardrobe, finding it stocked with fresh clothes and towels and extra pillows and blankets for the bed across the room. It's so unexpectedly normal that I'm not sure what to do with the information.

"You will never find it. Never break me," Marid's voice rumbles all around me, and I flinch at the sound. "You will be your own end."

I flip off the surrounding air.

His voice vanishes as I note a door I didn't see before. One just on the other side of the room, opposite the wall with the painting.

I take a deep breath and swing the door open.

"Fucking hell," I grumble as I step through, and the door slams shut behind me.

I'm in a room almost identical to the one I just left. This one has a blood-red carpet, but it's just as soft beneath my boots. Soft enough to leave prints in.

The walls are adorned with royal blue flower wallpaper this time, the same eerie painting hovering in the corner across from the massive bed that takes up half the room. The mattress is bedecked with comforters and pillows and blankets, and it looks more than tempting to sink into. The kind of bed you could sleep in for weeks and still not want to climb out of. Another wardrobe rests on the opposite side of the room, this one of black walnut instead of mahogany, and the same chandelier twinkles above it all.

I hurry across the room to the only door and fling it open.

The second I'm through, the door slams shut behind me, and another room appears, this one in colors of green and orange.

It's laid out exactly the same as the previous rooms, right down to the painting, but the solid walls are suddenly too close, squeezing the breath from my lungs. It doesn't matter that it has beautiful floral paper clinging to it, or the tinkling chandelier above. It doesn't matter that the size is decent. It feels like a trap. A beautiful, luxurious trap with pretty wrappings that has no business being inside a demon like Marid's mind.

I reach for the next door, step through, and it shuts again.

Another room. Fresh colors. Same horrific painting.

I run faster, throwing open door after door after door until I'm dizzy with the changing colors of the rooms. Until I can barely breathe from seeing so many walls without windows, without escape. Nothing but that same awful painting mocking me.

Marid's dark laughter is weak, but it sends spiders along my skin.

I look to that horrific painting, realizing maybe *why* that woman is screaming. Because she got stuck here for eternity with nothing but room after room after room she couldn't escape. I'd rather face a thousand demons than *this*.

My back hits the wall nearest the door, and I sink down, tucking my knees against my chest. I shake my head back and forth, fear and rage battling for clarity in my mind. "I don't have time for this. I have to find the tether. I have to get back to Ray."

The words leave me in a panicked rush, and I rock back and forth as if the motion will help draw air into my lungs. Dark flames circle my fingers. But I can't set the place on fire. I need to keep moving. Need to find the tether.

I can feel myself slipping, panic spiderwebbing its way through my mind, clinging to it, suffocating it, choking it.

Sanity.

This is Marid. He's doing this.

Fight him. Fight him.

"Sanity," I say out loud. "What is it they say about sanity?" I close my eyes, trying to focus through the ice freezing my thoughts. "Insanity is repeating the same action and expecting different results?"

I stand, scanning the room with new eyes. I've run through door after door after door for who knows how long, only seeing the next exit despite *knowing* I'd meet the same room over and over again. How the hell else can I get out of this place?

Kazuki warned me. Told me to not trust what I see, and still I keep reaching for a door that leads nowhere.

Draven would've probably already made it to the tether by now.

I can't stop the thoughts from seeping into my mind, can't stop the doubt and regret swamping me. But I *can* ignore it for the moment.

I move along the edges of the room, scanning each and every crevice for another way out. Because there has to be another way out. Marid's mind is not a prison to trap me. It's just another journey. Another mass of realms.

I stand before the horrific painting. Stare at the sad old lady screaming forever. The hair on the back of my neck bristles like something skitters across it. The artist who painted this rendered the fear so perfectly—I shudder to think that *they'd* been the one to put that terror on her face.

Every instinct shouts at me not to touch the painting because maybe I'll *become* the painting. But there is something else there, something in my power that urges me forward. To face the fear. To face the terror of being trapped in Marid's mind forever. To never set Ray free.

I step closer and reach for that frame.

The painting budges an inch, revealing a shadow behind it. I rip it from the wall and toss it behind me. A dark, startled laugh rips from my lips as I look at the tunnel dug into the wall.

"Not so clever, are you?" I snap into the ether, then climb into the tunnel.

It's squishy and cold, but I don't care. Not when I'm moving, winding and twisting down, down, down until my bones ache and my lungs burn.

And just when I feel the panic creeping back in, just when I feel my hope slipping, a light forms in the space in front of me. An orange, buzzing light. Bile froths on the back of my tongue, but I swallow it down, listening to the writhing inside me that feels a lot like rage.

Not mine.

Marid's.

I'm close, too close for his liking.

I haul ass through that orange light. Anything that makes him this angry is *good* for me.

I slip over a ledge, falling onto threadbare carpet I know all too well. The smell of vodka and sweat fills my nose. I scramble to my feet, and a strangled, startled gasp bursts from my lips.

We're inside my trailer on Earth, and that's my piece-of-shit father walking through the front door.

CHAPTER SIXTY-FIVE

Everything in me freezes.

That old instinct to make myself a small as possible flares to life.

He looks right at me but doesn't really see me.

I don't move.

I *can't* move.

There's a little girl by the couch, maybe just a year old, and she looks incredibly malnourished. Her red hair is a mess of oily curls on top of her head, as if it's never been brushed or washed. Her cheeks are sunken in, the bones sticking out at sharp angles, and her eyes are leeched of color. She reaches for my father, who sinks into his recliner, ignoring the girl, his eyes glued to the TV, a silver can in his hand. A stack of empties litter the table next to him. The little girl reaches for one of those instead. Picking one up, she brings it to her lips, a few drops of the liquid dripping in.

Tears stream down my cheeks, the wetness grounding me to the present. My soul curls inward with shame and anger and regret. I cry for that little girl, cringing as she reaches for him again.

Where is my mother?

Why isn't she here, putting a stop to this?

You know why. She didn't care. She left. She left you with that monster.

I know what will happen before it plays out, and yet I still flinch. He raises his boot and knocks her down. He doesn't pick her up, he doesn't try to comfort her, and he doesn't try to give her what she's so clearly starved for—food and love. Simple, *basic* things.

My lungs fill with cement as I watch her try over and over again to reach for him. So many attempts before she realizes that reaching for him only earns her a hard shove.

"Pathetic." Marid's voice fills the area around me, snapping me out of the spiraling rage threatening to consume me. "Always reaching for what you can't have. What you haven't earned. Who could love a thing like you?"

More haunting scenes play out in front of me, and I'm powerless to look away. Powerless to shut my eyes against the horrors I faced before. Useless against what my father subjected me to over and over again. Some scars on my body are explained after all these years of wondering. Memories I've tried to block out.

"Weak," Marid whispers, the heat of his breath at my ear, but I see nothing but my father. The girl I used to be.

Memory after memory, haunting and dark.

But seeing it from this angle, I see something I never have before.

Every harrowing attack, every scar I couldn't remember because I'd been too young when it happened…all of it. It *meant* something.

"I'm a survivor," I say, my voice tangled in tears and anger. My entire body trembles, fists clenched and hungry to feel my father's neck crack beneath it.

Not my father.

Not my real one.

Just a man who turned me into what I am, and for that alone, maybe I should thank the son of a bitch.

"I *survive*," I say, baring my teeth like I'd seen Wrath do back at the fighting pits when he was outnumbered.

Marid's anger shakes me to my core, and the memories continue to shift and play out in front of me until—

I'm ten. I sit alone on the couch, rocking slightly, staring down lovingly at the baby in my arms.

"No," Marid whispers, and the memory blurs in front of me like he's just hit fast forward.

I stumble closer to the girls on the couch, willing the movements to slow, but I'm too late.

"Stop," I command, using every ounce of strength I can to put power behind the word.

The memory slows, shifting to one of Ray at her drawing table. Her first sketch of Marid in progress. Her little brow furrowed in concentration as the pencil moves along the white paper.

Ice snaps against my skin, the room dropping in temperature so fast my teeth chatter.

But it doesn't stop me from seeing what I need to.

There, snaking its way out of the center of my sister's chest, is a ribbon of black scaled light.

Hands engulfed in flames, I reach for it, for what I know is the tether—

I'm hauled back by the roots of my hair by a grip I'm all too familiar with. I whirl around, eyes wide and furious as I look up at the person who used to be my father.

But now he looks like what he truly is.

A monster.

A real monster, his flesh stretched and rippling with muscle. He's four times my size, his teeth sharp and black and dripping spit. His eyes are solid black and glistening with malice. His hands end in sharp claws, his feet bare with curling and yellow toenails.

The man I've feared my entire life.

The man I would provoke in order to save my sister over and over again.

Now he stands between me and the tether to Marid. No doubt, Marid's mind battling me with what I've always feared most.

Flames erupt from my palms, and I shift to face my fear head on.

The simple movement sets him off like it always did whenever I tried to defend myself. He roars, loud enough to shake the small room we stand in. Ray continues drawing, totally oblivious.

The monster hurtles into me. His massive fist sinks into my stomach, and I fold around it, all the breath rushing from my lungs in one quick movement. Stars burst behind my eyes, and my flames flicker away from my fingertips as the wind is knocked from me. I bounce on my feet, dancing away but keeping my balance. If I fall down, that'll be it. My father always loved to kick me when I'm down. And with his size now? One kick to the head is all it'll take.

I find my flames again and swing. Hit him dead center in the chest. He's so much taller than me in this form. Looming over me like some demented Hulk.

He backhands me, and I fly across the room, my spine smacking against the opposite wall. My vision shudders, flickering from darkness to present and back again. I cling to consciousness, dig my claws into the present, force myself to focus. He's right there again, another hit, another attack, relentless. He bats me back and forth like a cat with a mouse, toying with me. Drawing out the pain.

Just like in real life.

Just like he's always done.

Another backhand, and I fall to my knees. Blood snakes down my nose, trickles from my split lip, dripping onto the floor. My entire body aches.

"The one enemy you'll never be able to beat." Marid laughs, his voice skittering along the edges of my mind. "Weak. Pathetic."

I look up from my kneeling position, lock onto the pair of black eyes, and realize something.

This isn't about defeating my father.

I've already done that. Because he isn't my father. I don't know where my real father is, and I don't care. I don't need blood family when I've *chosen* a family for myself.

Ray and Draven and Cassiel.

Maybe even Wallace.

Maybe Ryder.

Wrath.

They're waiting for me. Counting on me. Ray needs me.

I force myself to stand, shifting my feet so I have better balance.

This is about killing a piece of myself—that hard, brittle piece of my soul that my fake father created with every ounce of hatred he raised me with. With every ounce of disdain he covered me with instead of blankets. With every ounce of malice he fed me instead of food.

He'd told me he'd been paid to turn me into a monster.

But he *failed*.

I raise my hands between us, and flames of braided fire encircle his wrists, his ankles, his neck.

And I squeeze. Tighten those ropes of flame, gagging at the acrid smell as he thrashes. But he's no match for my power.

Mine.

He's the weak one.

The hulking monster of a man falls to his knees before me, his eyes pleading, *begging* for mercy.

"You never showed me any mercy," I seethe and yank on those braids of fire, removing his head from his body. It squelches as it lands upon the threadbare carpet beside his now-slumping body. Hard enough to rattle the room around us.

Marid's screech is terrifying, the anger tangy in the air as I whirl around.

Ray grabs at her chest, her body jerking at awkward angles. "Harley?"

I rush to her, grab the black, scaly ribbon, and squeeze. Curl my dark flames around it—

Her fear turns to sobs. "It burns!"

"Almost there."

"Harley! No, it hurts!"

Tears well in my eyes. "Just a little more, Ray."

She grits her teeth, her blue eyes scrunched in pain, but locks her body.

"You're so brave," I say, yanking on the tether. Scorching it with each sharp pull, each tug, until it jerks free.

I'm flung back by the motion but manage to hang onto the black ribbon. Manage to keep coiling my dark flames around it until it crackles. Until Marid's screeching weakens.

Then everything falls silent, the tether crumbling to ash at my feet.

"Harley?" Ray says. Her voice is weak and gurgled before she fades from sight.

My knees hit the floor, exhaustion pooling out of me as I feel myself yanked backward through the thick darkness.

CHAPTER SIXTY-SIX

"Harley, damnit, come back!" Draven's voice is loud, jerking to attention everything inside of me that just wants to sleep. To *rest*.

"I saw her," Ray says from somewhere beside me. Why can't I open my eyes? "She was…"

"She was what?" Draven asks, and I hate the panic in his tone.

"She was a mess."

"A hot mess," I manage to say through dry lips, my tongue feeling like it's caked in sand.

Warm, strong arms shake me gently, and I'm finally able to open my eyes.

Draven's gaze hits mine, and he glares at me. "Don't you ever fucking do that to me again."

"Don't bark orders at me," I groan as I sit up. My muscles feel like they've been run through the garbage disposal. My eyes widen when I see Ray, leaning limp against the wall. "Are you hurt?"

She shakes her head but doesn't lift her arms. "Just tired."

I nod at her, but my strength is returning with each deep breath I take. Draven shifts, moving out of my way so I can stand, but he keeps a steady hand on my lower back. Wrath is instantly at my side, and I lean into the hound's strong frame.

"Has he said anything?" I ask, eyes on Marid. They tied him to a table while I was out. The chains have a glass bulb between every link, and they glow with a bright white light.

"Told you those string strobes would come in handy," Wallace says, then shakes her head. "He's only growled. Thanks to you, right?"

I nod, limping over to him. "How are these string strobes holding him?"

"Watch," she says and nudges his side.

The motion moves the bulbs between the links, and electric sparks pulse over his form. He groans, the snakes coiling and constricting.

I scan the room, noting Cassiel by the door that is cracked open, his eyes watching for any movement in the hallway.

"How long did it take me?" I ask, watching as Ryder leans on the opposite side of the room, arms folded over his chest but seemingly unruffled.

We're all whole.

We're all here.

And the tether is broken.

We did it.

"Maybe an hour," Wallace says.

"Longest hour of my life," Draven snaps, and I flash him an apologetic look.

"You were knocked out for half of it," Ryder chides.

"And *you* were knocked out when I got here," Wallace fires right back.

Ryder glares at Wallace.

"Glad to see we're all still getting along." I shake my head, and Cassiel grunts from the doorway.

"See anything?" I ask.

He shakes his head. "That's what bothers me," he says coolly. "We need to leave—"

"Yes, dark princess," Marid says from the table. "*Leave*. Leave your people behind. Do what you're good at. *Run*."

I glare down at him, staring into his now-open eyes. He struggles against the bonds, each movement delivering another painful shock until he stills completely.

"What the hell does he mean, your people?" Ryder asks.

"Fuck if I know."

"Oh, don't be modest, your *highness*."

"Highness?" Ryder echoes the demon, and I roll my eyes.

"He's spouting lies," I say. "Like always." My dark flames slide around my hand, shaping into a dagger. "Any last words?"

"Yes," he says. "Dear Ryder, you spent many cycles here with me. You saw and heard my movements through time. You remember I spoke of the one who could open the gates and set us all free?"

"The one who could restore balance," Ryder whispers, his eyes distant.

"Repay those who stole from the Ather," Marid says. "It's her. It's always been her. The lone surviving daughter of the king of Ather himself. She could merge our worlds."

The floor tilts beneath my feet, the flame dagger slipping in my grip above Marid's throat. I turn to Draven, gaping.

"Is that the reason?" The question is a whisper, a choked plea begging for denial. "Am I his daughter? That's how I'm the Antichrist, isn't it?"

"Wait. You're the Antichrist?" Ryder says.

Wallace rolls her eyes. "Dude, catch up or shut up."

"He didn't say that to me," Draven says. "When I saw him…" He frowns. "I swear to you, he didn't say that. I told you I couldn't trust everything I saw, but he only said he wanted you. Wanted me to bring you to him."

My eyes widen.

"I would never do that, obviously," he says. "You know I wouldn't."

Here we fucking go *again*.

"When were you going to tell me, Draven?" I snap. "When were you going to tell me that the king of the Ather asked for me?"

"When I figured it all out," he says. "When I knew what it meant. He dangled Ryder's life in front of me, told me he'd trade Ryder's freedom if I brought you to him. I was going to come here myself, alone, and search for Ryder. I would never have given you to him. I tried to tell you that first day I came back, on Nathan's porch, but then he happened." He jerks his head to Marid. "And it didn't matter. None of it did. What mattered is getting Ray safe. We could figure it all out after that. Figure out what Rainier wanted with you."

My heart is racing, but I remember that night on the porch—my questions and him getting cut off in between our kisses, when he was about to tell me something but Ray's possession distracted me.

"Oh, I can tell you that," Marid says, his voice full of delight. "She's the only one who can restore his powers to their full strength. His only living heir. She's the only one who can free him. Together, they could put the Ather on the same level of importance to the universe as Earth, but her selfishness and greed will keep her from that."

"Shut up," I snap at Marid.

"You won't go to him?" Ryder asks, eyes wide. "You won't free your own father?"

I raise a finger at him. "I literally *just* found out. And right now? All I care about is getting Ray home." Draven is right. I can deal with everything later. We broke the tether. I'm seconds away from killing Marid. A few more realms, and we're back home.

"Selfish little thing," Marid says. "That's why I've been working on my own way out. I'll be the change the Ather needs. I will do *far* better than Rainier ever did."

The dagger flashes firm in my hands, and I stomp back to Marid, raising it above his chest—

He jerks, his entire body a coiled mass of power setting off every electric bulb in the chains. They shatter and crack, the force of the tiny bombs blowing me off my feet and across the room.

I scramble to my feet, searching for Ray among the shards of glass.

Ryder is draped over her like a shield, half his back covered in jagged pieces that look like red-dipped icicles.

Cassiel is in the hallway, wings flared, his hands splayed against the walls. Wallace staggers to her feet next to him.

Draven and Wrath are on either side of me, helping steady me as I redraw my flames into a sword and aim it at Marid, who lingers near a window across the room. He whispers in that ancient language I don't understand, and the room trembles.

I groan. Not this again.

Thousands of snakes dart into the room, some small and neon while others are huge beige-and-brown anacondas. The writhing masses shift around us, herding us closer to Marid.

I swing my sword of fire, turning every snake close to us to ash.

Cassiel flies into the air as Wallace leaps into the center of the room beside me. Ryder groans, scooping up Ray and hurrying over to us.

"Thank—"

"Don't thank me."

"Firestarter," Wallace says, pointing toward the window.

Marid flashes me a smirk, then waves his snake hand before leaping out of it.

"He can't get away!" I yell, swiping that sword at the wave of snakes lashing at our ankles. Wrath chomps a mouthful in half, spits them out, and reaches for more.

Draven steps in front of our group. Raising his hands, he shoots whips of liquid silver in every direction, catapulting each creature into the air, lopping off snake head after snake head. Their lifeless bodies plunk to the floor.

His breaths saw in and out as he leans over.

"Draven," I say, my throat tight. Too much, he's been using too much power. The entire time we've been here, he's been using so much.

"Get him," he says, his voice weak. "I'll be right behind you. End this."

I swallow around the knot in my throat, blinking back tears as I spare a glance behind me. My friends create a powerful circle around Ray, and it's the only thing that gives me the strength to do what I have to.

I lock eyes with Ray before leaping out of the window.

"I told you *I* want to kill him!" Ryder yells somewhere close behind me, but I don't pause to look back or contemplate why or how he'd leaped out of the window after me. Not when he's been so sure we'll die in this realm.

Maybe that's what he wants. I remember a time when that was never far from my thoughts.

Wrath's massive splash sounds seconds later, and in a blink, the hound is on my left, tearing through the water in a way that makes me envious. He quickly gains speed, making the trek in front of me, hot on Marid's heels.

Marid knows the swamp grounds better than any of us, and I mean, *yeah*. It's his fucking realm, but it's annoying as hell.

The murky water melts into a soft bank of tangled grasses, and Marid scales the ground a minute ahead of us. My legs burn with the weight of the water and the way the mud sucks at my shoes, but I don't stop. Not to catch my breath. Not to ease that damn stitch in my side. Not even to check the ground for any more of those poisonous snakes. I can't think of anything except for tearing my dark flames through each of Marid's limbs.

In the far distance against the dark skyline, I can see what looks like a city—like terrifying skyscrapers with sharp points that look ready to tear open the sky. But I can't think about his people right now, no doubt causing all kinds of gruesomeness in that city. I can only run faster, push harder.

I'm so close to finishing this.

To stopping him.

I just have to keep going.

The squelching of my shoes pulling free of the mud and slapping against the grass is almost louder than my heaving breathing, but barely. I clamber after Marid, drawing my flames into my palms. Footsteps sound behind me, but I can't tear my eyes off Marid. His dark form gains speed on the ground, hurtling toward a giant archway I can just see in the distance.

Oh, hell no.

He's going to use the archway, the one leading to Conilis. That peaceful, beautiful farm and mining realm I loved so much.

I don't fucking think so.

I dig my heels in, forcing my legs to propel me farther, faster. Wrath does the same just ahead of me, the giant hound a miraculous beast of speed and muscle. If he catches Marid before me, I'll have to give him a treat. What do hell hounds eat, anyway?

Priorities. I'll have to figure that out later.

Obsidian fire crackles on my fingertips, spheres of heat gathering as I draw my arms over my head. I jolt my arms forward, the breath shooting from my lungs as I hurl giant balls of black fire toward Marid.

He screeches as one barely grazes his shoulder, but he dodges the next one and ups his pace.

A burst of blue-white light zips past my ear, connecting with the ground in front of Marid's feet. The demon stumbles, barely righting himself before taking off again.

"Close!" I holler to Ryder, keeping my pace despite the burning in my lungs. Fuck, I thought I had it bad when that damn power-sucking bracelet kept my strength down, but this? New goal—*if* I live—is to totally work on my cardio.

I send waves of flame, this time opting to aim in front of Marid instead of hitting him directly. I call to the land, making it roll beneath his feet. If I can just slow him down—

"On your right," Ryder calls a breath before bolts of lightning streak to the right of me. I take the hint and veer left while Wrath darts down the middle. If we can corner him, I won't hesitate to remove Marid's head from his slithering body.

We gain ground, either because Marid is tiring or because he's nearing the archway—my money is on the latter.

"Together!" I yell across the distance, and Ryder nods. "One, two…" My power gathers at the base of my spine, snapping along every inch of my skin as I draw as much of it as I can into my hands. "Three!"

The swamp explodes in brilliant bursts of silver and black and blue-white. The air tastes like electricity and smoke as Ryder's and my powers crash together in a glorious display of searing light, forming a cage of fire and lightning around Marid's form.

Relief barrels through me at the sight. Later, I might give us props for creating something so damn cool—a life-size birdcage with lightning bars and fire bases—but right now? All I want to do is finish this.

Slowing my pace, I catch my breath, already gathering my fire into the shape of the sword I'd wielded earlier.

Marid spits black ick through the bars as Ryder, Wrath, and I meet in the middle before it. "You'd kill a trapped creature?" he seethes, pacing his cage. "Why am I not surprised, Princess?"

"Like you're so much better." My arms tremble as I clutch my sword of fire. "You're done," I say, my words ragged. I need a nap. A shower and a nap and at least two weeks of nothing but Marvel movies. "You're done with my sister. With the Ather. Everyone you've tormented. It's over."

Marid stops pacing, whispering in that old language again as those pits for eyes meet mine. Ice skates over my heated skin, and I spare a glance at Ryder, who's gone rigid as if his powers have turned on him.

"Ryder?" I ask, the point of the fiery blade still aimed toward Marid's cage.

"Run," he whispers, and his voice is so low and cold I'm sure I heard him wrong.

"What?" I snap, still stepping toward Marid's cage. "No. We have to—"

Ryder's jaw clenches as he roots his feet to the spot. Crackles of lightning spark between his fingers, his arms flexing like he's trying to hold them down. "Run!"

Wrath lowers his head, the hair on his neck standing on end as he growls at Ryder.

"Is he doing this to you?" I point the sword at Marid, who's still whispering in that damn language.

"Harley," he grinds out my name, and my heart lurches at the anguish in it. "*Run*."

"I'm not going anywhere." I bound for the space between the lightning bars. "Not until he's dead." I draw the sword back to plunge it into Marid's chest—

An explosion rocks the swamp. Immediately, I'm swallowed up in a swirl of unfamiliar indigo smoke drenched in the smell of almonds and spice. The scent is suffocating. Is this some hidden power of Marid's I didn't know about? Tendrils of it shove down my throat as my feet lift off the ground.

Ryder groans.

The sound is quickly snuffed out, like someone shoved a cloth in his mouth.

I fight against the smoke, but each attempt only pours more in my body.

My vision flickers in and out—indigo to black and back again.

I'm drowning, I realize seconds after my body has already submitted to the panic. I flail around, shooting fire every which way. It blazes through the smoke just enough for me to see Ryder and Wrath sucked up into the swirling mass, too. A demented tornado that closes around me too fast for me to see if our cage still holds. I reach for the earth in my blood, roots snapping and bursting from the ground, lashing out at the smoke.

But it has nothing to hit.

My muscles grow weak with each smoke-filled breath. Fuck, is this what Ryder felt when I made him pass out in the fighting pit? I immediately swear I'll never do it again. Because this is torture. Each second the strength drains out of me is one second

I don't have to waste.

Black bleeds into the edges of my vision, the flames flickering out on my fingers.

And that's when I hear it.

Marid is laughing.

And I can't stop it, the ice crystalizing over my heart at the victory in his laugh and the terror in my mind as I slip backward down a tunnel of smoke.

CHAPTER
SIXTY-EIGHT

An axe is buried in my skull. There's no other reason for the ache in my head.

These thoughts flicker weakly in my mind as I try and fail to open my eyes.

My heart stutters against my chest like it's tripping over obstacles.

Leaving Ray with Cassiel, Wallace, and Draven.

Jumping out the window to chase after Marid with Ryder and Wrath at my back.

Marid in a cage of lightning and fire.

Indigo smoke.

Flashes of memory twist the axe in my skull, and I jolt awake.

A thick fog covers my eyes, so heavy I have to blink it away.

Ryder sits across from me, eyes closed, head drooping toward his chest. His arms are bound by thin black chains. I try to stand up so I can round the long table between us, but twin bursts of pain scream around my wrists.

I'm bound, too, my wrists and ankles encased in black stone chains, securing me to the black wooden chair that arches high above my head in twin peaks that look like pikes. My heart is fully racing now, but I force myself to breathe. I can melt through these chains or, at the very least, I can summon enough strength from the earth to break them myself.

I close my eyes, reaching for my power—

That isn't there.

It's like a steel door has been slammed over the well of power

I'd grown so used to recently.

"Fuck," I whisper, dropping my head back against the chair. I've felt this before, only the wishing bracelet from my mother had never been this strong. The chains must be made of the same power-sucking stone.

I swallow hard, scanning the area. From this angle, I can see grand chandeliers that have seen much better days. Where there should be golden flickering light in the crystal cups that surround the bulbs, there is nothing but shadows. I narrow my gaze, studying those goblet-looking glasses around each bulb, and acid claws up my throat.

Moths. Hundreds of dead moths fill the cups, their lifeless wings pressed against the dirty glass in pathetic piles. A shudder wracks my body as I force myself to look down. Ryder's chest is rising and falling, so that is something good to cling to. The area behind him is all black stone, a fireplace carved straight into the rock that is large enough to swallow him whole. It's not lit, but soot marks drench the stone. To my left, grand purple-and-red rugs line the rock floor, and I gasp at the sight of the giant hound laying on his side in the center of one.

"Wrath," I whisper, tugging against my bonds only to be met with the same shocking hit of icy pain. It reverberates through my body, twisting up my muscles until it's hard to breathe. "Damn it," I squeeze out the words, willing my body to still so the pain will stop.

I glance to the right, noting the vast rock wall and the lone door carved in the corner of it. One exit, no windows. Fantastic. I slow my breathing, trying to sort through my racing thoughts.

Is this another trick from Marid? Had I somehow slipped into his mind again—

No. That doesn't make sense. I killed the connection between him and my sister and had successfully made it back to myself. I almost had him, until...

The indigo smoke.

I breathe deeply, prickles of cold raising chills on my arms. The entire place smells of almonds and spice, and if I wasn't bound to a chair right now by these damn power-sucking chains, I might actually welcome the smell. As it is, it only pisses me off.

"Ryder." I launch the word across the table between us. His head bobs slightly, but he doesn't open his eyes. "Ryder!"

He jerks in his seat, groaning against what I can only assume is the same burst of pain I had moments before.

"Don't move," I demand. "Just open your eyes."

Muscles in his cheeks twitch, like he's fighting an invisible barrier. I take slow breaths as I wait.

"Damn it," he groans, blinking several times before those turquoise eyes meet mine. "I'm so sick of this. You show up in the pits, and all I do is get knocked unconscious over and over again. I should've stayed in Conilis. At least they fed me."

"I didn't do this to you," I fire back, but I'm relieved to see his anger is still intact. It means he's whole, he's alive. I can't imagine how I'd ever live with myself if I got Draven's brother killed.

"Finally awake, I see," a deep, masculine voice vibrates the room.

It's not Marid's voice, so there is something to be said for that, but I can't tell if I'm angrier that it isn't him or not. Because it's not him, which means he's likely escaped. I highly doubt my and Ryder's powers held after the choking death-smoke got ahold of us, and can I just say what in the actual fuck is that all about?

"Show yourself," I demand, surprised that my tone isn't the least bit terrified. In fact, there is only a hint of fear in my blood. The anger there is smothering it too quickly to surface.

"Of course," the voice says, and seconds later, an ethereal figure glides into the room. He's tall with broad shoulders, a black cloak that looks entirely made of smoke drapes and flows over his body, and his face? It's shadowed by the updrawn hood, but I can see his eyes—just two of them, and they're an insanely crushing blue as they meet mine. "I've been waiting ages to meet you," he says, stopping at the head of the table.

"Who are you?" I ask as he folds into a chair, never once taking those eyes off mine.

He waves a hand over the table, his long, bone-like fingers twirling this way and that. "I'm the overlord of the king's realm of the Ather. You caused quite a disturbance."

"Sorry not sorry," I say, and Ryder heaves a big sigh that sounds like a plea for me to not snap at our captor. I glance at him and shrug.

"Why did you bring us here?" I ask, returning focus to the overlord. "I'm guessing from the painful power-sucking bonds and the worse version of the Addams' family mansion vibes we're not honored guests."

Ryder's eyes widen at me.

A soft, humming laugh rumbles the overlord's wide shoulders, his cloak fluttering around the chair. "You truly have no fear, do you, Princess?"

"Ugh," I groan. "I seriously wish people would stop calling me that. What is it? A masculinity thing? Any young girl you see is automatically a princess?"

The overlord blinks, and his face is the picture of calm again. He looks human, no older than Nathan, but I can sense the power radiating from him. Not to mention the smell of almonds and spice. He clearly can control smoke and wields it in a much worse way than Draven wields his shadows.

Draven.

His name clangs through me. Did he regain his strength after he saved us? Did he and Cassiel and Ray make it out? Because surely, they left Marid's realm, right? They would know Ryder and I were a lost cause, and with the connection broken between Ray and Marid, they could at least get her out safely.

"Like I said," the overlord says, drawing me back to the present. "I've been waiting for you for a long time." He spares Ryder a glance. "Finding you with your mate is just a bonus."

"Oh, for the love of the *Antichrist*," Ryder groans, and those splinters in his eyes flicker and shine like his lightning. "Wrong. Fucking. Brother. *Again.*"

CHAPTER SIXTY-NINE

"He is *not* my soul mate," I say at the same time Ryder says, "My hair is completely different."

I gape at him.

"And our eyes," Ryder continues with his rant. "Like, do demons just *not* see the difference? Or are twins interchangeable objects here?"

"What do you want?" I ask the overlord, ignoring Ryder because I cannot handle his tirade and simultaneously hold my shit together.

One step at a time.

First, figure out what this creepy creep wants with us.

Second, exploit it and escape.

Third, get us the hell out of Hell.

The overlord inhales deeply, his nostrils flaring. "He's not your mate?"

"*No.*"

He squints at me. "I was told a description. Informed that he'd likely be traveling with you."

"Again. *Wrong brother*," Ryder growls. "I can travel with someone without being their mate. Shit."

I roll my eyes. Doesn't look like he'll get over the mistaken identity any time soon. But, to be fair, after what's happened to him, I wouldn't either.

Ryder scowls. "Honestly. If this is the kind of security the king keeps, it's no wonder Marid and his brethren were able to take over."

Okay, let's not piss off our only way out of this place.

"Do you know my mother?" I ask the overlord.

"Excuse me?" he asks, so damn formal I almost laugh.

I glance at the shackles around my ankles and wrists. "She saw fit to chain my powers, too, though she clearly didn't have access to as much of this stone as you do."

He tips his chin, those eyes glaring at me down his nose. "As a matter of fact, Princess, I know both your parents."

Shock ricochets down my spine. I didn't expect that, but I guess that's what I get for being sassy. "Do tell," I say in my best Kazuki-like voice. I'm more than shocked he doesn't pop into my mind as I think his name, but I don't have time to worry on it. "I mean, with the chains and the smoke suffocation show earlier, I wouldn't doubt you'd love to hang with my non-biological father up on Earth."

The overlord grunts, shaking his head. "I only recognize blood," he says. "And their stories are not mine to tell."

"Of course not," I say, rolling my eyes. "Well, underling—"

"Overlord," he cuts me off.

"Whatever," I say, and Ryder snorts. "It's been super fun. I'd advise you to remove these chains from us both and wake up my hound. You won't want to know what I'll do to you if you don't."

"Darkness," he says, shaking his head. "You even *sound* like him." He motions toward Wrath still laying on the rug to the left. "You say that's your hound?"

"Yep," I say, nodding. "You suffocate him, too?"

"I didn't suffocate either of you," he says. "I gave you some sleeping smoke. Many of the Ather pay for such a luxury, and yet you're being awfully dramatic about it."

I glare at him, and Ryder snorts again.

"You did *not* just call me dramatic," I say. "Have you seen your house? All doom and gloom and moth carcasses? Wait, let me guess, it's called Moth Manor?"

Something cold and sad darkens his blue eyes as he leans closer to me, his long arms draped over the table. The smoke cloak goes right through it, and if that isn't unnerving enough, the look he pins me with is. "You have a habit of judging creatures based off their surroundings. You have no idea the life I've lived. The sufferings I and my kind have seen."

I swallow around the rock in my throat. I shouldn't care what this demon thinks, because hello, kidnapping...but his words cut deep. How many times had I been judged for living in a trailer? Wearing the same three outfits over and over again because I didn't have money for new clothes?

I dip my head. "Maybe it's these chains talking," I say, and at least it's the truth. Under different circumstances, I wouldn't have played the low-blow card, but he'd stopped me from ending Marid, so yeah, maybe I'm feeling a little on the bitchy side.

The overlord leans back in his chair, studying me. "That hound doesn't belong to you."

"Like hell he doesn't," I snap. "I saved him from a fighting pit."

"Truly?" He looks to Ryder, who nods.

"More like stole," Ryder says. "She took me, too. So, more thief than savior."

Really? I grind my teeth to keep from snapping at him. I don't have time to explain—again—that I honestly thought demanding his freedom would be a blessing, not a curse.

"She also tried to kill me," he continues, then shrugs. "So, murderous thief is more appropriate, I guess."

"You started it!" I shout, and yeah, it's totally childish, but I'm exhausted, I'm in pain, and I can't feel my powers. I'm terrifyingly close to slipping back into that girl who felt useless again, and I really, really don't want to go back there. Not when I just started to feel like myself for the first time in my entire life.

"The hound is fine," the overlord says, and another bit of relief uncoils inside me.

"Wake him up after you undo these bonds," I say, giving him a little smile to show my teeth.

Another laugh. "I will undo your bonds," he says. "I'm not your enemy, though if not for the blood in your veins, I would've punished you and your companion for the disturbance you caused. Seeing as who you're linked to, I will do no such thing. Like I mentioned, I've been waiting ages for you to cross into the Ather, and here you are." His blue eyes sharpen as he rises to stand. "But are you worthy?"

CHAPTER SEVENTY

The overlord towers over me, but I don't break our stare. "Worthy of what?"

He waves a hand over me. The chains pinching my ankles and wrists vanish. Blood rushes to my fingertips and toes, the pins and needles sensation a welcome sting. I can feel my powers climbing up my soul, doing their damnedest to return to full force after being shoved down by the magic of the stone. I stand up so fast I knock the chair over.

"Release him, too," I demand.

"What do you think I'm doing, Princess?" The overlord shakes his head and waves a boney hand toward Ryder. His chains disappear, but he isn't as quick to rise.

I keep one eye on the overlord as I cross the room and drop to my knees next to Wrath. Smoothing my fingers over his coarse fur, I try to coax him awake. He snarls with his eyes closed, his massive paws digging against the rug as if he's running in his sleep. A few more pleas from me, and his eyes snap open. In seconds, he's on all fours, if not a bit wobbly. His head swings back and forth as he surveys the room, his dark eyes landing on the overlord, who merely arches a brow at the hound.

The fur on the back of his neck relaxes. In fact, his *entire* body relaxes as he sits next to me.

Okay, that is…something.

I cast Ryder a quick look. He's standing, and faint blue-white bolts buzz between his fingers.

"Welp," I say, emphasizing the *p* as I stand, but keep one hand on Wrath's back. "It's been a nice kidnapping, but we have places to be, demons to see, you know how it goes."

The overlord shakes his head again, a soft laugh playing at his lips. He's abnormally tall, I suddenly realize, as he spans the distance between us, towering over me so much I should be trembling. But, as it is, I just survived a really bad trip through Marid's mind, so this guy isn't exactly making me shake in my boots.

Maybe that should worry me. The fact that I'm quickly slipping into an unmovable *numbness*.

"You can hide behind your sarcasm and anger all you want," he says. "I know exactly where it comes from. I know you better than you know yourself, because I know your heritage."

Even with the gathering clouds of numbness in my soul, there's a prick of curiosity, of longing. I've only known my father on earth wasn't my biological one for a short time, but it doesn't matter. Ever since he's revealed that tidbit, I've wondered who my real parents are. I can't be sure if the woman who put the bracelet on me all those years ago—the same bracelet that drained my powers—was my biological mother. From the blood in my veins and the power in it, I'm guessing not. But how would she know about the stone's ability? There's no way it was a coincidence. She'd put that thing on me on purpose, to keep me weak or to keep me hidden, I'm not sure.

And then there is the thing Marid said—that I'm the king's daughter—but seeing as that tidbit came from Marid, I don't believe it just yet.

"Fine," I say, shrugging as I try like hell to appear not as interested as I am. "Tell me who my parents are."

He folds his arms behind his back, his smoke cloak billowing around him. "That information is privileged and highly sought after. I'm under strict rules to only reveal it if the being proves themselves worthy."

I roll my eyes. "Okay, then. I've lived for eighteen years without knowing them, doesn't really change anything if I never find out," I say and head toward the lone door across the room. Yeah, I'm dying to know who they really are, if they have the same powers as me, and why the fuck they left me to the monster I called father…but I don't need to know *that* bad.

There are more important things than my curiosity, like ensuring that Draven and my sister and my friends have successfully made it back to Earth.

Ryder and Wrath are right behind me as I reach for the stone handle on the door.

"Regardless if you care or not," the overlord says, appearing directly to my left, "you *will* have to prove yourself."

"What about me?" Ryder asks. "I don't need anything but to get out of this place."

"You, former Judge, have no one to prove anything to but yourself."

He brushes his boney fingers over the handle I'm reaching for, and the door swings open.

The smell of salt and sulfur blow past us on a sharp gust of wind that nearly knocks me over, but I manage to steady myself. Ryder barely hides a laugh at my nearly falling over, and I resist the urge to flip him off.

There is nothing in front of me but shadows and thick curtains of indigo smoke. But beyond that, I can hear the crashing of waves against rock.

The overlord gestures toward the open door. "After you."

Something in my gut tells me stepping into that smoke will only lead to another spiral of terror, will only land us in another realm with new challenges. But again, I just can't find the energy to care. I can't possibly sit in Moth Manor for the rest of my existence. I mean, sure, the overlord looks like he might be able to hold an interesting conversation or two if he removed the stick from his ass, and there's a whole lot about Ryder that still needs explaining, but I don't have the time for that.

So, without looking back at Ryder, I walk through the door.

Wrath presses his muscled body against my hip, sticking close as we're engulfed in shadow. Ryder is behind me...I can *feel* him there more than hear him. It's like he carries his own signature sensation—a crackling energy that constantly raises the hair on the back of my neck, like a predator stalking me in the night.

"Want to clear this smoke away?" I shout into the ether. "I've left Moth Manor like you wanted."

"I know how badly you want to understand your powers." The overlord's voice is everywhere at once, rattling my skull. "I know how desperate you are for answers. To all the questions that have been left unanswered about where you come from. About what you *are*."

I swallow hard, wanting to deny it, but unable to make my voice work.

"Find your way free of this island," he continues. "Prove you are worthy of the truth, and it will be given to you."

"And if I don't?"

"You will spend an eternity here."

CHAPTER
SEVENTY-ONE

Jagged black rocks jut at awkward angles as far as I can see. And just beyond them? An ocean the color of red wine, raging and thrashing against the rocks, reaching toward a dark purple sky with no end in sight.

I whirl around, fully prepared to set the mansion on fire out of pure spite, but Moth Manor is nowhere to be seen.

There is nothing but Ryder and Wrath and an endless island of rock and caverns with mountainous peaks piercing the night sky.

I sigh. "Well, this is just fucking *peachy*."

The roar of Ryder's laughter is so shocking, I nearly fall off the rock.

He waves me off, reeling it in. "It's just so comical to me," he says, "that you took me from one cage only to plop me in another."

"*You* agreed to help." I take a steadying breath, raking my fingers through my hair. "I didn't do this."

"Didn't you, though?" he asks, crossing the small space between us.

Wrath steps in front of me, but Ryder doesn't blink at the hound's protective stance. His turquoise eyes are locked with mine as he looks down at me.

"You're the one who saw fit to knock me unconscious and drag me into your little quest."

I part my lips, then shut them. He has a point, sort of, and that guilt will likely eat at me for the rest of forever. "First off, you were really close to killing me. I wasn't about to let that happen."

"And yet, you didn't kill me."

"A decision I'm totally regretting," I lie as I scan the area. "We don't have time to play the blame game. I asked for your help. You agreed in an exchange for a favor. End of story. Stop complaining about it." I start heading toward the dark ocean crashing against the base of the rocks. "We need to get off this island."

"So you can find out the truth about yourself? Yay for me."

"This isn't all on me. You need to take a good look at yourself, too," I snap, not bothering to turn around. I can feel him following me like static electricity at my back. Wrath keeps pace with me, treading carefully when the rocks grow slick. "We have to get out of here," I say, reaching the outermost edge of the island. The air is damp and cool against my heated skin, and I breathe the salty smell of the ocean in deep. "I need to make sure Draven and Ray got out. Need to make sure they're okay." I close my eyes, wondering...

Kazuki?

I say his name in my mind several times, but the connection to the warlock seems broken. I wonder what the overlord did to block it for this whole *worthy* game he's playing.

Kazuki, if you can hear me, please find a way to tell Draven I'm okay. Tell him to get out. Tell him to get Ray out.

I repeat the words a few times, just in case Kazuki can hear me but I can't hear him.

"Do you have a plan?" Ryder asks. "Or are you simply making up shit as you go?"

"Does it really matter?" I ask, whirling to face him.

He grins down at me. "If you want to survive in the Ather, everything matters. Even when you think it doesn't."

"Oh fun, you're as cryptic as your brother."

"Don't," he warns, his tone lethal, "compare me to my brother."

I glare up at him. "Your brother is one of the most amazing people I've ever met," I say with equal coldness. "If I compare you to him, you should be honored."

Ryder rolls his eyes. "It's sad how much you don't understand."

I spin back around. If he's going to insult my intelligence, then

I can't give him the satisfaction of seeing the hurt and truth in my eyes. I really *don't* know a lot about what is going on. I don't know everything about Draven—hell, he felt it wise to keep the fact that he's my soul mate from me. So yeah, maybe there is an entire chunk of my own history I'm missing, but right now? I just don't fucking care.

I have to focus on the task ahead of me.

Another trial.

Another test.

One I have to beat if I ever want to see my sister again.

CHAPTER SEVENTY-TWO

"So, how many times do you think we've circled this island?" Ryder asks, the sarcasm in his tone so not lost on me.

My thigh muscles burn and an ache pulses behind my eyes. "I've lost count," I say honestly. I don't even have the energy to snap back. He must be stronger than me if he can still hold that tone.

I slow to a stop, bracing my hands on my knees. We've walked the outer edges of the island at least a dozen times and crossed it back and forth just as much. We've searched inside the various caverns, finding nothing but empty rock. And the sky has never changed color, keeping us in an endless night. Wrath looks just as grateful for the reprieve as I am.

"You've lost count?" he repeats my words, his tone softer. "Not, *as many times as you're annoying, Ryder,* or *the same amount of times I've thought about killing you, Ryder?*"

I huff out a laugh, shaking my head as I try to right myself. My breaths are shallow and sting, the sharp wind blistering my cheeks.

Ryder frowns. "Harley?"

His eyes are more lucid than I've seen them in what has to be hours…maybe days? How long have we been searching for a way off this thing?

I collapse then, no warning, no precursor. Just one second I'm standing and the next my ass is on the slick rock.

"Oh, damn it," he says, sighing as he reaches for me. "Come on." He hauls me up, shoving his shoulder beneath my arm.

"I can walk on my own," I grumble but totally use his strength to help me anyway.

Ryder just shakes his head and tightens his grip. I can't help but notice how easy it is for him to touch, either painfully or helpfully. It took Draven days to trust me enough to touch me, so terrified he'd kill me with his siphon powers. And Ryder can do it without even realizing how much of a privilege physical contact is.

I sigh, wishing I could figure out how to mend what is broken between them, but know that is the least of my problems right now. Ryder guides us toward a mountain of jagged black rock, a slit in its center.

"We've already searched that cave," I say, hating how winded I sound. I mean, the boy is holding up half my weight, for fuck's sake. But maybe it's a combination of the last few days—the last *month*.

It *feels* like it's been years.

"I know," Ryder says but continues leading us in that direction anyway. "You're going to keel over if you don't rest," he says. "And what good is a dead Antichrist, anyway?"

I laugh again, because I can't help it—he's funny when he's not lobbing insults my way or blaming me or my boyfriend for how miserable he is.

No, not boyfriend. Soul mate.

Draven.

Ryder situates me on an outcropping of bedrock in the cave, the sound of the crashing waves softer here. I lean against the wall, and Wrath instantly takes guard at the entry.

"Thank you," I manage to say as Ryder settles next to me.

"*Thank you*?" He shakes his head. "I think I like you better when you're threatening to kill me."

I laugh again and shrug. "I can say the same for you."

"Good," he says, but there is a softness to his eyes I haven't seen before. He glances at Wrath, pacing the entrance. "Who knew I only had to lead you around an island over a thousand times to wear down your defenses enough where you're actually agreeable to speak with?"

I roll my eyes, but I can't argue. He's right. I'm exhausted, and we *have* scoured the island with no escape in sight. Maybe my non-biological father was right all along. Maybe I'm not worth a damn. Because if I was, I'd be able to get us off this rock.

I clench my eyes shut against the doubt and the hurt, and my mind replays where everything went wrong—when the overlord took us just as I was about to kill Marid. But even before that—

"Why did you tell me to run right before the overlord showed up? Could you sense him or something?"

Ryder visibly swallows. "No."

"Then why—"

"I told you I never really escaped Marid's realm," he says. "He loaned me to Sage, sure. But he still has hooks in me. Found a way to manipulate my mind. That language you heard him speaking? If he says the right words, I slip away and turn into something he uses at his will. I didn't want him to turn me into his puppet and order me to kill you."

I gasp at the admission. "That's horrible."

"You see why I didn't mind the pits now?"

I nod, the words tangling in my throat. The Seven have similar power over him—over Draven, too—though they seem to not care that Ryder's been in the Ather all this time. And why is that, exactly? I need to figure that out once we're free of this place.

"I'm sorry," I say, knowing those words don't make anything better, but I can't not say anything.

He shrugs.

I hurry to reach for something else to steer us away from where I can see his mind is going. "Can we talk about something else?"

"What do you want to talk about?"

"I don't know," I say. "Tell me something."

"I'll tell you anything you want to know," he says, shocking the hell out of me. "But you won't always like what you hear."

I nod, respecting that. "I want the truth," I say, even though as I say the words, I'm doubting he'll tell me.

"I am the more attractive brother."

I laugh again. "You're identical twins."

"You asked for the truth, I gave it to you." He shrugs.

I purse my lips. "I want to know the truth about you and Draven. Was it Marid stealing you in his place that broke the bond between you?"

"Speaking of bonds," he says, totally ignoring me. "Can't you send something down that soul mate connection of yours and call my brother for help to get us out of here?"

I don't know what shocks me more—the fact that he mentioned needing help or the fact that he's so desperate for it he'd let his brother be the one to do it.

"Oh, gee, I hadn't thought of that."

"*There's* that sarcasm."

When we first started our trek around the island, I'd reached for that chain connecting Draven and me, but...I can't feel it anymore. Much like the connection with Kazuki. There is just nothing there. I assured myself that it was due to this twisted realm and not anything to do with his well-being. I have to believe he's alive. That they all are. That they'd made it out.

"You didn't answer my question," I say.

He cocks a brow at me. "You noticed."

"There isn't much I miss," I say. "You don't have to tell me, though." I of all people know how hard it is to open up. It's one of the reasons I keep letting it slide with Draven when he plays things too close to his chest. It takes time, earning trust enough to share. "You don't owe me anything, but we're trapped on an island, and I can't help but wonder if you're worried about your brother, knowing he's out there somewhere, or if you truly hate him so much you don't care. And if you do, then I'm curious if it runs deeper or if it's just that Marid took you in his place."

"*Just?*" he asks, his tone sharp. "As if that lone event—or, rather, that my brother vanquishing Marid's mate led to *my* capture—wouldn't be enough grounds to hate him?"

"Hate is a strong emotion. Plus, I know you're not all bad. I saw it in the Conilis realm when you entertained Ray and her new friends. I saw it when you shielded Ray from the glass in Marid's palace. And you chased Marid to fight with me."

"All three of those instances can be chalked up to boredom, accidental saving, and my bloodlust being bigger than yours."

I don't buy his deflection for one minute. "I feel like there is more to it than all that."

He parts his lips, a choked breath escaping before he shuts them.

"Look," I say, softer this time. "I can't pretend to know what it's been like for you. Trapped here for over one hundred years. I can tell you've tasted horrors I'll never understand. Living under Marid's rule for as long as you have? I'm surprised you can find humor in anything. But…Draven has missed you every day since Marid took you. He's carried the guilt and anguish for just as long. When we were searching for you…I've never seen him look that hopeful. And yet you are so ambivalent toward him."

"And?"

"*And*," I say, "I would do anything for my sister. Literally anything. I came here for her. I ventured into Marid's mind for her. I found *you* for her. I'd kill for her."

Something churns in Ryder's eyes, an understanding buried under years of anger.

"I know that kind of bond doesn't simply stop. And that makes me believe something broke it. Like an axe."

"An axe isn't too far off the mark," he says, his voice almost a whisper.

Ryder stares at the cave's slick floor, looking but not really seeing. "I found out Draven had been sent on what I—and many Judges—would call a suicide mission. The mission called for several seasoned Judges, and Draven was barely out of his training stage—if you can call what he went through at the Seven's headquarters training."

I tilt my head, and he shrugs.

"They didn't know what to do with him," he says. "His power is infinite. Dangerous to everyone he comes into contact with."

Except me.

His soul mate.

"So," he continues, "I convinced my mentor to tell me where he'd been sent, and I went after him. I found myself running headfirst into a nest of scrivenger demons. Nasty things straight out of the Old Testament era. They kill slowly and brutally and delight in every exquisite drop of fear. There were at least twenty of them who'd slipped through the veil where it was thinnest. That many demons called for at least six veteran Judges, but they only sent Draven."

"They wanted him to die," I breathe.

Ryder dips his head but continues. "Even with his powers, his mentor knew what he'd face but sent him anyway."

"Esther?" I ask, remembering the woman Draven had once spoken so fondly of.

"No," he says, shaking his head. "She heard about it when I did. And she was furious. She came with me, though she wasn't as fast as I was. Probably because she was trying to cover our tracks so the rest of the Seven couldn't find us. It's a crime to interfere or oppose Orders," he explains. "And we'd been ordered not to help under the guise that it was a test for Draven to control his dark power."

Adrenaline surges through my blood. "And if he died?"

"I believe they would've been relieved. They feared him. They thought he was a punishment sent by the Creator. If he died on a mission, then they would see that as the Creator forgiving them for whatever crime they'd committed to deserve a Judge like my brother."

I swallowed hard, my chest aching. Draven had been called to serve in a divine war and then was punished for the powers he possessed. They put him in the Divine Sleep, him so much more than others, because they were terrified of his power. Terrified he'd use it against them. His choices, his free will, and the chance to prove just how damn good he was had been ripped away from him. If that wasn't enough, he'd lost his brother and wore that guilt like a bloody crown sewn to his skin.

"He'd already beaten six of them by the time I arrived," Ryder continues, drawing me out of my rage. "But he was struggling. I'm sure you've seen him when he absorbs the powers of demons?"

I nod. I *had* seen it. Experienced it. The moments with the largitas and the drakels flash through my mind.

"I didn't think," he says. "I didn't blink before I dove into the fray. That was my brother. Despite the differences in our powers, our mentors, and the way we'd been trained, that was my brother. My twin. The person I thought knew and understood me the most. We may have looked at our Calling differently, but we were still two sides of the same coin." He looks at his hands, the blue-white light buzzing there. "He was the dark terror to my Creator-worthy light."

The line of Ryder's jaw hardens. "We were able to whittle them down to just a handful. Victory was on the horizon," he says sarcastically. "But one got lucky. Clipped me from behind. Almost knocked me out. My head split open here," he says, dragging a finger down the right side of his face, over his eyebrow and all the way down to the line of his jaw.

As he traces it, I can see the faint remnants of a silver scar. He has so many, I hadn't noticed this one.

"I was bleeding out, screaming from the pain of the creature's venom." Ryder shudders next to me like he can still feel the poison working through his body. "But Draven had already killed so many, touched so many, that he was shifting. Shifting into something I didn't recognize."

The cold wind slips into the cave.

"He either didn't hear me calling for help, or he ignored me. I was barely clinging to consciousness by the time Draven finished the last of them. Their ashes were piled all around us. Esther hadn't gotten there yet. We were alone. I didn't have much more time. Draven came to my side, finally looking like my brother again. I couldn't speak, to protest. Didn't have the strength to stop him as he *reached* for me." His eyes darken, his mouth going tight. "He saw that I was dying and decided to not waste my powers. Instead, he decided to steal them to add to his already vastly growing collection."

My lips part on a gasp. *No.*

"I remember the terror as my brother reached for me. He hadn't touched me in years, despite me offering myself as a test subject so we could learn to control his siphon abilities. And there, bleeding out upon the ground, after I'd risked everything to come and save him, he decided to lay his hands on me. Right over the fatal wound. Everything that I was slipped out of me like sand from a broken hourglass and funneled into him. I passed out after that."

Ryder shifts next to me. "My brother's selfishness is what broke our brotherhood in the end. I stood by him through everything, and instead of helping me, he *stole* from me as the life slipped from my body."

"You're still alive," I point out, anger swirling through me.

"Esther," Ryder says. "She saved me. I imagine she fought

Draven off since he was never a match for her. But she wouldn't talk about it when I woke at my mother's home, in my childhood bed. Despite everything, I instantly looked for my brother as if he'd be sleeping peacefully in the other bed, the one right across from mine. But it was empty. Draven was gone. And I never heard from him again."

The broken look in his eyes is crushing. There was a time I doubted Draven, too. Not anymore, though. Not after everything we've been through, everything we've shared. We both have walls to keep climbing and tearing down, but I know this in my bones. There had been a time when I needed a power that would kill him, *did* kill him, and he didn't hesitate to give it to me.

And it's that unshaking trust in him that has me going back over Ryder's story...and finding a major fucking flaw. "Draven didn't steal your powers. He couldn't have."

"You weren't even born yet," he scoffs. "You can't possibly know what he did."

"I wasn't there, sure, but I know Draven. If he had the divine light we needed to break the tether between Ray and Marid, he wouldn't have hesitated to use it to save her. He was insistent we needed you. That *you* were the only one who could do what we needed."

He blinks a few times. "He was lying."

"I don't believe that."

Ryder scowls at me. "Then you know nothing."

I shrug. "Well, I know you're as bad as the rest of them. You assume the worst of your brother with no proof. You've let this hate fester in you, and you have no idea why he really touched you that day. If he actually even *did*. You said yourself you were half dead already. Who is to say he didn't help save you? Did you ever think it was because he was siphoning the venom from your blood? Your soul?"

He stares at me, unmoving.

"No, of course not. Because it's easier to believe the worst about people, right?" I shake my head. "You have no idea what

Draven was prepared to do to get you back." He was going to kill me, before he knew me. Use my blood to open the gates. Use it to go around the gatekeeper who would never let him pass. He wanted to find Ryder, damn the consequences.

And now here I sit, with the twin he's always searched for, and he hates him.

"I hate the life that you and Draven both have had to live," I say. "It isn't fair, but life isn't designed to be fair. Or easy. I don't have the proof you need, but I'm hoping once we get out of here, you'll give Draven the chance to tell his side of the story. Because I know in my heart, in my soul, it's not the same story as the one you just told."

There. That's all I've got.

This journey has taken its toll on me, and I'm just so tired of the questions, of the trials. That numbness I felt earlier has spread over my entire body, and it has nothing to do with the cold.

"I don't hate the life I've been given," Ryder says, shocking me. "Would I change a shit-ton of things? Yes, yes, I would. But I didn't tell you that story to make you feel sorry for me. You asked me a question, and I answered you honestly. I told you, you wouldn't always like what you hear."

Especially when it's wrong. "Fair enough."

Ryder rises. "Rested enough?"

I groan. "Not remotely."

"Tough. We need to keep moving." He extends his hand.

I clench my eyes shut. The idea of traipsing around this island for one more second makes me want to puke. "I don't want to."

"You don't want to?"

I shake my head.

"You're joking, right?"

"No, not this time."

He huffs. "So, what? You want to hang out in this cave for eternity until you and I either kill each other or waste away?"

No. I don't want that, but I also don't want to keep moving. I'm just so damn tired. Tired of the questions, of all the creatures we keep running into who know more about me but won't tell me a damn thing. Of the guilt and the lies and the unease.

I'm just tired of it all.

And yeah, maybe it's childish to sit here and pout, but fucking hell, it's been a long month.

Ryder crouches so he can meet my eyes. "You're the key to everything, Harley," he says. "The power in your blood? The heritage the overlord spoke of? *You're* the reason all of this is happening. You, out of all of us, have to keep going."

His words hit the center of my chest. "I didn't *ask* to be the Antichrist," I snap. "I didn't ask for these," I say, showing him the dark flames dancing on my fingers. "I didn't ask to be given to a monster and be beaten nearly every day of my life. To be told how worthless and useless I am twice as much. I didn't ask to be forced to murder my best friend to stop the evil from spilling onto the world. I. Didn't. Ask. For. This. Life."

A muscle in his jaw ticks, and the motion is so much like Draven my heart aches.

Where is he? I hope they all got out. Hope they made the right decision and left us behind. If Ray is safe, then nothing else matters. Even being stuck on this island with no escape in sight.

"It doesn't give you an excuse to give up."

"Did I say I've given up?" I swear my flames curl up my arms, my neck, and radiate from my eyes.

"I can see it in your face. I can hear it in your words. You don't want to keep moving? Too bad. You're not allowed that luxury—"

"*Luxury*? The only luxury I've ever known has come from the kindness of my boss, feeding us when we were *starving*. Don't talk to me about luxury, Ryder."

"So you've fought to survive your entire life, only to give up when it matters most?"

"I'm not giving up. I'm tired. I need a rest—"

"You've rested. I shared my sweet little sob story with you. You didn't believe me. Now it's time to move. To face this trial head on—"

"I'm tired of trials!" I shout. "I'm tired of tests and trials and people kicking me when I'm down just to see if I'll get up! I'm tired of *proving* myself," I admit, my tone shifting to a whisper. The fight leaks out of me as quickly as it built.

Ryder smirks, his smile half angel and half demon. "Then stop proving yourself and just *be.*"

"Be what?" I ask, because honestly, who the hell am I?

"I can't tell you who to be," he says. "But I can tell you who *not* to be. Don't be the Antichrist, don't be my brother's mate, don't be this realm's *test*. Be all of them or nothing. Just be you, Harley. Only then will you escape this place."

I swallow around the rock suddenly lodged in my throat. "What if who I am isn't enough?"

"That's bullshit. I haven't known you that long, but almost killing each other has its bonding perks." He flashes me a wink. "If you didn't have what it takes to escape this place, then you would've died long before you made it to this realm."

His words sink into me.

I'm not just Draven's soul mate or the Antichrist or Ray's sister.

I'm all of those things and *more.*

I'm the girl who constantly got back up after a beating, woke up the next day to face another one.

I'm the girl who looked Draven in the eyes when he'd shifted into those monsters and told him *I* wasn't afraid.

I'm the girl who sliced my best friend's throat because I knew I had to save the world.

And my father on Earth may have said I was worthless…the overlord may have set this trial in motion to *test* my worth, but—

I jolt to standing, nearly knocking over Ryder in the process. He and Wrath follow me as I storm outside the cave, his words rattling in the back of my head. The ocean waves thrash against the rocks, a mirror to the rage swirling in my soul.

"Harley?" Ryder asks, and I whirl around, eyes on the purple sky. "What are you—"

"I have nothing to prove to you!" I shout as loudly as I can, letting every inch of my rage, my pain seep into my words. "Do you hear me, you sons of bitches?" My obsidian flames spark silver with each word I hurl toward the sky. "I don't have to prove my worth to *you*! I am worthy of the truth, of everything kept from me, and a whole hell of a lot more."

I'm enough.

I've always been enough.

Enough to keep Ray safe, to give her a good life, to make her laugh even after she's witnessed evil.

Enough to save the world despite being fated to ruin it.

Enough to soothe the darkness in Draven.

I am. *Enough.*

And my worth isn't determined by my father on Earth or whatever biological parents exist in the Ather. My worth isn't decided by a council of ancient beings on a power trip or even the boy I love.

I determine it.

From here on out, I decide my worth.

And if anyone doesn't like it, they can go to fucking hell.

CHAPTER SEVENTY-FOUR

A wave of almond-scented smoke streaks across the island, gathering at the rocks just in front of us.

"I anticipated you taking much longer," the overlord says as his form materializes in front of us. His blue eyes sear into mine as he folds his boney hands together before him.

"I'm nothing if not unpredictable," I clap back.

Ryder laughs. "That's the fucking truth," he says under his breath.

The overlord looks to Ryder. "You were able to put someone else's needs before your own," he says. "Told her what she needed to hear. You're not completely lost after all."

"Whatever you say," Ryder says, rolling his eyes. "We beat your little game."

"I'll take you where you belong now." The overlord reaches out his hand, and I eye the offer like it might turn into a snake and strike me. But he isn't Marid, and what choice do we have?

I glance at Ryder, the brother who helped push me past my breaking point to realize the truth. He shrugs, a silent gesture of *I'm just along for the ride.*

I step toward the overlord, extinguishing my flames as my fingertips hover over his hand. "If you take me to another Moth Manor or Dark Island, I'm going to incinerate you."

The overlord laughs, the sound rough and light at the same time. "I have no doubt you would try, Princess."

I reach behind me with my other hand, and Ryder slips his hand into mine. The tiny electric shocks make my muscles twitch, but I know he likely can't stop his powers in this heightened situation. Wrath leans into my hip, and I nod to the overlord. "Waiting on you now," I say and lay my hand over his.

"He's going to love you," he says, and the words barely have time to register in my brain before a whirl of suffocating indigo smoke engulfs us.

I become weightless, the smoke curling around my body as the overlord soars us to…wherever he's taking us.

My boots hit the ground in front of a wide door. The onyx castle it belongs to glistens like black diamonds under a deep gray sky. The door is open, and the light inside is inviting and warm. Something inside me stirs, a longing I can't place. A glimmer of hope in a sea of boiling rage.

My fingers flare with flames.

Wrath lets out a howl loud enough to let anyone within a hundred-foot radius know we've arrived, and I move to shush him, but he bolts inside the castle, disappearing around the corner.

I take off after Wrath, hearing the footsteps of Ryder behind me as I stay on the hound's tail. Damn, he's fast. I can barely keep up as he bounds up a flight of stone stairs that spiral so tightly that I'm dizzy. Clinging to the cool stone wall, I propel myself upward, higher, trusting Wrath, though I'm sure Ryder is cursing my name outside. I don't have a clue where he's taking us. He could be chasing some damn demon squirrel and I wouldn't know any better.

Sweat beads on my brow, but I push past the final step, catching sight of his bushy tail as he bounds through another open door. I race through it—

And slam to a stop.

A man in a slick black suit stands before a roaring fire, a glass tumbler in one hand, the other propping himself up as he leans against the mantel. His hair is the same onyx of the castle walls, and the way the suit fits him, he's clearly built of long, lean muscle.

I've seen him before—in the vision when Kazuki looked through my blood, the same night he branded me with the tattoo of protection. I *saw* this man, a reflection of my own soul.

Wrath's pants fill the room as he pads over to the man and sits, his tongue hanging out of his mouth.

"Ah, Lazarus," the man says; his voice is deep and rich and infinite. He sets his glass down and rubs behind Wrath's—Lazarus's?—half-bitten ear, the hound leaning into his touch as he's done to me so many times. "I haven't seen you in ages…" The man's voice trails off as he notes where the hound is looking. Frowning, he turns, and his eyes fly wide.

They're deep and red and black, sitting in a devastatingly beautiful face with a strong jaw, hints of a five o'clock shadow coating it. His lips part as those eyes take me in.

"You've brought her to me?" His voice, despite its strength, *cracks* as he glances from the hound to me and back again. "Lazarus, you old devil," he says, elation lighting up his features. "You found her. You *found* her." He grins, revealing straight white teeth, and walks toward me.

I forget how to breathe as the flames dance in my blood. A buried instinct sighs as if I've just found a piece of myself I never knew I lost. I rebel against the sensation, but I'm unable to move as he stops an arm's length away from me.

"Hello, daughter," he says. He's at least a foot taller than me as I look up at him. I feel small. Even the power crackling inside me somehow feels small in his presence. "I've been dying to meet you."

CHAPTER SEVENTY-SIX

Shock rattles through me, the sensation like tipping to the side even though I'm standing straight up.

Marid hadn't been lying.

I can feel it, the truth radiating in the power in my blood. I recognize this being, or at least something in my soul does.

I finally snap back into myself and raise a dark-flamed finger toward him. "First things first," I snap, then point to Wrath, who remains sitting by the hearth. "His name is *Wrath*."

The man laughs, the sound smooth and powerful as it fills the room.

"Daughter," he says, "we have much to discuss—"

"Holy shit."

I spin around just as Ryder stumbles into the room. His eyes spark with lightning as he looks over Rainier. "It's true. It's really—"

An explosion outside rocks the castle.

I struggle to keep my balance, and in a blink, Rainier throws himself in front of me, the enormity of his presence threatening to swallow me whole.

"What did you bring with you?" he yells over the rocks falling in the corners of the room.

"I didn't bring anything!" But my words die short, because *that's* when I feel it.

The chain between Draven and me flares to life, pulsing with a hunger that makes me shiver.

Darkness sweeps into the room, blotting out the light, and

then he's there—all golden, murderous eyes, his face a mask of pure rage and terror.

"Draven!" The shadows part, and I *run*. The sight of him alive, the sight of him whole, has me launching myself at him. "You found me."

He hauls me against his chest. "I will always find you," he says, his voice cracking with relief and pain—and fear.

"*You*," Rainier whispers, and I shift then to see his gaze pinned on Draven. "You brought her to me," he says, shaking his head. "I didn't think you'd remember. I didn't think the spell would let you give her my message—"

"I didn't bring her to you," he growls, placing himself in front of me as his shadows evaporate. "She is not anyone's to *bring*. She decides. Always."

My heart stutters at his words, but I get caught on what Rainier said. "The spell?"

Rainier resumes his place by the fireplace and picks up his glass, but his expression remains wary. "The same one that drained me of my powers and trapped me here. It prevents me from delivering messages to Earth, but I thought I'd found a loophole when your soul mate died. I yanked on his soul, preventing it from settling anywhere but here." His eyes meet mine. "And before I could finish telling him what he needed to know, *you* pulled him back."

I swallow hard, seeing the pride in his eyes. The unmistakable emotion I so desperately wanted from my father back on Earth in the early days. When I still had hope that I could magically turn into the perfect daughter and he'd stop beating me.

"You were a force to be reckoned with," he says. "You took him, *demanded* I release him. There are few creatures in existence who have ever attempted to demand things from me."

"I don't like people taking my stuff," I say, eyes flashing to Draven, who grins at me in a way that is so not appropriate in front of the king of the Ather—who is apparently my biological father—but I totally don't care.

"Neither do I," he says. "Now tell the rest of your friends to make themselves known, or I'll delight in educating them on what happens when beings other than my blood try to sneak up on me. It has been *eons* since I've had any fun." He takes another drink, his tone casual.

Friends? I thought only Draven—

Footsteps thunder up the stairs behind me, followed by my friends barreling into the room. Cassiel immediately scans the space, his fighting stance matched by Wallace, who looks ready to throw down.

Ray shoves her out of the way and flings herself at me. I catch her, smoothing back some hair that has come undone from her braid. "Harley!" she shrieks. "I was so scared, but you're okay! This place is so cool. When did you get here?"

"You should've seen this place in its conception," Rainier says. "You would've loved it."

I ignore the nostalgia in his voice. The way he jumps from nice to threatening and back is...unsettling.

"This is Ray," I say to him. "My sister." I hold her out at arm's distance. "You shouldn't be here."

"Yes I should. It's not up to you *or* them," Ray fires over her shoulder at Draven, Cassiel, and Wallace.

Judging by their irritated expressions, they'd tried.

"It's *not*," she says, her words final. "It's my turn to rescue you, Harley," she says, then glances up at Rainier, whose staring at her with curious eyes. "Isn't it?"

"Ah, the little seer," he says, reverence in his tone. "You look exactly like—" He stops short. Blinks. "Exactly like a seer," he finishes. He points to her eyes. "It's all there. The ancient wisdom."

"I'm eight," she says. "Not ancient."

I resist the urge to remind her that her birthday is a month away, but hell, who knows? Maybe we've been in the Ather longer than we know.

Rainier shrugs. "Numbers are just numbers. Your powers are not."

"You're safe right now," I manage to say. "That's all that matters." But I flash Draven a look that says we'll be talking about this later.

He's not having that, though. "*The minute I felt the bond between us, once it resurfaced and I knew where you were…I had to find you,*" he says through our connection. "*I told them where you were. I laid out the dangers, the risks, and they decided to come. I couldn't, wouldn't rob her of her choice. Even if that pissed you off.*"

I understand, but still. She could already be back at Nathan's. Would she be angry? Yes. But she'd be safe.

I glance at Wallace. She definitely should've known better. Plus, she didn't even want to go to Marid's, and now she's here?

She winks. "What?" she asks at my silent question. "I've always wanted to see the King's Palace." She dips her head toward Rainier. "Wallace, by the way. Ather guide. Since she doesn't seem too keen on introducing me as a friend."

Right. Introductions, I guess. I start to explain who my friends are quickly, but I realize pretty quick that the angel of death needs no introduction, and Draven…well, they've met.

Rainier studies Ryder. "A fallen Judge…and a siphon Judge, an angel of death, my favorite Ather hound, a guide, and a Seer." He lifts an eyebrow. "You draw a fascinating crowd, daughter."

"If you're keeping tabs, I'm also friends with an ancient warlock."

He gives me an impressed look, but then his gaze sharpens on Draven. "If you're not here to accept the bargain I offered, then why bring her to the Ather at all?"

"Hi again," I say, adding a little wave for good measure. "Just a reminder—I brought myself here, thanks."

Rainier arches a brow.

"Marid," I say in response to his question, then explain what he'd done to Ray. "And after that, the overlord took me and Ryder. He made me prove myself worthy of your presence and then dumped us here."

"He made you prove yourself?" Rainier asks. "And *Marid,*"

he snarls, and the room trembles with power. "He's always been one of the evil entities I wanted to expel. I would've, too, if the Seven hadn't stripped me of my powers and trapped me here." He takes a sip of his drink, reining in that chaos rattling beneath those red eyes, even though he's gripping the glass so tightly I'm afraid it'll shatter. "But I've heard no word about Marid amassing more Colis. To what end?"

Ryder steps forward. "I can answer that," he says. "I was Marid's prisoner for…well, for long enough to learn a thing or two."

Draven flinches at my side.

"He's buying his get-out-of-jail-free card," Ryder says. "Twelve passports to Earth are costing him nearly a mountain in Colis. And you know what they can do with that on Earth? Turning it into weapons and infusing it with their powers?"

My blood runs cold. Wallace mentioned this.

"They could wipe out a city in a matter of hours," she says.

"Damn him," Rainier says. "*And* the Seven. They're all wretches, and yet I'm the one the legends call evil?" He notes my wide-eyed expression. "I'm assuming you've heard the story of the Fracture?"

"Yes," I say. "So it's true, then? All of it?"

"Yes," he answers. "But there is one thing the legends have always left out. The Seven, those pompous, narcissistic creatures…" He waves the drink in his hand, as if he can see the memory of all of them standing before him. "Everything they do—regardless of right or wrong—they do in the name of the Creator. And yet, they had no issues betraying the Creator's *blood*."

CHAPTER
SEVENTY-SEVEN

I blink. Once. Twice.

Nope, we're all still standing here like Rainier didn't just say the Creator is his sister.

"Of course, my dear sister hasn't taken a *real* active role in the world since the dawn of time." He sighs. "Really. At this point, who could blame her?"

My mind races, rewinding to the story Delta had told us. "The legend said you were going to appeal to the Creator," I say. "Your *sister*."

And my biological aunt? Oh hell, I can't even digest that right now.

"That's why the Seven trapped you, isn't it?" I ask. Because if anyone could have the Creator's ear, it would be him, right? Family?

Rainier raises his glass, toasting a confirmation before taking another drink.

I'm kind of starting to want a glass for myself.

"Esther," Draven says her name, the member of the Seven who he once told me helped him, saved his life. The only one who ever believed in Draven. "She is not capable of that kind of betrayal."

"For once," Rainier says, "you're right. Esther is my ally." He presses his lips together for a moment. "Beings with divine blood are able to pass in and out of this realm, a loophole they built in so they could taunt me at their leisure. She's managed to sneak here a time or two, but the risk is great."

"All this time," Draven whispers, and I can feel his anguish down that chain between us. There is only little relief to hear Esther isn't in on all the schemes like the rest. "Every order. Every time I tried to question them…" He looks up at Cassiel, a silent, pleading look.

"They do have a thirst in their power, brother," he says to Draven, and Ryder glares at the term of endearment. Cassiel grunts, his wings ruffling.

"Which is why we need to stop them," Rainier says.

"Where do we even start?" Wallace asks. "They've been around almost as long as you," she says to Rainier.

Rainier looks to me, and all their eyes follow.

I feel the weight of their gazes like a steel blanket. "Me?"

"Yes."

Oh, that's rich. I choke on a laugh. "Am I the only one who thinks this is funny?"

I get more than a few confused glances.

"Um, pretty sure, yes," Wallace says slowly.

I snort. "My whole life I thought my father was a monster because he beat me. And it turns out my real dad is the Devil—at least, the creature the Devil legends come from. And the beings that were sent to earth by the Creator to help humans end up being the assholes trying to control and destroy us all. And here we sit, with the Devil himself, his Antichrist of a daughter, a hell hound, the angel of freaking *death*, and two Judges—I bet the Seven would shit themselves if they knew their divine soldiers were here, by the way—plotting to *save* the world."

The sadness of reality catches up with me, sending my emotions crashing over an edge that is not giddy or hopeful or finding irony in the situation any longer.

It's just sad. They've been robbing Draven and Cassiel and Ryder of their choice for longer than I can fathom. They've ruled over countless other creatures for millennia and somehow became power hungry and twisted enough to think they can play God with the world. They ordered Draven to watch me, to *kill* me if necessary. Did they know he was my soul mate when they gave him those orders? Could they be so evil and cruel to inflict that upon him?

Yes. Yes, they could. Because they hated him for his siphon powers. Ryder's story was proof of that. Feared him, tortured him when awake and put him in the Divine Sleep when he was of no use to them. And they trapped my father, they trapped the ruler of the Ather, leaving its people kingless and subject to the evil they forced into the realms. Their actions led directly to creatures like Marid taking control. Allowing him the power, the *arrogance* to possess my baby sister. Letting him create weapons for them as payment for his freedom.

Flames burst around my fingers, my body trembling with rage. Tears pool at the edges of my eyes.

Draven steps in front of me, holding my gaze. "You are stronger than your rage," he says. "More than its power. But you do what you have to. If you want to raze everything to the ground, I'll happily stand by and watch. Your choice."

My fire wavers and flickers out as a sob shakes my body. As I stop plotting the demise of people I've never met and let the rage trickle out of my blood. I fall into Draven's open arms, his lips instantly on mine as if he's fully prepared to kiss away the anger threatening to consume me.

I come alive under his kiss, under his touch at the back of my neck as he draws me closer to him.

"*Damn*," Wallace says from somewhere behind me. "Is there like a signup sheet for soul mates? Because I volunteer."

Power crackles in the room, a dark wave with a familiar taste of anger—bitter with a hint of spice. Rainier's power.

Draven tears his lips from mine, growling at that flicker of power as he releases me.

"Smarter than you look," Rainier quips, taking another sip from his drink but casting Draven a threatening stare as I unhook myself from him.

"Well," Wallace drawls, dropping onto the chaise on the other side of Ray, propping her boots on a little wooden end table.

Rainier snarls at her, and she instantly settles her feet on the floor. "*If* we're plotting," she says, "I need brain power. Got any snacks, King? I'm starved."

Rainier snaps his fingers, and a tray of strange-looking fruit appears, a decanter of that neon yellow drink beside it. Ryder crosses the room, he and Wallace not hesitating to dig in. Ray joins them at a slower pace.

"So how *do* we stop them?" I ask, raking my fingers through my hair. I'd planned on getting Ray home as soon as we broke the tether, but now, with the Seven and Marid and the Twelve threatening the world she'll live in, how can I send her back?

Rainier slides his hands into his pockets of his jacket. "You."

CHAPTER
SEVENTY-EIGHT

I arch a brow at him. "I'm exhausted from one unsuccessful battle with Marid. If the Seven are even more powerful than him, I'm not liking my chances."

Rainier sighs. "You know so little about your powers."

"Whose fault do you think that is?" I fire back.

He nods. "Fair enough, daughter. But if I had been allowed to raise you, trust me, I would've bargained anything for that honor."

I swallow hard, but he continues before I can say anything.

"When they trapped me here, I didn't think I'd ever see another being. For millennia, there was no one. But then my overlord arrived. Half angel, rare as that is, he was able to exploit that loophole in their magic. I expected others would follow, but as you might imagine, not many venture this far out to try their luck. Especially when the journey can be harsh for those who don't know the correct path to travel." He gives Wallace a grateful nod, and she grins. Had Anka not sent me to her, would we even have gotten this far?

His red eyes darken, a longing ache there. "But *she* came to me," he says, his voice almost a whisper. "I thought she was here to finish what the Seven started. To kill me. Honestly, I'd been here so long, powerless, I would've been happy if she had." He shakes his head. "But she...she had such kindness in her. And more power than I'd seen in so long."

He falls silent, withdrawn, as if he's reliving those memories. Something like true devastation flickers over his face, but it's gone in the span of a breath. "I didn't know she was carrying my child when she left this realm, assuring me she'd return. She didn't, and when Esther brought the news to me of what had been done to her…"

I'm not sure I'm breathing as his voice trails off, as the castle itself trembles with his dark power, his rage at the memory.

"And here you are," Rainier finally says, motioning to me. "I see her in your eyes. But I feel my powers in your blood. You *are* the chosen one to stand for both worlds. The piece to bring it all back together. *Heiress* to the Ather. You are beholden to no one and no spells. You're the only one capable of restoring my powers. And together, we are the only ones who can match the Seven's collective power."

I have so many questions about my mother. Was it the one I knew? Or someone different? And what had happened to her that made his power thick and searing through the room?

But now is not the time.

"How do *we* stop them, then?" I ask.

"The Seven Scrolls," he says.

"How will those help?" I ask.

"Finding the scrolls and uniting them to control their power is the only way to strip the Seven of theirs."

"And what's stopping me from getting the scrolls and using them?" Draven asks.

Rainier's strong jaw goes taut. "Because they were scattered across Earth." He flings his arm out. "Only those who are *made* of the same power can detect them. Only those with that same power can wield them."

My hand stills on Lazarus's head, and the hound huffs in protest. "How do you know they'll work?"

"As the Creator's brother, I helped make them," he says. "They were a failsafe. A counterbalance to the well of power the Seven possesses."

"So, we find these scrolls and use them to stop the Seven and hope like hell they don't set the Twelve free before then?" I ask, my shoulders sinking. I'm so fucking tired. Like, I can feel it in my bones tired. *Another* quest. I used to read fantasy books and wish on every star to be whisked away to another world, one where evil was easily overthrown and power was reserved for the heroes. This is *so* not like the books I love. This is hard. And I'm heavy from the constant buckets of shit that keep spilling over me.

"That's not even half of it," Ryder says around a mouthful of food. "The Seven have been stringing Marid and the Twelve along for *centuries*. Even when I was his prisoner," he says. "And after. It's why he tried to find you, Harley. He's done waiting."

A shiver races down my spine.

"But after you help restore my powers and we find the scrolls, we can stop them all," Rainier adds, as if he's trying to be the silver lining to this tragic little tale. "That's why I bargained with Draven—or *tried* to. Why I needed you to come to me. To save our people, my world, and yours."

The exhaustion only gets thicker. I feel emptied out. Hollow. I look at Ray, and some of the life in my blood is restored at the sight of her, munching away on snacks. Marid has no power over her anymore, and that is something to celebrate.

"How do I do that?" I ask. "Restore your powers?" Not that I'll do it. I mean, I don't even *know* this guy. What could he truly be capable of? I've been here mere moments, and he's already whiplashed between steady and calm and borderline chaotic. And sure, my power seems to recognize him—it's practically dancing in his presence—but that doesn't mean I trust him.

"You accept your ring of power," he says.

I choke out a laugh. "You're joking, right? *One ring to rule them all* bullshit?"

He furrows his brow.

Okay. Earth reference. I clear my throat. "That's it? I take a ring from you?"

He shakes his head. "It's *your* ring. Crafted for you when I learned you existed, fashioned from this mountain and forged in the same flame that runs through your veins. Accepting the ring means accepting your birthright."

Antichrist.

The word rips through my soul.

"It means accepting your role as the heiress to the Ather," he continues. "Its future ruler. It means you'll be of both worlds, but rule in one."

Wallace whistles. "So *that's* why everyone keeps calling you princess."

CHAPTER
SEVENTY-NINE

Ruler? Heiress to the Ather?

"I thought the Antichrist was meant to *end* the world," I croak.

Rainier scoffs. "You also thought I was going to be some malicious demon hell bent on tearing a hole through the world, weren't you?" He waves his hands innocently before my face. "Spoiler alert, I only want that on Tuesdays."

He laughs, and I can't tell if he's joking or not.

"The Seven robbed me of my chance to know you, to *raise* you," he says, all humor gone. "For that alone, they deserve to die. They cannot be allowed to set the Twelve free or to use them to create weapons to wield against both the Ather and Earth. We must stop them."

And then what will Rainier do? If I restore his powers and we stop the Seven? Will he become the new big bad I'll have to someday face? So far, the only problems I've had are demons wanting my blood to open the gates, Marid and his buddies trying to rip through the veil, and then Marid possessing Ray. And when I think about *that*, think about what I had to do to save her...go into Marid's mind, endure it...

It's more than I've had time to process. And who is to say that any of the Twelve don't have a dozen other tethers connected to innocent people at this very moment? Am I expected to sever each one? Is it selfish that I'm not sure if I have the strength to do it?

Rainier's asking too much. They all are.

"I'm not a princess," I say. "I'm not a hero. I *ruin* things. I fail.

I work at a deli, and all I've wanted my whole life is to keep my little sister safe." The confession spills from my lips. "I'm not a savior," I say. "I'm a survivor. That's all I've *ever* done."

"You are more than you'll ever know, Harley," Rainier says, using my name for the first time. "I've lived lifetimes. Eons. I've seen a world created and torn apart. I've tasted unlimited power and had it ripped from me. And nothing, none of that, compares to the faith I have in you. You *are* my daughter, rightful heiress to the Ather. You are everything. I will stand by your side. I will make up for the time we've lost, and I *will* shred every bastard who stole happiness from you." Flames dance in his eyes—black and glittering silver.

My flames.

His flames.

"But," he says, "I can't do that without you."

"I can't keep my sister here," I say, my mind splintering from all that's been laid at my feet. "And Marid is still out there. If he gets to Earth, she'll never be safe."

"I can't send anyone to Earth without my powers, without the spell removed on my realm once and for all. The Judges and the angel of death should be able to pass through, but your sister and Wallace will be stuck here until my powers are restored. But I *will* help you stop Marid. I'll help you end him."

I glance at Draven. *"How can I trust a father I've never known?"* I ask him. *"How can I make this decision, Draven?"*

"Nothing worth anything *in this life is ever easy,"* he answers.

I close my eyes and sigh. *"What if I'm wrong?"* I ask. *"What if my instincts are wrong, and I restore his powers and he turns out to be as awful and terrifying as all the legends say?"*

"Oh, he's fucking terrifying," Draven says. *"You felt his power seconds ago when I kissed you. He dragged me to hell just for the chance to speak to you. His power is endless. Especially if what we're feeling now are the barest flickers of what was stripped from him."*

"What do I do?"

"You do what you've always done. You survive. You conquer. You take ownership of every inch of your power and you use it to protect what you love. We'll find a way to finish this together."

A shuddering breath rips from my lips at his words, at the images he shows me. Flashes of my life, of me winning against all odds, of keeping Ray safe, keeping myself safe, despite everything stacked against us. I open my eyes to meet his gaze across the room.

"I've always known you were a queen," he says. *"The Ather would be lucky to have someone like you in their corner."*

"And you?" I ask, needing to know. *"How do you feel being mated to the daughter of the Devil? The princess of the Ather? The Antichrist."*

Draven pushes off the mantel, letting his arms hang loose at his sides. *"I've never been worthy of you, Harley,"* he says. *"But I'll stand with you. For as long as you'll let me. I love your scars, your darkness, your rage. I love your hope and your wishes for Ray. I love every piece of you, titles and birthrights be damned. I love my mate."*

My body trembles. He's given me the words I didn't know I needed to hear. I turn to Rainier.

He's *waiting.*

Letting me decide for myself what I want to do.

"I—"

A thundering crack splits the air and sends all of us soaring across the room.

CHAPTER EIGHTY

"Looks like the little princess has come home." Marid's voice fills the room.

I scramble to my feet, flames instantly flaring from my fingers.

"You're in the wrong realm, Marid," Rainier says, stepping in front of me.

Cassiel has Ray on his shoulders, backing toward the shadows of the room. If Rainier is right, his blood has enough divinity in it to leave this realm, to save himself, but I know he won't. Not as long as my sister is in danger.

Wallace is already glowing bright purple, her eyes indigo as she buzzes with energy. Draven and Ryder shift into defensive positions, blue-white sparks crackling over Ryder's raised fists.

But all I can do is gape as eleven more demons materialize in the room.

The Twelve.

They're here.

Greater Demons, the very depiction of every legend and horror story about Hell. Beasts with twisted horns, some made of shadow and smoke, others scaled and ruthless looking. And the power? Fuck, I can feel it. Feel it reaching across the room and snapping at my own, testing it, challenging it.

Lazarus lets out a low, warning growl, taking up my right side.

"I knew the overlord would bring you here," Marid says, ignoring Rainier. "Little girls are so easily manipulated."

I narrow my gaze, and Draven adjusts his position.

"I've bought us passage," Marid says, waving to his eleven

brethren behind him. "And I've come to collect what's *mine*." He looks directly at Ray.

"No—"

I'm so focused on Marid—we all are—that I don't have time to think or blink or react as one of his eleven lunges for me.

I try to dodge the outstretched arms, but sharp talons dig into my sides, dragging me back. My chest hits the floor, and I flail, trying like hell to shake the grip, but the demon only digs its talons in harder.

The room erupts into a mess of shouts and screams and the sounds of flesh hitting flesh.

Lazarus bounds in my direction, leaping over me, and slams his paws into the demon's thick, feathered chest. Its grip slips, and I hop to my feet. Lazarus rips out the demon's throat, black, viscous fluid spurting from the wound.

I whirl, tearing my eyes away from the gruesome sight, finding two demons heading for Cassiel, who herds Ray into a corner. He grabs a demon by the neck, his silver eyes lighting up like lightning. The thing goes limp in his hands, and he tosses it to the side, sizing up the other one.

But I'm already sprinting across the room, leaping onto the demon's scaled back. I become a living flame, and the demon screeches, bucking until it sends me hurtling across the room. It chases me, leaving Cassiel and Ray alone. I sigh with relief but quickly regret the momentary reprieve as the thing knocks me off my feet.

Twin bands of shadow lasso it from behind, jerking it to the ground with a sickening *crack*. Draven is there, battling another demon while also controlling his shadows. Protecting me.

So much power. Maybe too much.

I scramble to my feet. Across the room, Rainier smirks at

Marid. "This is your last chance. Leave, or be killed."

Marid apparently doesn't care about the threat because the fighting doesn't cease.

A yelp sounds, freezing me to the spot as I turn to see Lazarus flying through the air, whimpering as he hits the wall near Ray. The horned demon who threw my hound caws with delight.

I send a wave of rock toward her face, knocking her to the ground. I hurry toward Lazarus, but I'm hauled back by another demon.

They just keep coming.

There are five either knocked out or dead, I can't tell, strewn across the room. And six more, plus Marid, still actively trying to kill us.

I flail in the hold of the one that grabs me, spinning enough to clip it with a flaming hand. The thing—which looks like some half-demented bull three times my size—growls at me and wraps its clawed hands around my throat.

Everything slows in my mind, narrows to the breath struggling to get in my lungs around the thing's tight grip.

Wallace cries out, and I see her go down, two bird-like demons above her, scratching and slicing her skin until I see blood.

Lazarus is trying like hell to climb to his feet to stand in front of a sobbing Ray.

Cassiel is struggling to fight off two demons who are shredding his wings with their barbed teeth.

Rainier and Draven are fighting the largest demon in the room side by side. They both look drained of power, of life. Draven stumbles and catches himself on one knee.

And Ryder is having a stare-down with Marid, hurling bursts of lightning toward him, but Marid dodges him every single time.

Tears bite the backs of my eyes. My friends, my chosen family, we're *losing*.

Not just losing—dying. And if that happens, then there will be no one left standing to protect Ray. To protect all of the Ather.

I may not be ready to rule.

But I am ready to be the Antichrist.

My vision blurs with how fast my dark flames storm me, thrashing along my fingers, my forearms, and up.

The demon drops me, and I'm no longer thinking, calculating, crying.

I'm nothing but the fire and earth in my blood.

Nothing but glittering darkness with a hunger for the Twelve's blood.

Spears of sharp flame soar throughout the room, slicing necks and severing tendons.

I am darkness.

I am fire.

And I'm fucking *done*.

One by one, the Twelve fall beneath my flames, some cut, some reduced to mere ash, until I can't tell where one enemy started and the other ended. I reel my powers in, my entire body shaking with adrenaline as I search the room—

I'm jerked back by hands I recognize.

Snake hands, their scales and coiled bodies locking around my neck.

"Stop," Marid commands, his grip around my throat threatening to crush my windpipe. A brightly colored snake of purple and yellow slides from beneath the arm of his black cloak. It's coiled and ready to strike my face. "Stop now or I kill you."

"Too late, asshole. I don't think any of your Twelve are left," I seethe. Flames curl around my fingers, uncaring at the reptile staring me down. I'm not going down from a fucking snake bite. Wallace can use her pink potion and heal me—

"Harley, don't," Rainier says, the panic in his voice stopping my flames in an instant.

"Smart." Marid nods to Rainier, then Ryder. "You both know what this is."

Rainier raises his hands toward Marid, a demon the size of a dragon sprawled dead between where he and Draven stand.

Me.

I did that.

I spare a glance to the other bodies lying in the room. So much blood.

And my friends? They wear looks of unrestrained terror, and I can't tell if it's me they're scared for or scared *of*.

"Yes," Rainier says, his voice cracking. "I know the original serpent."

"Then you know it is the only one whose venom has no cure."

I swallow. Maybe I can turn the snake to ash before it strikes. Maybe my fire is faster than Marid's pet.

Rainier shakes his head, a subtle move as if he can read my mind. Ryder is a mirror image of plea, though his eyes are drenched in horrors of the past. Had he been threatened with this snake when he was a prisoner?

"What do you want?" Rainier asks.

Likely revenge, now that I've killed his friends, but he isn't showing remorse for them. Instead, he smirks, those hollow eyes shifting as they land on Ray.

CHAPTER EIGHTY-TWO

Everything in me goes cold.

"Not a chance," I choke out the words, the damn snake tightening around me. "I broke your tether. You're done with her."

"I'll never be done with her," Marid says and eyes Rainier, who is edging toward us. "Unless you want her to die," he says, "I suggest you stop moving."

And to my shock, he does.

The king of the freaking Ather *stops*.

For me.

And if I could shake my head right now, I would. Because, seriously? It's just us and Marid. Sure, I may die from the snake bite, but they can finish him. Get Ray out safely. That's all that matters. Her life is worth so much more than mine.

Marid's snake-form shifts slightly, his black eyes darting around the room, sizing up my friends. The odds are not in his favor, and I'm his last card to play.

But I don't want to play anymore.

"You. All. Can. Stop. Him." I have to squeeze out each word, and Marid grips me tighter, causing that poised snake to hiss. But it doesn't strike. Not yet. Marid knows the second I'm down, they'll rush him. All his plans, all his carefully laid calculations, will be for nothing.

"Let me go," I say.

"Shut your mouth," Marid hisses.

I ignore him. "You don't need me."

"Harley, no," Ray whispers.

Marid holds firm. Tears roll down my cheeks, my heart shattering at the truth of what I'm saying. They are strong, powerful. They can end this now. They have to win. I'll never see Ray again, but my friends will keep her safe. Draven will. I know it.

"I love you," I say to Draven, bracing myself for the blow I know is about to come. Fuck, I hope it's a quick poisoning. Knowing Marid? It'll be long and drawn out. I'll probably swell up like a balloon—

"No," Draven snaps. *"You* don't *get to say goodbye."*

"This is it," I say. *"He has to be stopped. He can't be allowed to live to take Ray again, to hurt her. He can't—"*

"We'll kill him together," he says.

But I know that's not true.

I'm not worth everything Marid is trying to do, to Ray, to the Ather, whatever he may be doing with the Seven. There has to be another way to restore Rainier's powers, and I know my friends will help him find it. They have to let me go.

Rainier's power rolls through the room as he glares at Marid. That's right, attack him. Do it and make it quick.

"It'll be okay, Draven," I say. *"Even after I die, you won't be alone."* I repeat the words he told me when he was prepared to die to save the world.

It's my turn.

It's not like we planned, not even close. But Ray will be safe. Everything will be okay—

The snake tenses, fangs dripping as it hisses at me so close I can feel its breath on my cheek.

And I stare the fucking thing down, refusing to give it the satisfaction of killing me with my eyes closed.

"You are my mate!" Draven roars inside my head. *"I just got you, and I will not let* anyone *take you from me."*

Fuck.

I see the shift in Draven before anyone else, or maybe I feel it. One second he's the gorgeous boy with golden eyes that I can't help loving. The mirror to my darkness. The other piece of my broken soul.

The next, he's the monster everyone has always seen him as.

In a blink, he shifts not into one creature, but all manner of creatures. A beast of smoke and shadow and light. A being of claws and fangs and venom.

The sight should terrify me, but all I can see is *him*.

My siphon.

My friend.

My mate.

And Marid really picked the wrong person to piss off.

A heartbeat, and Draven, in this beast form, is on us.

We hit the ground. The snake strikes and misses so fast I feel the wind from the force of it graze my cheek. Close, too damn close.

I scramble back, away from it, but the thing disconnects from Marid's body and slithers toward me.

Draven is on top of Marid in a tangle of fangs and snakes and cries of pain.

Rainier rushes toward me, reaching for the damn snake that won't quit.

A pained wail comes from Draven, and I stop my retreat, unable to ignore *that* sound. Marid is desperate. His snakes swarm Draven's beast form, striking so much that his true face shifts in and out of focus beneath all the teeth and snouts.

But then he's roaring, and sharp claws erupt, slicing clean through Marid's neck. He keeps hacking away, relentless, until Marid's form is no longer a collective of snakes, but a pile of shreds.

I breathe a sigh as his golden eyes lock on mine—

A sharp pain bursts on my leg, and I go ramrod straight as I hit the floor.

"No!" Rainier gasps, getting to the serpent one second too late. He rips the thing's head off in one yank, tossing it behind him as he drops to his knees at my side. "Daughter," he says, hands gripping my leg above the bite so hard I flinch.

But the pain is nothing, *nothing* compared to the venom.

Fuck. It hurts.

"Siphon!" Rainier growls, and Draven is there, shifting back to the boy I know, the one I love.

"No, no, no," he says, scanning me. He smooths some hair from my face. "Harley, it's fine. I'm going to make this okay."

I try to make my tongue work, to tell him it's already fine. He killed Marid. Ray is safe. I'm fine. But I can't move. The pain rushing through my blood is hot and cold at the same time, pressure grinding my bones, trying to shift me into nothingness.

My vision wobbles, darkening in and out of focus.

"Stay with me," Draven pleads, and the broken, ragged sound in his voice jerks on my heart.

Or maybe that is the venom trying to stop it.

"Harley, goddammit," he growls, his fingers roaming over my body, my leg, as if he's searching for something. "Move," he commands Rainier, who looks like he might strangle him. "Move or I kill you where you stand."

Rainier releases my leg, and the blood he'd been holding back with his grip rushes out in searing pain. I can't even scream. My body is a useless, agonized thing.

"Hurry, Draven," Cassiel says, his voice calm, cold. "I can hear her song."

Cold chills skitter along my bones at that, but the pain swallows it so damn quickly.

"I am," Draven says, frantic. "I *am*."

Something strong and angry and ancient slides along my skin. Something I've felt before, but only once. When Draven had been trying to scare me in Myopic. That felt like years ago. Centuries ago.

One of his powers, dark and terrible and consuming. He'd already used so much, if he keeps pushing it—

"There," he says, his fingers on my upper thigh.

I wish we were somewhere else. Somewhere peaceful where we have time to explore and linger and learn. Somewhere his hands are on me not because I'm dying, but because he's bringing me to life. I cling to that fantasy, hoping that when I slip away, I'll find someplace that bright.

"Almost done, Harley," he urges. "Don't let go."

I hear the strain in his voice, the life draining out of him as he wields that power under my skin and deeper, into my very blood.

A slipping sensation has me feeling like I'm falling backward, despite still laying on the floor.

Then there is a tugging sensation in my veins.

My blood slows, *stills* under that command.

A harrowing wail rips out of me, and I thrash.

"Hold her!" Draven demands, and Cassiel is there, pinning my shoulders to the ground.

The pain ratchets up so much I'm sure my insides will turn *outside* any moment. But Draven's powers dig deeper, tug harder. I scream as that wound on my leg pulses. As my blood soars out of me in a steady, controlled stream, hovering in the air next to my body.

A sheen of green clings to that blood, and I'm about to say how it's kind of pretty, but then my skin goes cold. The pain is gone, but I'm falling down that tunnel of darkness—

"Shit, that's too much blood," Draven says, almost as if he's scolding himself. I raise my hand, relief pulsing weakly at being able to move again, and I touch his face.

"It's okay," I whisper, my eyes drooping.

"The fuck it is," Draven snaps, and I can feel him again. That power, willing my skin to sew itself back together, to hold in what little blood I have left after he rid me of the venom coursing through it.

"Show," I say, my eyes closing. "Off."

My hand drops.

"Done," Draven says, right before he collapses on the floor next to me.

And everything goes black.

CHAPTER EIGHTY-THREE

Something heavy and hot is draped over my chest, the sensation oddly comforting.

I pry my eyes open, feeling as if I've been swimming in nightmares for longer than I can remember.

"Lazarus," I groan as I try to move under his weight.

The hound stands up—on a bed, I realize, a really big one—and starts licking my face. I gulp in deep breaths with the absence of his weight, then dodge his massive tongue. "Okay, okay."

"Harley." Draven's voice fills the room, and my eyes dart toward him. He's at the side of the bed in a second, helping me rise to a sitting position when I struggle. Lazarus lays at the foot of the bed, his tail wagging this way and that.

I scan the room, noting the giant bed, the luxurious room with its own hearth, the paintings on the walls. "What happened?"

My memory comes back to me in shaky bursts.

The Twelve falling under my flames.

Except for one.

Marid.

Dread builds in my stomach, but Draven is there, his calm, strength helping steady me.

"He's dead." He slides his arms around me, and I drop my head against his chest. Those words unshackle my sluggish memory.

I remember.

Everything.

"You saved my life," I say, drawing back to look up at him.

"Always," he says, and my heart climbs up my throat. The boy who was sent to kill me saves me. And I save him. It's our thing, and I love it.

"He's really gone?"

"Yes."

The Greater Demon who almost killed me to open all the gates connecting Earth to the Ather, who violated my sister's mind and body by possessing her, who tortured Ryder for longer than any of us know, who had such horrible plans for Earth…

Is dead.

Gone.

The relief is so instant it almost hurts.

I sob into his chest. He holds me tight against him.

Once I manage to breathe, I relish his cedar and citrus scent. "And you're okay? You used so much power, Draven. Too much."

"I'm fine. Just had to sleep it off," he says, kissing my forehead. "In this very bed, actually. With my arms around you. Too bad you weren't awake." His eyes twinkle.

I chuckle. Yeah, that's probably for the best. No way would either of us have gotten any healing done that way. I glance around the room again. "Where are we?"

"Rainier's still," he says, smoothing back my hair.

"Where's Ray?"

"She's safe," he says. "She's hanging with Wallace."

I sigh, nodding. "So, we're safe."

"For the time being."

Of course, there is my heritage to sort out, and the matter of accepting my father's power and help free him if I want to one day be queen of the Ather. I wish there was a way to break the curse without fully unleashing Rainier's power.

My entire life has been a battle of survival, all with the goal of making it to my eighteenth birthday alive. So I could take care of my sister.

But now that Nathan has adopted her and loves her unconditionally like I know he does…

"I have to talk to Ray."

He sighs. "You still want to stay here."

"Yes," I say, the decision only solidifying with the question hanging over my head of if I'll free Rainier or not yet. "It's the safest play. No demons hunting me for my blood. No one trying to use me as a weapon. Here? In the Ather? I can be just any other demon if I want." Sure, rumors had spread about who and what I was after my not-so-subtle displays on our trek through the Ather, but no one *really* knows what I am outside of my friends. "I just need to figure out how to get Wallace and Ray out of here."

"I understand," he says.

I sit up, shifting out of his hold to face him. "So…" I hate that my throat tightens. "What will you do?"

He may be my soul mate. He may love me. But asking him to stay in the Ather? That's a whole world of intense.

"Ryder and I have been talking," he says. "While you slept."

That had to be interesting. "How long was I out?"

"Two days," he says. "The venom—I got most of it out, but there were faint traces I couldn't reach."

"Have I said thank you for that?" I smile up at him.

"No," he says.

"Remind me someday."

He laughs.

"So, you and Ryder have been talking…"

"Trying to bridge some of those gaps between us. Clearing up miscommunications," he says, and I wonder if Draven told him his side of the story of when Ryder was attacked. A story I definitely want to hear, but later. "And he's decided he finally wants to return to Earth. We tested it. Our divine magic lets us leave this realm. Cassiel, too."

"But Wallace and Ray are stuck here until I break the spell."

Draven shakes his head. "We're not entirely sure about Ray. She says she needs to talk to you. Wallace, yes. Though she seems keen to stay regardless. She told me this morning that she's explored every realm in the Ather but this one. And

I kind of love the idea of her annoying Rainier for a little while, don't you?"

I can't help but smile at that idea.

But then I realize if Ryder is going back to Earth, then that likely means Draven will go, too. I mean, he's searched for his brother for a century. That totally trumps our handful of weeks of knowing each other. "That's really good about Ryder," I say and mean it.

Draven nods. "He says it's to monitor the Seven. See what their plans are or if they'll make any other moves now that the Twelve are gone and their supply to Colis will most certainly stop." I nod. "It's brilliant, really," he continues. "They will never suspect their golden Judge to be a spy."

I hear the slight hint of bitterness in his tone, and I climb onto his lap, straddling him until we're nose to nose, eye to eye. "Hey," I say, tangling my fingers in his hair. "Golden Judges are overrated," I say, planting a soft kiss over his lips. "I'm much more intrigued by siphons."

His hands slide to my hips, gently clutching there. "*Siphon. N.*" He squeezes my hips harder. "No plural."

"Never," I say, smiling against his mouth.

He kisses me then. Fast and hard and devouring, and I start to lose myself in the sensations he draws out of me. "I want this, Draven, I really do, but…"

"Mmm. But you need to talk to your sister," he says.

"Yes."

"I'll get her for you," he says, lifting me off of his lap. "You still need to rest anyway." He strides for the door across the room, looking back at me where I sit on the bed. "Plus, if we're staying here, the Seven can't reach me unless they find me. So we'll have eons to do *that*." His eyes darken as he points to the bed where I sit.

"You're staying?" I ask, breathless. "But what about Ryder?"

"I'll make sure he gets settled on Earth. I'll even visit. Perks of being a Judge, remember?" He smiles. "You're my mate. I stay where you stay."

Tears well in my eyes, but he's turning out the door before I can tell him how much that means to me, how much *he* means to me. I've barely wiped the tears away before Ray is bounding into the room and leaping on the bed.

Lazarus barely lifts his head as I catch her in my arms, holding her against me before she wiggles free.

"You scared me," she says.

"I know," I say. "I'm sorry."

"Don't do that again. Okay?"

I laugh. "I have no plans to fight twelve greater demons and get poisoned again any time soon."

"Good idea."

"You okay?" I ask.

She nods. "Wallace and I have been drawing. Mostly what we saw in the battle, some other things I've seen here." She shrugs. "It feels good. To be drawing without worrying it's Marid."

"I bet," I say, and I don't know how to breathe around the happiness, the safety net spreading out beneath us.

And here I am, about to break myself in order to make sure it's the safest net possible.

"You're staying here," Ray says softly as she fiddles with the blanket on the bed.

"Did Draven tell you?" I'm going to murder that siphon for stealing my chance to talk—

"No," she says. "I dreamed it. Last night."

The breath goes out of me, and that sadness is welling up inside me so much my chest hurts. "What did you see?"

"You were in Conilis," she says. "Happy. So, so happy."

I smile, a tear rolling down my cheek. Her eyes match mine, and she hugs me again. "Are you mad at me?" I ask, needing her to be okay with this decision. Because if she isn't? I'll face the risk of demons coming after me, risk being used as a weapon, if only to make her happy.

"No," she says like it's the silliest question in the world. "You belong here. I can see it. And Nathan will take care of me. I'll be safe."

"But Ray," I say. "You can't leave this realm. Not until we break the spell."

"I can," she says matter-of-factly. "That's why I needed to talk to you."

"How?"

"I also dreamed about me being home with Nathan. Cassiel dropping me off. He's going to take me home, Harley. I saw it."

Relief expands in my chest, but I tamp it down. I don't doubt her abilities—it just feels too easy. I'll let myself relax when she's actually home safe.

Or…kind of relax. That's not really my thing.

"I don't really know how to live without you." I choke on the words as the truth of my decision settles over me.

She squeezes me tighter. "You won't be," she says. "It'll only be a short ten years till I'm eighteen. Maybe I'll come to live with you. I just…"

"What?"

"I want to finish school first."

I laugh. Of course she does.

"I want that for you, too, Ray. I want you to have the best life filled with friends and movie dates and junk food. Proms and art galleries. I want you to experience life without the threat of attacks or demons. If I didn't bring all that to your world, I would be going with you. You know that, right?"

"I know," she says. "I love you, Harley."

"I love you, too, Ray." And even though my heart feels like it's breaking, it's also full. Knowing she'll be able to live a happy life without demons threatening her at every turn? That is worth everything. If her being a Seer turns out to be as problematic as an Antichrist, we'll deal with that when it comes. For now, she deserves to be a kid.

"Will you tell Nathan?" I ask. "Tell him what I have to do?"

"Yes," she says. "You know he's going to be mad, but I'll get him to understand."

I laugh. "I have no doubt about that."

"Can I stay for one more night before I go back?" she asks, and I nearly break down into sobs again.

I manage to hold them back. "Yes, of course," I say and crush her in another hug, resisting the urge to talk her into staying forever.

CHAPTER EIGHTY-FOUR

"You sure you're fine with me taking some time to sort things out?" I ask Wallace for the tenth time that day.

She rolls her eyes from where she sits at Rainier's table.

Cassiel and Ray left hours ago, and while I'm happy my sister gets to live the life she's always deserved, there is a tiny Ray-shaped hole in my heart.

Draven and Ryder left shortly after to get Ryder all set up on Earth.

Rainier is eerily quiet where he sits at the head of the table, his fingers wrapped around his favorite crystal glass.

"Yes," Wallace says. "I am more than happy to be stuck here for a while. Who else in all the Ather can say they have unrestricted access to the King's realm?"

When she puts it that way…

"Go to Conilis," she says. "Delta will gladly have you. *And* Draven. Take the time you need to figure out the next play."

I sigh from where I sit across from her and glance to Rainier. "I need time," I admit to him again.

The grip on his glass tightens, and while I can understand his frustration, I don't let it sway my decision. I can't simply free him without going over my options. And after everything that has happened?

I need a break.

I need to breathe.

I need to clear my head before I make life-altering choices. Like freeing Rainier and accepting my role as heiress to the Ather.

"I've grown accustomed to waiting," Rainier says, his jaw tight. He pushes away from the table, striding across the room to a decorated mantel above his hearth. "You'll want to take this with you," he says, returning to stand before me. He sets an intricately carved wooden box in front of me.

A ring box.

I swallow hard, staring at the thing like it'll bite me.

"Your ring," he says when I make no move to open it. "In case you decide to accept your birthright while you're in Conilis." He lingers, those red eyes casting me with a look I can't quite place, before he spins around and leaves the room.

"Are you going to open it?" Wallace asks, eyeing the box.

I shake my head and pocket the box instead. "Not now."

With how *torn* my mind is? I don't need any sort of temptation to increase my powers. And if I saw the ring? Who knows, it may have some magical pull on me I won't be able to refuse. Better to make my mind up first, then look.

"Well, Firestarter," Wallace says, shoving back in her chair and propping her feet on the table now that Rainier is nowhere in sight. "You think you'll suck at farming as much as you do decision making?"

I gape at her, but a welcome laugh bursts from my lips.

She grins, and there is something there in her rich brown eyes. Something I've never had before like this. Friendship.

Huh, who knew I needed to come to Hell to find my best friend?

"Let's hope," I say, pushing away from the table to stand. "For Delta's sake."

EPILOGUE

I pluck a ripe piece of fruit from the magenta stalk and drop it into a half-full bin. I'm working solo today, but there is a certain kind of peace in my secluded little section of crops.

The sky in Conilis is shifting toward night, and I breathe in the silence.

It's been three weeks since Marid nearly killed me.

Three weeks since I left Wallace at Rainier's, with her using her powers to leap all across his realm and back, badgering him with hundreds of questions about it.

Three weeks of uneventful breakfasts and blissful nights with Draven.

Three weeks to *breathe*.

What better place to sort out my mind than here? It only made sense to try my hand at farming. In Hell.

I've carried the ring Rainier gave me every day since, just in case the perfect ah-ha moment hits me and I decide to take hold of my destiny.

There have been plenty of times that I've wanted to go to his realm, ask him to tell me about my mother, but I never found the courage to.

That's why we're here, Draven and me. To find strength, to grow together in love and trust. If only for a little while. And, holy hell, it's been nothing but bliss with him. We spend our days helping contribute to the peaceful realm, and our nights?

Heat storms my body, wondering about what all we'll do tonight when he gets back from helping Ryder on Earth.

Whenever he leaves—which has been twice this week—I always worry the Seven will chose that *exact* moment to snap their fingers and put him to sleep. Draven always assures me the odds of that are incredibly slim, especially with how quick he keeps his visits. Short and to the point, only long enough to help Ryder adjust to the new-to-him world. The Seven don't even know he's there.

I move on to the next stalk, pride rising in me at how much fruit I've collected for Delta's people today.

The rage and anger that usually live just beneath the surface of my skin are slowly ebbing out of me like a river polishing rough stone. Knowing Ray is safe, knowing I'm taking ownership of my life and not allowing anyone to use me as a weapon or a Key to unleash Hell on Earth, knowing that Ryder is keeping an eye on the Seven, informing us they have no plans in place for now...

It's a happily ever after I never thought I deserved—

A burst of bright light flashes through the area just to my right. Joy pumps through my veins at the angel of death's sudden appearance.

"Hey, Cas," I say. "Got something for me?" He'd already brought me a letter from Ray since she left. Helping me stay in contact with her whenever he's in the Ather to transport demons in is definitely making the whole separation thing easier.

But he doesn't answer. His chest rises and falls too quickly, and my blood runs cold as I see the horror in his silver eyes.

I drop the bin, my fruit spilling out all over the ground.

"It's Ray," he says, and the breath stalls in my lungs as I wait for him to say more. "They...they took her. I didn't know. I didn't know until it was too late."

My body trembles, my mind fracturing as all the calm chips off of me like chunks of ice. The powers in my blood rise, swarming me so fast it hurts. "*Who?*"

"The Seven."

He says more, but I can't hear him over the ringing in my head.

I *left*. I stayed here. Peaceful, content. Not a *hint* of a threat from me, the Antichrist, against Earth. I took myself off the gameboard, and they...

They *dare* to take her?

How did they even know she was there?

Have they been watching this whole time?

The rage I keep bottled, the anger I thought dormant—

It explodes.

And the entire area around me bursts into flames.

Nothing stops the waves of fire pouring out of me.

Nothing stops the flames from licking up the stalks of crops in my little section of the farm.

I clench my eyes shut, drawing my power as fast as I possibly can. My breath comes in great gasps as I lock down my power, hating the sight of the ash all around me, but not fully capable of caring.

Cassiel's great wings flap, blowing the hair back from my face as he lands. I want to apologize, but I can't. I don't have the words.

All I have is rage and hate.

The Seven...they took her. I thought not accepting my role as Rainier's daughter would help keep them from looking too close at me, at what and who I loved, and they just proved me the fuck wrong.

They'll regret it.

I reach into my pocket, pulling out the ring Rainier gave me before I left.

My ring. A band of silver holds up a stone of purest black, the shape of both a diamond and a hexagon combined. The sharp points glisten as if it's winking at me.

Cassiel's silver eyes track my movements as I poise the ring on my right-hand middle finger.

One heartbeat, then two, and I slip it on, knowing the decision I'm making and not caring.

It sears against my skin for a heartbeat before settling with a comforting weight. My powers ignite, the well shifting to an infinite, endless pit. Suddenly, I'm not so tired or scared. For a few precious moments, there is only power pulsing and healing and ebbing in every crevice of my soul.

If the Seven want a fight? Then me and Rainier will sure as hell give them one.

I arch a brow at Cassiel.

"Who?" I say again, grinding out the word. "Who, exactly, took her?" I need specifics so I can kill the right person. Slowly.

Anger and panic shape his features. "Draven."

ACKNOWLEDGMENTS

Awesome reader, you're always the first one I want to thank. I'm blown away by the love you all have sent Harley and Draven's way! I'm so honored you picked up this book and have gone on this journey with me!

Dare, my mate. Thank you for the cheeseburgers, the late nights, the carpool shuffle, and just genuinely being my inspiration for seriously steamy heroes. Thanks for talking sense into me when I was spiraling over plots and prose. Thanks for never once doubting my ability to do things under pressure. And finally, thanks for being my favorite snack.

Thanks must be given to my family for supporting this dream of mine, even when I started dreaming about it in the second grade. The encouragement to chase my dreams no matter how hard it is stays with me every single day.

Liz, thank you so much for believing in these characters and helping me shape this awesome new world!

Heather Howland, you are officially my own personal Doctor Strange. I can't thank you enough for the late night texts, edits, calls, and inspiration. I know I'm a better writer because of your guidance. Thanks for working some serious time stone magic on this!

Elizabeth Turner Stokes, I'm forever your fangirl. This cover is stunning and fits Harley SO well!

Also want to give a huge shout out to _lulu_lucky, natasha. reads_, and flourishing_fables. The fanart you all have created for the Ember of Night series SLAYS me! You're all fire! Thank you for taking the time to bring my characters to life in such visually stunning ways!

To Jessica Turner, Riki Cleveland, Jessica Meigs, Heather Riccio, Stacy Abrams, Meredith Johnson, Alex Mathew, Curtis Svehlak, Toni Kerr, Greta Gunselman, Megan Beatie, Stephanie Elliot and all the wonderful people who are at my Entangled home, thank you for all the work behind the scenes! Each one of you has put so much into this series, and it wouldn't be the same without all of your incredible talents! I'm so honored to be part of this awesome family.

To Beth Davey, my amazing agent, thank you for constantly being in my corner and helping me achieve dreams I've had since I was eight! You're simply wonderful.

Molly McAdams, you will always be the coolest half of #MollySquared. Thank you for always being a beacon on light even when I'm in my darkest moods. You are fire. And I love you.

Stoney, my woman, the way you approach life and always see the positive side of things amazes and inspires me. I love spending whole hours of the day laughing with you, even when we have no clue what's funny. Also, T-Rex was close. You never get to pick movie night again. And you need to admit that S'mores donuts are way better than lemon-blueberry. Just saying.

Esther. I love you. Then, now, and always.

To the amazing bloggers who constantly work on the behalf of authors and readers alike, you are EVERYTHING. I'm grateful and honored and appreciative of every single one of you who sacrifice time in the name of love for books!

And finally, for anyone who relates with Harley's character in more ways than her being a genuinely snarky badass, I want you to know you're in my thoughts. You're not alone. You are worth it. You find your joy and chase the hell out of it.

Thank you again for choosing this book. You are the reason I write!

*Don't miss the global sensation
everyone is talking about!*

crave

NEW YORK TIMES BESTSELLING AUTHOR
TRACY WOLFF

My whole world changed when I stepped inside the academy. Nothing is right about this place or the other students in it. Here I am, a mere mortal among gods…or monsters. I still can't decide which of these warring factions I belong to, if I belong at all. I only know the one thing that unites them is their hatred of me.

Then there's Jaxon Vega. A vampire with deadly secrets who hasn't felt anything for a hundred years. But there's something about him that calls to me, something broken in him that somehow fits with what's broken in me.

Which could spell death for us all.

Because Jaxon walled himself off for a reason. And now someone wants to wake a sleeping monster, and I'm wondering if I was brought here intentionally—as the bait.